INVASION
AMERICA!

INVASION AMERICA!

A Novel

Alan D. Wing

iUniverse, Inc.
New York Lincoln Shanghai

Invasion America!
A Novel

iUniverse books may be ordered through booksellers or by contacting:

iUniverse
2021 Pine Lake Road, Suite 100
Lincoln, NE 68512
www.iuniverse.com
1-800-Authors (1-800-288-4677)

First Edition

ISBN-13: 978-0-595-37661-2 (pbk)
ISBN-13: 978-0-595-67538-8 (cloth)
ISBN-13: 978-0-595-82047-4 (ebk)
ISBN-10: 0-595-37661-4 (pbk)
ISBN-10: 0-595-67538-7 (cloth)
ISBN-10: 0-595-82047-6 (ebk)

Printed in the United States of America

To my lovely wife, Shannon. Your love and
encouragement strengthens me.

To every Soldier, Sailor, Airman, Marine and
Law Enforcement Officer who stands in the gap
between the American people and those who
would do us harm. Thank you!

PART I

▼

The Towers

The towers, they stand so high,
Reaching up, up, up to the sky.

Side by side, so imposing they stand,
Majestic, imperious, so grand.

Now they are broken and fallen down,
With a loud, ear-shattering sound.

The smoke rises, rises high,
The devastating evidence tells no lie.

The giants fall, brought to the ground,
Weeping and gasping the only sound.

-Donna-Rae Standley

Prologue

───────────▼───────────

"To win the objective in an attack, strike them where they are undefended"-Sun-tzu, The Art of War.

Terrorism has long been a threat that has failed to receive its proper attention from the United States Government. Our national attitude continues to be one of deep apathy. The American people, as a whole, tend to believe it is a problem that only Europe, Asia, Israel and the rest of the world must be forced to deal with; as long as the attacks take place somewhere else, it isn't our problem.

The average American does not truly comprehend the deep-seated hatred that dwells in the hearts of our enemies. A poll conducted in the United Kingdom in the summer of 2005 revealed some very startling statistics. Of Muslims residing in the UK, fully twenty percent held the belief the western world should be brought to its knees through violence. If Muslims in the US hold the same belief then we have a recipe for disaster.

According to some reports there are nearly nine million practicing Muslims living in the United States and if that twenty percent figure holds true, then there are possibly 1,800,000 who believe violence should be used to bring us down. Suppose only ten percent of that one point eight million are actually radical enough to put their convictions into action; that would mean we have a potential army of 180,000 militant zealots prepared to wage war in the cities, streets and homes of the American people.

Terrorism, we thought, raged across the vast oceans separating us from the rest of the world. For years there were those warning we should give it more thoughtful consideration. They cautioned we should be constantly prepared for the ominous threat that would no doubt one day strike our shores. They warned, secure your borders and ports of entry and be aware of who is allowed access. We were urged to increase security at all national monuments, banks, vital government buildings, railroads and airports. And they warned that our entire infrastructure was much too vulnerable to a determined and well-armed attacker. For years those warnings were virtually ignored; as a nation, we buried our heads in the sand. Meanwhile, our enemies endeavored to take advantage of our apathy and plotted our destruction.

*   *   *   *

Islamic terrorists chose February 26, 1993 to bring international terrorism to American soil. On that cold, brisk Friday morning, a stolen van packed with several hundred pounds of explosives entered the public parking garage of the World Trade Center in New York City. The men driving parked in a predetermined location, locked the doors and calmly walked away. At 12:17 PM a bomb exploded, blasting a crater twenty-two feet wide and over fifty feet deep. Fortunately the ensuing fire burned up the cyanide gas the terrorists had placed inside the bomb, saving countless thousands of lives. Still, the damage was enormous; six people were killed and one thousand forty-two others were injured. The Trade Center suffered severe cosmetic damages exceeding three hundred million dollars, however, it suffered no structural damage and was repaired in less than thirty days.

The resulting panic and fear had never previously been experienced in our nation's history. The FBI, joined by other law enforcement agencies, went to work, and six days later announced the capture of one Mohammad Salameh, a twenty-six year old Palestinian who entered the United States on a Jordanian passport. Also arrested was a twenty-five year old US citizen named Nidal Ayyad; both, up until the attack, had reputations as decent, law-abiding young men. Although it would be several more years before either was tried or convicted of the crimes, the quick work of the authorities provided a face that America could attach to her enemy. The nation exhaled a sigh of relief; she had her villain and life could now return to normal.

*   *   *   *

On the sunny spring morning of April 19, 1995, a few minutes shy of 9:00 AM, a yellow Ryder rental truck was parked just a few feet from the north side of the Alfred P. Murrah Federal Building in Oklahoma City. The driver climbed down from the cab and casually walked away. The vehicle contained a bomb constructed with over four thousand eight hundred pounds of ammonium nitrate. It was set off at 9:03 AM and all hell broke loose. Obviously timed to detonate when the ultimate number of people would be entering and exiting the building, the explosion was so violent, the north face of the nine-story building was entirely ripped away. For nearly two weeks America and the world watched as the broken and twisted bodies of one hundred sixty-eight men, women and children were removed from the rubble.

Within days of the attack, the authorities found that their primary suspect, Timothy McVeigh, was already in police custody pending other charges. Shortly after McVeigh was charged with the vicious attack, so was a Herington, Kansas man named Terry Nichols. Once again, through expeditious police work, the American people were given a face they could point to and say, "That's the bad guy!" The land of the free was once again safe. We could all return to our boring everyday lives, resting peacefully and vainly believing our sleeping families were no longer in any imminent danger.

*   *   *   *

Terrorists struck again on the morning of September 11, 2001. Nineteen Arabs armed with box-cutters, perfectly legal to carry on planes at the time, hijacked four US airliners. At 8:45 AM, terrorists forced their way into the cockpit of American Airlines Flight 11, with ninety-two people onboard. They diverted the plane from its flight path and crashed it into the north tower of the World Trade Center in Manhattan, New York City. Although having received minimal training at a Florida flight school, these hijackers first murdered the pilots and then flew the aircraft themselves. Eighteen minutes later United Airlines Flight 175 with sixty-five passengers and crewmembers onboard was flown into the south tower. A little over thirty minutes passed when American Airlines Flight 77, en route from Dulles airport in Washington, DC to Los Angeles, with sixty-four people aboard, smashed into the Pentagon in Arlington County, Virginia. Carrying nearly twenty-four thousand pounds of fuel combined, the terrorists had transformed the planes into gigantic guided missiles.

Massive fires erupted in the upper floors of both towers, melting steel support beams and severely weakening both structures. Fire suppression systems were completely overwhelmed and the south tower collapsed at 9:50 AM, pancaking down upon itself one floor on top of the next; thirty-nine minutes later the north tower followed in the same fashion.

At 10:00 AM an emergency operator in Pennsylvania received a distress call from a passenger on United Flight 93, traveling from Newark to San Francisco.

The caller reported the plane had been hijacked; other calls confirmed four ter-rorists had hijacked the plane and some of the heroic passengers were preparing to retake it. Two minutes later the plane crashed into a field eighty miles outside of Pittsburgh, ending the lives of forty-five passengers and crew.

The 9/11 attacks are by far the worst this nation has ever suffered. The terror-ists originally planned to use ten aircraft, striking high profile targets all over the country; by quickly suspending commercial air travel in the continental US, thousands more lives were likely spared.

The deaths of two thousand nine hundred and seventy-three souls, from many different countries, exceeded those from the attack on Pearl Harbor on Novem-ber 7, 1941. The lives of the nineteen hijackers were not included in the final tally of victims.

Within hours of the attacks, the federal government had identified the nine-teen hijackers and several co-conspirators. Authorities quickly laid the blame on the terrorist organization al-Qaeda and its leader Osama bin Laden. The United States declared war against terrorists and their supporters worldwide. Once again the American people had a face in which to direct her powerful rage. Through the assurances of the government that the guilty would be brought to justice, the wounds started to heal and painful memories of that dreadful day slowly began to fade away.

*   *   *   *

In years past, the United States government was provided many opportunities to stand up to the ever-growing terrorist threat and say 'enough'. The US has the best-trained and equipped intelligence services and military in the world, but for some unknown reason refuses to employ them in an effective manner. We have always had the ability to deal with terrorism; we just have not, evidently, always had the political resolve.

President Jimmy Carter, after Americans were taken hostage in Iran in 1979, allowed the crisis to go on for more than a year before taking any offensive action to free them. When he finally authorized a rescue, it was poorly planned, sloppily executed and was a dismal failure.

In 1983, after a suicide bomber killed hundreds of US servicemen in Lebanon, President Reagan withdrew US forces before they had completed their mission. To the world America appeared to be running. The Arab world was watching.

Having driven Iraqi forces out of Kuwait in the first Gulf War, President H.W. Bush ended the war leaving Saddam Hussein, a known supporter of terrorism, in power. Bush's reason for not pressing onward to dethrone the dictator was that the US did not have global support or sanction from the United Nations.

Not until the early nineties did terrorism truly rear its ugly head within US borders. The administration occupying the White House at the time was quite content to casually turn their eyes away from the threat and play nice guy to those that were hell-bent on our destruction. Even when they did decide to take a stand, it amounted to nothing more than a few missiles being fired into tents in the middle of the desert. This half-hearted action resulted in two things: good press for the president and absolutely no deterrent to the terrorists.

The United States had an excellent opportunity to take a stand when the US military was part of a peacekeeping force in Somalia back in 1993. After US forces came under a guerilla loyalist attack in October of that year by the local warlord, General Muhammad Farrah Aideed, we found how truly unprepared we were to fight terrorism with any kind of long-term commitment. Although our forces fought valiantly that bloody day by defeating an enemy possessing far superior numbers, the battle did rage all day and throughout the night. When it finally ended we'd lost eighteen brave men and suffered injuries to seventy-nine others. Although an accurate count of Somali deaths was never kept, estimates place guerrilla and civilian deaths at between five hundred and one thousand, with more than three thousand wounded.

Lacking the political will to stay the course, shortly after the battle, President Clinton ordered all military forces out of Somalia. This sent a loud and clear message of capitulation to terrorist forces worldwide; give America a bloody nose and she'll retreat. Pulling out told our enemies that America no longer had the stomach to fight a long and bloody war as we did a generation before in Vietnam. Osama bin Laden was believed to be behind the attacks in Mogadishu and all we did by leaving was to encourage him and his 'true believers' to fight with an even stronger resolve.

It was only after the second attack on the World Trade Center that the American government found the courage to face the threat the rest of the world had been battling for many long years. President George W. Bush stood on top of the rubble, once the World Trade Center, and said, "No more"; he then proceeded to back up his words. No longer would the words of Uncle Sam be hollow and without merit. President Bush took the war to the enemy; unfortunately, even his efforts were not enough. While we fought a protracted and surprisingly effective war against terrorism worldwide, we failed to give proper attention to the ever-growing danger faced here at home.

Terrorism, and the boldness of attacks against America, continued to grow through the early years of the 21st Century, but to this day, as a nation, we remain blind to the enemy within.

CHAPTER 1

▼

Day One

Summer, 2009

Friday

Three men made their way through the thick woods, crossed the dry creek bed and approached the rear of the brightly lit house with a quiet confidence. They stopped and listened for several minutes but all they heard were the sounds of music, laughter and frivolity coming from within. This informed the men that the party was in full swing, just as expected. The celebration was not one of the rich or affluent, but rather of your average small town, middle class family.

The house was a modest ranch style home built on a small knoll on the outskirts of Redding, California. There was a tire swing hanging from a limb of a withered oak tree near the center of the large back yard. Nearby lay one of those small, blue plastic children's wading pools, soiled with leaves and residue from a close by sandbox. The house would soon require yet another coat of paint, frequently necessary in this climate of extremely hot, dry summers and wet, cold winters.

One by one the men climbed over the chain link fence and began making their way across the yard. Though the moon was out, one of them failed to see a tricycle and stumbled over it as he crept across the yard; "Americans and their playthings!" he cursed. His leader motioned to him, with a quick finger to his lips and a stern look, to be silent.

The people inside were having a family reunion of sorts having gathered to celebrate the homecoming of two young United States Marines, just returned from the war on terror. Their duties had been to provide security for supply convoys that were attacked almost daily and sometimes hourly. The Marines had seen enough carnage and mayhem to last a lifetime. It had not taken them long, fresh out of infantry training school at Camp Lejeune North Carolina, to discover everything they knew, or thought they knew, about combat was nothing more than an illusion. Both quickly learned reality is far more brutal and neither would view a Hollywood war movie with such flippant and carefree attitudes ever again. The two witnessed several of their fellow Marines talking and laughing one moment and the next, seen their bodies blown apart by booby traps and car bombs. These frightful images helped keep them ever vigilant during the day and haunted their dreams at night. But this night they would concentrate on much happier thoughts. Though both would soon return to the war and an uncertain future, but tonight would be the beginning of two weeks of peace and relaxation with their loved ones.

The darkly clad men outside knew of the party because this was one of the many families they had been watching on and off for the past several weeks. The red and gold Marine Corps flag flying proudly from a column on the front porch of the home was what had attracted their attention to this particular family. One early mid-summer morning an old man was working in his flowerbeds and two of the men, who happened to be working in a culvert nearby, walked over and struck up a friendly conversation with him. One of them made reference to the flag and the old man, who they learned was named Jonathan, was proudly eager to boast about his twin sons. He mentioned they had been in Syria for twelve months now, fighting the enemy and how happy he was that they would both soon be home on leave. He added the entire family was coming over for their homecoming in just a few more weeks and this last bit of information was all the men needed to know.

They split up as they neared the house, each going to their assigned areas. The tallest of the three crept into the open garage, past a late model Buick and waited at the inside door to the house. He remained still for several seconds listening for any indication someone might have been alerted to his presence. Several minutes passed before he decided it was safe to move. Taking advantage of the light from an open dryer door, he began to look around. He took note of the numerous shelves stuffed with boxes identifying such things as Christmas ornaments, picnic supplies and winter clothing. *These people have more belongings in their garage than most Egyptian families have in their homes,* he thought. It was unfathomable how much emphasis Americans placed on material possessions and personal wealth.

The intruder placed his ear against the door and listened to see if anyone was near. After several seconds he was satisfied that his initial entry into the home would likely be unobstructed. There was no dead bolt on the door and he gently turned the knob, verifying it was unlocked. He smiled, bent down and opened the small sports bag he had brought with him. He removed a machine pistol, attached a foot-long sound suppresser to the end of the barrel and then loaded it with a thirty-two round magazine. Slipping several more magazines into his waistband he turned back to the door, said a silent prayer and stood ready for action.

The second man moved stealthily toward the house, past a large, black gas grill and several patio chairs and flower planters. He crouched next to the back door melting into the shadows thrown off by a small porch light. After taking a few brief moments to survey the area to ensure no one had noticed his approach, he stood up and peeked into the small kitchen window to the right of the door.

The first thing he saw was the Marines were the center of attention. A pretty little girl with blond pigtails was in the arms of the shorter one, her head resting on his shoulder, appearing to be fast asleep. The other had his arm around the waist of a rather striking young woman who looked to be about twenty years old or so. The man didn't see any wedding band and assumed she must be his girlfriend. There were several other party guests gathered closely around laughing, perhaps from a funny joke someone had just told. He could see what appeared to be an animated Disney movie playing on a monitor in the living room just beyond the kitchen. Several children were sitting Indian style on the floor, sharing a large bowl of popcorn and completely immersed in the adventures of Peter Pan. There were numerous bowls and trays of food and drink spread out on the kitchen counters and dining room table. From his vantage point he could clearly see the front door. The intruder reached for the weapon slung across his back, checking to make sure it was ready to go. He then settled back in the shadows to wait, taking solace in the fact that this little celebration would shortly be coming to a quick and brutal end.

The third man walked around the side of the house and passed through an open gate. Continuing around to the front of the house, passing Jonathan's flowerbeds, he approached the front door. There he paused, glanced casually around the yard from left to right and then behind him to ensure he had not attracted the attention of some nosy neighbor. He made note of the fact there were no windows in or near the door, assuring himself no one inside the house could see him. The swarthy man dried the sweat from his hands on his trousers and then withdrew the .40 Glock pistol from his holster. He checked the weapon once again verifying a round was in the chamber and the magazine was fully loaded and properly seated in the pistol grip. Taking a deep breath to settle his nerves, he glanced at his watch and then pressed the doorbell. From inside he heard a distant and faint, "Just a minute." A few seconds passed before a middle-aged woman, with a broad smile on her face, opened the door, the smell of freshly baked goods hitting him square in the face. "Yes?" she asked.

She looks so happy, he thought, guessing she was likely the hostess of this little get-together. She was wearing a yellow apron covered with colorful butterflies and ladybugs, and her graying hair was pulled tightly into a bun on the back of her head. When she saw who was at the door, the expression on her face changed to one of surprise and then, just as quickly, to one of deep concern.

"Can I help you, Officer? Is there a problem?" she inquired, straining to see over his shoulder, as if scanning behind him for some reason as to why he was here, and then back to his eyes. The woman didn't seem to notice the absence of a police car in the driveway and if she had it wouldn't have mattered.

"No, no problem, not for you. Not anymore," he replied. Then he raised the pistol from behind his leg and shot her in the forehead, instantly robbing her of all future hopes and dreams.

Hearing the gunshot the twenty or so startled partiers inside abruptly stopped what they were doing and turned toward the earsplitting noise not certain what it was they'd heard.

The hostess' body struck the floor with a resounding thud, a pool of blood spreading rapidly over the slate tile, a shocked expression frozen on her face. At that same instant the Marines recognized the gunshot for what it was and instinctively reacted, shouting for everyone to get down. Hearing the shot, the other two gunmen entered the home, immediately located targets and began firing their M-10 9mm machine guns. These weapons are small, compact and with a cyclic firing rate of eleven hundred rounds per minute; no one in the house stood a prayer of surviving. The shooters had practiced together many times and knew right away what their area of responsibility was.

The Marines turned at the sound of the two gunmen entering the home and seeing the new threat sprang into action. The one holding the little girl threw her onto a nearby couch, as they grabbed wooden chairs, raised them to strike and charged the killers. Before either had taken more than a few steps, a hail of bullets swiftly cut them both down.

Plates and drinks were cast aside as panicked family members, suddenly realizing what was happening, tripped over furniture and one another trying to flee to safety. The gunmen did not discriminate between man, woman or child and fired at anything that moved. Jonathan was shot several times as he attempted to escape out a bedroom window. A teenage boy was shot in the back as he sprinted down a hallway. Several people, unaware that two more shooters had entered the home, turned and ran for the back door as a means of escape. Sadly, there was no safe place for the traumatized family members to flee to and in short order most everyone in the house was either dead or dying.

A wrinkled old man, probably a grandfather, was found in a bathroom, cowering behind a shower curtain. In his twisted old hand, he was clutching a cell phone and attempting to press the buttons with severely arthritic fingers, in all likelihood trying to call 911. Seeing the shooter raise his pistol to fire, the old man threw up his hands, vainly trying to ward him off. The gunman who had rang the doorbell shot through the outstretched hands, striking the frail old man twice in the chest at point blank range.

The body crumpled to the floor of the shower and the killer bent down and retrieved the phone from his dead hand. Glancing at the screen the killer was gratified to see the message, "No Signal Available." He looked down into the dead accusatory eyes of the old man, dropped the phone onto his ravaged chest, then turned and left the room.

The assassins walked calmly through the house checking closets and under beds for anyone that may have eluded them. They paused occasionally to nudge a body with their boot. If anyone moaned or simply did not look quite dead enough, another silenced round was fired into the victim's head. After checking the entire house, the three intruders returned to look down at the bodies of the two Marines. One of the killers commented that although both of them were shot several times in the torso, very little blood was visible against the dark blue material of their dress uniforms.

*   *   *   *

Across town, a man and a woman crouched in the darkness under a tree, watching a house in a quiet residential neighborhood. The couple was married and had legally immigrated to the United States from Jordan eighteen years earlier. Through special tax breaks not granted to the average American, they were able to purchase a small Shell convenience store. The business provided sufficient income for them and their two small children to maintain a reasonably comfortable existence. Both were told many years ago they would one day receive orders to carry out their mission but until then to live normal, quiet lives and to keep their faith a secret.

The mission requirements were laid out for them before they left Jordan, and those orders had never been altered. Instructed that when the signal was received, they were to cause as much mayhem and chaos as humanly possible and both were trained in just how to go about it. After ten years had passed, they started to think maybe they would never receive that order and decided to fulfill their dreams of being parents. Understandably surprised when they received the green light six weeks ago, the couple was still willing and ready to do Allah's bidding. They contacted the other four operatives in their cell and began making preparations. The six zealots had been getting together nearly every evening and weekend since, utilizing the time to revise and refine their plans. All maintained the equipment they had so carefully procured long ago. Each traveled around the city looking for targets that met the team's specifications.

There was no party at this house, for this was a group home for special needs people. With the exception of two in-house caregivers, everyone living here was either physically crippled in some manner or mentally challenged. This particular target had been selected not only for its tremendous shock value, but also for its high probability of success; those inside would stand little to no chance of escape.

The two religious fanatics had been waiting forty-five minutes when they heard a toilet flush followed several minutes later by the last light being extinguished. They waited another twenty minutes allowing all to fall fast asleep and then, at last, it was time to begin.

The house was a perfect choice with its high privacy fence crossing the back and sides of the property with heavy foliage and drooping trees in the front. The couple moved cautiously out of the shadows and crept around to the rear of the house, entering the back yard through a side gate to begin their work. Listening and watching the home for several more minutes, ever alert for the slightest indication someone might still be awake.

Using everyday garden sprayers, they had purchased from a nearby Mom & Pop hardware store that very afternoon, they started spraying the house with gasoline. Both took their time ensuring the entire house received a thorough soaking, giving all the windows and doors extra attention. No part of the house was left untouched, including the roof. Ropes, treated with a fire retardant, were even tied around shrubs and fastened to the doorknobs, preventing anyone from opening doors from the inside. To reduce their chances of discovery, a thorough investigation of nearby homes assured no barking animal would interfere with their carefully laid plans. In fact, neither was overly concerned about the neighbors either. The infidels were all warm and cozy inside the protective cocoon of their homes, watching television, playing video games, making love or sleeping; totally oblivious to the terror that was at that moment being unleashed upon their country. By the grace of Allah, this land of moral corruptness would be shaken to its foundations.

They finished wetting down the house and then struck matches, tossing them onto the accelerant. Satisfied, they then turned and walked just as casually down the street as one would make a trip to the mailbox, taking the sprayers with them. They might still have some use.

There'd been no rain in the area for more than two months and it left the structure as dry as a tinderbox. The house was rapidly transformed into a raging inferno. It only took a couple of minutes for flames to seek out and find the natural gas lines supplying the house and with a *whoomp*, alerted everyone in a five block radius that life had forever changed in their quiet and safe little world.

Neighbors ran outside in their nightclothes gasping at what they saw and several ran to call 911. Many residents grabbed garden hoses attempting to douse the flames but soon realized their valiant efforts were in vain. The fire grew stronger crackling and exploding as people watched in horror; cringing and sobbing they slowly backed away from the scorching heat, unable to process what they were witnessing.

By the time the police and fire departments arrived ten minutes later, the house was fully engulfed and little hope was held that anyone could be saved. Firefighters went through the motions of trying to rescue those trapped inside, their efforts, however, were more for the people watching outside than for any real hope of saving anyone.

Glowing embers shot into the air spreading flames to neighboring houses and more engines were called to battle the blazes. In the end, no one managed to escape; onlookers would later describe hearing the most agonizing and horrific screams coming from within the dwelling, as if from the fires of hell itself. One man reported briefly seeing a teenage boy, he remembered as having Down's Syndrome, in one of the windows trying to break it with a chair, a look of sheer terror on his face. "God have mercy on them all," he said. "At least the boy didn't suffer for long," he hoped.

It would have shaken the onlookers to the core had they known that at the same moment the man was expressing his horror, the two responsible for that horror were three blocks away, dressed in their pajamas and crawling into be, having already kissed their sleeping children goodnight.

Several hours would pass before fire investigators determined the cause of the fire to be arson and the deaths to be murder.

CHAPTER 2

▼

Day Two

Saturday

As the sun rose in the east over Mount Lassen, people awoke all over town to begin daily routines, only to be shocked at what they would soon learn. Many of their daily rituals involved turning on televisions, radios and retrieving newspapers from their front yards and driveways. Jaws dropped, people stared, stunned at what they were reading, seeing and hearing. Redding was a quiet town, this sort of thing just didn't happen here. Even though the area was quickly becoming a getaway for people from the San Francisco Bay area and other big cities, it remained, as it had for years, the outdoor playground Mecca of northern California. The Redding area boasts little industry, deriving most of its income from tourism and a constantly growing tax base, made up of an ever-increasing number of retirees from across the region.

The small city was fortunate to have only a few homicides each year and these were usually of a domestic nature. The scale of mass murder that took place the previous night only occurred in the big cities, always elsewhere, right? The sheer number of deaths was too shocking to accept. The police were saying they had no suspects at this time, but were continuing to investigate. Most people understood that was pretty much what they always said this soon after a serious crime. Most residents were certain the authorities would quickly apprehend the culprits.

Chief of Police Mitch Baker and Homicide Detective Phil Scott knew differently. They were looking over two notes that were exactly the same in every respect, with the exception of where they had been found. Each had been discovered in the mailbox of one of the invaded homes just a few hours ago. The notes had already been checked for fingerprints, DNA and other trace evidence, neither cop was surprised to discover that nothing of any value had been found.

"What do you think, Mitch?" Scott asked.

"I don't know what to think yet," Baker replied. "What do you say to something like this? I mean, we all knew someday something like this might happen, you know? I just never really thought that it would."

"I know," Scott said. "The public is going to demand some quick answers and I'm not sure what we should tell them. Hell, we don't exactly know a whole lot at this point to tell them. All the training in the world doesn't prepare you for something like this. I think most people understand that."

Baker thought for a moment before responding, "I think we should call in the FBI, immediately."

"I don't know about that just yet," Scott quickly replied. "Let's not be too hasty, all right?"

"Hasty?" Baker snapped in a tone completely out of character for him. "We've got thirty-three dead people, Phil. Dead! A great majority of them children and handicapped, and you don't want to be hasty?"

"Let me rephrase that." Scott said, a bit taken aback. "What I mean is, let's not get in a hurry until we know exactly what we're dealing with."

Baker, who followed dramatic world events very closely, responded in a firm, harsh voice. "We're dealing with terrorists, Phil, that's what we're dealing with."

"Terrorists? We don't know that with any degree of certainty. This could be nothing more than a serious domestic situation gone horribly wrong," Scott said, not sounding too sure of himself. "I just think we need to collect all the facts before we make a decision to involve the Federal Government in this," he clarified.

"What more facts do you think we need?" the impatience and fatigue very evident in Baker's voice from lack of sleep. "We've got two different houses attacked within fifteen minutes of each other. Fifteen minutes! This was a very coordinated operation and we've got two identical notes claiming responsibility. You read them Phil, how can you think this could be anything other than a terrorist's attack?

"On the surface that's exactly how it looks," Scott conceded, "but it might be nothing more than a simple case of misdirection to throw us off the real killers."

"That is a very remote possibility," Baker noted. "Is this something we really want to keep quiet and better yet, can we really afford to?"

"Not necessarily quiet," Scott replied, "let's just give it forty-eight hours and see what shakes loose. Give my men a chance to look into the victims' backgrounds. Maybe we can find another link between the attacks other than the notes and the seemingly obvious terrorist connection. Maybe someone had a score to settle with one of the victims. Come on Mitch, stranger things have happened," Scott almost pleaded

"If we were talking just about the first family, I would tend to agree with you. However, with the second house being handicapped people, I find it a bit difficult to believe someone had a score to settle with them, especially one that ties into the other killings."

"I see your point, but I'd still like to wait."

"I don't know," Baker said. "Everything in my being tells me to call the Feds in right here and now." *This is a big case,* Baker thought, *But if we can manage to solve this quickly on our own, it could be my best and only chance of getting out of this one horse town and on to something better, my family deserves it and I'm not getting any younger.* He thought over what they knew and then quickly made his decision. "Have the contents of the notes slipped out to the media yet?"

"Not yet. But, they are screaming to know what happened. They're swarming the crime scenes and haranguing my men trying to learn something, but we're keeping things close to the vest."

"Who knows about them?"

"Just you, me, two lab techs and the officers who found them. They've all been ordered to keep the details to themselves."

"Do you think they will?" Baker asked cautiously.

"I'm reasonably sure. I may have subtly implied there could be criminal charges if word were to leak out," Scott grinned.

Baker thought for another minute, "I'll give you forty-eight hours, no more. Monday morning I'm calling the FBI and that's final."

"Great!" Scott said, a little too excitedly for Baker's comfort.

"I'll do what I can to appease the Mayor until then."

"My men and I will break our backs and come Monday morning, if we haven't resolved the case, I'll dial the number for you myself."

Baker sighed and nodded his head in consent, "You better call the local Marine recruiter and notify him that two Marines are dead and won't be reporting back for duty. I'm sure he'll know who else to notify up the chain of command."

"I'll take care of it right away," Scott said, then stood up and walked out of the room. Baker's eyes drifted over to the notes on his desk and he wondered if he would end up regretting the decision he'd just made.

Not only would he regret the decision, so would a lot of other people, not that an additional two days would really have made much of a difference. The die was already cast; nothing anyone could do at this point could possibly alter events that were already set into motion.

CHAPTER 3

▼

Day Three

Sunday

Sunday is a day for church, a day for picnics, watching baseball and shopping at the mall. Whatever activity people choose to do, it is supposed to be fun and relaxing. For most it's a day spent with family and friends enjoying one another's company. For others it may involve feeding ducks at the river's edge, kids riding bicycles in the parks and old men hauling in rainbow trout from their favorite stream. Or 'the old man' simply lying in a hammock under a shade tree in the back yard, sipping on ice cold lemonade, watching the condensation collect and then dribble down the sides of the glass onto his tee shirt. In the end, it doesn't much matter; it's all about being able to celebrate life and the fruits of one's labor.

Today offered the blessings of a comfortably warm summer morning, the Rev. Moses Sharp thought as he watched his flock make their way into the Full Gospel Missionary Baptist Church. The building sat at the end of a narrow, pothole-ridden gravel road in the middle of a small stand of scraggily oak trees.

The church had about seventy-five faithful, tithe-paying members and that was enough to provide a sufficient income for Moses and his wife of forty-two years to live a frugal, yet comfortable life. Most Sundays they saw a few guests come to the morning service and today was to be no exception. Moses preferred to call them guests, not visitors; he felt the term 'guest' sounded more warm and friendly. Sharp noticed, just before he commenced with the service, two men and a woman walk in and sit near the back of the auditorium. *The back seems to be where the guests usually choose to sit,* he thought, watching the usher walk over, shake their hands and offer them a visitor's card to fill out. They seemed to politely accept it and one of the men began to fill it out.

Moses noted that these guests wore light jackets, and he thought it a bit peculiar, considering what time of year it was. *Oh well,* he thought, dismissing it and making a mental note to shake their hands and introduce himself at the conclusion of the service. *Perhaps they would accept an invitation to supper.* Inviting new guests to share the Sunday afternoon meal was a practice he and his wife had started more than thirty-five years ago; it was a great way to make them feel appreciated and welcome. Moses believed this to be a very valuable and under-utilized tool of Christianity.

The service followed pretty much the same pattern each and every week. They would start with hymns, then the offering and announcements. Following a special song by Sister Betty, Moses would bring forth the Word. Today's message, taking into consideration the events of Friday night, would be about forgiveness. Forgiving one another, forgiving one's self and forgiving one's enemies. It was a message that Rev. Sharp preached somewhat frequently, although he tried to change it up a bit so it wouldn't get too boring.

It was painfully obvious to the old preacher that people possessed a nasty habit of judging each other very harshly; especially when it was perceived the other person had done some terrible wrong. Moses knew no one walked on water, other than Jesus Christ and the Apostle Peter, and he thought mankind should keep their judgments to themselves. Moses also believed a lot of the evil which people do toward one another could be greatly diminished, if everyone would take this one simple message to heart, forgiveness. Unfortunately this Sunday's message would never be delivered, at least, not at the Full Gospel Missionary Baptist Church, and not by the Rev. Moses Sharp.

As Sister Betty finished her song to the Lord and stepped away from the pulpit, the three 'guests' stood up. The two men walked to the rear exit doors on opposite sides of the sanctuary; ushers were paying too much attention to the activities in the front of the church to notice. The woman split off from the others and walked toward the pulpit down the center aisle. Rev. Sharp noticed the woman approaching as he stood up to begin his sermon. He smiled at her and briefly wondered why she was wearing gloves; he did not notice her two companions moving towards the exits, if he had he would have seen that they were wearing them as well.

Without breaking stride, the woman withdrew a silenced M-10 machine gun from under her coat, pointed it at the reverend and fired. Her movements were so fluid that even those closest to the front didn't realize what was happening. That was, until Sharp was flung backwards, landing half in the baptistery, the crimson hue of his blood instantly turning the water a hazy brownish-red. The woman didn't pause to observe her work; she rapidly adjusted her aim and shot the three other church members on the platform, including the assistant pastor and the Sunday school director. Then effortlessly reloading, she spun around and fired into the mass of stunned worshippers behind her. Emptying the thirty-round magazine in seconds, she reloaded with a smooth proficiency one could not have managed without many hours of practice.

The realization of what was happening settled on the stunned congregation like a cold, wet blanket and they began bolting for the exits, the stampede feeding itself with many people still not exactly sure why they were running. The other two gunmen, holding their weapons at the ready, opened fire into the brethren charging toward them. Fear quickly turned to panic when the severity of what was taking place became evident and the terrified parishioners realized they had no safe place to run. Horrified people were falling over one another crying and screaming repeatedly, "Oh JESUS, Oh JESUS!" Bodies were dropping one upon another; some fell right where they stood, others were thrown violently over pews each already on their way to judgment. The three assailants continued reloading and relentlessly firing until no one was left moving.

Throughout the small sanctuary wounded people were weeping and moaning, but soon their pain and fear would come to an end. The killers began to calmly and methodically walk around the room systematically shooting anyone that was still breathing. One very large woman had managed to squeeze her ample frame halfway under a pew in an attempt to shield a small boy from harm. The female killer found them and simply shot through her, killing them both. A young man was found crouched down in the sound booth at the rear of the church begging for his life. The gunman dispatched him just as swiftly and coldly as the others. The killers, having finished their bloody work, looked at one another and smiled with satisfaction. The female walked up to the pulpit, which was miraculously still standing and placed a folded piece of paper upon it. They all took one more look around the slaughterhouse and then walked out of the Baptist Church closing the door behind them.

The three killers climbed into a white van and drove slowly down the bumpy road. They had people to meet and other things to do, but first they needed to make a phone call.

*   *   *   *

After more than twenty-four hours of hard investigating, Baker's men had come up with not one promising lead. They hadn't been able to find any connection between the two groups of victims and were quickly running out of investigative options. Officers were still digging into the financial records of all of the victims and had found it difficult, in the early going, with banks being closed on weekends. Luckily, after surprisingly little persuasion, bank managers volunteered to come in and open their files in the hopes some nugget of information could be found that would help the police break the case. Detective Scott was right now at Bank of America, while other detectives were scouring through the records at other financial institutes, looking for a proverbial needle in the haystack. Still more officers were beating the pavement, knocking on doors and re-interviewing neighbors, friends, coworkers and relatives on the outside chance they might glean one tiny and seemingly insignificant clue that would turn out to be the bombshell they were seeking.

Mitch Baker was at Police Headquarters wracking his brain hoping to stumble on something they had, until now, overlooked and which might lead them to the killers before they could strike again. So far, he had no such luck, and in all his many years in law enforcement, he never felt so utterly useless.

"Chief Baker?" his assistant said over the intercom.

"Yes?"

"Nine-one-one operators have just received a call reporting a shooting at a Baptist Church on the south side of town. Police, fire and medics are already responding."

A hollow feeling filled his stomach. "How bad is it?"

"I don't know sir. The dispatcher said the caller only reported there was a terrible shooting and hung up without elaborating," she answered.

"What's the address?" Baker asked, grabbing a pen and sticky pad. He quickly jotted it down, "Thanks." he said disconnecting the call. He grabbed his weapon from the desk drawer; his suit-coat from the back of the chair and ran out the door.

Ninety seconds later he was racing through the city in his unmarked car, siren blaring and a small, blue bubble light spinning and flashing on the roof. *Please don't let this be connected to the other attacks,* he prayed fervently. In his heart he knew it was, and all the prayers in the world wouldn't change it now. *What in the world was I thinking? I shouldn't have waited to call the feds. Please God, forgive me.*

Speeding south on Market Street, he could see several emergency vehicles far ahead and still others in the rearview mirror screaming away behind him. Baker heard the first officers report to the dispatcher that they had arrived at the scene and were preparing to enter the church.

A few tense moments passed before a frantic voice suddenly came across the radio. "Merciful God in heaven…it's a bloodbath! There are bodies everywhere; they've killed them all! They're all dead!"

*   *   *   *

The Mount Shasta Mall is the nicest one for a hundred miles in any direction. Like in other cities all around the world, the mall is where teenagers gather to socialize and hang out. Normally, around eleven on Sunday mornings the food court begins to fill with shoppers and by noon the place is packed. Groups of teenage girls sit around sipping soft drinks and nibbling french fries, donuts and chips, while gossiping about boys. Groups of boys hang out boasting about their latest conquest and who the next lucky one on the list would be. Usually it's all a bunch of hot air, but embellished stories always make for more entertaining conversation than the boring truth ever does.

There were old men discussing favorite fishing holes, and young families and couples grabbing a quick bite before dispersing throughout the mall to spend more than they could really afford.

The cleaning lady scurried from table to table, quickly clearing and making them presentable for the next patron. Sometimes she thought she was invisible to those she served and that bothered her.

Leaning against a concrete column, in the center of the food court, was the lone security officer, and although making minimum wage, he was standing ready to protect all the nice people with his sparkling uniform, flashlight, two-way radio and John Wayne attitude.

Several doors along the glass front of the building allowed easy access to the food court from the south parking lot. Through these doors walked five men, each wearing blue jeans and light green windbreaker jackets with the word 'security' plastered on the back in big yellow letters. From under their coats they withdrew their instruments of death and without warning, three of them opened fire directly into the center of the crowd, steadily sweeping their weapons back and forth. The remaining two gunmen stood motionless, as if waiting for someone to say 'go'.

Within seconds the shooters emptied their machine guns and quickly and proficiently reloaded. The security officer nearly succeeded in getting the button on his radio pressed to call for help when three bullets ripped into his throat. The young man was thrown over a table and lay on the floor with blood gurgling and air whistling from his ravaged neck. People were running and screaming in all directions like chickens after a fox had gotten into the Henhouse. Some parents grabbed small children and attempted to flee, while others elected to cover their children's bodies with their own. Four teenage boys wearing varsity letterman's jackets dove for cover behind the counter of the Orange Julius, saving their lives. The cleaning lady took refuge behind her cart, screamed and wet her pants when several bullets smacked into the mop bucket beside her head. Finally the other two gunmen opened fire, quickly shooting down several people making a mad dash for the safety of the interior mall. Bodies were dropping too fast to count, many shot, while others slipped and fell on the blood-slickened floor.

The shooting lasted less than two minutes, and then suddenly stopped, as if some unseen movie director had yelled 'cut'. The killers turned and bolted from the slaughterhouse they had just created. They slammed through the doors, brushing by several people just entering the mall, sprinted past a water fountain, and headed for a waiting Ford van parked at the curb. Jumping in, one of them shouted, "Go!" to the woman in the driver's seat. She stomped on the gas and left a long streak of burning rubber behind as she made a getaway. Running stop signs and red lights the vanload of killers quickly reached the interstate and just minutes later were out of town and calmly driving down backcountry roads.

The six terrorists abandoned the vehicle behind a two-story farmhouse several miles from the mall. Soaking the van with gasoline, one of the killers placed a burning cigarette inside a book of matches on the floorboard. It was a simple fuse, but allowed the killers to be two miles away, in a Jeep Cherokee, when the getaway vehicle exploded. In short order, the nearby house caught fire and was fully involved when the Palo Cedro Volunteer Fire Department arrived.

$$* \qquad * \qquad * \qquad *$$

The food court at the mall was eerily quiet, devoid of the usual chatter of a hundred patrons, even the faint moaning and weeping of the wounded was barely audible. Those fortunate enough to have survived without wound or serious injury slowly began to emerge from behind the relative safety of tables, chairs and trashcans. Several had even used the fallen bodies of strangers for cover. Two off-duty trauma nurses from one of the area hospitals, shopping on their day off, were the first to recover their bearings and began tending to the wounded. People's shock gradually wore off, those with first aid training started to help. The task was overwhelming, as there were far more dead and injured than there were qualified people to attend them.

Grief-stricken mothers and fathers wept over the bodies of their children, wives for their husbands, husbands for their wives and children for their parents. In some cases, whole families were completely eliminated. Shocked people staggered around in dazed confusion, while others just sat and stared in disbelief at the carnage before them. Shouting and cursing began as horrified victims questioned where the police and ambulances were. "Why is there no one coming to help us?" one distraught woman wailed loudly, rocking back and forth clutching the limp body of her dead infant to her breast.

After waiting more than twenty minutes and still no help having arrived, many bystanders began loading the grievously wounded into their own vehicles and racing them to the hospital. Other shoppers gently placed garments they'd just purchased over the faces of victims that were obviously beyond any earthly help. A few Arab shoppers, receiving hostile looks from bystanders, panicked and raced to their vehicles, leaving before they could become victims of someone's misplaced rage.

The reason no help had yet arrived was there was no one available to come. At the time of the attack, all emergency personnel were at the Full Gospel Missionary Baptist Church thirteen miles away. The Redding Police and Fire Departments, as well as all ambulatory services, were already fully deployed when the calls for help from the mall began to come in. The emergency dispatchers' only recourse was to call in volunteer fire departments from outlying areas, as well as the Highway Patrol and Sheriff's Department. These additional resources were spread out all over the County, and it took time for them to respond. Nearly half an hour had passed before the first ambulance drove up. As a result, many people, who normally would have survived, succumbed to their injuries.

CHAPTER 4

▼

Chief of Police Mitch Baker collapsed into the chair behind his gray metal desk and placed his head in his hands, an expression of grief and utter exhaustion upon his face. Coming to grips with what had transpired over the past several hours and days was a monumental undertaking. Since his arrival at the church this morning, he had not been able to stop questioning his earlier decision to postpone calling in the FBI. Even though his head was telling him it wouldn't have mattered, his heart was singing a far different tune, and he couldn't stop kicking himself for it. His eyes strayed over to the picture of his own family sitting on the corner of his desk, and he grieved for all the other families that would be forever changed. He had only been at his desk for a couple minutes when the intercom buzzed. It was his secretary informing him an agent with the FBI, out of the Sacramento field office, was holding on line two.

Baker took a few moments to gain his composure, and force down the bile that was rising in his throat, before picking up the extension. "Chief Baker," he said firmly, in an attempt to sound more in control of his emotions and the situation than he really was.

"Chief, this is Special Agent Dalton Ryker with the FBI in Sacramento. I've just been informed that things have been a bit eventful up your way the past couple of days."

"That, Agent Ryker, would be the understatement of the year," Baker replied, his nerves calming a bit. "I was just preparing to call you guys for some help."

"You've had four major terrorist incidents in the past forty-eight hours Chief," the agent said sharply. "And you're just now getting ready to call?"

"I'm well aware of that *Agent Ryker*. The last thing I need is for you to start busting my chops over it," Baker retorted forcefully.

"What I don't understand," Ryker continued, ignoring the irritation in Baker's voice, "is why in the hell didn't you call us right away?"

"Well…we weren't too sure exactly what we were dealing with…to be perfectly honest with you, we still don't."

"Chief, by the figures I have in front of me, you've got a lot of dead people on your hands, and I don't know how many wounded…"

"But…"

"What I'm trying to say is, even if you didn't know for certain what was going on, after what happened Friday night, you should have called us, immediately."

"I realize that now, but at the time we thought we were taking the appropriate actions."

"Did it not occur to you to err on the side of caution?" Ryker asked with an edge to his voice. "We've now wasted over thirty hours! Thirty hours we could have used chasing down the killers! Even though, in all likelihood, today's attacks wouldn't have been prevented, that's very valuable time we could have utilized to get up there and prepare for when they did hit again."

Baker took a moment to compose his thoughts before replying. "My senior detective and I discussed it Saturday morning after the first two attacks. We decided to take a couple of days and see if we could break the case, then in the event we had no luck, we were going to call you in."

"Did you really think you could solve the case in two days with the limited resources at your disposal?"

"Agent Ryker, I realize in your eyes, we may be just a hick-town police department, but we're still expected to do our jobs. Give me a break will you? We've never dealt with anything like this before, you know? And yes, to answer your question, we did believe we had a halfway decent chance of solving this in two days. And even with our *limited resources,* we have managed to solve murder cases before in less time!"

"Yeah, well that also left you with a halfway decent chance of failure, didn't it? And with what's at stake, that's an unacceptable risk for you to have taken! Furthermore, I do realize that it's the first time you've dealt with this type of thing and that's exactly why you shouldn't have waited! How many more people may die due to your procrastination?"

"I know," was all Baker could think to say, knowing too well that what Ryker had just said was dead on the money.

"I damn well hope you didn't wait too long!"

"Me too," Baker humbly replied.

Ryker decided to reel things in just a bit. "Chief, we're not going to accomplish anything if we continue to bicker. The FBI has a satellite office in Redding; first thing in the morning I will be up there with a counter-terrorism task force; we'll operate from there and I will need your full cooperation, understood?"

"I understand." Baker replied.

"Alright, I'll see you in the morning." Realizing they would have to work together, Ryker extended an Olive branch. "Oh…and don't let it get to you about waiting to call us. You and I both know it wouldn't have made much of a difference." Ryker said and hung up without waiting for a reply.

Baker's hand was shaking as he replaced the receiver on its cradle and leaned back in his chair. *What in the world was going on,* he thought? *Who were these savages? Why here? Why now?* They were like ghosts, coming out of the shadows to strike then vanishing just as quickly. Other than the notes, he had no evidence and no leads. When the third note at the church was found he hoped they'd caught a break; no word on that yet. All the attacks were obviously connected, of that he was certain. But so far not one bystander had been able to give them any kind of a decent description. And the only place anyone was left alive was at the mall, and people there were too busy running for their lives to get much of a look at the shooters.

Baker looked up to see Phil Scott coming his way. Scott rapped once on the glass and came on in, not waiting to be invited.

Baker looked up at him and asked, "Well, what have you come up with?"

"A big fat zero!" Scott replied, dropping into a chair with a huff. "Most of the survivors are in too much shock to be of any help."

"Has forensics come up with anything of value?" Baker asked hopefully.

"Not so far."

"All right, let me have it Phil, how many victims do we have?" Baker asked, not really wanting to know.

Scott removed a small spiral bound notepad from his breast pocket and went through the motions of checking his notes. In reality, this was not necessary. He knew only too well what was in them.

"Well, the church was the worst," Scott began, "there are sixty-three fatalities."

"Sixty-three? My God!" Baker exclaimed. He sat back in his chair slowly dropping his gaze to his hands and intermeshed his fingers. "Any survivors?" he asked softly without looking up, already knowing the truth but hoping someone had somehow slipped by the killers and survived.

"None. It appears the killers took extra care to tidy up…you know? They made sure no one was left alive, just like at the first house Friday night." Scott answered.

"I was told there was another note?"

"Have you seen it yet? I sent it over to you as soon as it cleared forensics?" Scott inquired.

"Not yet. From what I was told it was identical to the first two. Did they find anything useful?"

A dejected Scott informed him they hadn't.

"Well, whoever these monsters are, they certainly want us to know they did it all. What about the mall?" Baker asked. *Please, please give me some good news?*

"There were not as many fatalities, but it was still bad, forty-seven dead. However, there are another fifty-seven wounded, some really bad and many of those probably won't survive the night," Scott explained. "More than a hundred and fifty others didn't get a scratch," he added.

Baker did some quick math, "Merciful Jesus Phil, a hundred and forty-two dead in two days?

"I know." Scott said bowing his head, as if by reporting the details it somehow made him responsible for them. "We do have a general description of the gunmen however."

Baker's head came up, "A description?"

"Just as we assumed, they appear to be Middle Eastern, late twenties to mid forties. From the amount of shell casings we found, they had to be using fully automatic weapons, most likely M-10's or Uzi's; same as the other attacks."

"Has the lab been able to lift any usable prints from the shell casings?"

"They haven't had all that much time, they did dust a random sampling of the casings, but it's pretty evident the shooters wiped them clean before using them."

"What else?"

"We also have a report that a female may have been driving the get-away vehicle. Evidently they made their escape in a white Ford van."

"A woman…?" Baker said a bit surprised.

"Yes, a woman."

"Let's concentrate our efforts on her. She'll probably be easier to track down than the men will be."

"Why do you think that?"

"There are a lot less Arab females in this county than men," Baker explained.

"I agree. Do you want me to give this information to the Sheriff? There's no guarantee the terrorists live within the city limits."

Baker thought about it for a few seconds. "Yes, that will be fine."

The telephone on Baker's desk buzzed. He picked it up, "Yes?" Baker listened for a minute or so and hung up. "There was a house fire a few miles out of town this afternoon, about twenty minutes after the incident at the mall."

"Do you suppose it's connected to the shootings?" Scott asked.

"I wouldn't bet my house on it, but probably so. It looks as if the fire started inside a van parked up close to the back of the building," Baker explained. "Apparently the owners of the house have been on vacation for the past several weeks and the house has been vacant."

"Do you think this is where they were staging their attacks from?" Scott asked.

"Could be, with the exception of half the living room, the house was almost completely destroyed. Why don't you get over there and talk with forensics, see if they have been able to find anything promising? I doubt they will, but we can always keep our fingers crossed and hope. You'll have to coordinate with the Sheriff as it is his jurisdiction."

Scott was already halfway to the door before Baker was finished speaking. "I'll let you know as soon as we find anything out," he said, walking briskly away.

Baker sat for a few minutes pondering what his next move should be, and then picked up the phone and called a junior detective into his office.

"Hal, I want you to get over to the County Tax Collector and get me a list of everyone in the county who is Middle Eastern. I also want you to get ahold of someone at the County Schools office and get me a breakdown by nationality all students on their roles."

"Sir, I'm not sure the Tax collector would have that information. Perhaps the Census Bureau or the Controllers office?"

"I don't know who has it, just find it!"

The young detective turned to go and then hesitated.

"What is it?" Baker asked impatiently.

"Sir, all of those offices are closed until tomorrow. What should I do?"

"Why don't you exercise some initiative and ingenuity? Find a way to make it happen and don't come back until you have."

No sooner had the detective left the office did Baker regret how he handled the young man. *I shouldn't have taken my stress out on him.* He would make a point to apologize the first chance he got.

So far Baker had no leads and very little evidence to tell the FBI man in the morning. Hopefully his detective would be able to find something useful. It was a good a place to start as any.

CHAPTER 5

▼

Day Four

Monday

Abraham Dewalt Nicholson was the first black president in the history of the United States. He had been sworn in just a month after the sitting president was diagnosed with terminal pancreatic cancer. He had now been in office six months, after serving only two as the vice president. Being the great-great grandson of slaves, he tended to hold a strong position when it came to civil rights issues. He didn't believe he displayed any unfair bias toward people with fairer skin, but he worked hard to ensure a level playing field for all minorities. The more radical right wing groups out there were frequently accusing him of using his position to further his personal agenda; he knew, in his heart, these allegations were false and without merit. Yes, he had strong convictions, and opinions; however, his integrity was not for sale or compromise. He was determined to carry out his duties, the way he saw fit, and his critics would just have to get over it. The way he saw it, if at least fifty point one percent of the voters agreed with him come the next election, that was all the justification he needed.

It was Nicholson's position that the previous Republican administration had handled the nation's war on terror poorly, and evidently so did the majority of Americans, from the lop-sided voting that had taken place in the last national election. The United States citizens could no longer stomach the constant images flashing across their televisions almost daily of flag-draped coffins containing the remains of their young sons and daughters being rolled from the back of cargo planes at Andrews Air Force Base. And they had grown heartsick and tired of the hourly news updates reporting that another innocent American had been tortured and beheaded somewhere in the Middle East by Allah's 'true believers'. Added to this was the media coverage of badly burned, disfigured and crippled children, and the expansion of the war to include Syria.

The reason given for invading Syria was Republican claims that Saddam's weapons of mass destruction, still conveniently missing, had apparently been moved into the neighboring Arab country just prior to the US invasion of Iraq. Although no WMD's had yet been found, the Republicans did claim to have 'credible evidence' indicating they were present somewhere. All of this finally led to the weary American people saying 'enough', and the previous administration was voted out of office in a landslide election by an all time record voter turnout. Republican politicians later publicly admonished the American people and cautioned them they would rue the day.

President Nicholson had been working tirelessly to change the way the conflict was currently being handled. He believed the United States needed to withdraw her troops out of the Middle East and work toward forming a much stronger international coalition. He was convinced diplomacy would provide the path to a viable and lasting peaceful solution with those heads of states that were allegedly harboring terrorists, not invasion and destruction.

Nicholson was familiar with all of the intelligence supporting the theory WMD's were present in Syria, and yet to this very day, he questioned the validity of those reports. He believed much of the information was simply fabricated and embellished by the Republican controlled intelligence services in an attempt to justify their actions and their bloated budgets. He believed it was time America be held to the same level of accountability as the rest of the world, and he was going to see she was.

He had gone round and round with the Joint Chiefs of Staff about the necessity of such a large US military presence in the Middle East. The military leadership stood firm in their belief that a strong presence was essential in the Middle East to ensure the continued protection of vital US interests in the region. Nicholson, on the other hand, argued countries in the region should be left to govern themselves in whatever manner they wished. If the United States would remove herself and her influence, then a lasting peace could be achieved. With this in mind he had just given the Chairman of the Joint Chiefs orders to begin making plans for an incremental and eventually complete withdrawal of US forces from the Middle East. "If they don't want us there, then we should leave," he'd told the starchy Marine General. "We sure wouldn't allow another country to deploy forces off our coasts or on our soil, not without severe repercussions, so why should other countries allow us the same freedom, just because we're stronger?" With great power comes great responsibility, and he would not condone the United States' continual misuse of that power for one more day, if he could help it.

National Security Advisor Mark Gooden walked into the Oval office past the two serious looking Secret Service Agents standing guard. Gooden was one of the few Senior White House staff members Nicholson had retained from the now-deceased former president's cabinet. This was only because he and Mark had been friends for many years, having gone to the same college and pledged to the same fraternity. Through the years they had moved in the same circles and had grown to trust one another, as much as two people in the Washington elite were able to. Their families had regularly spent weekends together, that was until Nicholson was sworn in as president. Now those frequent weekend get-togethers were practically a thing of the past. Their families had managed to squeeze in one weekend together at Camp David, but that was all; they were now both far too busy for such luxuries.

"Good morning Mr. President," Gooden said, handing the president a folder marked top secret and taking a seat across the desk from him.

"Good morning Mark, have a good weekend?" Nicholson asked as he took the offered folder and placed it on the desk in front of him.

"Yeah, Marjorie and I spent the weekend out on the Chesapeake with the kids, thanks for asking."

"Great, hope you enjoyed yourselves," the president said, taking a drink from his can of Coke. Since he'd stopped smoking he found he relied more and more on the caffeine rich beverage; no matter the hour of the day he could usually be found with one close at hand. Unfortunately, it was also slowly packing on the pounds and he knew he'd have to tend to that problem soon enough.

"Thank you. We did."

"All right, let's get started," Nicholson said, indicating he was ready to begin the presidential daily briefing.

"Sir, we've got a real bad situation developing. Preliminary reports indicate as many as four different potential terrorist attacks have been successfully carried out in the Northern California City of Redding within the past forty-eight hours," Gooden handed the president the summary of what they knew so far.

"Potential terrorist attacks…we're not sure?" the president asked while scanning quickly through the file.

"No, not entirely. Evidently the local police chief didn't notify the FBI until sometime Sunday afternoon, several hours after the fourth attack. So, they're running a bit behind in assimilating all of the details"

"Why in the hell did he wait so long to call for help?"

"The locals were not entirely sure they were dealing with terrorists until after the second two attacks took place."

"What are we doing to deal with it?"

"We've checked with all our intelligence services and those of our allies, none of them report receiving any information that terrorists were planning anything at all in CONUS," Gooden explained. CONUS was Washington lingo for the Continental United States. "Other than that, the FBI Director has dispatched a terrorism task force to Redding. Its 5:15 AM out there and the team should arrive about 8:00."

"Has this hit the news yet?" Nicholson inquired.

"Yes, in addition to the local stations, CNN and FOX have crews on the way. So far, no one has made the leap and started publicly reporting them as terrorist attacks. But, that's only because the details are being kept from them, and that will change quickly enough. We'd better come up with some answers before then."

"If and when the terrorist connection is made, what do you think our position should be?"

"What do you mean by our position?'

"Well, do you think we should downplay the terrorists connection to prevent a panic, or do we provide full disclosure?"

"I think we tell them the truth, that details about the attacks are still developing and when we know more we'll let them know."

"All right, get the Press Secretary on it. I'm quite certain the American people will want to hear from the White House immediately. And have him throw in something along the lines of 'we're going to hunt down the perpetrators and bring them to justice'. The voters like to hear that kind of stuff. It helps them feel safe. Also make it known the Redding area will receive the full support of the government in her time of need."

"Sounds good."

"If this does turn out to be the work of terrorists, I'm sure glad they didn't choose a larger city like San Francisco or Los Angeles, the political fall out would be much worse."

"I know. I feel the same way," Gooden concurred.

"Now, to other matters. Late yesterday I directed the Chairman of the Joint Chiefs to begin making plans for our military withdrawal from Iraq and Syria, and eventually the region itself."

Gooden smiled, "Mr. President, it's about time. You know I agree with that move and I'm convinced most of the country does as well. We've been meddling over there for way too long; you do realize, however, that the conservative right is going to do its best to crucify you in the press?" he cautioned.

"I don't really care what my detractors do, or say. Getting out of there is the right thing to do and I'm going to see that it's done. We've lost a lot of fine young Americans because our involvement there was the wrong move from the get go. Wars are nothing more than young men dying and old men talking, I intend to change that too, if I can. We've got to get out, because the alternative is even more flag-draped coffins on the evening news and that's unacceptable."

"Does your desire to withdraw from the Middle East include Israel?"

"I haven't yet decided exactly what our future involvement there will entail, why?"

"If we stop supporting them, public opinion will turn against you even faster than it did against the Republicans."

'I'm not quite as convinced of that as you seem to be," Nicholson said.

"Mr. President, you know as well as I do, the threat of US military intervention is the only thing preventing the Arab world from driving the Jews into the sea. That has been their ultimate goal since Israel once again became a nation in 1948. Most Christians believe the rebirth of Israel is Bible prophecy being fulfilled. If you turn your back on Israel, the Christian Coalition will burn you at the stake."

"Oh very well, we'll maintain a carrier battle group in the Eastern Med as a deterrent, and we'll keep supplying Israel with arms to defend herself. But, as far as the Gulf goes, we're out of there."

Gooden thought for a second, "Aye, Aye sir. How do you plan to sell all of this to the American people? You will have to justify these moves. We've had a military presence in the gulf for years. Even though people are tired of the war, they're as equally afraid of not having fuel to put in their vehicles. If OPEC cuts oil exports to us any further, the people are going to run you out of office."

"First we'll get assurances from OPEC that oil supplies will not be interrupted anymore than they already have been."

"What makes you so sure we can get those assurances or even trust them once we do?"

"Because, I'm convinced that with the guarantee our military is gone, they will boost oil exports and gas prices will stabilize and eventually fall to more manageable figures."

"What if they don't?" Gooden argued.

"They will!"

"But how can you be so sure? That's a big risk you're proposing," Gooden persisted.

"I don't anticipate any further problems…!" Nicholson stopped talking and took a moment to regain his composure. "Mark, they know we can just as quickly send our forces back in, that's why. Besides they crave our money just as badly as we need their oil."

"How will you convince the country?"

"I will simply tell the nation we have fulfilled our objectives and it's now time to bring our boys and girls home. Saddam is gone and his regime is destroyed. There is now a democratic government in Iraq and things are steadily becoming more stable." The president chose to ignore that without the war he so strongly opposed, Saddam would most certainly still be in power and he would likely still be killing thousands of innocent people. "Al-Qaeda is all but destroyed, and what's left is scattered, although recent *intelligence* indicates they may be regrouping for another push, we have nothing concrete that says they will pose a legitimate threat to the United States. We've been in Syria for months and have found absolutely nothing, and it shouldn't be too hard to convince people that we won't."

"What about the conflict between the Palestinians and the Israelis?"

"Arafat is dead and his successor seems to be much more moderate. Additionally, the Israelis pulled their people out of the Gaza and gave it back to the Palestinians. So, it would seem the threat of further conflict in Israel is, at the least, greatly diminished."

"But our reasons for invading Syria were to find the WMD's. If we pull out short of discovering them, we'll be crucified in the court of international opinion and all the lives we lost in Syria would be for nothing."

"Not exactly Mark, don't forget thousands of terrorists from other nations were allowed to enter Iraq through Syria's open borders and attack our troops. Not only allowed, but assisted by the Syrian government. If push comes to shove, we can use that as justification for our going in, to protect our troops. And remember, if all else fails, we can simply lay the whole thing at the feet of the Republicans."

"How will you manage that?"

"Just like after World War Two, the Korean Conflict and Vietnam, America wants to go forward. They want this whole thing to just go away. They're tired and they're afraid. I don't think it's going to take a whole lot of convincing. Besides, we didn't send the troops in, like Nixon in his day, we're pulling them out."

"I hope you're right." Gooden said, not sounding all too confident.

CHAPTER 6

▼

Special Agent Dalton Ryker arrived with his team in Redding just after 8:30 Monday morning. He dropped them off at a motel on the edge of town, so they could check in, and then proceeded to the FBI satellite office not far from the last attack. He arrived to discover that reporters were already gathered outside waiting for him. *How did they know I was coming?* he thought. *It's because they're vultures; vultures are always looking for fresh meat,* he snickered to himself. He parked his car and got out, locking the doors. As he walked toward the tall gray building, one particular reporter from FOX News recognized him. She ran quickly towards him with her microphone cocked and ready, the cameraman struggling to keep up.

"Agent Ryker, were these attacks carried out by Islamic terrorists?" she demanded to know.

Ryker continued walking as he answered. "Is there any other kind?" he said, the sarcasm dripping from his words.

"You're kidding, right?"

"Sure…sure, I'm kidding." He took a few more steps, "At present we have no reason to justify making that conclusion."

"Is al-Qaeda involved?" she asked, as if she hadn't heard a word he said.

"I repeat, there is no evidence, at this time, linking these heinous acts to al-Qaeda, or any other terrorist group for that matter," though secretly he'd bet his upcoming two-week vacation that they were.

"My sources tell me there was notes claiming responsibility for the attacks. Can you confirm this?"

"I don't know anything about any notes."

"Then why did the FBI bother coming all the way up here from Sacramento if it's just a local issue, and there is no terrorist connection?"

Damn! I should have seen that coming! "I have no further comment at this time."

"If this is not a terrorist incident, why do the local police need the FBI's assistance in catching the perpetrators?" a local reporter with ABC asked.

"And why did you get up here so quickly?" another reporter yelled.

"Details are a bit sketchy at this time," he answered.

"Are all the attacks connected?" NBC chimed in.

"Details are a bit sketchy at this time," he answered again, trying to walk faster without being obvious about it.

"Do you have any leads?" CNN joined the fray.

"Details are a bit sketchy at this time."

"Agent Ryker, please give us something to go with!" someone pleaded.

Ryker stopped at the door, paused briefly, then turned toward the anxious faces of the media horde. He smiled politely, more to give himself a moment to think than of any heartfelt desire to be courteous. He cleared his throat, "Ladies and Gentlemen, let's everyone take a deep breath, shall we?" making quite a show of taking in a huge breath, holding it for several seconds and then exaggerating the exhale. "Now, doesn't everyone feel much better?" He found himself staring into what seemed to be a sea of faces, none of which appeared to be the least bit amused by his poor attempt at humor. He smiled. "I know you've been standing here waiting, and that you're all extremely hungry and want to be fed, but please understand, I am only just arriving and need some time to prepare your meal. I realize you're eager for some answers, so am I. However, when I say details are sketchy, that's exactly what I mean. When I have something substantial to tell you, I'll make an announcement." With that he turned and disappeared into the building, leaving the buzzards to fight over the scraps.

He took the elevator to the third floor, stepped off and turned to the left. He approached a door marked "Fullerton Breyer Industries and turned the knob. Few people in Redding even knew there was an FBI office in town. Since the attacks on the World Trade Center and the Pentagon that information was being kept quiet for security reasons.

Inside he found a short, stocky man with a receding hairline sitting in a chair glancing through a manila folder. "Good morning, you are…?" Ryker asked.

The man stood and extended his right hand, "Chief of Police Mitch Baker, we spoke yesterday."

"Oh…right," he said shaking his hand. "Follow me please," Ryker directed as he stepped into the first vacant office he came to and sat down behind the desk. Baker followed him and sat in a chair facing him.

"All right, what have you come up with?" Ryker immediately asked, dispensing with any further pleasantries and getting right down to business.

Baker took a deep breath. "Friday night we had two separate attacks. Both took place in private homes on opposite sides of town. They both occurred within twenty minutes of one another and were well organized. In all, there were thirty-three fatalities. Twenty-three at the first house and ten at the second."

"Any survivors or witnesses?"

"None, the killers made sure that everyone died."

"Could both attacks have been carried out by the same individuals?"

"Not a chance. The houses were too far apart for that to be a plausible possibility," Baker explained.

"Have you been able to link the victims at the first house with those at the second?" Ryker asked.

"Other than the two notes, my investigators have found no obvious connection between the two groups of victims, at least not one we've been able to track down. They appear to be completely unrelated. In fact, the MO (Method of Operation) of the attacks was completely different."

"Was there anyone missing or unaccounted for from either home that should have been there?"

"None that we could determine."

"Let me see the notes," Ryker requested, extending his hand toward Baker.

Baker slipped his hand inside the manila folder and handed Ryker Xeroxed copies of the first two notes. "The originals are being kept in the evidence locker back at headquarters," he explained.

Ryker read the documents and then placed them on his desk without comment.

"Yesterday morning there was an attack on a small Baptist church, and a little more than an hour later there was another one at the mall."

"Which mall?"

"We only have one, Agent Ryker."

"Oh…uh…how many victims from the last two attacks?"

Baker looked down, referring to his notes. "Sixty-three people were killed at the church and there were no survivors there either." He paused to give Ryker a chance to comment; when none came, he proceeded. "At the mall we had an initial body count of forty-seven; that figure has since risen to fifty-one and will most likely go even higher. There are still another fifty wounded, and five on the critical list."

"Why so many fatalities at the mall, surely the people were running and had more escape options? And I'm gonna guess that the shooters didn't have the time to walk around and make sure everyone was dead that time, did they?"

"No, they didn't, but the food court was crammed full of shoppers and it was like shooting fish in a barrel. They couldn't miss. They also made sure all emergency personnel were at the church; obviously to ensure as many deaths as possible."

"Well, how did they manage to do that?"

"Emergency dispatchers received a call reporting the attack on the church. The timing of the call indicated that it was made almost immediately after the third attack. It came in from a pay phone two miles from the church, and no witnesses have yet come forward. We surmise that one of the killers made the call to draw the first responders to the church and away from the mall.

"That makes sense. In fact, I'd say it was a brilliant move. Did you recover any usable prints from the pay phone?"

"No."

"I want a copy of the nine-one-one call so we can send it off to Quantico and have them run a voice print analysis on it." Voice print identification was still a relatively new science that was performed by taking a recording of an unidentified voice and washing it through a computer to compare it to other known voices on file. Though it was difficult to get an exact match without many samples to work from, it did aid in paring down the list to a more manageable figure.

"The nine-one-one call was from a woman," Baker added. "There are not a lot of females on the terrorism watch-list but the number is growing daily."

"That could certainly help narrow things down a bit; if she's on the list. How many shooters do you think we're dealing with here?"

"Our best guess is no less than five and as many as seven, possibly more."

"And you arrived at those figures how?" Ryker inquired.

"Forensics determined that the first and third incidents involved only three shooters."

"How did they arrive at that conclusion?"

"The shell casings only came from three weapons. I suppose there could have been more than three of the rodents present, perhaps a driver, but that's all speculation."

"Okay, go on."

"Two of the weapons involved in the church shooting were also used in the first attack, and this was all verified through ballistics."

"That would imply that two of the shooters took part in both attacks. Do we have four different shooters and weapons, or six shooters?"

"I think both. Through ballistics and eyewitnesses we've been able to determine that there were five different killers at the mall, and likely a sixth driving the getaway car. Four of the five weapons used at the mall matched up to shell casings found at the previous shootings."

"Anything else?"

"Other than the notes, we have nothing connecting the second house to the other three incidents, as no guns were used."

Ryker thought for a minute, "What do we know about the shooters themselves?"

"From eyewitness accounts, all five of the shooters at the mall were men. They appeared to be in their mid-twenties to early forties, possibly Middle Eastern and all clean-shaven. We don't have a good description of the woman, but we believe she may have been the driver."

"That's quite a wide range on the killers' ages. Most terrorists who take these kinds of actions are young, early to mid-twenties. Why do you believe they were Middle Eastern, since most Americans when put to the test can't tell the difference between Mid-Eastern and Hispanic people?"

"I know eyewitness identifications are not all that reliable either, most of the time. However, one of the survivors is a professor of Cultural Studies at the community college, and she is dead certain they were from the Middle East."

"Has anyone put her with a sketch artist yet?"

"Not yet, we've been a bit busy, but I'll get someone on it as soon as I get back to the office," Baker said, making a note on his clipboard.

"Has anyone else been able to give a description of the shooters?"

"No. I guess when idiots start shooting, people just don't take the time to look around to see who is doing it. They just scatter."

"Right. How about the surveillance cameras at the mall? Were those able to capture anything useful?"

"Nothing, it seems the killers knew where the cameras were located and covered their faces on the way in and out the door."

Ryker sighed, "Another wonderful piece of news. You mentioned a getaway vehicle was spotted racing away from the mall; have your people found out anything there we can use?"

"It was recovered just outside of town; both it and the house it was hid behind were gutted by fire. The vehicle belonged to the owners of the house. We're fairly confident it was just a target of opportunity. No forensic evidence was found that could lead us to the shooters."

"Any chance the homeowners are involved?"

"Not unless sixty year old Irish Catholics are now involved with Islamic terrorists."

"Point taken. Are you sure this is the correct vehicle?'

"As sure as we can be. A white van burning at this particular time seems a little too coincidental not to be."

"What other steps have you taken to try and locate or identify any suspects?"

Baker hesitated to answer, thought about it and then plunged forward. "I have requested local government agencies to forward to my office any information in their possession concerning persons of Middle Eastern origin living in the county."

"That's a pretty politically incorrect thing to do, don't you think?" Ryker prodded.

"I don't care, I'm trying to save lives, not get elected or win a popularity contest," Baker countered. "Besides, I'm convinced these people are living right here in the community."

"Why?"

"Just a hunch."

"Isn't it amazing how many cases are actually solved by cops following their hunches?" Ryker grinned, "Very well, I'm going to schedule a press conference for 1:00PM."

"What are you going to say?"

"I think we need to reveal all that we know. Keeping it quiet will only assist the terrorists. Besides, we need all the help we can get; and if we don't give those 'journalistic professionals' outside something to write, they're likely to start making it up themselves."

Baker grinned, "It has happened before, hasn't it?"

"Yes it has, far too often."

CHAPTER 7

▼

At exactly 1:00 PM Monday afternoon, Special Agent Ryker and Police Chief Baker walked out of the lobby of the FBI office to face the throng of reporters gathered outside. Ryker had mentally rehearsed several times what he was going to say; because he knew he had to be very careful with, not only *what* he said, but also *how* he said it. He was quite aware what he was going to say would not be popular, but he believed it to be the only viable course of action available to him at this time. *Drastic problems sometimes require drastic solutions,* he thought.

Ryker nodded to the members of the press standing before him, "Ladies and gentlemen, over the past forty-eight hours there have been four horrific and evil terrorist attacks conducted against the innocent members of this community and this country. These attacks have resulted in the deaths of one hundred and forty-seven American citizens, and that number will no doubt climb further, though we all hope and pray that it does not. The killers made no distinctions between man, woman or child. They attacked without provocation our homes, a place of worship and those among us who are the most vulnerable," the crime scene photos from the group home still glaringly fresh in his mind. "I believe these targets were specifically chosen for the severe emotional impact they would wreak on us as a nation. The attacks were meant to rattle our state of mind and destroy faith in our way of life. We, as a people, must unite and refuse to allow that to happen."

"Those claiming responsibility for the cowardly acts, left notes at three of the four locations. Through these notes and other forensic evidence, it is clear that the same group of people conducted all four attacks. The notes are identical to each other and I will now read them to you.

"Praise be to the great and merciful Allah. The Great Satan has imported its poison to our lands for years. You corrupt our governments and our children with your lies, your propaganda and your immoral entertainment. You use your powerful military to enforce your will and way of life upon us. We will make the streets run red with your children's blood until you stop. The two bombings of your World Trade Center were simply the first steps designed to bring the war to your shores. No longer will the fight be waged in Iraq, Syria, Afghanistan and other Islamic nations, the battles will now be fought in your own streets, and homes as well. The justice you have witnessed these past few days is only the beginning. Prepare yourselves, retribution is at hand. Allahu Akbar, Allahu Akbar, (God is Great!).

"The note is signed, The United Islamic People. We believe this letter to be authentic," Ryker continued. "However, no demands have been received from the killers at this time. We also believe there are at least six terrorists involved, five men and a woman." Ryker gave them what descriptions they currently had. "For them to have appeared and then disappear so quickly indicates to us that they are a part of this community, although that in no way is a definite. More than likely, they are working jobs and raising their families here. They would have to be if they want to blend in and avoid any unwanted attention. Therefore, I am calling on all good citizens, Muslim as well as non-Muslim, to be watchful of anyone of Middle Eastern origin. If you see anything suspicious, or just out of the ordinary, report it to the police or FBI immediately. Now please be fair in your assessments, we're not conducting a witch-hunt here. Do not attempt to take any action on your own; these people are extremely dangerous. If we work together, I believe we can root out this evil and restore order to the community. That concludes my statement," Ryker said. "I will now take a few questions."

The CNN reporter was the quickest to act, "Agent Ryker, are you actually advocating the profiling of Islamic people?"

Ryker smiled slyly, "Not in the way the tone of your voice would imply. By all the evidence we've been able to gather, as well as eyewitness accounts, the individuals responsible for these attacks appear to be Middle Eastern. So yes, I guess I am advocating the profiling of *Arab* Islamic people. If we receive further *credible* information that convinces us the description of the killers is inaccurate, then we will modify our search criteria accordingly."

"Could the eyewitnesses be mistaken? I mean, quite frequently Middle Eastern people are confused with being Mexican or Latinos. If that turns out to be the case, then you would be going after the wrong people, and whipping up the citizenry of this community against Arab Americans for no reason," the reporter rebutted.

"That is true, however, it is not a Latino's custom to walk into a church and gun down innocent men, women and children, all in the name of Allah."

"But how is what you are advocating any different than what African Americans have been subjected to, in every city in this country, for hundreds of years now?" she persisted. "I don't see how you're advocating the profiling of Arabs as any different. You're still targeting a segment of the population based solely on their appearance."

Ryker had already heard enough of what he considered to be bleeding heart liberalism being spewed in his direction. "All right, listen, all of you! If a fat, forty-year old white guy with a limp and a goiter on his neck robs a Circle K, you don't expect the police to put out an All Points Bulletin on a twenty-five year old African American female nun, you target the fat white guy. This is no different. I do not intend to subject everyone in this community to the FBI's scrutiny when the terrorists fit a specific profile. We're already having enough of that in our airports. Law-abiding citizens can't even carry matches and lighters on planes anymore and why? Because some idiot may decide that the all-loving Allah wants him to blow the hell out of it. Arabs are the ones who hijacked and crashed the planes on 9/11, which has resulted in the rest of us enduring long hours at security checkpoints. These Islamic whackos are intent on changing our way of life, and because we continue to play patty-cake with them, they're succeeding. We need to hold *their* feet to the fire-not those of innocent, peaceful citizens."

"There are currently one hundred and forty-seven cold bodies lying on concrete slabs at the morgue as we speak. And make no mistake, if these cuddly, misunderstood Arabs get their way, they'll gladly put every one of us standing here today on the slab next to them. If I have to resort to *profiling* to prevent that, then that's just what I intend to do. Now, how's about someone ask a question that may actually do some good here, instead of trying to get a spine tingling sound bite for your next newscast?"

Surprisingly the reporters were speechless for several seconds. "Do you have reason to believe that these attacks may continue?" the FOX news reporter finally asked.

"Yes I do," Ryker replied, with conviction.

"How can you be so certain? Previous attacks on US soil were never followed up with immediate attacks. Why are you so sure they will be this time?'"

"That's a good question, I'll tell you why. First, all four attacks were carried out too easily and with unconscionable success. This will no doubt give them the confidence they need to continue. Secondly, I believe these attacks have been planned for a long time, perhaps even years. They were just too well orchestrated.

Third, they have made no demands; therefore, there is nothing we can give them to compel them to stop, even though it is our national policy to not negotiate with terrorists. Finally, they said that very thing in the notes. They made a point to state very clearly that the attacks would continue and that the battles would be *fought*, future tense, in our streets. So no, I don't think they're done, I think they're just getting started.

"Does the White House condone the course of action you've just advocated, Agent Ryker?" ABC asked.

"The President has clearly laid out the foundation on how he wishes the fight against terrorism to be handled. I am following his written directives, in conjunction with sound law enforcement principles. These actions are not being carried out to offend or hurt any law-abiding citizen. They are simply being enacted to apprehend the killers as quickly as possible and hopefully save lives. I think that the president, as well as the American people, would concur with that and provide their unwavering support."

A reporter with National Public Radio spoke next, "Agent Ryker, have you been able to directly link these attacks to al-Qaeda, Hezzbollah, Hamas, Islamic Jihad, or any of the other internationally recognized terrorist organizations?"

"Not yet, however, I would not be the least bit surprised if we do so in the near future."

"How can you sound so confident?" The NPR reporter persisted.

"The attacks have so far shown a lot of forethought. They knew when and where to hit, and how to get maximum results. They conducted the attacks on Sunday in such a manner as to overload our emergency resources and greatly hinder our ability to respond effectively. Many more people died as a result of this."

"Do you have reason to believe a nation state may have been behind or supported the attacks in any way?" CNN again.

"While that is definitely always a strong possibility, and I personally wouldn't be surprised if there is, we have no evidence at this time to support making that kind of conclusion."

"Why do you feel that a foreign power may be behind this?"

"For the same reason I believe they're behind practically every Islamic terrorist group in the world. The terrorists are too well funded for one. Another reason is they're allowed to train and take refuge in foreign countries right under the noses of the government. They don't even hide their activities from the governments that shelter them. They operate in the open, knowing full well the host country will do nothing to dissuade or stop them. Why should they? The terrorists are carrying out a policy that they themselves condone, but can't accomplish by using their own military."

"And what policy would that be?"

Ryker smiled sarcastically, "Why, the destruction of the United States and Israel, of course."

"Chief Baker, what steps have you taken to further protect your city?" a USA Today columnist asked.

Ryker moved to the side and allowed Baker access to the microphones, "I have ordered mandatory overtime for all officers, canceled all vacations and recalled those that are on vacation. I have requested that the California Highway Patrol significantly increase their coverage in the area, and the Sheriff has called in all reserve deputies, as well as increased overtime."

"Has any consideration been given to calling in the National Guard? To me, that seems to be the logical next step."

"That option has been considered, just like in any other significant event or disaster; however, we have not made a firm decision either way as yet."

Ryker stepped up and leaned in front of Baker, "That is all the questions we have time for. We will advise you when anything of interest further develops. Thank you." The questions had started going in a dangerous direction. Ryker believed that calling in the National Guard would no doubt help to increase security; it was also likely to send the wrong message to an already frightened populace. Although he had said that further attacks are likely, he didn't want the public to start thinking that the military was the only option of preventing them. Not just yet.

Special Agent Ryker could not have known that a few National Guard roadblocks might very well have prevented what happened next.

CHAPTER 8

▼

Day Five

Tuesday

Late Tuesday morning the trucker pulled into the truck stop and waited his turn to fuel up. The tank on the right side of his truck was still full, but the left side was down to about a half. He knew it was always wise to start up the northern mountains with a full fuel load. The driver stopped here several times a week, as it was on his assigned route from the gas refineries just outside Oakland, to Eugene, Oregon. He had been making this same trip three times per week for the last four years and knew just about everyone working here.

His turn came and he pulled forward, topped off his tank, then drove out into the parking lot. He liked to park so he could see his rig from the restaurant, and boy was he hungry. He parked the truck and got out, leaving the engine running. He wasn't sure whether leaving the truck running was supposed to save fuel, or if it just saved wear on the engine from being repeatedly turned on and off, anyway, that's the way he had been taught to do it.

He started across the parking lot, and then stopped to look at majestic Mount Lassen, standing in all her glory more than thirty miles to the east. The view was awesome and no matter how many times he saw it, he was still amazed. At more than ten thousand five hundred feet above sea level, the active, although 'sleeping' volcano, grabbed his attention each and every time he came through. Finally, he walked the two hundred feet or so to the restaurant, bought a copy of USA Today from the machine, and was a bit surprised to find that it now cost a dollar per copy. Slipping a thumb inside his waistband, he tugged on his britches pulling them up snugly under his large gut. He then stepped inside, immediately feeling refreshed as the chilled air slapped him in the face. Entering the restaurant he took a seat in his regular booth near the window.

"Morning Earl, what can I get for you?" the waitress asked him as she flipped over the coffee cup already on the table, filling it to the brim. She knew not to leave room for cream and sugar. Earl liked it black.

This particular waitress had been working here since before he first started coming in. She wasn't much to look at he admitted, but she really was sweet, smelled nice and was very talkative. After hours in a truck by himself, a little feminine conversation was always a plus.

"Howdy, Edith, howze bout' a little kiss?" he joked.

"Sorry sweetheart, we're all out today, maybe next trip. Perhaps something off the menu would satisfy you?" she smiled, opening it and placing it on the table in front of him.

"No thanks, I'll just have the buffet," Earl smiled back.

"Okay. Just coffee?"

"Yeah, that's all. Are you guys serving lunch yet?"

"Sure are, help yourself, you know where the plates are." Earl watched her ample hips sway from side to side as she turned and walked towards the next table and thought *maybe…nah.*

*   *   *   *

Jose pushed his broom across the pavement sweeping up cigarette butts, soda cups and candy wrappers that were constantly being kicked out of trucks by careless drivers.

He saw the big, shiny red truck with all the chrome on it and decided this was the day. He had watched this trucker for quite some time and knew he always left the engine running and the door unlocked; *far too trusting,* he thought.

*   *   *   *

Earl is a big man and he rarely ordered anything off the menu, as a result he usually asked for the buffet. He liked his food and he liked to feel satisfied. He was just returning to his table with his third heaping plate of food, gravy dripping off the side onto the floor, when he glanced out the window toward his truck. *Is that someone lurking around the driver's door?* He took a few steps to his right to get a better look, and then realized it was just Jose, the nice young fella' who cleaned up around here. He dismissed the young man from his mind and proceeded to his table.

The sad fact was that Earl should have been more concerned. What he had actually seen was indeed Jose, also known as Mushin Ali Yasim, getting into the cab of his truck.

Yasim had been born to a poor family in Qatar, a largely barren peninsula in the Persian Gulf bordering Saudi Arabia and The United Arab Emirates. He had been recruited at the tender age of eleven by al-Qaeda; the terrorist group who all too frequently preyed on the young and impoverished. Yasim had been groomed and trained for more than ten years to carry out the bidding of Allah. It never occurred to him to question why Allah's wishes were always conveyed to him through a third party, never from the *deity* himself.

At the age of twenty-two he moved to Brazil, where through the use of falsified papers, he changed his name to Jose Ramirez. A year later he *legally* immigrated to the United States and took on menial jobs, eventually ending up in Anderson, California, a small town about ten miles south of Redding. He landed a job as a janitor at the truck stop located about halfway between the two cities. That was two years ago, and he was still there.

Yasim had waited patiently after the events of 9/11 for orders to carry out his mission; at times he started to question whether those orders would ever come. Having been in the west for several years he'd been exposed to every morally corrupt and evil thing that Islam was opposed to. America was filled with a people that pretty much believed that if it felt good, do it. Yasim had sampled just about every sin of the flesh known to mankind since arriving here, however, his faith in what he had to do had never wavered. He still believed that his mission was a righteous and pure one, and that he would go to Paradise and receive the seventy-two virgins he had been promised by Allah. Finally, two weeks ago, the signal was given and it was now time to act.

Yasim had attached two bombs to the underside of the tanker trailer, one near the front and the other near the rear. He had constructed each bomb with six sticks of dynamite and remote detonators that he had stolen from a construction site over a year ago. He climbed into the truck, closed the door, placed the detonator switch on the console and fastened his seatbelt, more out of habit than of any real concern for his own safety. He reached towards the dash and pushed in the large, yellow button releasing the airbrakes. Then pressing down on the clutch he shifted the big rig into gear and then slowly drove toward the exit and his destiny.

Inside the restaurant, Earl happened to look up from his second steaming plate of peach cobbler and saw his truck exit the parking lot, turn left and drive off toward Interstate Five. He jumped up and ran to the door shouting, "Hey! Someone's stealing my rig!"

He stood there staring for a few seconds watching his truck, and his only form of livelihood, veer onto the on ramp and head north towards Redding. Earl ran to the cashier and demanded to use the telephone. He quickly tapped in 911 and told the emergency dispatcher what had just occurred. He identified himself, gave a description of his truck and assured the operator that he would remain where he was. *Where else am I going to go,* he thought? He hung up the phone, and with nothing else to do, returned to his table. Earl glanced down at the newspaper and read the headlines, "Terrorists Strike!!!" He quickly scanned down through the first few lines of the article and when he saw just where they had struck, he looked back towards the interstate, his shoulders slumped and his face went pale.

*   *   *   *

Yasim worked his way through the gears as the truck rapidly gained speed. His destination was only a few miles away and by the help of Allah he would succeed in this greatest of missions. He'd only driven about two miles when he saw a police cruiser, with its emergency lights flashing and siren blaring, dart onto the Interstate behind him. He hadn't expected the police to respond quite so quickly. *Oh well*, he thought, *what can that little car possibly do to stop me?*

By the time he had traveled another mile, two California Highway Patrol interceptors had joined the chase. Yasim pushed down his right foot firmly and the speedometer crept past the seventy-five mile per hour mark. *Just a few more miles*, he thought, *Allah will be pleased*, he reassured himself.

Directly behind the fleeing tractor-trailer was CHP Officer Steve Chapman. He had been in the middle of making a routine traffic stop on the southbound side of the interstate when he received the call concerning the hijacked truck. The events of the past few days instantly leapt to the forefront of his mind. He quickly told the motorist it was her lucky day, tossed her license and registration in her lap, and sprinted back to his car. As he was getting into his vehicle, he observed the stolen truck pass him on the northbound side with two other law enforcement vehicles racing behind in close pursuit. Chapman spun the steering wheel hard to the left, and stomped on the accelerator. Hardly looking for oncoming traffic to his rear, he shot across the road, bounced roughly through the grassy median and joined the chase.

Chapman didn't know anything about the driver, or his intentions, he only knew that the truck had been reported stolen just minutes ago. Neither he, nor the other officers in pursuit could possibly know how this chase would end.

Chapman accelerated to over one hundred miles per hour and brought the Ford Crown Victoria up along the left side of the speeding tanker. Easing back on his speed to match that of the fleeing truck, he looked up at the driver and motioned for him to pull over, but the driver acted as if he didn't exist. Chapman radioed in that the hijacker appeared to be Iranian or of similar ethnic background. Upon hearing this, every officer in radio contact suddenly found that their stomachs were twisted in knots, more than was normal for any other high-speed chase. This was a feeling of impending doom and they would find that their feelings would prove to be right.

Innocent motorists braked, swerved and darted to the side of the road, fleeing to get out of the path of the rampaging truck. One driver, who was unaware of what was rapidly approaching, failed to evade the truck and was slammed from behind. The tiny Ford Focus was shoved along the asphalt for over a hundred yards before being flipped up and into the air, spinning twice end over end and finally landing with a tremendous crash on its roof, glass and shredded metal flying in all directions. One of the tires was ripped off the axle and went spinning down the side of the interstate, eventually coming to rest under a sign that read, 'Parking and Stopping Prohibited.' The driver of the demolished vehicle died instantly, even though both air bags had deployed.

By the time Yasim had reached the turn-off for Highway 299, there were eight police vehicles clamoring away behind him. Ignoring their commands to pull over, he grew ever confident that he would succeed. He swerved the racing truck onto the off-ramp for the Highway 44/299 split. West would take him toward Eureka and east toward Mount Lassen; he chose west. Looping around and under I-5 he accelerated toward the heart of downtown Redding. His destination was now less than two miles away and he believed nothing could stop him now. *Allah, please give me strength,* he prayed.

Officer Chapman was still to the left rear of the fleeing truck. When he saw it abruptly swerve onto the off-ramp and veer towards downtown, he quickly followed. It was painfully clear to him that 299 would stop being a highway at the edge of downtown and city streets would begin. There would be many more cars, as well as pedestrians, and they were traveling much too fast. Chapman decided that this whole ugly situation was going to end tragically; he had to terminate the chase, and fast. He quickly made a snap decision, and although it was a dangerous one, it was the only thing he could think of at the moment, let the consequences be damned.

Chapman reached over and retrieved the twelve-gauge shotgun from the security lock between the seats and then lowered the front passenger's window. With a practiced hand he wracked a shell in the breach of the Remington 870. While fighting to control the vehicle, Chapman sped up parallel to the truck and rested the barrel of the gun on the window ledge. Taking careful aim and ensuring there was nothing beyond the truck that he couldn't chance hitting, he fired a round into the left rear tires. Two of the huge tires shredded and hot chunks of flying rubber shot into the air. Several large pieces struck a pursuing CHP car and shattered the windshield, causing the officer to lose control and swerve into a guardrail. The car spun in two complete circles before coming to a jarring stop. The officer driving, though pretty shaken up and addled was not injured.

Chapman pulled the shotgun back to work another shell into the chamber. Even though he had practiced this maneuver many times, while sitting in front of the television watching ESPN, with an unloaded weapon of course, it was much more difficult to achieve while handling a steering wheel and racing over eighty-five miles per hour in hot pursuit. Crucial time was passing and the truck was now less than one mile from the edge of town.

One of the pursuing officers accelerated up close behind Chapman and repeated the same move that he had just executed himself. Firing at the tires on the tanker trailer, two more tires were blown apart. The truck swerved sharply to the left and collided with the right front quarter panel of Chapman's patrol car. The collision was powerful and although Chapman was a seasoned officer with much experience in high-speed chases, he still struggled to maintain control of his vehicle. The truck pulled away from him and there was now less than a half-mile to go.

Yasim knew he could not strike his intended target from this side of the highway, at least not at the speed he desired. As he crossed over the bridge spanning the Sacramento River, he jerked the steering wheel to the left, barreled into the median, smashed through the guardrails separating the two sides of the road, tore through the oleander bushes and bounced into oncoming traffic.

Like a flash, Chapman followed him, suddenly understanding just where the truck was heading. He knew there would be little room to maneuver in the tight city streets up ahead, and that left only one likely target. "My God!" he yelled. With everything in him Chapman hoped and prayed that he was wrong, but somehow knew that he wasn't.

There was only one other way he could see to stop the deranged lunatic and he only had time for one attempt. He knew he'd better make it count; if he failed, the consequences would be catastrophic.

Onrushing cars were veering sharply off the road into the trees and bushes lining both the sides of the highway in an attempt to escape the crazy truck that was racing toward them. At over eighty miles an hour, those that didn't react fast enough were crashed into and shoved out of the way by the eighty thousand-pound battering ram. An elderly couple, driving slowly down the road in an old '65 Chevy pickup, didn't see the truck speeding toward them. The wife was choking on a piece of cookie, and her husband was slapping her on the back, not exactly looking for oncoming traffic. The big rig slammed into them at close to ninety miles per hour, the smaller vehicle disintegrating like a firecracker set off inside a piece of fine china. The grandparents never knew what it was that instantly ended their combined lives of one hundred and forty-eight years.

Amazingly enough, none of the flying wreckage struck Chapman's vehicle and the truck did nothing more than bounce a couple of times and kept going, barely even slowing down. Chapman sped up to the driver's side door and again aimed his shotgun out the window. To get the angle he required to make the shot, he had to lean way over into the passenger's seat. Looking up to locate his target, he found the driver grinning at him with a triumphant expression of pure evil and hatred.

The two speeding vehicles raced side by side and entered the last small curve that would take them into the final quarter mile stretch. Chapman realized he was running out of road and with no time left to take proper aim, he fired from instinct. The nine thirty-two caliber pellets exploded from the end of the barrel and blasted into the driver's door of the truck. Only one of the lead pellets managed to find the intended target. It shattered the window and ripped into Yasim's body. The lethal projectile entered him slightly under the left arm, passed through his lung, and stopped to rest just two millimeters from the outer wall of his heart. Those two millimeters would make all of the difference.

Officer Steve Chapman had leaned over much too far to get his shot; the kick back of the weapon firing caused him to lose control of the car. It veered sharply to the left and smashed through the guardrail, flew off the steep embankment and slammed into a large oak tree at over seventy miles per hour. A split second after the patrol car struck the tree, so did Officer Chapman. In his haste to join in the pursuit, he had failed to fasten his seat belt and was thrown through the windshield even before the air bag could deploy, not that it would have helped a great deal. At that speed, the only thing for certain, was that he would never know how the chase that stole his life would momentarily end. He left behind a pregnant wife and two small children.

Yasim felt a sharp, fiery pain bite into his left side and he abruptly lost all feeling on that side of his body. He didn't know what had hit him, only that it was the most excruciating pain he had felt this far in his young life. Whatever the cause, at this point it didn't matter. With his right hand he somehow managed to steer the truck at the target and stomped down on the accelerator. The truck veered slightly to the right and would not strike the target exactly where he had planned, but that wouldn't matter much. The large vehicle crashed into the side of Shasta Regional Medical Center.

Yasim sat there slumped over behind the huge steering wheel, blood running down his side and gasping for breath; each one shooting laser bolts of agony through his body. Several moments passed before he shook his head vigorously from side to side attempting to clear his thoughts. At last some semblance of clarity arrived and he remembered what he was supposed to be doing. He looked out through the shattered windshield and saw broken bodies lying everywhere. *I did it!* From off to his left he heard crying and groans of misery. Looking in their direction, he saw several people trying to open a door to get away. Yasim, with his last ounce of strength whispered, "Allahu Akbar," and pressed the detonator.

CHAPTER 9

▼

The tanker tore into the northeast corner of the hospital at over sixty miles an hour. As the forty-ton guided missile smashed through the outer wall of the conference room, a steel support beam punctured the side of the tanker, ripping a gash in it eight inches high and fifteen feet long. Over eight thousand three hundred gallons of hi-octane gasoline began pouring out of the massive rupture in the side of the truck. However, the gas itself would not present the biggest problem; eight thousand gallons of fuel produces an enormous amount of vapor, and this would ultimately be the cause of the greatest damage.

At the time the truck was bearing down on the hospital, all of the departmental supervisors were just sitting down to begin their scheduled monthly board meeting. Surprisingly, taking into account recent events, most of them were thinking of other activities; shopping, golfing, and going to the movies, were amongst the favorites. The hospital director was discussing how the recent increase of patients, due to the terrorist attacks, was overtaxing their resources. This meeting would center on the possible short-term solutions to what, at present, was believed to be a short-term problem. She had just asked for suggestions when the tanker burst through the outer wall.

The calloused hand of the Reaper reached out, instantly claiming the lives of seventeen people. The dead would never know what had happened, at least not on this side of eternity. Thoughts of golfing and shopping were swept from survivor's minds, overwhelmed by the instinct to survive. Many, who were able to stand, began trying to do exactly that, staggering toward the exits. A huge section of falling ceiling pinned several more supervisors under its crushing weight. Only a few of the dazed and confused victims succeeded in reaching the door. An older man, with blood gushing from a head wound, was just turning the knob, when Yasim gave praise to Allah and pressed the detonator.

The twelve sticks of dynamite exploded, blowing fuel, steel, wood, furniture and torn body parts in all directions. The sound wave was audible more than twenty miles away. The blast ripped into the heart of the building and claimed the lives of every employee, patient and visitor within one hundred and twenty-five feet of ground zero. Then the fuel vapors ignited, creating a secondary explosion ten times greater than the first. A massive fiery shock wave shattered windows and shook the foundations of several nearby buildings. Concrete and steel were shredded as easily as a child makes confetti. The detonation opened a crater in the floor thirty feet deep, and thirty-five feet across. The polished stainless steel from the tanker was blown up through three floors, taking with it tables, chairs, glass and water pipes from the fire suppression system. The lives of two hundred and seven more were instantaneously added to the merciful Allah's rapidly growing body count.

The force of the explosion threw people out of windows, depositing them onto streets, sidewalks and parked cars seventy feet below. Flesh was ripped from people's bodies; bones were not only broken, they were shattered like a crystal bowl dropped on a concrete floor. Arms and legs were ripped from torsos, while other bodies simply vaporized. Agonizing minutes passed and then finally dazed, confused and wounded people began to slowly emerge from the suffocating black smoke and dust.

Seeming to have a mind of its own, the scorching fireball advanced rapidly through the building, searching out random oxygen cylinders and adding those to the bedlam. As each one exploded, more carnage resulted, and the angel of death claimed even more victims.

Water pipes burst, shooting water in all directions as doctors, nurses and other staff members rushed around trying to deal with the sudden madness as best they could manage. Although the staff was regularly drilled in fire evacuation, this by far exceeded anything they had been trained to handle. Bedridden patients were burned alive, screaming in their beds, as employees grabbed fire extinguishers and rushed in to save them, all in vain. Staircases crumbled and elevators were rendered useless, cutting off all avenues of escape, condemning scores more to their deaths. Faced with no other alternative than to surrender to the searing flames, people began jumping from windows. Those jumping from the second floor received broken limbs and other non-life threatening injuries; any who jumped from higher up, simply perished. Agonizing memories of 9/11 leapt into the minds of horrified onlookers.

Walls and entire floors started to collapse from stress, as the fire grew more powerful, feeding on a bountiful supply of fuel. Panicked hospital workers, overcome by their fear and their own will to survive, finally gave up trying to save those in their charge and fled, darting around sparking electrical wires and looking for any means of escape. Very few would find a way out.

Fire engines and rescue workers responded from all over the city and county. The besieged community was throwing every resource at its disposal toward fighting the blaze. Calls went out to the California Department of Forestry, pleading with them to send helicopters loaded with fire retardant in a desperate attempt to gain some measure of control over the blinding inferno. However, this only aided in extinguishing the flames shooting out of the roof several floors above the ground; the fires inside raged on undeterred.

On the east side of the building a large outer wall succumbed to the flames, shuddered and crumbled into a nearby parking lot, crushing ten valiant fire fighters under its massive weight. Fuel tanks in cars ignited and detonated, creating a chain reaction that jumped from car to car, forcing the remaining firefighters in the area to retreat from the furious heat, surrendering it to the intensity of the ravenous fire.

Hundreds of people stood watching on nearby rooftops, streets and sidewalks in horror and disbelief. Most of them had been in this particular hospital at one time or another for various reasons, recalling how many employees, patients and visitors they had seen in the building at the time. Then they started talking amongst themselves, remarking on how very few seemed to be coming out. The citizens of Redding began weeping and praying for the innumerable people that had already perished, and for those that would surely follow.

News helicopters were soon hovering high above the inferno, broadcasting the vision of the Armageddon below to every television set across the country and most of the world. Seeing this, off-duty firefighters, police officers and paramedics scrambled to their cars and rushed to assist. As word spread, doctors and nurses from every office and clinic in town canceled appointments and hurried to the scene to render aid. Most were disheartened to find that there was little they could do for the wounded once they arrived; most were beyond help.

Grievously wounded people were staggering into the streets, hands clasped over their bleeding heads and throats. Everywhere people lay bleeding on blankets and coats that onlookers had thrown down as makeshift beds. One woman walked in circles looking for her missing left hand, blood pumping from the stub of her wrist. Bystanders ran up with towels and tore away pieces of their own clothing in an attempt to staunch the bleeding. One young man was in such shock, that he was walking around on a leg so badly damaged, a bone could be seen poking out through a gash in his thigh. A police officer knelt over the body of a small child, clamping off her nose, attempting to blow life into her badly scorched lungs. A man held the bleeding, lifeless body of his wife, looking toward heaven with tears streaming down his face, screaming, "Why! Why!" All around were grief-stricken people, their lips quivering, wailing over the limp, broken bodies of friends, coworkers and family-members.

A light blue Jeep Cherokee drove slowly past the hospital. Inside were six people, five men and a woman. They all glanced over at the great display of carnage and human suffering. One of them smiled, "Praise be to Allah," another one uttered. The others grunted in agreement.

A police officer standing nearby directing traffic happened to look into the vehicle as it passed by. He couldn't see into the rear of the Jeep because of the tinted windows, but he did see the man in the front passenger seat; *was he smiling?* The officer didn't have a whole lot of time to think about it, but he did take a moment to make a note of the license plate number, as the vehicle turned the corner and disappeared.

CHAPTER 10

▼

National Security Advisor Mark Gooden strolled into the Oval Office with slumped shoulders, and sat down across from President Nicholson who was talking on the phone with the Prime Minister of Israel. Gooden's day had been very long and it looked as if it was going to get even longer. He had spent numerous hours burning up the phone lines with the heads of the FBI, CIA, Joint Chiefs of Staff and Homeland Security on and off for the last two days, trying to come to an agreement as how to best handle the current crisis in California. While everyone agreed that something had to be done, no one could come to any consensus about how to accomplish it.

The President was in full support of allowing the FBI and other law enforcement agencies to conduct their normal investigations, and the Director of the FBI Chuck Alexander concurred with him. CIA Director Stuart Minetti, and Homeland Security Director Iverson James, were both pushing to promptly take into custody all persons of Middle Eastern origin residing within one hundred miles of the Redding area for intense questioning. Meanwhile the military, led by the Chairman of the Joint Chiefs of Staff, General Donovan Slade, was in favor of immediately declaring martial law in the city, restricting freedom of movement, and bringing things rapidly back under tight control, if there was any in the first place.

Throughout the crisis, Gooden found himself strongly agreeing with the president; that is, until he found out the latest attack had taken place. Now, the seed of doubt had been firmly planted in his mind, and it was quickly sprouting roots of confusion. The more he thought, the more he listened to all the 'experts', the more confused he became. So far they had come up with no solutions, only more and more unanswerable questions.

Finally, the president hung up the phone and looked toward Gooden.

"Mr. President, there's been another terrorist attack, this one is much worse than any of the others by far," he sighed.

A look of deep despair spread slowly across Nicholson's face. "What now, where?" he asked somberly.

"In Redding again, sir. The lousy maggots hit a hospital and it looks pretty bad. From what I've seen they struck it hard. The entire building is in flames, large sections of it are collapsing and the death toll will be extremely high."

"What did they do, use a bomb?"

"You could say that, sir. The California Highway Patrol was in high-speed pursuit of a stolen truck just prior to the attack. The hijacker rammed the truck into the side of the hospital and blew it up."

"Why didn't they stop him?"

"They had no way of knowing they were chasing a suicide bomber at the time. They assumed it was nothing more than a random hijacking."

"You've got to be kidding! What in the hell did they think he was going to do with it, take it to the Burger King for a Whopper?" Nicholson retorted sarcastically.

"Well sir, with the current gas shortage, it made perfect sense at the time," Gooden tried to explain.

"Just what kind of truck did they use?"

"It was an eighteen-wheeler tanker truck taken from a local truck stop and it was loaded full of gasoline when he plowed it into the hospital."

"But how did he...?"

"Preliminary reports, by local authorities, indicate a bomb must have been used to blow it up; the truck would not have exploded the way it did, if it hadn't."

The President's face grew even paler, if that was possible. He leaned back in his chair and reached for the pack of cigarettes he kept hidden in the back of a desk drawer. He had been trying, on and off, for a year to kick the nasty habit, but every time he made a little progress, another stressing situation would come along and it was back to square one again. Striking a match, he lit the stale non-filtered Camel, "How bad is it really, Mark?" he asked, taking a long draw of smoke into his lungs.

"We're not sure just yet. Its 3:30 PM out there and fire fighters are still battling the blaze. However, all indications show that this is going to be bad, there's very little doubt about that. There's going to be a lot of dead bodies on the six o'clock news this evening, and for many more evenings to come, I'm afraid."

The President reached for the can of Coke on his desk, now warm and flat, and took a long swallow. Retrieving the remote control from the top drawer of his desk he switched on the television across the room. It was always tuned to CNN, and it amused him that many conservatives still referred to it as the Clinton News Network, even though the wildly popular and controversial former president had been out of office for close to ten years now.

Immediately he saw a huge building, or what was left of it, fully engulfed in flames. The plume of acrid black smoke reached far into the sky and blanketed the entire city for miles in every direction. There were ladder trucks with huge water cannons pumping hundreds and hundreds of gallons of water into the flames. From what he could see, the firefighters seemed to be having little to no success, and the fires raged on. On the left of the screen, there was, what appeared to be close to two hundred sheet-draped bodies lined up in a nearby parking lot, evidently waiting to be carted away.

Nicholson sat there dumbfounded staring at the holocaust before him. He could tell, just from the picture, that the hospital, once a refuge of safety and healing, was a complete and total loss. "It looks like an entire Marine Air Wing hit the place. Mark, casualties are going to be huge, what can we do to help?"

"I think you need to mobilize the National Guard and declare martial law out there until order can be restored. People are going to panic and pure pandemonium will surely follow," Gooden advised, surprised by his sudden change of attitude.

Nicholson was also a bit taken back at Gooden's uncharacteristic position. "Declaring martial law may be a bit premature, however, notify the Governor to take preliminary steps in that direction. Have him notify his guard commanders to place their troops on a twenty-four hour call up alert, but he's not to take any further action until directed to do so from this office." It would, no doubt, come as a big surprise to the president, that the governor of California did not need his permission to deploy the National Guard and that the troops fell under the authority of the governor, not the president.

"Abe, are you sure you don't want them to go ahead and deploy? I mean, come on, the local police cannot possibly handle a crisis of this magnitude on their own. They're just not properly equipped and they lack the manpower. Public outcry will demand that the government put a stop to any further attacks. Local law enforcement and the small FBI contingent present there cannot possibly do it all alone," Gooden cautioned. "Have you forgotten that aborted fiasco that took place after the flooding in New Orleans?"

"No Mark, I haven't forgotten and I understand your concerns. However, I am not willing to subject the citizens of this country to military rule, unless we absolutely have no other options." Of course the passive attitude he was now adhering to would no doubt necessitate that very thing. "Instruct the Governor to transfer State Police Officers to the area and request that other police departments throughout the state do the same. Let's see if we can manage this crisis without involving the military, shall we? Surely we can deal with an isolated group of radicals, right?"

"Very well, sir," Gooden said, not sounding the least bit confident in the president's judgment, and carefully avoided giving any indication that he agreed with his appraisal of the situation.

"Also, get me a very detailed report on exactly what happened out there and what the FBI is planning to do about it." Nicholson sat silently for a moment. "I'm going to have to address the nation concerning all of this pretty soon. I know this is not as catastrophic as the events of 9/11, but it's still pretty bad. The American people will want to know that their government is still in business and equipped to protect them."

"Anything else?"

"Yeah, is it true the Special Agent in Charge out there really told the public to watch their neighbors, paying especially close attention to Arab-Americans?"

"Not in those exact words, but that was pretty much the gist of it."

"What an idiot! That's just what we need! What in the world was he thinking?" He took another pull on the cigarette, held in the smoke and exhaled it into the air. "I have, at no time, authorized or justified the profiling of Arabs. Now we'll have every civil rights lawyer in the country beating at the door, trying to make a name for themselves. If that's not enough, every special interest group with connections to the Islamic community will be raising cain on every television and radio news program from coast to coast demanding justice and screaming that their clients' rights are being violated!"

"That is a strong possibility," Gooden conceded, "However, it shouldn't be too difficult for you to clarify your position to the country during the press conference."

"And say what? That in light of recent events I am now condoning the singling out of Arabs? That just can't happen. I have to protect the rights of all Americans; not just those with pale complexions." The president chose to ignore that a great majority of those individuals that were to be profiled, were here illegally and therefore, not entitled to any protection under the constitution. "If we start down that road, where does it end? Just because people are stirred up emotionally and scared to death right now, doesn't mean we should start setting aside the rights of a segment of our population, just to appease those fears."

"Abe, don't you think…"

"No Mark, don't you understand, it doesn't stop there. We've pretty much told the entire world that al-Qaeda is all but destroyed, and that the war on terror is practically won. People have started to believe those reports and are finally feeling safe again, now this happens. You and I both know that when all this gets resolved, al-Qaeda's fingerprints will more than likely be found all over it. What do I tell the citizens of this country then? Whoops, I was wrong, sorry…better luck next time? Well you can forget that, I won't allow it."

"I wouldn't expect you to sir, we'll put a spin on it."

"Yeah…*how?*"

"Make the case that our biggest efforts should have been directed here on the home front from the beginning, not fighting a war ten thousand miles from our shores in a country a very small fragment of our people will ever see. Help them see that we have been so busy trying to clean up the Republican mess in the Middle East, that you haven't had the time or resources available to concentrate on the dangers we were facing here at home."

"You think that will work?"

"Sure I do. You've only been in office a few months; the American people will give you the time to make changes, if you sincerely ask them for it. But changes will have to be made, and soon."

"What sort of changes do you propose?"

"To start, we need to take a long, hard and serious look at taking drastic measures toward securing the borders."

"We've already done that. We've added more officers to the Border Patrol, and are working with both the Canadian and Mexican Governments to assist us in controlling the flow of immigrants entering from their countries."

"I'm not talking about just adding a few more border agents and endlessly blowing hot air back and forth across a conference table, never making any progress…"

"Well, what are you proposing?" Nicholson interrupted.

"I'm talking about performing a complete overhaul of our border security and our immigration policy from top to bottom."

"Just what…are you suggesting?" Nicholson asked, suspiciously.

"I'm not necessarily suggesting anything. All I'm saying is that the borders are like a sieve. Illegals, terrorists included, are pouring into this country unchecked. There are close to nine thousand illegal border-crossings every single day, many of those are Islamic radicals who've shaved their beards and are impersonating peaceful Mexicans. Hell, if the voters ever find out that we really have no idea who, or what is finding its way across the borders, we're screwed with a capital S."

"And how do you propose we stop it?"

"Well, I hate to admit it, but that O'Reilly guy over at FOX has been extremely vocal about a very probable solution for many years now, and you and I, along with everyone else have ignored him, because it's not the politically correct thing to do."

"Please enlighten me," Nicholson said, with drudgery. "You know I don't pay any attention to that fruit cake closet conservative."

"Well, he has suggested we use the military to back up the Border Patrol, in nothing more than a security role, of course. He presented a study that claimed that both borders could be closed with as little as thirty-six thousand troops. The border agents would conduct all arrests, and the military would provide security under the Border Patrol's strict authority."

"*Of course,*" Nicholson said snidely. "What, are you suggesting that we become isolationists?"

"No sir, not at all. I am suggesting that we start protecting the borders, and that is within our mandate. That's what you and everyone in elected office took an oath to do."

"I know my responsibilities, Mark, I don't need them pointed out to me."

"I'm not trying to point them out to you. I just think that somewhere along the line, many years ago, the country somehow lost its way. We've become so concerned with not offending anybody, that we've pretty much exposed every decent man, woman, and child in the country to mortal danger. It's time we corrected that, if it's not already too late."

"You might as well forget O'Reilly's preposterous idea. Do you think for one minute, with everything you know about me, I would give those military war mongers that kind of authority? Not while I'm still in this office and drawing a breath. What in the world are you thinking, Mark?"

"I was just giving you options, sir. Popular or not, that's my job," Gooden said defensively.

"I understand, but I'm not putting armed military troops on the borders."

"Very well, sir."

"As far as this whole profiling thing goes, instruct the FBI to tone things down a bit. I want that agent to publicly retract what he said, and soon."

"Sir, that would make him appear like the idiot that you just claimed he was."

"Better him than me!"

"If he does that now, he'll lose all credibility with the public and the terrorists will know that the FBI will not go to whatever lengths necessary to stop them…sir, I just wouldn't recommend it."

Nicholson thought for a moment, "Very well, but I don't want any more public comments about profiling…period."

"I'll pass along your wishes, sir."

"As far as addressing the country, I think I may elect to do it from the Oval Office, and avoid having to deal with the media's probing queries for just a few more days. That should give us a little time to get things firmly under control."

"Very well, Mr. President." Gooden believed it was a good idea, for no other reason than the President's current position wouldn't be very popular with the presently enraged population. The country may be politically polarized most of the time, but when hit, the nation wanted to hit back, and the lets-see-what-happens attitude the President encouraged, just wouldn't go over very well.

"Get to it, Mark."

"Right away sir." Gooden said, standing to walk out of the room.

Privately Nicholson believed what Gooden had proposed was not entirely without merit. Even he believed that placing troops on the border would more than likely put a stop to most terrorists coming into the country. However, how would that be any different than what the former Soviet Union had done? Look at what they had accomplished. They no longer existed. Furthermore, his voting base would never stand for it. Mexican-Americans would raise Cain, and where would the number of troops it would take come from; and how would it be paid for? So far, he had a lot of questions and very few answers. The obvious solution was not always the most popular or the most doable. No, another way would have to be found. The problem was, President Abraham Nicholson, in office now less than seven months, didn't have the foggiest clue what to do, or where to even start looking for solutions.

*   *   *   *

For decades the United States' energy policy has been to conserve its natural resources and rely more and more heavily on those of other nations around the world. As a result, new oil exploration off the coast of California, Alaska and in the Gulf of Mexico was halted. In light of US over-reliance on foreign oil, OPEC, (Organization of Petroleum Exporting Countries) saw it as the perfect set of circumstances to strike. Knowing the strong US economy relied heavily on cost effective energy sources, OPEC worked tirelessly to incrementally drive up oil prices and the cost of fuel at the American pump. This helped make their primary goal a reality; bring down the American juggernaut economy, and put an end to the Great Satan's dominant position as the world's only true super power.

George W. Bush tried, during his eight-year presidency, to open up the Alaskan wilderness to new oil exploration in the hopes of ending US reliance on foreign energy sources. While he enjoyed some limited success, during the early part of his second term, other political parties, as well as special interest groups, opposed him at every turn, which resulted in a failed policy and US continued dependence on imported petroleum.

In addition to the United States failing to capitalize on alternate sources of new oil within her own borders, her oil production in the Gulf of Mexico was decimated by huge and destructive hurricanes slashing through the Gulf damaging many oil-drilling platforms, resulting in Gulf oil production being reduced by an astounding sixty percent. Instead of ending US reliance on foreign oil, it was increased two-fold.

OPEC, whose members are virtually all Arab or Muslim countries, saw this as an opportunity too good to pass up. They started to fabricate industrial 'accidents' to artificially reduce oil supplies, and inflate fuel costs. Over the period of just a few short years, the price of oil rose from around forty dollars, to more than seventy-five dollars per barrel. The cost of diesel at the pump in the US surged to over four dollars a gallon, and the wheels of America's thriving economy began grinding to an anemic pace.

The most crucial area in which this sharp increase was felt was in America's extensive trucking industry. As the cost of fuel rose, so did the cost of goods transported by those trucks. Nearly one hundred percent of all US retail products, at some time or another, were all transported aboard trucks.

Farmers could no longer absorb the huge cost of keeping fuel-guzzling equipment in the fields and they started to go out of business. The shortage of farmers caused demand to overwhelm supplies resulting in the price of food to rise dramatically and the consumer suffered.

The building of new homes and businesses slowed to a snail's pace as the wary American consumer held onto every dollar they could. The tight-fisted consumer caused thousands of businesses to stop hiring new employees, and the downsizing of others. The US economy was in its worst shape since the late 1970's and early eighties when interest rates hovered around twenty percent.

Little by little, real fear began to grow in the hearts of the American family. No longer were they taking vacations, or making casual trips to town. Impulse buys went by the wayside, and concerned housewives began hoarding food, whenever they got the chance. Many beautifully manicured back yards were tilled up, and thousands upon thousands of vegetable gardens took their place. The American consumer was preparing for the worst.

Gas station owners instituted a policy that everyone must pre-pay before pumping, because the sheer number of drive-aways was staggering. Thousands of motorists across the country awoke each morning to find that the fuel in their cars had been siphoned away while they slept. This resulted in consumers putting enough fuel in their vehicles to get them to and from work for only a couple days. The high cost of fuel was seriously affecting the day-to-day lives of millions of Americans.

The President believed the oil crisis was legitimate and that it would soon be rectified. In a bold attempt to stabilize prices and kick-start the economy, he authorized the release of America's huge strategic petroleum reserves. The sudden influx of new oil, coupled with a huge tax cut, the Republican controlled Congress shoved down the throats of Democrats, did help for a few months. The economy began to slowly bounce back, some jobs were again being created, and new home construction started to rebound. The President was confident America had dodged yet another bullet, and the country's dominant economic position in the world was again secured.

However, the United States Government was completely fooled by the underhanded trick played on them by their oil rich *friends*. Within a few short months the oil reserves had been all but depleted, and oil 'shortages' in the Middle East had worsened, not improved. Even with the increased oil imports from South America, Canada and Mexico the president was able to negotiate, fuel prices began to steeply climb once again. The price of gasoline and diesel shot above six dollars a gallon and again, the trucking industry was the first and worst hit.

While all of the larger trucking companies had large cash reserves on hand, and were able to withstand the price increases, hundreds upon hundreds of smaller companies and independent drivers couldn't survive, and shut down operations. Desperate to stop the economic landslide, the government stepped in with a huge financial aid package in an attempt to get the trucks rolling again; unfortunately, it was too little, too late, the damage had already been done.

Grocery stores nationwide keep roughly a two to three day supply of product on hand. Stores that would normally receive a supply truck every day or two, were now lucky to receive one every four or five. Managers were no longer able to keep their shelves as well stocked as before and consumers began to panic, the hoarding of food increased. Many of the larger grocery store chains instituted policies that placed limits on the number of individual items customers were allowed to purchase; this only caused people's fear to deepen.

New laws were passed outlawing the hoarding of food and fuel. Fuel rationing was instigated, carpooling was made mandatory, and the freedom that America all too often took for granted, was slowly beginning to slip away.

CHAPTER 11

▼

Day Six

Wednesday

Special Agent Ryker flipped through the summary of yesterday's attack, shaking his head. Preliminary estimates indicated as many as eight hundred seventy citizens had been killed, with another four hundred sixty-three still missing and presumed dead. Add to that, two hundred and sixty-seven wounded, and the whole ordeal was just completely overwhelming. The one remaining hospital in town was not equipped to care for all the wounded that came flooding through its doors. The less serious patients were being tended to at urgent care centers all over the city and in surrounding counties. As bodies were recovered from the still-smoldering hulk, they were being transported to the Convention Center just under a mile from the hospital. Tim Conway and Harvey Corman had been scheduled to perform there tonight-now it was serving as a makeshift morgue and things were much less joyful.

Ryker didn't know where to begin. He knew what he wanted to do, but those options would never be allowed. He had been with the FBI going on fifteen years, but had never been faced with something like this. After 9/11, he was one of the hundreds of agents assigned to track down the numerous investigative leads. Most of them resulted in two things: hours of grueling legwork, and a lot of dead ends. Through it all, he never got close to ground zero in Manhattan or the Pentagon. Now he was facing his own 9/11 of sorts and he had absolutely no worthwhile leads.

Agent Steve Roland knocked on the door and Ryker motioned for him to come in.

"What's up, Steve?" Ryker asked.

"We just got the background check finished on the suicide bomber. Guy's name was Jose Ramirez and he emigrated from Brazil a few years back. He only lived there for a year or so, and before that, he just doesn't seem to exist. The CHP officer who died during the pursuit reported him as looking Iranian. The coroner says there wasn't enough left of him to make a determination one way or the other."

"How did we find out his name so quickly, if that is his real name? Did they strain his remains for fingerprints?"

"Not hardly, the owner of the truck he hijacked saw him snooping around it just minutes before it was taken. Ramirez has worked at the truck stop as a handyman and janitor for the last few years and the driver recognized him. He didn't think anything of it though, he assumed Ramirez belonged there and left it at that."

"How did this Ramirez get the truck? Did he hot-wire it, if that's even still possible?"

"The driver seems to have a habit of leaving the engine running and he didn't lock the door."

Ryker shook his head slowly back and forth, "Well, I guess we can assume he's not on Mensa's short list for potential candidates."

"Who?"

"Mensa."

"What in the world is Mensa? I've never heard of it, sounds like a cooking ingredient."

"It's a club for geniuses. I can see it's safe to assume you're not on the list either," Ryker grinned.

"Ha, ha...very funny!"

"Anyway, how in the world are we supposed to prevent these kinds of things from happening when guys like this won't even do the simplest of things to help us?" Ryker fumed for a minute then asked, "What else?"

"The fires have been brought under control and engineers are making preparations to go in and shore it up before emergency personnel are allowed to proceed with potential rescues; it will still be a few more hours before that happens."

"Rescue or recovery?" Ryker asked, knowing all too well the chances of finding anyone still alive were slim to none. Those not killed by the blast, or the fire, surely suffocated from the smoke, or bled to death trapped beneath the rubble. *What a sad way to go!*

"We can pray. Surely they'll find someone alive," Roland said hopefully.

"I wouldn't count on it." The intercom on the desk buzzed, Ryker pressed the button, "Yes?"

"Agent Ryker, Chief Baker is holding on line one for you."

"Thank you." Ryker picked up the extension and selected the appropriate line, "Yeah Chief, this is Ryker. What can I do for you?"

"Agent Ryker, yesterday one of my officers observed a vehicle near the hospital shortly after the attack. He said the two people in it appeared to be Middle Eastern and…"

"What do you…?" Ryker interrupted and then reconsidered, "Sorry, please go on."

"Anyway," Baker resumed, "he said he couldn't be a hundred percent positive, but he's fairly confident the passenger was looking at the burning building after the explosion and he didn't look too upset about it."

"Didn't appear too upset? So what? What exactly am I supposed to conclude from that?"

"Ryker, this particular officer is extremely street savvy. He wouldn't have wasted my time by telling me, and I sure wouldn't be wasting yours if we didn't honestly believe there may be something to it."

"I'm listening," Ryker said, the impatience quite evident in his voice.

"He said he remembered you directing people to report anything suspicious involving Middle Eastern people. What he thought was so unusual is that the man was smiling; in fact, he said the guy had a huge grin plastered across his face. He added, that for the entire eighteen hours he was at the scene, that smile was the only one he remembered seeing on anyone, period."

"Even so," Ryker said, his voice softening, "that's not much to go on."

"I know, but what else have we got? Do you have anything more promising? Besides that, with him appearing Middle Eastern, that at least justifies taking a closer look, don't you think?"

"You got me there, Chief. Did the officer by some chance get a license number?" Ryker asked, sounding a bit more optimistic.

"He sure did, and we already ran it through the DMV. The car's registered to a Raissa and Mikal al-Nasser." Baker read off the tag number to Ryker.

"A woman?" Ryker asked, his voice raising an octave. "Could be the same one who made the nine-one-one call and if so, she's quite possibly the driver of the van at the mall."

"That's right. He also said there were more people in the rear of the vehicle, but he couldn't get a very good look at them through the tinted windows."

"Where do the al-Nasser's live?"

"Right here in Redding."

"Is the address current?"

"We believe so."

"Pull both occupant's drivers license photos and send them to me as soon as possible, will you?

"Will do," Baker replied.

"In the meantime, find out everything you can about their local doings; business, friends, personal interests, anything that might help. Contact Agent Roland in my office with whatever you find, but whatever you do, fly low under the radar, we don't want to spook them in any way."

"We'll get right on it."

"Oh, Baker?"

"Yeah?"

"You need to look past my little moods. There's a lot of pressure coming down from upstairs to solve this thing quickly and the faster we can put a face to these monsters, the better, understand?"

"You got it, I didn't take it personally," Baker said and hung up.

Ryker handed Roland the sticky note he'd written the tag number on. "Get on this right away. I want everything you can learn on these two people in three hours; bank statements, tax returns, the works."

"Consider it done," Roland answered. "Dalton, my gut tells me these two are involved in a big way, I just know it!"

"Let's not hinge our hopes on it though. Chances are it will turn out to be a big goose egg, but you and I know cases have been broken on much less. Let's keep our fingers crossed and hope the good Lord has just smiled down upon us."

Roland held up the crossed fingers on his right hand smiling, then turned and walked out of the office to carry out his orders.

Could this really be the break we've been waiting for? Ryker thought. He would make sure not get his hopes up. The worst thing to do was to become hopeful and then have the rug yanked out from under you. For some unexplained reason he didn't think this tip was going to be a waste of time.

CHAPTER 12

▼

Raissa looked at the faces of her sleeping children dimly aglow from the moon-beams shooting through the bedroom window. Watching them, she thought about the amazing success of their mission so far. Every step of the operation had gone much better than they had dreamed, and with the help of Allah, the next one would as well. It had become difficult at times over the years, to stay focused on the cause. Life in the United States was much more comfortable than she and her husband's lives had been in their native Jordan. Here they had not one car but two and the drinking water was always clean. *These infidels are always complaining that the water doesn't taste good,* she thought. *Perhaps they should visit my native land. There, if the water weren't boiled before drinking or cooking, you would likely develop severe diarrhea, or worse. It would serve them right to experience how much of the rest of the world lived; Americans are so fat and selfish.*

Most Americans did not know what it felt like to go hungry either; not just skipping a meal or two, but to not eat for days on end and listening to the young ones cry from the piercing pain in their empty bellies. Then, when one did manage to get a meal, it amounted to boiled goat meat, with no seasonings, a little broth and perhaps a carrot or a potato thrown in if you were lucky. Here, they just drove to the nearest McDonalds, or one of the many thousands of restaurants that seemed to be on every street corner advertising "All you can eat," in big, neon flashing letters.

The time had finally come for America to face the wrath of Allah, as well as that of the rest of the world. She was even convinced that the United States' closest friends and allies were sick and tired of constantly groveling at the feet of the Americans and their superior attitude. This country had, for far too many years been dictating to the rest of the world how to live, how to conduct their business and then continually legislating morality to the poor and uneducated people across the globe. *Every infidel in this godless country has an overwhelming expectation they deserve to have all that is good*, she thought. *But, it even goes further than that. 'I want it, you have it, give it to me,' seems to be the American mantra.*

In her mind, the ridiculous number of people receiving government handouts alone was staggering; in Jordan, if you don't work, you don't eat, period. There are no food stamps and welfare checks. If you can't afford children, you don't keep having them, expecting someone else to pay for them. *In America*, she thought, *if someone can't get handed what they want for free, they just simply walk into the nearest store and take it. If by some chance they do get caught, so what, it's not their fault. They're chemically dependent; forgotten is the fact that they freely chose to start taking drugs or drinking alcohol in the first place. Or they cry out they were abused as children, misunderstood, or a variety of other excuses are spewed to place the blame on someone else, anyone else, as long as the guilty party is never held responsible for their actions. They're often taken before a liberal judge who takes mercy on them and dispenses some token punishment with no realistic expectation of deterring future bad behavior. In Jordan, their hand would be cut off, end of story*, she thought. *People never got caught stealing more than twice.*

Americans just don't have the will, or the stomach to do what is required to fix their sick society. In the end, this will ultimately be their downfall.

The attacks on the World Trade Center in 93' and on 9/11, as well as the bombing of the Alfred P. Murrah Federal Building in 95', had been nothing more than the opening rounds of what she hoped would prove to be a long and bloody war with the unholy Americans. Raissa was in complete awe at how the ingenious planning of Osama bin Laden had led Americans to believe that two men, acting completely on their own, with a truck full of cow manure, had been the cause of so much destruction and death in Oklahoma City. *Americans were so gullible and stupid.* Oh yes, the American government knew better, but the average citizen believed what the government-run media monster told them to believe. The political elite did nothing more than simply march two evil men in front of the cameras, and that was the end of it, case closed. For the most part, Americans were satisfied and went on living their obscene lives. Of course, there were some extremist groups and conspiracy fanatics who believed there was more to it, but nothing ever came of it because these kinds of people are never given any credibility from major media venues…*they should have listened.*

Americans further believed that since no attacks had occurred on US soil since 9/11, they must be safe; and because the unjust war being waged against Raissa's

Islamic brothers and sisters throughout the world seemed to be succeeding, further attacks were being prevented. That belief could not have been further from the truth. Osama was a very patient and thorough tactician. The previous attacks were for no other reason than to misdirect the attention of the American people and her militant protectors. If the 'evil terrorist monsters' ever attacked their country again, the entire nation was convinced that it would be much more dramatic and heinous than the last. Once again, this was because that is what they were told to expect from their leadership. Americans firmly believed future attacks would most assuredly involve biological, chemical or nuclear weapons and target another big city or landmark of extreme emotional or financial value. Not so, the stupid American people had been misled. The attacks her cell were carrying out were designed to be of a much more personal nature.

The operations of the previous few days, and those that would follow had been carefully planned to strike fear and terror into the heart of the great American melting pot! When this Jihad was finished, no longer would people leave their homes for work, or kiss their children and send them to school without wondering, what next? The true war was just getting started after many, many years of careful planning. When completed, every American would be forced to sleep with one eye open. Raissa again looked at her sleeping son dressed in his Spiderman jammies; soon she would take her children home to Jordan, she thought warmly.

She gently kissed her children on their foreheads and adjusted their blankets, picked a teddy bear up off the floor and tucked it under her daughter's limp arm. Raissa turned and crept from the room, gently closing the door behind her and walked down the stairs to the living room where her husband, Mikal, was praying with the other four men in their cell.

Just like she and her husband, three of the men had emigrated here from the Middle East many years before; one had even taken an American wife. They all held respectable jobs and were active in the community. Abdul was from Yemen and had a Spanish mother; his lighter skin had helped him gain access to America by way of Mexico ten years ago and he had taken the fictitious name of Jesus Olarte. *How ironic*, Raissa smirked. He worked at a uniform supply shop, which allowed him to acquire, among other things, police uniforms that had proven very useful up till now, and would so again.

In his spare time Abdul Abida, often volunteered at the YMCA teaching rich people's children to swim. This of course, was part of his elaborate cover to fit in. In reality, he would have much rather drowned the spoiled little brats. It would be much better to eliminate them now, before they reached adulthood and were taught to take the lives of Muslim children with their high-tech weapons of destruction. Or worse than that, corrupt them with their debauched lifestyle.

Abdul's father had been assassinated over twenty years ago by the Israeli special intelligence unit Mossad. Mossad has the responsibility of gathering human intelligence, and carrying out covert action and counter-terrorism operations for the Israeli government. Everyone knew that Mossad was nothing more than a puppet of the United States Government. Yes, they did often carry out missions of their own choosing, however, this rarely occurred where American interests could be adversely affected, without first getting the approval of the White House.

Israel could not risk losing the political, financial and military support of their Zionist protectors; that would leave them entirely on their own, smack dab in the middle of the most hostile region on the planet. The eventual destruction of Israel was what *true* followers of Islam really sought, all bogus talks of peace aside. The United States must be forced to withdraw from that part of the planet if the Muslim world's goal for Israel were to ever be achieved.

The peace the rest of the world hoped for, worked for, begged for would never be realized; that could never be allowed to come to fruition. Even the Christian Bible was correct on that particular point, and when the US was forced out of the way, then true Jihad could begin, but not until.

Rashiid and Mustafa Baraka were brothers who had been, for the most part, raised in the United States. Their existence today could, in large part, be attributed to the CIA; while at the same time, so could their hatred for the clandestine organization. The CIA had helped their family flee from Iran, shortly before the fall of the Shah. Their father, who was a major in the Iranian military's intelligence division, had for years been spoon-feeding the CIA information about the inner workings of the Iranian Government. All of the top-secret information he supplied was, of course, carefully fabricated and screened by his superiors to help him gain the confidence of his handler. The major's plan had worked perfectly, and just days before the overthrow of the Shah, his family had been covertly whisked out of the country in the dark of night to safety. Yes, some might question the timing of their escape, but the US Government was not as surprised by the coup as they would have the rest of the world believe. Both brothers believed that very little happened in the world without Washington pulling on the invisible strings.

Only six short months after their midnight escape, Rashiid and Mustafa were orphaned at the innocent ages of three and five, respectively. Their parents had been killed in an automobile accident one stormy night on the way home from a rare date night away from their children. That was the official story, of course. It would be many years before either of them would learn the brutal truth.

A couple of months after the 'accident', a young Egyptian couple took in the boys and soon thereafter adopted them. As they grew, the orphans were taught the great mercy, love and power of Allah, and his faithful prophet Mohammed. They were carefully schooled about the evil ways of their host country and, when they were in their early teens, they were finally told the terrible truth surrounding their parents' deaths.

Their parents had indeed been coming home from a night out. In fact, they had died in a horrible car wreck, however, it had been no accident. The official story was that brake failure had sent their vehicle careening out of control on the wet, curvy mountain road, through a guardrail and over a two hundred-foot cliff, to their fiery deaths on the jagged rocks below. The problem with this *story* was that the brakes had been serviced the day before, and the police could never explain the mysterious black swipe marks down the side of their parent's red Pontiac. People, in the Islamic community believed that the CIA had learned of the misinformation their father had passed them, and this, coupled with the fear that he would one day reveal the true nature of his relationship with the US government, led to he and his wife's elimination. It was also strongly believed that the CIA's plans called for the boys to be in the car as well. The fact they weren't, only proved that the merciful Allah had plans for them to some day serve as mighty warriors in the holy crusade against the infidels.

The boys, now men, had eventually moved to Redding, where they both found employment with the city's street maintenance department. The very nature of their work provided them access to any part of the city they wished to go, without drawing the slightest bit of suspicion from the casual observer. Just recently they had even been told by their handler to loosen several long sections of guardrail on one of the bridges spanning the Sacramento River, and only yesterday did they learn the reason why. Their freedom of movement had served them well in planning out their missions thus far, and would be critical to the next one as well.

Omar Fadillah had been born and raised in the United States. He attended West Valley High School in Cottonwood, California, a few miles south of Redding, where he lettered in football and track; he was a swift runner. Omar sat in the school's library one early spring afternoon studying for an upcoming exam when he observed the large man in a stunning dark blue uniform talking with several of his fellow classmates. He eavesdropped on the conversation as the recruiter laid out to the impressionable young men the great future and benefits of serving in the United States Marine Corps. Omar, who was not the greatest of students and coming from a lower middle class family, had no realistic hopes of ever attending college, found the colorful picture the striking Marine was painting greatly appealing. Within two months, after tremendous grief from his worried parents, he found himself at the Military Enlistment Processing Station (MEPS) in Oakland, California and soon thereafter at the Marine Corps Recruit Depot in San Diego. Here he would attempt to complete twelve weeks of intense and grueling training in the hopes of becoming one of the few and the proud.

Omar excelled as a Marine and with his knowledge of Arabic was soon assigned to Force Recon Battalion, where he received specialized training in Counter Terrorism. Within a year he was transferred to a special unit attached to the Amphibious Assault Ship USS Nassau, cruising steadily toward the Red Sea. Their mission was to infiltrate Yemen and hopefully capture and bring out a Muslim cleric believed to have been responsible for the bombing of the USS Cole in the Yemeni port of Aden several years before. This was when Omar learned what the term 'need to know' truly meant.

The mission went like clockwork. They were able to infiltrate the country by sea at night and found the cleric exactly where intelligence had told them he would be. However, Omar would quickly learn that capture was not the true intent of their mission. The lieutenant in charge of the operation, upon locating and securing the cleric, made no attempt to interrogate the prisoner, he just walked up to him, placed a 9mm pistol to the back of his head and blew the man's brains out. There and then the veil of innocence was ripped away from Omar's eyes. He realized his government was not as righteous and just as he'd been conditioned to believe. There was no justice here, the cleric was simply executed with no trial to determine his guilt or innocence; where was the justice his country claimed to triumph? This was a major turning point for him. On this mission, he observed firsthand the squalid poverty his Arab brothers lived in and he made the decision, right then, to no longer take any part in furthering that misery. And by no means would he allow himself to be used as a weapon in the destruction of his hereditary people for one more day.

Soon after returning to Camp Lejeune, North Carolina, Omar sought treatment from a psychiatrist for combat stress and shortly thereafter was assigned to a non-combat unit. He completed his enlistment and was honorably discharged from active duty, returning to Redding, and using his five-point veteran's preference was able to get a job as a postal carrier. One of the stops on his route was a convenience store owned by Raissa and Mikal al-Nasser. It did not take long for them to completely open his eyes about the evil nation in which he lived. The al-Nassers embraced Omar, helping him to find the direction and purpose his life would serve. That had been three years ago and he was now a committed warrior in Allah's army.

The six freedom fighters sat around the kitchen table, after completing their prayers, snacking on chips and salsa and planning their next mission. It would be their final operation and would be the worst this country, and perhaps the world, had ever seen. The death toll would be enormous, the financial impact horrendous. America's spine would crack and her heart would break from the trauma. They all laughed because the plan, while complex, was also so simple. The will of this godless nation would finally be crushed, and they would no longer be able to ignore the mighty power of Allah.

CHAPTER 13

▼

Wednesday Evening

Even though it was only about eight paces from his own desk, Agent Roland practically ran to Ryker's office with a sheet of paper clenched tightly in his fist that was just faxed over from the Department of Homeland Security in Washington. What it said was almost too preposterous to believe. He flung open the door without knocking, to find a rather startled Ryker choking on a bite of sandwich due to the sudden intrusion.

"Dalton, this just came in from Washington!" Roland blurted out, not waiting for acknowledgment; he handed the sheet of paper to a still coughing Agent Ryker.

Ryker took the document from Roland's outstretched hand, took a drink of his Dr. Pepper, coughed again into his clenched fist to clear his throat and then calmly began to read. It revealed some quite surprising details about Raissa and Mikal's lives, both here in the United States and in their homeland. It described very vividly their family, their business interests and where they lived. It summarized how the two had immigrated to the USA nearly two decades ago. It went on to say they had both been intensely questioned by the FBI after the events of 9/11. The agent who conducted the interrogation was unable to find anything directly linking the two to al-Qaeda or any other terrorist organization for that matter. However, many years of experience convinced him that they warranted a much closer inspection. For some unknown reason they slipped through the cracks and further investigating never happened.

After some further digging, Agent Roland was able to discover some particularly interesting and quite unsettling information. Evidently, both Raissa and Mikal had been members of the Palestinian Liberation Organization for more than six years back in the late seventies and early eighties. The PLO was established in 1964 and is one of the most well known terrorist organizations in the world and its leader, Yassir Arafat, was probably the most recognized terrorist in history. At least he was, before the liberal media whitewashed his reputation and painted him in a much more positive light.

Following his death in 2005, the media suddenly forgot that he was the father of the term 'suicide bomber' and that he invented airline hijackings, hostage-taking for political gain and school massacres. Gone also were the decades of evil Arafat perpetrated on his own people. While he lived a life of luxury, they lived in squalor, while he ate the best foods and wore the finest clothes, they struggled to survive. In the end, he would be remembered as winner of the Nobel Peace Prize and would be airbrushed as a patriot and freedom fighter for the rights of the Palestinian people. Not the monster that embezzled his countrymen's money for his own greedy ends or the man that had sent countless young Palestinians off to kill themselves and others in the name of Allah.

Within three years of its creation the PLO leadership determined their primary mission would be the complete and total destruction of Israel and the Jewish people. For more than thirty years the PLO has conducted a brutal terror campaign against the Jews, both inside and outside of Israel. The PLO is most well known throughout the world for two separate, despicable attacks, although there are a slew of others.

The first of these attacks took place in Munich, Germany during the 1972 Olympics. The Olympics had not been held in Germany since 1936. In the '36 Games Nazism had fully reared its ugly head and most Germans hoped that the '72 games would, in some small way, help redeem their reputation in the eyes of the rest of the world.

On September 5, with only six days left until the end of the Games, the terrorists struck. Shortly after 4:30 in the morning, five men wearing tracksuits climbed over the six-foot high fence surrounding the Olympic village, entered the building and met up with three of their comrades who had gained entry using forged credentials. At 5:00 AM, they knocked on the door of wrestling coach Moshe Weinberg. Upon answering the door and seeing the threat, Weinberg and weight lifter Joseph Romano, tried to block the door in a futile attempt to allow the other athletes to escape. Both men were killed and nine Jewish athletes were taken hostage.

The terrorists demanded the release of 234 Israeli-held Arab prisoners, along with two renowned German radicals. They also demanded safe passage on a plane to Cairo, Egypt. After a day of intense negotiations, the German government agreed to the terrorists' terms, and transportation was arranged to carry them from the Olympic Village to the NATO air base at Firstenfeldbruck. There they would board a commercial aircraft for Cairo. The rebels took the athletes along, not knowing that German snipers were in position with orders to shoot and kill them without harming the hostages. During the transfer, the Germans discovered there were eight terrorists, instead of the five expected, and realized they did not have enough snipers to effectively deal with all of them.

After the helicopters carrying the killers and hostages arrived at the airport, German snipers opened fire, killing several terrorists. At first, the news media reported the hostages had been saved, however, nearly an hour later another gun battle broke out and a rebel grenade blew up one of the helicopters, containing some of the hostages. The remaining hostages were shot to death by a surviving terrorist before rescuers could reach them.

Later that morning a weary and tearful ABC news correspondent Jim Mckay announced, "They're all gone." Five of the PLO militants were killed, three were captured and one policeman was killed. More than a month later, a Lufthansa Airlines jet was hijacked and these terrorists demanded that the Munich zealots be released. The liberal German government, wanting to avoid any further conflict, acquiesced, and they were freed.

Following the release, Israeli Prime Minister Golda Meir covertly directed an Israeli assassin team to hunt down and kill each and every one of the terrorists, as well as those responsible for ordering and planning the attacks. Over several years the team tracked down and killed five of the Munich killers, and three more were killed with the help of the Mossad and the Israeli Defense Force. The mastermind of the massacre was never identified and is presumably still at large.

The second infamous attack was the seizing of the Italian cruise ship Achille Lauro in 1985, by four heavily armed radicals. The hijackers demanded the release of fifty Palestinian prisoners. In a truly despicable act, the terrorists shot to death a sixty-nine year old, Jewish-American passenger named Leon Klinghoffer, and flung his wheelchair-bound body into the ocean. World leaders were quick to condemn the reprehensible act and after two days the terrorists agreed to surrender if they were promised safe passage. Once again, an Egyptian commercial aircraft attempted to fly the zealots to freedom, but was forced to land in Sicily by a US Navy F-14 fighter jet, and the radicals were taken into US custody.

On September 13, 1993, the Israeli Government and the Palestinian leadership finally signed a peace agreement in Washington DC. The agreement commonly referred to as the Oslo Accord derived its name from the secret negotiations held outside Oslo, Norway. Mahmoud Abbas, representing the Palestinians and Shimon Peres from Israel signed the document while US President, Bill Clinton, Israeli Prime Minister, Yitzhak Rabin and PLO Chairman, Yassar Arafat oversaw the historic signing.

Since that peace agreement was signed, terrorist organizations in league with the PLO have ignored its goals, committing more than one hundred twenty-five attacks, resulting in more than three hundred fifty killed and more than four thousand wounded. While most of the attacks involved suicide bombings, many were executed by car bombs, ambushes, rockets, mines, grenades, mortars, snipers and any other means the militants could manage to think of.

With all the peace talk espoused by the Palestinians, the official emblem of the PLO includes a picture of the entire nation of Israel, not just the areas publicly claimed by the Palestinians. The Israeli government contends that this is proof that the PLO doesn't simply envision Israel withdrawing from the disputed lands, but that they secretly intend to destroy Israel and take all of the land as their own. Many Israelis believe no matter what 'peace agreement' the PLO signs it will never result in a lasting peace, for they are convinced the Palestinians will not be satisfied until all Jews are killed or, at the least, pushed out of the Middle East.

In the early eighties Raissa and Mikal publicly renounced their involvement with the terrorist organization, and several years later the Immigration and Naturalization Service (INS) allowed them to legally immigrate to the United States. The document went on to elaborate that there were strong indications Raissa had at one time been the secret lover of Yassir Arafat himself and had reportedly even bore him a son. It concluded by implicating Mikal in the planning of the bombing of the Marine barracks in Lebanon in 1983, which resulted in the deaths of two hundred forty-one US servicemen.

"How in God's holy world did these two manage to get approved for citizenship in this country?" Ryker thundered.

"I don't know, boss," Roland answered. "Pretty unbelievable, isn't it?"

"Unbelievable? This is scary as hell!" Ryker grabbed the paper off his desk, shaking it in his fist, "This says all of this information was in the hands of the INS prior to approving their immigration request, and they still did it!"

"I know, I read it," Roland responded calmly.

"What gets me is if these two are involved in these attacks, and after reading this I'll bet you two round trip tickets to Pluto they are, these two freaks shouldn't even be here in the first place, I don't care what they supposedly *renounced.*"

"You know what really makes my liver quiver? If these two were able to get INS approval, with everything we knew about them at the time, how many more were allowed in we know absolutely nothing about?"

A dead silence filled the room as Ryker looked up from the wrinkled piece of paper, all the color draining from his face. "Steve? If these two are involved with this nightmare, that means twenty years ago someone went to a lot of trouble to plant them here and they have been patiently waiting, looking for the right time to strike. Reminds me of the German-planted moles during World War Two."

"Scary, huh?" was all Roland could think to say.

"Scary doesn't begin to describe it. For years it's been reported by the CIA that thousands of suspected terrorists are already in the country and nobody seems to be listening. What I want to know is, are these two just the tip of the proverbial iceberg? I mean sure, we have most of the ones we suspect under some sort of surveillance, not the greatest in all cases I concede, but some. What if we've been watching the wrong people all this time?"

"What do you mean, the wrong people? Are you suggesting that everyone we've had under surveillance for the last, I don't know how many years, are not terrorists, that we misidentified them all?" Roland queried.

"No, nothing of the sort. I'm sure that every one of them has some sort of tie to terrorism. What I am saying, is that none of them appear to be doing anything significant. As you said, we've been watching them for years now and so far we haven't pinned anything more serious on them than a traffic violation or stealing a candy bar."

"So what? That doesn't mean that tomorrow they won't go out and try to blow up Grand Central Station or something!" Roland countered.

"No, it doesn't, they very well could, and that's exactly what we've all been waiting for. That's what we've all been told to expect from the government and the media for years. But what if they have been carrying out their true mission right in front of us all along, and we failed to see it?"

"Dalton, if they were planning attacks, or carrying out attacks, surely we would have seen or caught a whiff of something by now; nobody's that careful. But you're right, it doesn't appear as if they're doing anything of any concern to us."

"And I'm certain we would have caught them if they were, but what if their real mission is not to attack?"

"Not attack? What, then?" Roland asked, a perplexed expression on his face.

"Suppose their only purpose here is to drain our resources?"

"Drain our resources?"

"Yeah, say for instance they were instructed to come here and just be visible, stand out, nothing more?"

"You mean, actually let us see them?"

"Exactly. We have thousands of agents from different law enforcement and intelligence agencies all over the country trying to keep track of them, all ready to pounce at the first sign of trouble. Where we may have it wrong, is that they apparently have no orders to do anything, except keep us jumping at shadows and running around in circles. From a tactical standpoint, it's brilliant."

"So, they give us exactly what they want us to see, what we *expect* to see. We're so busy watching the wrong people, that we've failed to dig deeper and go after the *right* people."

"Bingo, and our real enemies have not yet revealed themselves." Ryker took in a deep breath. "Okay, first things first. Get the Sacramento office on the phone and request reinforcements. I'll get in touch with Chief Baker and go over the details of getting surveillance set up on our two friends. I'll also call the Director and tell him exactly what's going on, what we've learned, and what we think it might mean. I'll also request that he send a Hostage Rescue Team out here ASAP."

"HRT?" Roland asked sounding a little confused. "Don't you think that might be a tad bit premature?"

"Possibly, but I don't think so."

"Dalton, we don't even know if this lead is going to amount to anything. It surely doesn't warrant repositioning an HRT clear across the country."

"I'm well aware of that, however, if and when it does, I intend to make sure we have all the resources we need in place."

"Why can't we just pick up the suspects right now? If we wait, who knows what will happen."

"Because, if they turn out to be innocent, we'll have lawsuits up to our necks, and you and I will be tied up in court for the next three years trying to explain ourselves to the ACLU, the Arab Coalition and every other bleeding heart in the country. If they're guilty, we have to be able to prove it with absolutely no doubt. Besides, that only gives us two of the killers. Remember, there are at least six of them and if we act too soon the others will go to ground and pop up someplace else. And don't forget who is in the White House…everything has to be done by the book."

"I know. He's got the Liberal handbook and he's following it step by step," Roland said sarcastically. "Why does it seem like law enforcement's job gets easier when the Republicans are in the White House?"

Ryker chose to ignore Roland's snide comments. "Anyway, I'm sure that if these are the ones we're looking for, then they've been very careful to cover their tracks. We sure don't want to alert them prematurely; God only knows what other rotten deeds they're preparing to carry out, and I don't want to give them any reason to speed up their schedule."

Roland grunted in agreement and walked out of the room, intent on getting things moving.

Ryker pressed the intercom, "Get Baker on the phone."

Less than sixty seconds later the intercom buzzed, "Chief Baker on two."

Ryker snatched the receiver from its cradle, "Chief!" He quickly updated Baker on the latest developments.

"What do you want me to do?" Baker asked.

"These two own a convenience store and a house in the suburbs," he gave Baker the address. "I'd like you to assign your best officers to the surveillance team. I don't want these people making a move without us knowing about it five minutes before they do. If they eat lunch, I want to know if they prefer regular or extra crispy, got it?"

"Anything else?"

"Yeah, get me a list of everyone they know; friends, family, coworkers and anyone they do business with. These people can't live in a vacuum. If they are terrorists, then someone is helping them, and there has to be some sort of connection between them and I want it found, yesterday."

"You got it."

"Also, see if you can get in touch with that professor from the college. Ask her to come by my office for an interview and set it up with my assistant, will you?"

"The one who witnessed the mall shooting?"

"Yeah. We're assembling a photo lineup, and Mr. al-Nasser will be the guest of honor. Let's see if she can ID him for us. That's something we should have already taken care of."

"Sounds good."

"Chief?"

"Yeah?"

"Tell your men to be extra careful and to stay out of sight. We can't afford for the bad guys to get tipped off we're onto them."

"I'll see to it personally."

"Oh...and keep your fingers crossed." Ryker hung up the phone. Remembering his earlier conversation with Agent Roland made him think about, of all things, the ancient city of Troy. The Greek army, led by Agamemnon, besieged the city for ten years. In the tenth year of the siege, the great warrior Achilles learned that his closest friend, Patroclus, had fallen in combat to a mighty Trojan warrior named Hector. Achilles immediately challenged Hector to a fight and slew him. Soon thereafter, Achilles also died after being struck in the heel by a poisoned arrow.

Following the death of Achilles, and seeing that the vast and mighty Greek army could not take the city by force alone, the Greeks wanted to give up and go home. However a daring and cunning plan was devised by the Greeks to infiltrate their army into the city. An immense wooden horse was built and many warriors were hidden inside its hollowed out innards. Leaving the great horse at the city gates, Agamemnon withdrew his mighty army and sailed away so as to deceive the Trojans. Ignoring the warnings of several advisors, the Trojan king allowed the horse to be brought inside the city walls, believing that it was a gift of peace.

That night, while most of the Trojans were asleep, or in a drunken stupor, the Greek army quietly returned. The warriors inside the horse slipped out, overcame the guards and opened the city gates. The entire Greek army entered and dispersed throughout the city, setting it on fire. The Trojans awoke to find their city ablaze and attempted to flee, only to be slaughtered by the Greeks.

Ryker could not help but wonder if America appeared to her enemies like that old, ancient city, only instead of walls, there were oceans. Was Osama bin-Laden their modern day Agamemnon? The al-Qaeda leadership knew the US military was too large, too strong and too well equipped to defeat in open combat. They also knew that they could not spend America into submission, as the United States had done to the Soviet Union in the eighties. No, their plan must be even more cunning, more daring and brilliant than the Greeks' had been. Just as it had taken ten years to besiege and sack that city so long ago, was al-Qaeda as equally patient and committed to destroying America? Ryker believed that they were, and then some.

What if, instead of using a Trojan horse to get inside America's 'walls', enemies were resorting to the use of green cards, work visas and apathy? Was it not apathy, laziness and overconfidence that had led to the fall of the Roman Empire, the Egyptians? In their day, they were the only super powers, just as the US was now. Was America, like the Trojans and the Romans, asleep to the real threat? Ryker believed so, from the government all the way down to Joe citizen. It was time to wake up.

Ryker thoroughly enjoyed reading books of fiction and watching movies. They both provided him an escape from the reality of life for just a little while. What concerned him was that every book he read, and every movie he watched on terrorism followed the same basic storyline. First, the terrorists attacked, and of course had much more evil and hideous plans in store. Then the FBI, CIA or some other top-secret covert spy agency assigned their best agent to track down and kill the evil zealots. Along the way he met the beautiful woman with whom he fell in love, and together, at the last possible second, just as the terrorist was preparing to carry out his most evil deed, they swooped in and stopped him and America won again.

That all made for great entertainment and escapism but Ryker thought that the American people had started to believe that that was the way things worked in the real world, that America would always come out victorious. Ryker knew when that illusion was finally shattered, and it would be, the results would be cataclysmic.

The liberal media had sold the American people on the belief that Islam was a 'peace loving' religion. That could not have been further from the truth; the Koran itself stated that Islam was the only true religion. It went on to instruct all Muslims to either convert all infidels to Islam, or failing in that, spill their blood. Nowhere was it encouraged to compromise or to peacefully discuss differences with the followers of other faiths. *Peace loving, right? What other religion justifies the massacre of anyone who disagrees with them, all in the name of God?*

In recent years, many Muslim leaders have been aggressively pointing to a scripture in the Koran that forbids the killing of innocent people. What they don't bother to elaborate on is that only believers in Islam are considered innocent in the eyes of Allah; that everyone else is fair game, for they are basically considered non-persons.

Comparisons were constantly being made between Mohammad and Jesus Christ. However, there was one glaring difference between the two. Christ did not rob, rape, pillage and murder to spread his faith. Mohammad did! That bit of history, conveniently, never found its way into the curriculum of public schools and it certainly was never shown the light of day by the mainstream media. It was not politically correct or *sensitive* to the true peace loving Muslims in the world; so therefore, it was being incrementally erased from history and the minds of all civilized people.

Sensitive or not, America had better wake up to the bitter truth. Ryker believed that radical Islamists did not want to talk, they didn't want to understand and they did not want to compromise with people of other religions. You had to either believe their way or suffer a bloody fate at the end of their dull knife or scimitar to your throat. While the great majority of Muslims were indeed peaceful, law-abiding citizens of the world, they remained blind to what Mohammad truly stood for.

The time had come for America to wake up, put aside political correctness, and do what she had to do-anything she had to do-to be safe. Because, her current path would likely lead to the American paradise being destroyed.

CHAPTER 14

▼

Day Seven

Thursday

Corky Rollins had been in and out of trouble with the law since he was thirteen. In fact, of the twenty-eight years he had been alive, he'd spent nearly ten of them in and out of county jails and state prisons for a variety of reasons. The son of an abusive father and an alcoholic, drug-addicted mother, it was no surprise that he turned out the way he did. When he was eleven years old, the school he attended reported finding numerous round scars on his arms, legs and back. Social Services investigated and found that his father was burning him with cigarettes whenever he felt the boy required discipline, or was deemed guilty of the slightest of infractions. Corky was removed from his home and placed in a foster home. His father received a six month suspended jail sentence, placed on probation and given sixty hours of community service. His mother elected to take his father back and Corky found himself banished to the state's foster care program.

Corky spent several years shuffling from home to home, and soon realized that he was in no better shape now than before. His caregivers showed very little concern for his welfare, but great concern for the government check his presence brought to them each month from the state. Often times he pretty much did whatever he wanted, and could come and go as he pleased. That is, as long as he was home, bathed and dressed in his finest clothes when the social worker made her monthly visit. After missing one of these appointments, as punishment, his foster mother locked him in a basement closet for three days with no blanket, food or water; Corky made it a point to never miss another one.

Corky made fast friends with two brothers living in the neighborhood whose living conditions were not too different from his own. No, they were never placed in a foster home, but their parents were just as uninvolved and disinterested as his own had been. Billy and Danny Whitby seemed to have no problem taking risks, and that daredevil mentality would prove to be the cause of Corky's first brush with the law.

The boys were out late one night, looking for mischief, as they frequently did, when they walked into a convenience store to get some sodas and snacks. Upon entering the store, Billy suspected that something wasn't right, since there was no employee visible. Taking a brief look around they found the clerk on the floor behind the empty cash register, unconscious and bleeding from a severe head wound. The proper thing to do would have been to immediately call the police. Instead, the boys, at the prompting of Billy, the eldest of the three, seized the opportunity to grab bags stacked by the register and began filling them with cartons of cigarettes, candy and as much beer as they could possibly carry. Just as the boys were making a break with their loot, three police cars skidded to a stop in front of the store, responding to the silent alarm that the now dead employee had pressed just before being shot. The juvenile delinquents were quickly arrested, taken to jail and questioned about the murder.

It took until the next day, through the use of security tapes, to determine they were not guilty of killing the clerk. However, all were charged with felony theft and released to their parents. Although their public defender tried to make the case that they had not left the store with any of the stolen goods, the judge didn't buy it and two months later he sentenced all three to ninety days in juvenile detention. The judge determined that although the boys did not contribute to the death of the man, they could not have known this at the time they chose not to call for help and their actions showed wanton disregard for the well being of another.

That was fifteen years ago, and Corky had just been paroled from prison after serving three years for strong-armed robbery and assault; now he was free and looking for trouble. *It had served that uppity broad right,* he thought. All he had asked for was five dollars to get something to eat. She'd looked at him with disdain, scoffed, then turned and walked away without saying a word. Corky had grown tired of people looking down their noses at him. A powerful rage, which he could not explain to this day, welled up inside him and before he knew it, he had grabbed a large rock off the ground, ran up behind her and smashed it against the back of her head. The woman collapsed to the ground, her skull cracked and bleeding profusely. Corky quickly grabbed her purse and jewelry and fled. Two days later he was arrested attempting to use one of her stolen credit cards. He'd later be sentenced to seven years in the state penitentiary at Folsom.

Upon his release from prison, Billy and Danny met Corky at the front gate and gave him a ride back to Redding. Amazingly, this was as close as either brother had ever gotten to a prison. Through the years they had somehow managed to avoid getting into any serious trouble; at least, for which they had been caught. Sure, they had run-ins with the law over the years, but it amounted to nothing more than nickel and dime stuff and was dealt with at the local level.

Two days after Corky's release, they were all down at the creek, and had been since early afternoon, drinking beer, smoking pot and celebrating Corky's return home. The boys spent most of the afternoon throwing rocks at birds and the occasional squirrel that unfortunately wandered into their free-fire zone. Every so often one of them would jump into the creek to cool off. Their conversation centered on women, their lives growing up together, and the trouble they'd gotten in to and out of. One popular topic of conversation was the stuck-up broad who had been born with a silver spoon in her mouth. If she had just given Corky the five bucks, he would never have hit her and gone to prison.

As the day wore on and the sun began to set, hunger pangs hit and the beer was all gone prompting them to drive to a nearby store and stock up for the evening. Walking into a Shell convenience store around 6:30 they began picking out desired items for purchase. Danny grabbed the beer, Corky the chips and other snacks, and Billy got six hot dogs from the deli area.

Billy observed the two clerks watching them very intently and was instantly ticked off. *Why are they watching us for? We're not here to steal nothing, we got money. Stinking camel jockeys,* he thought. *They come over here; sneak into our country and then look at us like we're the ones breaking the law.* It never occurred to him the clerks were the ones working a job, and he wasn't. He walked over to Corky, tapped him on the shoulder and then leaned over to whisper in his ear.

"Hey man, you see those two towel heads watching us?" subtly pointing toward the counter.

Corky glanced toward the front of the store and saw the male and female clerks eyeing Danny suspiciously. Corky snipped, "What do they think he's gonna' do, stuff those three six-packs down the front of his britches?"

Billy thought for a few seconds and then said, "Hey, you remember that cop a few days ago on TV?"

"Exactly what cop you talkin' bout, man? There ain't been nothing but cops on TV the past few days." Corky responded.

"You know, that FBI guy. He said that one of the terrorists was a woman and that we was supposed to keep an eye out for them," Billy said, pointing again toward the female employee.

Corky looked directly at Billy, "No, I don't remember that, I was in prison, remember *stupid*?"

"Oh, right. Anyway, what if she's the one he was talkin' bout?"

Corky continued to rifle through the bags of chips, pretending to be looking for a specific brand. After a couple of moments he said, "I don't know. There are more and more of them sneaking over here every day, but what are the odds she's the one?"

"I'd say pretty good," Billy answered. "Honestly, how many of their women do you ever really see?

"Come to think of it, not too many."

"Right! Stay here a minute." Billy said, handing the hot dogs to Corky. "I'll be right back." He then turned and walked out to his pickup, the eyes of the clerks following him closely. Less than a minute later he was back.

"You ready to have some fun?" Billy asked, lifting his shirt, revealing the handle of the pistol in his waistband.

Corky looked surprised to see the gun, not knowing, up till now, that Billy even had one. Then he thought of all the crap he had gone through in his life. He thought of every raw deal he'd been dealt, and every day he'd spent in prison as a result. Looking around the store and parking lot and seeing no other customers, he made a snap decision. "I'm with you, Billy!"

Billy didn't have to ask his brother what he thought; they always backed each other's play, without question. In fact, that was one of the main reasons neither one had ever done time in prison. They always provided each other with ironclad alibis that the cops could never seem to break; no matter how hard they tried.

Billy waited for Corky to get the chips and snacks and then walked toward the cash register. Corky followed and Danny quickly joined them. Danny knew his brother too well not to realize when he was up to something. At times it bothered him because he feared someday they'd both end up in prison, or worse.

They all met at the register, dropping the booze and food on the counter. The female clerk began to hurriedly ring up the items while her husband bagged them.

Billy looked at both of their nametags, attempted to read them and failed. "Hey, Corky, how in the world are we supposed to read those names? Man…looks to me like gibberish." The male clerk stared at him with a sour expression, but didn't say anything.

"I don't know, man," Corky responded.

"I'm told if you have a cold and ya got a little phlegm caught in your throat it really helps," Danny chimed in. They all laughed while the clerks kept ringing up and bagging their items.

"Do you like killing innocent women and children?" Billy suddenly asked the woman, very coldly.

She froze, slowly looked up at him and then toward her husband, speechless.

Her husband was the one to finally answer in heavily accented English. "What does that mean?"

"What I mean," Billy said, as he drew the Taurus .357 Magnum pistol from his waistband, "is do you enjoy killing innocent women and children?"

Terror instantly replaced the confused looks on the couples' faces. "We kill nobody!" the man answered, his voice noticeably breaking as he backed away from the counter. "Get your things and leave, don't pay. Just go."

"Just go? You hear that guys? He wants us to leave!"

"I heard him. He's not a very friendly camel jockey is he?" Corky said.

"No, he's not. Are you really sure you didn't kill anybody?" Billy asked the clerk again, waving the gun-barrel in front of his eyes.

"No, we kill nobody, we are not filthy Muslims, you leave now, please go, no pay, just please go."

"You know, I almost believe you…almost," Billy said without the slightest bit of emotion in his voice. "I guess if you're innocent, you can both go to Allah with a clear conscience." Then he shot the man in the stomach, then quickly turned and did the same to the horrified woman. He shot them so fast that they struck the floor at the same time, their blood rapidly mixing on the freshly waxed tile.

"Damn, Billy, what did you go and do that for?" Danny exclaimed.

"Just following my president's orders, of course."

"What are you talking about?" Corky screamed.

"I'm fighting the war on terror," he smiled. "Danny, run out to the truck and get the can of gasoline, hurry…move your butt! Someone could show up any minute!"

The couple lay on the floor moaning and weeping. Unlike on television, in real life if the victim was not shot in the head or heart, or a major organ or artery was not damaged, then death was most assuredly a slow and agonizingly painful process to endure. The couple had managed to crawl toward one another and was weakly embracing as their life's blood pumped steadily from their wounds and tears ran freely from their eyes.

Danny returned swiftly with the gasoline and handed it to Billy. He told Corky and Danny to take the food, beer and as many cartons of cigarettes as they could carry to the truck. While they did, he set the gas can on the floor and walked around behind the counter. Stepping over the moaning couple, and keeping the pistol trained on them, he opened the cash register. Taking out the eighty-seven dollars it contained, he stuffed the money into his pocket. He took a step and then turned back to the register, reached in and pocketed three rolls of quarters as well. He returned to the gas can, picked it up and opened the spout. He began to hurriedly pour its contents all over his victims. He poured a stream all the way to the door and struck a match. Billy yelled to the dying couple lying on the floor, "Al Yahoo Yakbare to you too!" and tossed the match. "Enjoy your virgins, you psychos!"

Though grievously wounded, Salila and Amal Swaji, would not die from their gunshot wounds. Having legally immigrated to the United States five years earlier from India, a non-Muslim country, they would die a screaming, horrible death.

Corky, Billy and Danny jumped in the truck and spun the tires out of the parking lot. Looking in the mirror Billy could see flames dancing in the windows. Before firefighters could respond to the store the killers were already sitting on the banks of the creek, popping the caps on some Coors Lights, smoking pot and stuffing their faces with the hot dogs.

CHAPTER 15

▼

Seymour Murphy's hands were sweaty and shaking on the steering wheel, as he drove slowly down the dark alley and parked behind the brick building.

He was a dealer of fine area rugs, and represented the third generation of his family to be one. His grandfather had opened a regular carpet store in San Francisco back in the late nineteen-fifties, and business proved to be good. However, through the years his grandfather decided that the family's fortune would be better acquired by selling another kind of product. By the time Seymour's own father was preparing to take over daily operations in the late seventies, his grandfather was already cautiously making the transition to the more expensive area rugs. The smaller rugs required far less room to store, thus allowing them to get a smaller building, while more than tripling profits in the first year alone. As an added bonus they didn't have to pay laborers to install them, unlike they did with wall-to-wall carpet.

In nineteen eighty-seven his father, growing more and more dissatisfied with the hustle and bustle of the big city, decided to take a huge risk and relocate his family and his business to Redding.

For more than five decades the business had provided a steady income for the family by first dealing mostly to the rich in the San Francisco Bay area, then later to the numerous tourists and wealthy that were steadily moving into the Redding area from the big cities. His family had managed to live quiet and comfortable lives and for the most part, they were very happy and content. That, of course, all began to change when the owner of the store he was presently parked behind opened his doors for business three years ago. Seymour was on the verge of closing his doors forever, due to the stiff competition.

*   *   *   *

Ahlam Kabala had moved his family to the United States from Pakistan, shortly after the US declared war against the Taliban dictatorship in Afghanistan. His request to legally immigrate had been submitted to the US Citizenship and Immigration Service, formerly known as INS, and approved long before the arrival of the US war machine to the poverty-stricken neighboring country, so the American authorities had honored it. Ahlam was also a dealer of fine rugs, especially Persian rugs. He was fortunate to have made contact with an exporter in Iran, just before he came to America, who agreed to give him an exceptionally good deal, as long as Ahlam agreed to order all of his stock from him. The price was so unbelievably good that Ahlam felt he had no other choice but to agree.

Initially, business had been slow and he came close to closing up shop, or perhaps relocating, but sales were starting to pick up and the overall outlook was becoming more promising. Ahlam decided to take a huge risk and invested almost all his capital into one of the finest shipments of rugs that he had ever seen. That shipment was now tucked safely away in the warehouse in the rear of the building. A very rich collector from another state had been scheduled to pay a visit to his store this very week, but he'd been forced to cancel due to the recent events. Ahlam was at first, very disheartened and knew, without a doubt, that he was ruined; however, the collector assured him that once things returned to normal and it was again safe, he would make a special visit to Redding and promised to purchase several nice pieces. To think that all of his hopes rode on the acts of a few misguided Muslims was frightening.

Ahlam did not understand what was wrong with his fellow Muslims. Even some of his own, close family members back in Pakistan had chosen the way of violence and terror in an attempt to attain their lofty goals. He was not unsympathetic to what they were trying to accomplish but why did they believe that the killing of innocent people here, or anywhere for that matter, was justified in the eyes of Allah?

Islam was a peaceful religion and he felt that its spiritual leaders must begin to speak out against this perversion that was taking place, they must take a stand for what is right and just! His Muslim brothers and sisters must realize history showed that America, when faced with a direct threat to their interests, struck back with the quickness and the venom of the Cobra. Ahlam believed the United States would very soon lose patience with the cold and calculated attacks on her homeland. Then she would lose faith in the diplomatic arena as well and would then resort to waging total war against his people. America must not be forced to choose that option; that just could not be allowed to happen. Muslim children would be the ones to suffer the most and the thought of that saddened Ahlam greatly.

He had seen, just as he was leaving Pakistan, the powerful might of the US military when it was unleashed to fight a war that America believed in. *But surely cooler heads would eventually prevail and peace in the world would be the result, wouldn't it?* He did not know what the eventual solution to this madness would be, but he did know that someone had better come up with some answers, and they had better do it soon. He flipped over the closed sign in the window, stepped out and locked the door of his shop. *Tomorrow would be a better day…*he hoped.

∗   ∗   ∗   ∗

Seymour had come mentally prepared tonight; he was determined to put an end to his constant worry, permanently. He'd checked out Kabala's store several days before and noticed that it was not equipped with a burglar alarm nor did it have any type of fire suppression system. *Why would this man take such unnecessary risks when his whole livelihood rested on what was contained within these four walls?* He didn't know and to be perfectly honest, he didn't truly care. All he knew was that it made his task all that much easier.

From where he was parked, he could look up the alley and see Kabala's red Ford Taurus parked at the front of the store. He was relieved when he heard the front door of the building shut and saw his hated competitor walk toward the car. Seymour watched him get in and make a call on his cell phone before finally backing the Ford out and driving away. Murphy waited another fifteen minutes before shutting off his engine and getting out of his vehicle.

He walked around to the rear of his van, ears perked up for any sound that might alert him trouble was on the way. When he didn't hear anything but the crickets and a random car passing by out front, he opened the rear door of his van and retrieved a crowbar and flashlight from the cargo area. He took a quick look around and seeing no lights on in adjacent buildings, assumed it was safe to proceed. Seymour walked over to the rear door and, using the three-foot long crowbar, quickly pried it open. Taking one more look around he stepped inside and closed the steel door behind him. Shining the flashlight around he found the light switch and since there were no windows in this area of the building that could reveal his presence to the casual passerby, he flicked it on.

What he saw immediately took his breath away. These rugs were much more exquisite than anything in his own inventory by far. Seymour quickly regained his composure and began appraising which of the rugs were the most valuable. He set the crowbar down and started stacking the expensive rugs by the door. He wanted to take them all, but he knew that wouldn't be the wisest thing to do. Ten minutes later he had what he believed was the cream of the crop set aside and ready to load.

One by one he carried the twenty-five heavy rugs out to his van and after making the last trip, retrieved a can of kerosene and returned to the store. He thought what a shame it was to leave any of them, but if he didn't it would surely draw suspicion from the insurance company. He opened the can and began wetting down the remaining stock.

"What in the hell are you doing?"

Seymour spun around, spilling kerosene on his shoes and trousers, to find an angry looking Ahlam standing in the doorway behind him.

"What are you doing to my store?" Ahlam raged, finding that his suspicions had turned out to be accurate.

Seymour stood frozen in place, completely surprised and speechless by his being discovered. He couldn't believe it; he was so close to getting away with it, now everything would fall apart. Not only would he lose his business, but his freedom and reputation as well. Five decades of hard work by his family would vanish in a matter of minutes. He would be ruined.

"I saw you come in my store a couple of days ago, you didn't think I was here but I was. Watching you from my office I thought you were checking out my prices, that I could accept, it's good business. But the more I watched you the more I realized you were more interested in my doors, windows and ceilings than in my prices and inventory. I let it go because until today, I didn't understand what you could be doing."

"So why did you come back tonight?"

"I saw your truck in the alley as I was leaving. No one in the surrounding buildings owns a vehicle such as yours and I have also looked over your store from time to time and remembered seeing it there."

"What are you going to do?" Seymour asked with a quivering voice.

"I'm going to my car and call the police. You would destroy me to satisfy your own greed, why should I show you any mercy?" Ahlam turned to leave.

Seymour, faced with complete ruin acted without thinking. He raced after Kabala, but what could he do to change the angry Arab's mind? *There, by the door, the crowbar!* He grabbed it as he ran out the door and saw Kabala open his car door and reach inside. Without pausing to think about what he was doing he swung the steel club with all his might, striking his victim between the shoulder blades.

Ahlam fell to his knees hitting his forehead on the threshold of the door, opening a wide cut near his hairline. Groggily he managed to climb to his feet wiping the blood from his eyes with his shirtsleeve. Facing Seymour and with slurred speech he asked, "You would kill me over a handful of rugs?"

"Why not? Your people do much worse for far less," he said trying to justify his actions. Not waiting for a response, Seymour swung his weapon again with as much force as he could muster, hitting Ahlam hard across the left side of his head. The savage blow cracked his skull open from the temple to just behind the ear and he collapsed to the asphalt.

Seymour moved closer and looked down at the competition. Aided by the dome-light from inside the car, he could see the Arab's brains through the ragged fissure and knew that he was dead. Setting down the murder weapon, Seymour reached down and grasped Ahlam under the arms from behind and dragged him back inside the building.

He placed the body near the door to make it appear as if Ahlam were trying to get out when the smoke overcame him. Murphy suspected it wouldn't pass the muster of a close and detailed autopsy, so he had to divert the blame away from himself some other way. He retrieved a sheet of paper and a black marker from his van and began to write. Hopefully he would catch a break and the police would never come knocking on his door.

Seymour got a bucket of water from a janitorial closet, went outside and washed away the blood that had seeped onto the roadway as best he could. After doing so he couldn't understand why. What would it matter where Kabala was murdered? He closed the man's car door with a rag to avoid leaving fingerprints, placed the crowbar in his own van and returned the bucket to its place.

He finished saturating the rugs with the kerosene and then stood in the doorway. Seymour's guilt almost got the better of him, but he pushed it aside and struck a match throwing it into the fuel. Then he turned and ran to his van and as calmly as possible drove away.

Murphy was three miles away and nearing the storage building he had rented two days before, under a fictitious name, before anyone saw the flames and called the fire department. By the time engines arrived, the store was a total loss. Ahlam had always meant to get insurance, but now it wouldn't matter.

The police later found a note nailed to the wall of the building across the alley. "*Go back to your own country! If the attacks here continue, we will continue to hit back! We will kill your families too! GO HOME WHILE YOU STILL CAN!!!"* Three hours later, investigators found the remains of Ahlams's body and drove to his residence to break the devastating news to his wife and children.

CHAPTER 16

▼

Day Eight

Friday

Dalton Ryker tossed and turned all night. He tried reading, taking a long hot shower and as last resorts, drank warm milk and even tried counting sheep. Nothing worked; he lay there until 5:30 AM getting absolutely no sleep. Finally he got up, got dressed and drove in to work, stopping by McDonald's on the way to grab a Sausage McMuffin and black coffee.

Dalton sat at his desk scanning through a report detailing the latest casualty figures from the hospital attack. He saw that the building was virtually a total loss and the few parts still standing would no doubt have to be demolished. A new hospital would have to be built from the ground up and hospital beds in Redding would be in short supply for a long time to come.

As more bodies were recovered overnight the death toll rose significantly from just over eight hundred to around eleven hundred and fifteen as of six o'clock this morning. In addition, there were two hundred twenty-five wounded, and another three hundred forty-three still missing; it was just mind blowing. Thirty-five of the survivors from the mall were at the hospital when it was blown up. Sadly, of those, seventeen had died in the explosion. Three of the mall survivors, who managed to make it through the hospital attack, later died from their original injuries as well as two other victims, who had been sent to the other local hospital, from injuries sustained at the mall. That brought the total fatalities to one thousand two hundred and sixty-seven. Ryker knew the figure would climb dramatically, as more bodies were removed from the still-smoldering rubble and trying to keep all the numbers straight was mind numbing. When compared to the events of 9/11 and taking into account the other attacks here in Redding, this could potentially turn into the worst terrorist attack in US history if not the entire world.

What was ironic, thought Ryker, was that no biological, chemical or nuclear weapon had yet to be used. Even though for years both the government and news media had been warning us about it. Now it wasn't a question of *if* the terrorists would use them, but *when*. These recent attacks had been well thought out and coordinated by an intelligent someone who knew exactly what they were doing. What was really frightening was that killers were still out there plotting. Even though they had two people under close surveillance and the college professor was scheduled to be here shortly, to hopefully make a positive identification of Mikal as one of the killers, things were still not looking too promising. If she could implicate the al-Nassers that would still leave at least another four terrorists, possibly more, out there somewhere, preparing to do God only knew what. *We have to catch a break pretty soon,* Ryker thought, *or things are going to go from bad to worse in a hurry.*

Ryker's secretary buzzed in to notify him the professor had arrived. He gave instructions to have Agent Roland greet and escort her to his office. Ninety seconds later there was a knock at the door, "Come in," he said.

Roland opened the door and motioned the middle-aged, gray-haired African-American woman to go in ahead of him.

Ryker stood and walked around from behind the desk smiling with his hand outstretched, "Professor Gomillion, thank you for coming, it's a pleasure to meet you. I'm Special Agent Dalton Ryker, Agent Roland you've already met," he said shaking her hand.

"Yes, you're welcome, officer," she smiled, returning the handshake.

Ryker dismissed her reference to him as an officer and motioned to a chair. "Please have a seat ma'am." He returned to his own as Roland sat down next to the professor.

"Now professor, before we get started, I would like to ask your permission to video tape this interview," Ryker said, pointing to a video camera on a tripod standing in the far corner. Professor Gomillion looked over to where he was pointing and with a nod of her head indicated that she would have no objections.

"Great." Ryker motioned to Roland, who stood up and turned on the camera. After Roland returned to his seat, he continued. "Professor…"

"Please, call me Amanda," she politely interrupted.

"Okay, Amanda. For the purposes of identification would you please look toward the camera when I state your name and affirm by saying *here*? Present here today at FBI headquarters in Redding, California is Special Agent Steve Roland with the FBI."

Roland looked at the camera and said, "Here."

"Amanda Gomillion, Professor of Cultural Studies at Shasta College."

"Here," she said.

"And myself, Special Agent in Charge Dalton Ryker, of the FBI counter ter-rorism team here in Redding." He concluded by stating the date and time of day.

"Professor, were you present at the Mount Shasta Mall this Sunday past?"

"Yes, I was there."

"What, if anything, did you see?"

"Five men walked into the food court and begin shooting everyone with machine guns."

"How do you know they were machine guns?"

"Because that's the way they sound in the movies, you know, like one contin-uous shot."

"Okay. Approximately what time did this incident occur?"

"I would say about twelve noon, perhaps a little after; I'm not entirely sure."

"What was your physical position in relation to the suspects when the shoot-ing started?"

"I was just finishing shopping with my granddaughter. We were about to leave, so I could take her to a movie, when they pulled out their guns and began shooting. I pulled my granddaughter behind one of those wooden vendor carts you see at all of the malls nowadays."

"I understand…but where were you hiding in relation to the shooter's posi-tion?" Ryker attempted to clarify. "What I mean is, was there anything between you and them that may have obstructed or impeded your view?"

"No…I was almost directly in front of them when they walked in and there was nothing between us. They came through the doors and turned immediately toward the food court. I was about thirty feet away," she answered.

"You say that they turned away from you and walked toward the food court?"

"No. I guess I should say they sort of angled their bodies away from me but I could still see their faces quite clearly."

"Would you say you got a clear enough view of their faces to identify them, beyond any reasonable doubt, if you ever saw them again?"

"As I said, I saw them when they came in and I also peeked at them through the merchandise on the cart during the shooting." She thought for a minute, then added, "To answer your question, yes, I saw three of them quite clearly and would have absolutely no problem whatsoever identifying those men in the future. The other two I saw only briefly; they were the furthest away and there was a concrete column between them and myself."

"Profes…Amanda, the reason I ask is that if you are able to identify any of the potential suspects and if and when this case were to go to trial, the defense coun-sel is without a doubt going to bring into question your state of mind at the time of the shooting. He will raise the issue that you must have been in a state of shock and therefore could not possibly remember his clients as clearly as you claim. With that in mind, how is it that you had the presence of mind to look at them when everyone else was panicking, running for their lives or hiding? Most people in that situation would have ducked for cover or ran like hell, but few would have had the presence of mind, as you did, to risk a look at who was shooting at them."

She smiled and then said "Several years ago I went on a trip to Israel with a group of my fellow professors. Our party stopped to grab a bite of lunch at an outdoor diner. We had only been seated for a couple minutes when two masked gunmen pulled up in a car got out and started shooting. Many people were wounded and killed that day, including two of my closest friends. All I can guess is, perhaps having gone through it once before, maybe I wasn't as shocked the second time around. I don't really know why I looked or even how I was able to look, I only know that I did."

"Very good." Ryker looked down at a list of items he wanted to make sure that he covered. "Amanda, have you been paid or received favors or promises of favors, for your testimony here today?" he asked.

"No, I have not!" she answered, sounding a bit insulted by the veiled implication of the question.

"I'm sorry, these questions are necessary. Have you ever met with either Agent Roland or myself prior to today or discussed this incident with either of us or any other law enforcement officer prior to this video taped interview?"

"Other than the brief statement I gave police officers on the day of the shooting, I haven't spoken to anyone in law enforcement concerning these events."

"Have you been coached or counseled in any way concerning the testimony you are freely providing here today?"

"No, I have not," she answered indignantly.

"Do you wear corrective lenses and if so were you wearing them at the time of the shooting?"

"No, I don't. My vision is 20/20 uncorrected," she said proudly.

"I know I'm kind of repeating myself but how certain are you that if you saw the gunmen again you would be able to identify them?"

"I will never forget those despicable men, never! I have no doubts that if I ever saw them again I would easily recognize them." She paused for a second. "I assume this is all leading to a lineup, at least I hope so."

Ryker smiled and motioned to Roland, who once again stood up and retrieved three large sheets of poster board from the corner of the office. Keeping the blank sides pointed toward the professor, he walked around the desk and stood beside Ryker.

"Ma'am, what we are about to show you are three sets of ten photographs. All thirty photos are identically the same in every respect, size and color background, with the exception of their faces. With the help of the DMV, we have chosen thirty random people who look as much alike as possible." In fact, they had even mixed in the faces of several Hispanic men who closely resembled the suspects. "When I show you the photographs, take your time. Study them carefully and please don't offer any identifications unless you are absolutely positive that the one you identify is one of the gunmen you remembered doing the shooting at the mall, okay?"

"I understand. Are the men I saw on those?" she said, pointing to the poster boards.

"I can't answer that. You will have to look and make that decision for yourself. Okay?"

"Okay."

"Very well, Agent Roland, if you would?" Roland placed the first poster board face up on the desk. Professor Gomillion leaned forward and looked closely at the faces. She saw that all the men were indeed quite similar in age, skin color, hairstyle and facial structure. She spent several minutes carefully looking at each of the faces several times before looking up, "I don't remember any of these men doing any of the shooting at the mall."

Ryker looked at Roland who then turned over the second set of photos. Amanda leaned forward once again, looking closely. After several more minutes she again sat back. "None of these were there either," she said, sounding disappointed.

Neither of the two agents was surprised. They had left the set of photographs with Mikal's picture until last. They had to be sure of her identification. Witnesses were commonly known to jump at the first photo they saw that closely resembled the suspect, thereby tainting the identification when they later saw the right person. Roland turned over the last set of photographs and then crossed his fingers behind his back. If she didn't ID the photo of Mikal, they were back to square one.

Once again she leaned forward and scanned over the photo lineup. However, this time it took her only a few seconds to lean back in her chair. "Number twenty-three!" she said, tapping the picture repeatedly with her index finger. "He was there!"

Both agents repressed the smiles that were threatening to break out on their faces. They looked at the picture she selected, and indeed it was the picture of Mikal al-Nasser. "Are you positive this is one of the men you saw shooting at the mall?" Roland asked.

"Without a doubt." she said, "I'm positive. He was the first one through the doors and the first one to start shooting. He shot that poor security guard…" Amanda removed a tissue from her pocketbook and dabbed her eyes.

The two agents again looked down at the picture, not believing their good fortune, when the professor spoke again.

"This one too!" she said.

They both froze and slowly looked up at her in surprise. "Excuse me?" Ryker said, "What did you say?"

Amanda Gomillion huffed, "I said, this one too," tapping her finger on the bottom right photograph, "he was there also, number thirty!"

The stunned agents were motionless, staring at her like two deer caught in headlights, for several seconds before speaking. Roland recovered first; pointing to the photograph he asked, "Are you certain this is one of the gunmen you saw shooting at the mall?"

"I'm absolutely positive," she answered. "I'll never forget that face."

Ryker could barely control his enthusiasm. He had to refer to a page of notes in his desk in order to identify the second man that she had recognized. Using two pieces of blank paper, he covered the other names on the list, leaving just one name visible. He then showed it to her, "Professor, would you please read the name on this piece of paper and verify that the number on it corresponds to the first photo you identified from the lineup?"

She leaned forward and said, "Mikal al-Nasser and it does match the number on the photograph I identified."

Ryker repeated the process with the two sheets of paper and asked her again.

"Omar Fadillah," she said.

"And does the number match the second photo you identified?" Ryker asked.

"Yes, it does."

"Ma'am, are you one hundred percent certain that these are two of the men you observed walk into the Mount Shasta Mall last Sunday and begin shooting innocent people?" Ryker asked.

"Yes, I am certain that's them," she answered, without the slightest bit of hesitation in her voice.

"Is there anything else that you wish to add that you feel is important and we have failed to ask?"

She thought for a minute before answering, "No, sir. Just get them."

"Very well, that concludes this interview." He again gave the time and Roland walked over and switched off the camera.

"Professor Gomillion," Ryker said, standing to once again shake her hand, "I want to thank you for your time, you've been a big help."

"You're welcome Agent Ryker." He smiled when this time she got it right.

"Amanda…how's your grand daughter. Was she injured?" Ryker asked.

"No, she's fine. Still a little shook up, but fine. Thank you for asking."

Ryker smiled, "Agent Roland, would you please escort the lady to her car?"

"Yes sir, I would be honored," Roland said as he gently guided her from the office, with his hand at the small of her back.

Has lightning just struck, not once, but twice? Ryker thought. *Could this professor have really positively identified two of the shooters? What are the odds that by pure chance, another one of the terrorists had inadvertently been placed on the list? And what was the connection between Mikal and Omar?* Ryker did not yet know, but he was determined to find out. He had to find out.

Roland returned to the office and closed the door. "Well boss, what do you think?

"I think we need to find out all we can about Mr. Fadillah and quickly! If Amanda is right about her ID's, we could have this whole thing wrapped up by week's end." Ryker hit the intercom, "Get me Chief Baker and please make it quick."

A few seconds later Baker was on the phone. "What can I do for you Agent Ryker? I do hope you've got some good news for a change," Baker said, knowing that Ryker had scheduled a meeting with the witness this morning.

"Chief, we just got a positive identification on not one, but two of the shooters at the mall." He quickly briefed him on what had just transpired.

Baker was momentarily stunned by what he heard. "That's unbelievable!"

"I know, we're pretty amazed about it ourselves."

"Are we certain the ID's are accurate?"

"As sure as we can be, so far. She sure would have convinced me if I were on the jury. At any rate we should know more in a couple of hours."

"Anything I can do to help?"

"Do a background check on an Omar Fadillah; just the local stuff, we'll take care of everything else."

"I'll get someone on it right away."

"Great…what's going on with our two store owners the al-Nassers?"

"Not too much. They went to work yesterday morning, worked a full day without leaving, and went home about six o'clock. Surveillance just reported in and said it looks like they're heading back in to work. The officer following the woman said she just dropped off the kids at the daycare and is driving in the direction of their store. The husband went by a uniform shop, picked up some new shirts and is also heading that way."

"Anything else I should know?"

"Yeah, surveillance also said they had several guests over last night."

"Guests? How many guests?"

"Not quite sure, but I can find out."

"Do it, I'll hold." Ryker waited with the phone to his ear while Baker got the requested information.

Two minutes passed before Baker spoke again, "Surveillance officers say just two, a man and a woman. They said it looked as if they were just having dinner." Ryker knew he couldn't act just yet. Even if the guests were two of the terrorists, that still left at least two more unaccounted for. Besides, there was only one woman involved, as far as he knew. So that left at least three more. Great! No, he had no choice but to wait as hard as that might be. He wanted to get all the terrorists in one fell swoop. If he grabbed these two now, it would, no doubt, alert the others and then they may never be caught. *God*, he thought, *I hope and pray nothing else happens until then.*

"Have you checked out the guests yet?"

"My men are still looking into them, but so far they appear to be clean. However, we won't clear them until we're certain."

"What about their employees, any chance they're involved?"

"Not likely," Baker responded. "They all appear to be Caucasians or African-Americans. We've done cursory background checks and, as best we can determine, none of them are practicing Muslims."

"Isn't it a bit odd that Arab shop owners are not employing other Arabs?"

"I'm not sure."

"Well unless your town is completely different than other American cities, most Arabs tend to employ their fellow Arabs."

"That hadn't occurred to me, but it does seem strange now that you mention it."

"Have your men reported seeing anything unusual in their behavior yet?"

"Nothing, everything looks to be pretty much routine stuff; kids, work, home, school…"

"Okay. Chief, I'm going to keep your men on surveillance for now. They certainly know this town better than mine do and they're less likely to be spotted and can definitely do a better job of blending in."

"I understand."

"Thanks Chief. Oh…and tell your men no mistakes, I think we may be getting close to ending this whole mess."

"Got it," Baker said and hung up.

"Roland, I want copies of all their phone records, both at home and at their business. Also find out if they have cell phones; running a business, I'd lay odds that they do."

"I'll have to get a warrant."

"Then get it. Submit the request to Judge Potter, that should help us avoid any problems, and speed things up at the same time."

"Anything else?" Roland asked, starting to stand.

"Get with the surveillance team and have them let you know when the house is empty. I want the house wired for sound and video. Also, add wiretaps to that warrant, all phones."

"I'll get on it immediately," he said, on the way to the door.

"And place GPS locators on their vehicles. I want to be able to find them in case they give the locals the slip."

"10-4," he said, opening the door.

"Also, assign a couple of agents to the guests and two more to the phone records when we get them. I want to know everyone these two talk to. Pay close attention to new numbers that may have shown up in the past few months or numbers that have been called more frequently during that time. Once you have the list, eliminate all non-Arabic people from it. It's a risk but I think it's a safe one; we can always go back and check them later."

"Where am I supposed to get all these agents? You know we're spread kind of thin as it is."

"The fifteen additional agents I requested are supposed to be here later today; until then, do the best you can."

"Have we found out when we can expect Hostage Rescue to get here?" Roland asked, changing the subject.

"Supposedly mid to late afternoon tomorrow," Ryker replied.

"What's with the delay? We need those guys like yesterday; there's no telling when this thing will blow wide open."

"Apparently some white supremacists robbed a bank in Boston. Things didn't go as planned and they couldn't make their escape. They've taken more than thirty people hostage and are demanding the usual plane and unmarked money, or they start killing. The special agent in charge of the scene is reporting things are going downhill pretty rapidly; they'll probably have to breach the bank and take them down sometime tonight. As soon as they finish things up in Boston they'll jump on a plane for Redding."

"But isn't there another team that the Director could send out here?" Roland persisted.

"What I'm being told is that this particular bank is in a rather large building and that there are at least eight hostage takers inside. It looks as though they've spread the hostages throughout the building to make things much more difficult for any potential rescue, so both on duty teams are in Boston. Anyway, when I talked to the Director, we didn't have anything real solid to go on. He said that when we did he'd send out the team."

"Well, I hope our chickens stay in the coop until he does," said Roland worriedly.

"Me too Steve…me too."

∗   ∗   ∗   ∗

In Redding, like most cities in America these days, talk radio had become a very popular news source and in many cases was nothing more than another form of entertainment. While most listeners were content to just sit back and listen to the host's monologues or opinions of a special guest, others chose to phone in and verbalize their views on a particular subject. Today, on News Talk with Ken Roberts, the subject was once again the terrorist attacks and the effect they were having on the city and the surrounding community.

The station manager, due to the enormous call volume, extended the late afternoon weekday show into the early evening. The host had been doing his dead level best to try and calm his listeners. But despite his best efforts, they just would not accept his premise that everything would soon be resolved and that things would return to normal. In fact, the tone and attitude of his callers convinced him there was a real and growing fear that he believed could be bordering on uncontrolled panic.

The show up to this point had mostly been a regurgitation of people's fears and ideas about what was going on and what the police should or shouldn't do to stop it. While it was getting a bit repetitious, there was no shortage of callers nor listeners.

The host answered line seven, "Michael, you're on News Talk…Michael are you there?"

"Oh yeah, I was thinking about the previous caller's comments and didn't hear you, sorry."

"That's okay, what's your question?"

"I don't really have a question….more of a statement."

"Go ahead."

"Ken, I just got off the phone with my brother-in-law who works for a large trucking company that supplies grocery stores here in Redding. He told me that his company has suspended all shipments to our area indefinitely."

"Why are they doing that?" the host asked, more than a little concerned in light of the increasing shortage of truckers due to the ongoing fuel crisis.

"Well, from what he said, insurance companies are threatening to refuse coverage if anything happens because it's getting so dangerous here."

"I've not heard anything like that," Ken said, in an effort to calm people before they allowed their fear to overwhelm them and run off half-cocked.

"My brother-in-law also said that other companies are considering whether to cease shipments as well and that we might want to consider getting out of the area until things calm down."

Ken was not sure how he should respond to this latest bit of information. If it was true, life here was going to get even worse, not better like he had been saying all afternoon and evening. If it wasn't true and this was just someone's idea of a sick joke or someone letting their fears get the better of him, then something would have to be done quickly to allay people's fears. Either way he'd have a word with his call screener for even letting this guy on the line.

"Thank you for your call," Ken said, disconnecting the line. "Folks, I don't know if what we just heard is true or not but I will do my best to find out and let you all know either way before the end of the program. Until then, let's all stay calm and wait and see. We've got to take a commercial break but when we come back we have a former New York City police officer who was on duty during the 9/11 attacks. He'll be giving us his advice on how he believes we should handle this crisis and what we can all do to better protect ourselves and our families from future attacks. We'll be back in a minute."

Even though Ken had tried his best to calm his listeners, the damage had been done. Worried mothers and housewives picked up phones and began calling friends and family members, sharing the latest news. The news was already spreading like wildfire by the time Ken was able to verify that the caller had been ill informed. He told his audience that although there was still a severe shortage of trucks, and deliveries were slow, those that were scheduled would still be made. But it was too late, the cat was out of the bag, so to speak. Wary people had already gone through their pantries and determined that their families could not survive for more than a few days on the meager supplies they had on hand. The great majority decided that first thing in the morning they would go to the grocery store and stock up. Many did not wait until morning, electing to hit the twenty-four hour grocery stores tonight, avoiding the morning rush.

CHAPTER 17

▼

Day Eight

Saturday

The City of Redding lies about sixty miles south of Mount Shasta, in the north-ernmost part of California. Mount Shasta, at fourteen thousand one hundred sixty-two feet high, is the largest mountain in California, the second highest in the Cascade Mountain Range, behind Mount Rainier in Washington State. Shasta is also a dormant volcano whose peak rises more than 7,000 feet above the tree line, and on a clear day, can easily be seen from a hundred miles away. The dazzling mountain, snow-capped for most of the year, is a huge drawing point for tourists and a big reason why more and more people every year are making the Redding area their home.

August mornings in Redding do not differ too greatly from those in other rec-reational towns of similar size across the country. There is always a steady flow of traffic into and out of the area. The local population, while culturally diverse, is mostly made up of retirees and folks migrating from the larger cities in search of a quieter and safer place to raise their kids. Saturdays tend to draw a huge influx of people from out of the area, driving in to either start their vacations or seize a quick weekend away at one of the area's beautiful lakes, just a short drive outside of town.

In fact, two of the largest lakes, Shasta and Whiskeytown, supply much of the northern part of the state with fresh water through an elaborate array of canals and aqueducts. Billions of gallons of fresh water are pumped every year as far away as Los Angeles, five hundred miles to the south. Without it, residents of Southern California might find they could no longer fill their swimming pools each spring. Most of the locals believe Lake Shasta is refilled every year by the snowmelt but that's not entirely true. While the melt does help in maintaining lake levels, it is the annual rainfall that carries most of the burden; for every inch of rain in the area, the entire lake rises by as much as one foot.

It amazed Virgil Stokes how many people seemed to think that life must be better someplace else, never being satisfied with where they lived or with what they were doing, thinking somehow the grass must be greener and the skies bluer in another city or state. Virgil was a realist and understood that yes, sometimes the grass was greener on the other side. However he was also a cynic and knew that the grass that grew in the immediate area of a septic tank always appeared much darker and richer in color as well. *And we all know what causes that,* he thought. Virgil was a staunch believer that you should stay where you were, stick with what you knew, and the world and your life, would be a less complex and better place as a result.

It became strikingly apparent to Vigil that this hot August morning, already a searing and balmy ninety-four degrees, was different than any other he had witnessed in the more than sixty years he'd lived here. Surprisingly, he had never traveled more than two hundred miles in any direction from Redding his entire life. Working as a logging truck driver for more than thirty years, he and his wife were able to pay off their modest home and sock away a little money for their golden years. Virgil was one of the lucky few that retired from logging before the liberal tree-hugging nature lovers or greenies, as he liked to call them, gutted the logging industry in the Pacific Northwest through the Spotted Owl fiasco.

In 2003, the US Fish and Wildlife Service released a statement decreeing the California Spotted Owl did not warrant any protection under the Endangered Species Act. In fact, due to the over-regulation that virtually stopped logging in the Pacific forests, wildfires burned more than six times the acreage than when heavy logging was taking place. Ironically, the owls, when threatened by the fires, simply flew to safer places and were seemingly unaffected in any adverse way. The legal industry and activist groups made money hand over fist, which they paid zero taxes on because it was considered charitable work and for the public good. In the end, it appeared as if the owl, and its habitat, was never in any serious danger; all the legal wrangling had been for nothing. Now, more than seventy percent of wood product in California was imported, western timber mills were now decimated and thousands of families had lost their source of income as a result.

As he drove his 1979 Chevy stepside pickup into town from Millville, a small rural community roughly ten miles to the east of Redding, he saw very little traffic going in his direction. Traffic heading out of town, however, was nearly bumper-to-bumper, which may not have seemed all that dramatic to people from the big cities, but for this area it was very uncharacteristic. The worst traffic jam you got into here was a ten-minute delay getting into or out of the mall during the Christmas shopping season. *This looks like the mass exodus from Egypt,* Virgil thought. Only these people were not walking or riding camels, they were riding in RV's. It looked as if every RV in the county was on Highway 44 heading east away from town, just as fast as their frantic drivers could push them and the traffic would allow.

About half of the RV's that Virgil saw belonged to tourists, who evidently had had enough and were escaping the madness while they could. Most had been at the lakes, rivers and campgrounds outside of town during the attacks and had suffered little direct effect from them. The rest of the self-imposed evacuees were retirees and other local residents who were fortunate to possess the equipment or the means to flee; terrified people were heading for the hills.

A mirror image of what Virgil was currently witnessing was being duplicated on Highway 299, and also on I-5 in both directions, the only other major thoroughfares leading out of the area. The panicked residents had decided that any other place on the planet must surely be safer than Redding. Word was spreading concerning the 'suspension' of food shipments and that had been the proverbial straw that had broken the camel's back.

Virgil's destination this morning was the Costco warehouse less than a mile from the mall. He was making his monthly trip in to stock up on some needed supplies. He didn't particularly enjoy coming to town because he'd reached a point in his life where he didn't like large groups of people; actually never had, if you asked his wife. Hazel used to be the one to make the trip, sparing him the aggravation, but she was now in the early stages of Alzheimer's and could no longer be trusted with the responsibility. She was fading fast and Virgil had been wrestling with the idea of placing her in a home for the past two months now. He would have to make a decision soon.

Virgil exited Highway 44 at the Dana Drive off-ramp and as he approached the traffic signal, he looked off to his right and what he saw nearly stopped him in his tracks.

The Costco parking lot was completely packed, cars were overflowing into the side streets. Frantic people were hurrying into the store. Others, having completed their shopping, were loading vehicles and driving away just as fast. Although the store always did pretty brisk business throughout the day, this was way beyond what any rational person would consider normal.

Virgil drove around and around the parking lot for nearly ten minutes before finally spotting a pickup backing out of a spot, its cargo bed stacked to the top of the cab with provisions. He sped up to get the space, just beating out another weary motorist by a couple of seconds and received a friendly hello by way of her middle finger. He parked, got out and retrieved a shopping cart from the basket return. Walking through the front door, he fished inside his wallet for the Cosco membership card, which he flashed to the door monitor. He always wondered why they even bothered to check it when everybody knew no one could make a purchase without showing it again to the cashier. *It's not like they're guarding some secret military facility, for grief's sake!* He had a hard time believing that their Brussels sprouts and garbanzo beans warranted that kind of protection.

The inside of the store was literally bursting with shoppers. As Virgil maneuvered his way through the throngs of people, he saw every register was open and the checkout lines were strung clear to the rear of the store. Seeing this almost caused him to turn around and leave right then and there. People were standing in line with two and three carts heaped full of groceries and other supplies. Evidently the policy of restricting the number of any particular item one could purchase was being ignored today. Looking at the anxious expressions on shoppers' faces easily explained management's decision to err on the side of self-preservation.

Carts were crammed with bottled water, dry goods, canned goods, breads, cereals, medicines, hygiene products, fresh produce and meats. He saw mouintains of toilet paper, sleeping bags, lanterns, ice chests and various other camping items. It looked as if people believed a great storm was on its way and that they had better be prepared. He personally had not heard the comments on the radio last evening and had no prior warning of what he was driving into the middle of.

Virgil made his way through the store, occasionally picking up an item from his list and placing it into his cart, when he managed to find one remaining. He reached the back of the store to find hordes of shoppers ripping into pallets of food that had ironically just moments before been off-loaded from the eighteen wheeler backed up to the dock. At first employees attempted to unpack the pallets and restock the shelves, but finally they gave way to the frantic mob and just stood back helplessly watching the melee ensue as people pushed and shoved each other to get to their fair share.

Virgil, finally seeing that he was wasting his time and that he would never get what he came for, left his cart in the middle of the aisle and started for the exit. Before taking ten steps the items in his abandoned cart were scavenged by other shoppers. Two minutes later he reached the parking lot, backed his truck out and drove away. The spot he had just vacated was immediately filled behind him. He decided to drive the short distance to the Wal Mart and see if things were any better over there.

What he found was an exact duplication of what he'd just fled from. In fact, every grocery and discount store in town was experiencing the same thing. As the city's one-hundred-thousand-plus residents heard about what was going on they were choosing to leave their homes and jobs and enter the fray as well. Virgil saw several fistfights break out over disagreements concerning the ownership of a particular item of seemingly drastic importance. Store employees were reluctant to intervene in the altercations and simply waited for the police or security to arrive and restore order. Help was slow in coming.

Shoppers rapidly lost patience with the extremely long lines and some elected to push their carts out of the store without paying. When others saw they were not detained or even challenged in any way, more quickly followed. Astonished employees could only stand back and helplessly watch as one customer after another walked out the doors, crossing the invisible line from law-abiding citizen to felon in just under five seconds.

Throughout the city stores swiftly ran out of merchandise and what had been, up to now, a rather organized chaos, dissolved into mayhem. Desperate people were running up and grabbing food from other people's carts or out of their vehicles as fast as their victims could load them. An elderly woman attempted to stop a man from taking her small cart of meager supplies only to be forcefully shoved to the ground, striking her head hard on the curb. As blood gushed from her wound unconcerned people rushed by without seeming to notice; it was now every one for his or herself. A teenage boy eventually stopped to help, using the T-shirt from his own back to staunch her bleeding. He sat there, holding her head in his lap, stroking her hand while quietly reassuring her that everything would be all right. Paramedics arrived forty-five minutes later, she died two minutes prior.

Gun stores were running a brisk business as well. Shop owners, to ensure record sales, were electing to ignore the mandatory waiting periods and anyone with a valid driver's license, and cash, could get on-the-spot service; for one day only. People were buying shotguns, rifles, handguns and as much ammunition as they could carry. Some stores still had a large supply of banned assault weapons in storage and although they could no longer legally sell them, several storekeepers chose to ignore the law and sell them anyway. When the authorities finally managed to catch on, if they ever did, to what had taken place, they would find most dealers had long since closed up shop and retired. With sales this strong and the fact that every firearm in the store had been conveniently marked up, as much as five hundred percent in some cases, that was a forgone conclusion.

Two men, trying to take advantage of the chaos, attempted to walk out without paying, not a very wise thing to attempt in a firearms store. Unlike other businesses, employees in gun stores all carried pistols while working. When the shop owner yelled for them to stop, one of the thieves made a terrible error in judgment; he drew a revolver and pointed it at the owner. In an instant another employee drew his own weapon and without a moment's hesitation shot the thief twice in the center of his chest. The man dropped heavily to the floor with a shocked expression on his face. Everyone stood still as a deadly silence filled the room, the smell of burnt gunpowder permeating the air. The other thief dropped his booty and ran from the store forgetting all about his 'friend'.

After a few tense moments the owner retrieved a blanket from under the counter, walked over to the body, scooted it into a corner with his foot and then bent over and covered it. He then returned to help the next customer in line. Amazingly, not one customer left the store before completing their purchase. Patrons and staff alike ignored the body on the other side of the small store. It wasn't their problem; besides, it was his own fault and he no longer seemed to mind. It was ninety minutes later when the shop owner phoned the police, no customer had even bothered.

Generator sales were through the roof, as well as that of fifty-five gallon drums, which had been loaded into the backs of pickup trucks and were being filled at service stations. Again, mandatory restrictions were being ignored. Cars were lined up around the block of every gas station in town as worried motorists rushed to top off their tanks, all concerned that fuel trucks would be the next deliveries that would be 'suspended'. Even the more than six-dollar-per-gallon price was not dissuading patrons in any way and sales were strong. As word spread throughout the community, every item that people thought they might need was quickly sold out, leaving store shelves bare citywide.

The volume of calls coming in rapidly overwhelmed the emergency 911 dispatchers and police officers as well. Business owners were demanding that police respond and stop all the fighting and looting. Ambulances were falling behind, unable to keep up with the high volume of calls. Not only did they have the normal amount of calls to deal with, but also the injured from the numerous incidents of fights and assaults. The police and the Sheriff's departments were inundated and simply could not keep up.

It didn't take long for the criminal element to become aware of the ripe opportunity all the sudden chaos was providing them too. Jewelry, electronics, and computer stores all became victims of the madness; any semblance of a peaceful and civilized society had vanished. People who would normally never think of breaking the law were being caught up in the whirlwind of fear and panic that was gripping the very heart of this once serene community. Their sense of right and wrong was cast aside and self-preservation took its place, as they seemingly lost the ability to control themselves. More and more frequently banks were opening their doors on Saturdays and three of them were robbed in a matter of fifteen minutes forcing managers throughout the city to close and barricade their doors.

Marauding bands of rioters swept through the city, vandalizing cars, breaking windows out of businesses and looting the few stores that had the foresight to close in the face of anarchy. Within a couple of hours the tiny mobs had all but destroyed more than twenty businesses and wreaked severe damage on more than thirty others.

Chief of Police Mitch Baker had finally heard and seen enough. He and his men, with the help of the Sheriff's Office, had done their dead level best to control things here at the local level. That was no longer feasible and outside help would be required. He telephoned the mayor, who in turn telephoned the Governor. Within fifteen minutes the National Guard, which had already been placed on alert, was ordered to fully deploy and restore order. For the first time since the floods in New Orleans in late 2005 an American city was now under the control of the military. A state of martial law was present in Redding, California, population one hundred thousand and shrinking.

Virgil, having driven to several different stores looking to fill his grocery list, finally gave up and stopped by a Shell convenience store on the way back to his home. He walked in and quickly gathered several bags of groceries. Most convenience stores almost always carry a small selection of food items, although at a much higher price than supermarkets, and Virgil bought most of what was left on the shelves. He added six cases of Budweiser and two full plastic containers of beef jerky to his selections. He paid the nice lady who owned the store; he could never seem to remember her name, *what was it? Risa, Reza,…something like that.* Anyway, after making three trips to load his purchases into his truck he bid her a good day and left. As he drove off he grabbed a beer and a stick of jerky from one of the bags and headed home. Using only back roads, he was able to avoid the ever-increasingly dangerous situation on the highway.

*   *   *   *

The C-5B Galaxy heavy cargo transport landed at the Redding Municipal Airport at 4:30 PM. The C-5 is one the largest aircraft in the world. Its length measures two hundred forty-seven feet and is almost as long as a football field, excluding end zones, of course. It is as tall as a six-story building, has a wingspan of two hundred and twenty-three feet and its cargo compartment is as big as an eight-lane bowling alley. This mammoth aircraft can carry unusually large and heavy loads and utilizing the front and rear cargo openings, the Galaxy can be loaded and unloaded at the same time. Both the nose and rear doors open the full height and width of the huge cargo compartment within the giant aircraft. In fact, the cargo area is so large that it can facilitate the drive-through loading or unloading of wheeled and tracked vehicles and even faster loading of bulky equipment such as huge M1A1 main battle tanks. The C-5 simply performs missions that no other plane in the US inventory can.

The FBI Hostage Rescue Team immediately began unloading their equipment. From inside the huge transport two small helicopters, with their rotors folded back, were rolled out and quickly pushed inside a remote vacant hanger at the end of the runway. These helicopters were the MH-6H Little Birds. The Little Bird, having no weapons, is a light assault chopper that has an unrefueled range of two hundred and fifty miles and is designed to carry troops into combat. Two to three fully equipped combat troops can be carried inside, with up to six more on fold-down external platforms. They also have a fast roping system installed to facilitate the quick insertion of troops into the combat zone. Upon getting the choppers into the hanger, the maintenance crews got right to work preparing them for operations that everyone involved secretly hoped would be needed.

CHAPTER 18

▼

Redding National Guard Commander, Lt. Colonel Jake Searcy, began his military career in the United States Navy. He joined the Navy more than twenty-five years ago and completed boot camp at the Naval Recruit Training Command in San Diego, California, closed in 1997 due to military downsizing and realignment.

Recruit training demanded a complete change in lifestyle, discipline, and responsibility, as well as the overall physical and mental make up of the young would-be sailor. All recruits underwent swim tests and then went on to receive stringent training in order to bring their skills up to the Navy's tough standards. In addition to classroom instruction, recruits received extensive training in seamanship, ordnance, fire fighting and water survival.

After completing boot camp and finishing specialized training at the Naval Air Station twenty-one miles north of Memphis in Millington, Tennessee, Searcy was assigned to duty on the re-commissioned battleship, USS New Jersey. He didn't know that soon after his assignment to the World War II era man-of-war he would find himself smack dab in the middle of a bloody Middle-Eastern civil war.

*   *   *   *

A yellow Mercedes truck, crammed full of explosives, slammed into the Marine Barracks in Beirut, Lebanon at 6:20 AM on October 23, 1983. Marines who witnessed the attack reported seeing the vehicle enter the parking lot in front of the barracks and circle once around the lot. Before the Marines could bring a weapon to bear and fire in their defense the truck ripped its way into the lobby where it detonated with a force of twelve thousand pounds of TNT. The explosion killed two hundred forty-one sleeping US servicemen. Although most US citizens remember the bombing, few recall that merely ten minutes later the headquarters of the French contingent was also struck killing more than fifty soldiers there as well.

The Americans and the French were in Beirut as part of a multi-national peacekeeping force backed with troops from the United Kingdom and Italy. The MNF was sent to facilitate peace between warring Christian and Muslim factions and restore order to a country ravaged by civil war. Responsibility for both attacks was claimed by a previously unknown terrorist organization called Free Islamic Revolutionary Movement. Although their involvement with FIRM was never confirmed the two suicide bombers were later identified as Abu Mazen and Abu Sijann. In response to those attacks, the New Jersey, already deployed to the Mediterranean Sea, was ordered to provide naval gunfire in support of the remaining Marines ashore.

While the Jersey sat off the coast, Searcy was assigned to a shore detail and there he witnessed firsthand every kind of suffering and misery that one human being could inflict upon another. Without so much as a second thought, he saw people who claimed to be doing God's work, slaughter others as easily as one would squash a spider on their kitchen floor. He frequently pleaded with his superiors to explain why he and his fellow sailors and Marines were even here, because the butchery he observed taking place was not limited only to the 'other side' and there always seemed to be plenty of evil to go around.

Daily he saw apartment buildings, school buses, and hospitals bombed with impunity. Women and children were slaughtered in the streets for no other reason than they were in the wrong place at the wrong time and happened to hold a different view of how things were supposed to be. Old men were used for target practice simply because no other more worthy target had presented itself. Some would say these religious differences were valid reasons for disagreement, but not justification for wholesale massacres.

It wasn't until May of 2003, that US District Judge Royce Lamberth ruled that the Iranian Government directed and funded the terrorist group Hezbollah, or party of God, to carry out the attacks. He also ruled the militant group was formed under the auspices of the Iranians, and was financially dependent on Iran during 1983. Only with the help of Iranian security agents could Hezbollah have been so successful in carrying out their mission.

Even though the court ruling came twenty years later, the US State Department was in possession of this intelligence shortly after the assault in '83. It was blatantly clear the attack was nothing less than an act of war upon the US by a sovereign foreign government. The reasons why America did not declare war, or take other drastic measures to see justice was done, are still unclear to this day. What is abundantly clear, however, is that 241 US servicemen died, many more were wounded and the lives of their friends and loved ones at home were forever changed.

Searcy believed all the US presence accomplished in Lebanon was to give the 'holy warriors' more fodder to shoot at and he was not surprised in the slightest when the US withdrew from the war-ravaged country in 1984, her mission a complete failure. It was also the first signal to the Islamic world that America had a big bark but when it came to backing it up, she had no bite.

Searcy served four years in the service and then decided he wanted to try his hand at becoming a Navy SEAL. The Navy SEALS are the most feared and respected commandos in the US military and the most elite and highly trained warriors in the world. SEALS have operated in the worst hellholes on the planet and their mission success rate is unmatched by any other special operations unit on the planet.

He applied for BUDS, Basic Underwater Demolition/Seals, training and transferred to Naval Warfare Command at the Naval Amphibious Base in Coronado, California. He received high marks in his preliminary physical fitness evaluation and was accepted for training. Of the seventy-two trainees in his class, Searcy was one of only thirty-seven who managed to successfully complete the course. After serving two years in the SEALS, he applied and was accepted to Officer's Candidate School, there graduating at the top of his class and commissioned an ensign.

Searcy served another ten years before deciding he wanted to get married and start a family. Realizing the Navy was not the ideal place to do this, what with the constant deployments to hot spots around the world, all with little or no forewarning, he left the Navy for civilian life. However, after less than twelve months out of military service he realized he couldn't live without it, at least in some fashion. To stay near his family he returned to duty in the Army National Guard as a Lt. Colonel and had been the commander in Redding going on fifteen months now.

Searcy's commanding general had telephoned him three days ago instructing him to place his unit on alert, but to not mobilize or deploy them until he received further orders. Those orders had just come in. The City of Redding, for all intents and purposes, was to be placed immediately under martial law.

His first official act was to alert all local radio and television stations of what was taking place. It took less than three hours for all National Guard troops to muster and prepare for deployment. Their first assignment was to suppress the rioting and looting that was running rampant throughout the city. These riots didn't fit the general definition of the word but in Searcy's opinion that was exactly what they were. People were fighting, stealing from each other and the police were utterly powerless to stop it. In addition, closed businesses were being broken into and Arab-owned enterprises were being burned by angry people wanting some payback; whether or not the owners were guilty of anything didn't seem to matter. A panicked populace was taking desperate measures to ensure self-preservation.

Within six hours, Searcy's troops had brought things more or less under some semblance of control; the guardsman had arrested one hundred and thirty people. Most of them were simply cited by the police and released, but many were taken to jail for various crimes and booked.

Once the looting was stopped and order had been restored, the next step was to set up roadblocks. Searcy ordered them placed at all major intersections and all ingress and egress points to the city. He then instructed his troops to create a perimeter around the only remaining hospital in town. With the exception of ambulances, no vehicles were to be allowed within three hundred yards of the building. Visitors, would-be patients and even employees were directed to the parking lot of a vacant grocery store two miles away. From there, anyone requesting access to the hospital was subjected to bodily searches and thorough security screenings, which included information from the DMV and NCIC (National Crime Information Center). It was an agonizing and time consuming process but only after the checks were completed would those wishing access be loaded onto waiting shuttle buses. From there they would be escorted to and from the hospital by armed guards; those without proper identification were denied access, no exceptions.

Vital structures in the city were also placed under tightened security. Armed soldiers, sandbags and iron barricades were visible outside the police department, fire stations and other crucial government buildings. In addition to these security measures, Searcy instructed that two Humvees, equipped with fifty-caliber machine guns, be posted at the gates of all power and water treatment plants in the county. This all came as the result of a report one of his men had made after driving by the entrance of a Redding power plant in the southwest part of town.

He informed Searcy that the only visible security there appeared to be two ten-foot-high chain link fences topped with barbed wire, an unmanned guard-house, and card-activated security gates. It amazed Searcy that given the volatile climate, those in charge of protecting vital structures believed this to be adequate security. *Hell,* he thought, *a kid with a box of Fourth of July fireworks could take the place out.*

In addition, all day care centers and schools as well as businesses that did not provide an immediate and vital need to the security and functioning of the city were ordered closed until further notice. A strict curfew was established mandat-ing no one was to be on the streets after dark without prior approval from the authorities. Anyone discovered out after curfew would be arrested on the spot, there would be no exceptions. Still, several people were arrested and jailed and one looter was even shot in the leg before word got around that the soldiers meant business; after that, even the criminal element stayed indoors.

Searcy stood outside the hastily erected temporary command post near city hall. He was looking over a report of their progress thus far and a list of his avail-able resources. He was pleased by the first and concerned by the second. While his soldiers were doing an outstanding job of getting things settled down, he knew he couldn't maintain this level of security with the personnel he currently had available. He instructed an aide to get the commanding general on the phone; he had to get more troops.

A private walked up handing him yet another report detailing several attacks that had taken place against Arab-owned businesses, including a double murder at a convenience store and the burning of a rug store not two miles from his cur-rent position. Added to this were the random muggings and assaults on Middle Eastern people and anyone that looked like them made it quite the daunting task. Searcy knew that somehow he had to do something to protect them. He instructed the private to get a list of foreign-owned businesses from city hall and assign four armed, roving patrols to them. It wasn't enough, he knew, but that was all that could be done for now.

Considering everything that had taken place there was little doubt that enact-ing martial law had been the proper step to take. *Sure it should have been done sooner, but kudos to the Chief anyway. Apparently he had the stones to make the tough decisions after all. Now, if we can only catch the terrorists and return order and nor-mality to this community before panic begins to spread to the rest of the country.* Searcy had already received reports that attacks on Arabs were occurring all over the nation. He said a silent prayer the FBI would catch a break soon.

CHAPTER 19

▼

The headlights of the white Ford Crown Victoria reflected off glistening wet pavement as it turned onto a dimly lit street and made its way towards a large house at the end of the cul-de-sac. Its owner pulled into the driveway, parked and cut off the engine. He sat there quietly listening to the heavy rain patter the roof for several minutes gathering his thoughts before getting out, opening an umbrella and walking toward his yellow stucco house. Shaking the moisture from the umbrella, he set it on the porch, unlocked the door and stepped inside.

There his smiling wife and three children, ages nine, seven and four greeted him. Dressed in pajamas the kids gave him quick hugs and kisses then, just as quickly, ran away to resume whatever entertaining activity their mother had, only minutes ago, managed to drag them away from.

His wife reached up, wrapped her arms around his burly neck and kissed him, her affection showed more interest than the children's had, and lasted just a bit longer. Running her fingers through his receding gray hair she asked, "How was your day?"

"Long. How was yours?" the man responded. This little interlude had taken place between them almost every day for the last eighteen years. Though it was repetitive it never grew old for them; it was one of those little things that make people feel normal and comforted and which folks tended to take for granted.

"Grueling," she answered, as she helped him out of his suit jacket. "Sarah," their youngest, "has done nothing but whine and complain all day how her stomach hurts and she ended up spending most of the afternoon in bed. "William," the middle one, "has back-talked and tested my patience at every opportunity. I had to spank him once, put him in time out three times and take away his Play-Station."

The man smiled warmly at her, "And how was Jason?"

"Oh, Jason was a perfect little angel. He has learned that when one of the others is acting up, to let them have my complete and undivided attention," she giggled.

"Smart boy. He must get that from his father."

"You'd like to think," she smiled.

"What's for dinner? I'm starving!" he said, patting the round bulge of his stomach.

"Peanut butter and jelly sandwiches with the crusts cut off and Cheetos."

"Sounds good, do I get milk with it?" he said, playfully poking her in the ribs.

She nimbly dodged his attack, "Very funny! How does Chicken Alfredo, Caesar salad and garlic bread sound?"

"Even better. Have the children eaten?"

"Fed and bathed."

He looked toward the top of the stairs and yelled, "C'mon kids."

Moments later the children came tearing down the stairs, joining their parents in the family room. They piled on top of their beanbags sitting on the floor in front of their father's high-back leather chair. While the man took a seat, his wife walked over and lit gas logs in the fireplace. Even though it was the middle of summer, they still lit a fire to properly set the atmosphere for this special time; of course they set the air conditioner on high. All knelt on the floor together, joined hands and bowed their heads.

"Dear Father, thank you for bringing us safely through this day," the man began praying. "Thank you for the day that is to come and help us to honor you in our behavior, our speech and our thoughts. Please forgive those that have done evil to our town, they know not what they do. Bring them understanding of who you are and the love you offer, in Jesus' mighty name," and they all said together, "Amen."

"All right, who can recite today's memory verse for me?" the man asked.

"Me! Me!" Sarah cried.

Her father nodded.

"Jesus loves me this I know, for the Bible tells me so, little ones…"

"No, Sarah," the man said smiling. "Your memory verse, the one we worked on last night out of the Bible."

"I don't know it. It's too *hard.*"

"William can you say it?"

William stared at him, but didn't say a word.

"All right Jason, I guess it's up to you."

Jason sighed, "Then Peter said unto them, repent and be baptized every one of you in the name of Jesus Christ for the remission of sins, and ye shall receive the gift of the Holy Ghost."

'Very good, Jason," Julie said. "And where is that verse located?"

"Acts 2:38."

"Wonderful. Who can tell me what the shortest verse in the Bible is?"

"Jesus wept!" Sarah screamed with a gleeful smile.

The man stood up, "Good job guys!"

As all returned to their seats, the woman stood, "Honey, it's late so I'm gonna' go ahead and prepare our dinner while you handle things here."

"Okay Julie. I guess we can manage this alone tonight, right kids?"

"Right!" they replied in three-part harmony.

"I'm sure you can," she smiled, walking out of the room.

The man turned toward his children, "Okay kids, whose turn is it tonight to pick a story?"

Sarah raised her hand and again exclaimed, "Me! Me!"

The man smiled, "Okay, go to the shelf and choose a book."

The little girl ran to a nearby shelf, her blond pigtails bouncing behind her as she went. Moments later she returned, flopping down on the fluffy beanbag, she handed her father her selection.

He took the book from her tiny hand, rustled his hand through her hair affectionately and read the title, "My, my, The Many Adventures of Winnie the Pooh."

"Aw, man…" Jason said dejectedly. "She always picks that one."

"Well son, it is her turn and this is the one she wants. Tomorrow night it'll be your turn, I believe."

"I know but I get tired of that one."

"And I'm sure your little sister gets tired of your Harry Potter books as well."

"Okay…" the boy said begrudgingly, dropping his chin ever so slightly toward the floor.

The children sat quietly as their father read of Pooh Bear's grand adventures. When he finished twenty minutes later, Sarah was curled up fast asleep with a thumb tucked loosely in the corner of her mouth, the flicker of flames dancing across her peaceful face. Julie came in, smiled, stooped down and lifted the little girl into her arms.

"William, Jason, give your father a kiss and go get into bed."

The boys followed their mother's instructions and raced ahead of her up the stairs, Jason taking two steps at a time and William struggling valiantly to mimic him. A few minutes later, she returned to find that her husband had kicked off his shoes and was half-asleep in front of the fire. She sat down on his lap slipping her arms around his neck and kissed him lightly on the nose.

"Honey, are you ready to eat?" she asked softly.

He slowly opened his eyes. "Do I have time to grab a quick shower first? I feel cruddy."

"Sure. With the kids in bed perhaps we'll be able to sit and enjoy a quiet meal together," she winked.

"Quiet meal, huh? That would be nice." The man grinned as he slid her gently off his lap and hurried up the stairs to their bedroom.

Having taken a nice long hot invigorating shower and now refreshed, the man emerged twenty-five minutes later dressed in sweat pants and T-shirt and walked back downstairs. He found his wife sitting quietly in the dining room reading her latest issue of People magazine under the dimmed lighting of the chandelier. The house was silent; the kids were nowhere in sight and candles were burning in the center of the table.

"Feeling any better?" she asked, setting aside the magazine.

"Much," he said, bending down to kiss her softly on the forehead. "Something smells really terrific…I hope you made enough…I'm famished."

She smiled, "I'm sure there will be plenty. I guess that means you're ready to eat?"

"Whenever you are," he said taking his seat. He started flipping through her magazine and wondered how the movie stars could possibly be happy when their every move was photographed by the paparazzi. *What a way to live. A life shared by millions,* he thought.

His wife stepped into the kitchen and in a few minutes returned to pour them both a tall glass of iced tea. She stepped back into the kitchen, retrieved a tray containing two salads, two steaming plates of pasta and freshly baked bread. Julie served her husband then herself, sat down across from him as he took her hand in his own. The man said the blessing over the food, picked up his tea and said, "A toast," as his wife raised her own. "To a long life together. May the rest of it be as rich and fulfilling as what has already passed."

"I'm sure it will be," she said.

"Happy anniversary, sweetheart."

"Happy anniversary to you too," she replied warmly. "I love you."

"I love you too. More than you'll ever know."

Julie smiled.

The man reached for his fork, wound a huge portion of pasta around it, and raised it to his mouth and the doorbell rang.

"Oh for goodness sakes!" the man exclaimed, dropping the fork onto his plate and leaning forward to stand up.

"I'll get it, honey," his wife said. He'd had a very long day and was more than happy to let her.

The man sat at the table, drumming his fingers, impatiently waiting to resume his meal. He could hear his wife open the door and greet whoever was there. A moment later he heard her call out to him.

"Honey, it's for you."

With disgust he wadded up his napkin and tossed it onto the table as he stood. *Can't we have just one night alone without some sort of interruption?* He walked to the front door to find three sheriff's deputies waiting for him. *Now what?* As he approached them the deputy on the right drew his weapon and aimed it directly at his chest.

"On the floor, now!" he ordered, stepping inside the door.

The man stopped in his tracks, shocked confusion on his face, "What is the meaning of this? Do you three have any idea who I am?" he demanded to know.

"Yes, we know exactly who you are, now get on your face…move!" he yelled. He shifted his gaze toward the stunned woman, "You too!"

Julie looked at her husband, hoping that he had some sort of explanation as to what was happening. The man thought quickly and then told her to go ahead and get on the floor. "I'm sure this is all a big misunderstanding, Julie, just do what they say. We'll get this all worked out later."

The confused couple finally did as they were instructed.

"Put your hands behind your back!" one deputy commanded. They did as they were told and two of the deputies knelt down, one of them placing his knee in the middle of the man's back, and his hands on the back of his head. The other also placed a knee on his back and took a firm hold of the man's hands, shoving them sharply up toward his shoulder blades, eliciting a sharp groan.

The remaining deputy holstered his weapon and did the same to Julie.

"I demand to know what we are accused of doing!" the prone man shouted.

"Shut up!" one deputy ordered, pressing his knee more firmly into the man's back and giving his arms another jerk upward.

"Ughh…take it easy," the man gasped. "I will report this treatment to the Sheriff!"

The deputy kneeling over Julie withdrew a large black knife from behind his back, reached down and grabbed a handful of her hair, yanking back sharply. Placing the edge of the long glistening blade to her tightly stretched neck he drew it across, smoothly slicing through both jugular veins; blood erupted from her savaged throat, all the while the three intruders were chanting, "Allahu Akbar, Allahu Akbar!"

Her husband, lying on his stomach not three feet away, did not at first comprehend what he was witnessing and was stunned, unable to move. When he heard the rasping, gurgling sounds escaping from his love's windpipe as she struggled to continue breathing, he began fighting violently, twisting and thrashing his body from side to side trying to free himself from the large men kneeling on his back. The deputies fought to hold him still while their partner rushed over to assist.

Reaching down, the deputy grasped the man by the chin from behind, attempting to still his jerking head. He was finally able to gain some measure of control long enough to cut his victim's throat. Due to his struggling, however, the knife only managed to partially sever one of the vital arteries. Even so, it was sufficient for his racing heart to begin pumping huge amounts of blood out onto the bright white marble floor. Though his wound was no less fatal than his wife's, his death would come a little slower and would be more agonizing.

The man lay dying on the floor, trapped under the weight of the three killers, staring at the dead vacant eyes of his wife. He felt the men stand, the heavy pressure of their weight releasing from his body. He knew that he would soon follow his wife into eternity, but his fears multiplied when he saw the killers step over Julie's corpse and walk towards the stairs. *The children!* Gathering every bit of strength he could possibly muster he forced himself to stand and lunged toward the men, his hands outstretched like the talons of an angry eagle.

The killers heard the labored efforts of the grievously wounded father and turned to face him. It took little effort for the tallest of the three to shove the weakened man aside, causing him to collapse on top of his wife's body. Feeling her warmth beneath him enraged him even more. *I will not leave my children to these monsters!* With great effort, he managed to drag his bloody body several feet across the floor, clawing his way toward the killers, refusing to surrender to his fatal injury. At last he knew he was finished, that his battle with the Reaper had been lost. He struggled once more to rise, buckled and stopped moving. *Oh God, I'm sorry kids, Daddy tried. I'll see you in heaven.* Several more labored, sputtering sounds escaped from his lips, then Police Chief Mitchell Wade Baker drew his last breath and died.

Omar Fadillah, Rashiid and Mustafa Baraka watched the chief die and they smiled, as they knew he would soon stand before Allah and his judgment. In his last minutes they had even gained a little respect for him. If all Americans would fight as valiantly as this man, the brothers realized that they and their fellow Muslims might not stand a chance of winning this war. Rashiid bent down and wiped the blood from his knife in Julie's blonde hair. He rose and joined his compatriots, walking up the stairs to the rooms of the sleeping children. Their task was not yet complete.

CHAPTER 20

▼

Day Nine

Ryker was once again up early after another restless night's sleep. He was standing alone in the pouring rain, a rare occurrence here in the summer. It was just after daybreak Saturday morning and he was looking at what was left of the hospital. The overnight showers had finally managed to suffocate the smoke from the few remaining smoldering hot spots. He was simply amazed a structure that had taken literally years to construct was completely leveled in a matter of minutes. Ryker began walking slowly around the perimeter of the building, occasionally stopping to take note of something that grabbed his attention. One particular thing he saw, which left him feeling even more emotionally drained than before, if that was possible, was a soggy, soot-covered teddy bear lying on top of the remains of a crushed heart monitor.

Occasionally he'd come across a purse, a briefcase, or some other item signifying that there had once been living human beings working here. He circled around to the side of the building that had collapsed and crushed the brave firemen less than four days ago. Their bodies had all been removed, taken to the morgue and had no doubt already prepared for burial by their grief-stricken families. Ryker had learned that most of the men were young, married and either had children or their wives were pregnant. It was all so tragic, so senseless. He said a silent prayer, not so much for the dead, but for the living left behind.

Ryker continued walking around the rubble and stopped dead in his tracks. In front of him was a mangled baby stroller but that was not what shocked him so badly. Inside it was a charred baby's shoe, a sock still in it. He couldn't tell if it belonged to a boy or a girl. The shoe was still tied, it looked as if the force of the explosion had left the sock in its wake but jerked the baby's foot out. His heart broke; he had seen enough and he turned around, heading back the way he had come.

Rescue workers had been working furiously to find someone alive, but in the last twenty-four hours all they recovered were another fifty-seven bodies. The death toll now stood at one thousand two hundred and seventy-two. There was some good news, though. Most of the critically wounded had been upgraded to serious or guarded condition, surely not home free, but much more optimistic.

Vast numbers of construction workers, firefighters and civilian volunteers had arrived from all over California, Oregon and Nevada to lend a helping hand. Local church groups were providing sandwiches and coffee to the weary workers and area motels were putting up those from out of town free of charge. Ryker found it particularly disturbing how people could be so kind and helpful to one another one minute and then practically killing each other over a sale at Wal Mart the next. There was no doubt in his mind that humans were, by far, the strangest and most complex creatures on the planet; and the most evil! At least the savagery wild beasts displayed had a purpose and made sense, humans were not so easily understood.

Hostage Rescue was on the ground and ready to deploy at a moment's notice. They were being staged out of an unused hangar at the airport. The media had obviously heard about the giant cargo plane landing there for they were clamoring to know just what was going on. The Mayor's office initially considered avoiding their queries, but had soon thought better of it. Ignoring them would only fan the flames of curiosity. He decided to release a brief statement explaining the C-5 was supposed to be on display for the upcoming Air Show next week, but in all the confusion nobody had thought to cancel its arrival. He even made a point to clarify that the plane had been quickly refueled and returned to its base that very day. Surprisingly enough, with all the increased security around the airport, no one managed to see its cargo unloaded at the end of the runway.

Ryker received a phone call early that morning from the FBI director informing him that the President wanted to see significant progress, sooner rather than later. The American people were demanding the terrorists be caught and brought to justice and were rapidly losing patience. The Director added that consumer confidence was growing weaker by the day and the Dow was already down twelve percent, its lowest point since the Carter presidency in the late seventies.

The president had held a press conference within hours of the attack on the hospital. He'd denounced the heinous acts as cowardly and assured the nation the perpetrators would be quickly hunted down and held accountable for their despicable and evil deeds. This had done very little to assuage people's fears and even less to restore their faith in his administration. Nicholson's vice-presidential campaign had centered mainly on the diminished threat of terrorism to the US mainland and right now people's confidence in his ability to fulfill that boast wasn't all that strong.

Ryker suspected the President's primary concern was not of the economy, or of people's fears, but more about the fact his poll numbers were beginning to dip sharply. Not only were they slipping amongst the swing voters, but also with the strong liberal voting block as well. During his campaign for Vice President, he had gone on the record many times boldly stating how strongly he believed the war on terror would shortly be coming to an end and that our brave troops would soon be coming home. Frequently he made it known that there had been no attacks on US soil since 9/11 and that the threat of further attacks was very unlikely.

It was a known fact he strongly disagreed with the US military's involvement in the Middle East and that behind closed doors he was doing his best to arrange for the withdrawal of forces. The liberal left applauded his position, while the conservative right strongly criticized him as just another liberal Democrat who was weak on defense. Those in the middle, who tended to lean one way on some issues, and the other way on the rest, were not sure what to believe. Most people were either socially conservative or liberally fiscal, vice versa, or a mix of both; it all depended on the issues. However, these voters who had listened to both sides claim for years to be speaking the truth, were now even more unsure of what to believe, so most just voted according to their heart. Either way, Ryker didn't care. Right now he just wanted to catch some bad guys in the worst possible way.

What Ryker really wanted to know was when was Congress going to get truly serious about the war on terror and quit treating it like a routine police investigation? He knew that if they took the shackles off the military and let them do what they were trained to do, this war would be won inside of twelve months. Not just in Iraq, Syria and Afghanistan, but worldwide. He also knew that was not very likely to happen, because it was not the politically correct thing to do.

He was sick and tired of politicians using poll numbers to dictate every move this once-great nation made. They were so worried about offending the rest of the world that they were endangering Americans as a result. *Our nation used to have a backbone. When other countries pushed us, we pushed back. Now the politicians run to the United Nations whenever something goes wrong or they conduct a poll before taking any action. Sooner or later, our leaders in Washington are going to have to either wake up on their own, or they'll be forced back to reality kicking and screaming...or bleeding,* he thought.

The UN did not always have the US's best interests at heart. That political body was made up of too many countries with conflicting values and loyalties contrary to those of the United States. In fact, the American people did not go to the ballot box and elect the United Nations to protect their interests, they voted for a President who was supposed to be protecting them and right now his ability or willingness to do that was in serious question. Ryker was afraid it was going to take a twenty-five kiloton nuclear blast in the heart of New York City to finally get the President's attention. *Maybe they should blow up an abortion clinic, cut down a tree, or kill a snail darter…. that would surely fire up the Libs!*

What was even more surprising was that the nation, as a whole, was not reacting to this brutal situation quite the way one would expect it to. Sure public support for the victims was strong and people were showing obvious disdain and anger toward the terrorists. However, the fear and panicked spending that followed the events of 9/11 was amazingly non-existent, at least beyond the Redding area, he corrected himself.

Coast-to-coast radio and television talk show hosts were even curious as to why this seemed to be impacting the country so lightly. Had the nation grown so used to the possible threat of terrorism that now, in some strange way, it was becoming an acceptable way of life? Or was it that these attacks were not occurring in larger cities, with more high-profile targets or in their own backyards? Personally, Ryker believed America had grown indifferent to the repeated and numerous terrorist alerts. *Threat level orange, yellow, mauve, fuchsia, who in the hell knew what to believe anymore?* Had the magnitude of this latest violence not completely sunk into people's minds? *Has the constant blood and gore of television desensitized people to the point they don't even care anymore?*

Perhaps, with everything taking place, America still believed it was somehow untouchable. Within twelve months of 9/11, the millions of US flags that had been so prevalent on every car, business and house across the nation had all but disappeared. The yellow ribbons tied around thousands of trees had faded, tattered and blown away in the wind. *Along with our vigilance, it would seem!* As the colors in those flags and ribbons slowly faded so had the memory of the heart-wrenching events that spurred those patriotic displays in the first place. The fact that the mainstream media, for reasons known only to them, conveniently stopped broadcasting video footage of 9/11 on their television news programs was in no doubt partly to blame. For who better than they to decide what was needed to be seen?

Or maybe the fact that no foreign military had laid foot on US soil in more than two hundred twenty-five years had lulled the country into a false sense of security. Somehow, somewhere in the collective subconscious, American's truly believed the US was too big and too powerful to be conquered. That even though the smaller kid may sometimes land a lucky punch and bloody a nose, in the end, the bigger, stronger kid always comes out victorious.

Whatever the reason, Ryker was convinced something far more hideous was on the way, something dark and evil. He had nothing specific to point at but somehow he just knew the storm clouds were gathering beyond the not so distant horizon and that the excruciating wait would soon be over.

He saw Agent Roland park his car, get out, raise his umbrella and begin walking briskly toward him. "Dalton, I've got some really bad news."

"What now?" the sound of dread clearly evident in his voice.

"I don't know how to say this."

"Just spit it out, Steve."

"It's Chief Baker, he and his family were killed last night in their home."

"What! Killed? How? Who?" A startled Ryker demanded. Pausing briefly to calm his nerves, he asked, "What happened, Steve?"

"Their throats were all cut. He and his wife were found in the foyer at the foot of the stairs and the two kids were found in their beds."

"My God…you said two kids? I thought I heard someone say he had three?"

"He…they did. The oldest one survived."

"How, wasn't he home?"

"Yeah, he was home. Apparently there is a crawl space between the upstairs closets. The access panels are small and difficult to see if you don't know what to look for. We found out that the boy likes to pretend it's a fort and he sometimes hides in there. He evidently fell asleep in the access last night and the killers didn't find him or perhaps they were unaware there were three kids."

"Well, thank God for small favors," was all Ryker could think of to say.

"Yeah…I guess. Evidently the boy got cold and awoke sometime during the night only to come out and find his younger brother already dead. When he ran to get his parents they weren't in their bed so he ran to his sister's room and found her. By then he was really starting to come unglued and ran downstairs and that's when he found Mitch and Julie. Somehow, I don't know how, he was still able to call 911."

"Tough kid, managing to keep it together long enough to phone the police. How's he doing?"

"In a state of shock. He's with his grandfather now and I've been told the two are pretty close, so that should help a little. There's also a grief counselor and the family pastor keeping an eye on him."

"What do we know about what happened?"

"The Coroner says that it's very likely the children didn't suffer, it was over really fast and they probably didn't even wake up."

"Go on," Ryker said, again finding he was at a loss for words, and fighting down the lump in his throat.

"Looks like the wife was the first one killed. RPD guesses her throat was cut while Mitch was forced to watch. The Coroner believes Mitch didn't go so easily. The killers only partially cut one of his carotid arteries and although it produced a lot of blood it was not instantly fatal. Blood splatter patterns indicate he tried to fight them off, even with his throat cut. Coroner thinks he probably saw them going for the children and tried his best to stop them, he even managed to get to his feet at least once before succumbing to his wound."

"Good for him, I hope he got a piece of them before he died." They both stood there quietly in the cool rain for several minutes watching as another body was removed from the 'hospital' and placed on the sidewalk. "He was a good man with a good heart. He'll be missed," Ryker noted.

"Yes, he was, I liked him."

"What do we know about the killers...anything?"

"A neighbor was walking her dog last night around eight o'clock and reported seeing three deputy sheriffs at the door to the Baker's house. That time matches up with the Coroner's estimated time of death. She didn't think much of it though, what with Mitch being the Police Chief and all. She said that there are uniformed officers there all the time, day and night, and thought it was normal."

"Three deputies? Have we had any luck identifying them?"

"The Sheriff reports that none of his employees were anywhere near the residence at the time of the incident, at least not officially."

"So what do we have, impostors or three rogue deputies?

"Not sure just yet, but I'd go with the impostor line if it was left to me." Roland's cell phone rang and he stepped away to answer it. He listened to what the caller had to say, made a couple of inaudible comments, doing his best to juggle the phone, the umbrella and scribble in his notepad at the same time. He ended the call by dropping the phone with the snap of his wrist and walked back over to Ryker.

"That was the Assistant Police Chief. He says the Coroner was able to lift a partial bloody palm print off the banister to the staircase. The blood matched Chief Baker's, but the print doesn't belong to any of the Sheriff's employees or any member of the Baker family."

"So where does that leave us?'

"Well...apparently all County and City employees are fingerprinted when they're hired. When the print was checked against the Sheriff's personnel, nothing popped up, but..."

"Please, tell me I'm gonna' like your but," Ryker asked hopefully.

"We got a hit, but not to any deputy sheriff's."

"Well, who then?"

"The print matched a city worker named Mustafa Baraka, he works with the City's street maintenance department."

"Baraka?" Ryker thought for a moment. "His being with the city would help explain a great many things, like how the terrorists have managed to get all over the place without drawing any suspicion to themselves."

"Do you think it might be a little early to connect these murders to the terrorists?"

"Possibly...I know we have nothing connecting this Mustafa to the other attacks and the murder of Baker's family could be for any number of reasons but I'll bet he's one of the guys we're looking for."

"You're probably right. Oh, by the way, this Baraka guy has a brother who also works with the city."

"A brother? The plot thickens. What's his name?"

Roland checked his notes before replying, "Rashiid. They were both hired at the same time several years ago. According to the city manager, their immediate supervisor reports that they're both outstanding employees. He says they tend to be a couple of loners so he lets them work together and for the most part by themselves. He also said they've never missed a day's work and they do the work of four men, so he doesn't mind them working by themselves."

"If these are the guys that killed the Bakers where did they get the uniforms? Has the Sheriff reported any missing deputies?"

"No, he hasn't. In fact, all of his employees have already been accounted for," Roland added.

"Were any of them assigned to work in or near the Bakers' neighborhood last night?"

"No, the one's on duty were assigned to other areas, the others were at home with their families during the time of the murders. Sheriff Kidd said that since the attacks started they've all been staying pretty close to home when they're not on duty."

"I can understand that. Do we know where these Baraka brothers are? Please...tell me that we do."

Roland once again referred to his notes; "They share an apartment off of Churn Creek Road on the other side of town. We've got two teams watching it, but no one has come home yet. We've also put out a BOLO," Roland added, using department slang for 'be on the lookout', "with strict orders for anyone who spots them to notify us immediately, they are not to attempt to apprehend the suspects."

"If these are three of the terrorists, then that makes potentially five we've identified, assuming Baraka's brother is involved and not counting the unidentified third man. Where do you suppose they got the uniforms, or better yet, who gave them to them?"

"I don't know. Perhaps they stole them from a dry cleaners?" Roland offered.

"Perhaps, maybe not." Ryker's phone rang and he answered it. Listening for a minute he hung up. "They found another note at the Bakers', it was left in the mailbox."

"What did it say?" Roland asked curiously.

"It was the same as the other ones with the exception of a post script informing us that we should know that nobody is safe."

"That's it?"

"That's it."

"I guess there's no longer any doubt these are some of our terrorists."

"Not as far as I'm concerned there isn't. Call the Sheriff again; have him poll his uniformed personnel. Find out if any of them are missing any uniforms. With everything that's been happening they should all be in radio contact with the department 24/7, whether on or off duty. It shouldn't take too long to find out. Also find out which businesses supply their uniforms here locally."

"Right away." Roland reached for his cell phone to carry out his orders.

Ryker proceeded to walk around the burned out hull of a building whose purpose had once been to sustain life. Now it was nothing more than a temporary tomb that was defiantly refusing to give up her lodgers. He watched two rescue workers gently lift the twisted and charred body of another small child from the ruins. They carefully placed it in a body bag then carried it over and added it to five others that had been removed since he'd first arrived. Ryker felt a tear well up and roll down his cheek. He hurriedly wiped it away and looked around to see if anyone had seen. He realized he'd managed to get little to no sleep in the past week and the grueling hours were beginning to take their toll.

He looked up to see Roland approaching. "Sheriff says no one reports missing any uniforms," handing Ryker a piece of paper, "that's the name of the store where all city and county employees get their uniforms."

"It's still early, but have two agents find out where the owner lives and quietly pick him up and bring him to headquarters."

"You think he's one of the terrorists?"

"Probably not, but let's see who he's got working for him, shall we? I've got a nagging suspicion we just might be surprised by what we find."

$$*\qquad*\qquad*\qquad*$$

The city maintenance vehicle turned onto Clear Creek Road. It drove just over a mile before slowing down as it passed the City of Redding Power Plant. The two men inside saw there were two military vehicles with large machine guns mounted on top sitting in front of the gates. There were also concrete barricades and armed guards spread out in strategic positions all along the fence line, which had not been there two days before. They decided that this was no longer a feasible mark and sped off before they drew unwanted attention.

The men would eventually check out several more electrical and water treatment plants before giving up and scratching them all from their list of likely targets. Security was just too tight to risk getting caught over such insignificant targets. They would have to regroup at Mikal and Raissa's tonight and discuss alternatives.

CHAPTER 21

▼

Members of the terrorism task force were gathered in a conference room at FBI headquarters in Redding. Information had come in from the surveillance team on Raissa and Mikal's home an hour prior. Through wiretaps they learned that the members of the terrorists' cell would be gathering there tonight to discuss plans for future missions. No longer was there any doubt in anyone's mind they had the right group under surveillance. Through the use of listening devices covertly placed throughout the home two days before, as well as other investigative means, the task force was able to glean a lot in a short period of time.

They learned Omar Fadillah, identified by Professor Gomillion as one of the attackers, was employed as a mail carrier with the US Postal Service. Further investigation revealed he was also the carrier responsible for the delivery of mail to the al-Nassers' place of business. That was all Ryker needed to connect those two dots in the puzzle.

It was also learned one Abdul Abida, now going by the name of Jesus Olarte, worked for the uniform shop in question and that he routinely hung out with the Baraka brothers during his free time; a huge mistake on their part, however, another dot connected. And it was already a known fact the al-Nassers purchased their employees' uniforms at the very same store. Mikal was seen going into the shop by the surveillance team a few days ago. Another dot.

Field agents had earlier reported that all of those unsavory individuals would be at the al-Nasser's home tonight for a planning session.

Ryker had just received instructions from the FBI Director, who, having conferred with the Attorney General and the President, ordered him to take the terrorists down, hard. The Hostage Rescue Team was placed on full alert, the warrants had been approved and now they just had to cross the T's and dot all the I's.

Ryker decided to roll the dice and wait until all the known terrorists were gathered in the same location before making a move. He knew it was a risky decision and there was a possibility that any, or all of them, could strike another target before they could be apprehended. With security on them being as tight as it was, he believed the zealots' chances of success had been greatly diminished.

Equally risky would be trying to apprehend them individually. The possibility that one of them might slip through their fingers and warn the others was worse. Besides, with everything they had learned in the last several hours, he felt it was a relatively safe bet that they had no further attacks planned until after their get-together this evening.

Present in the conference room were the interim Police Chief, Peter Bond, Shasta County Sheriff, Levi Kidd, Agent Roland, Special Agent in Charge of HRT, Mike Daniels, Lt. Col. Jake Searcy, Ryker and several other agents and aides. They were here to decide how to quickly and safely take down the terrorists without injury to bystanders and the children present in the home. They had already decided the meeting at the al-Nasser's would likely be their best and only opportunity to grab them all at the same time.

"First of all," Ryker began, "Does anyone here not believe that the al-Nassers and their friends are the terrorists?"

"No doubt about it, it's them, everything adds up. We have eyewitnesses, forensic evidence like the bloody palm prints, video and audio surveillance putting all six of them together...it's them," Roland said, confidently, everyone else nodding in agreement.

"Alright, next question, are there any more of them we haven't stumbled onto yet?"

"It's always possible but in this case, not likely. We've seen no indications that anyone else is involved. From the audio we picked up from the house, as well as cell phone intercepts, they have not even alluded to the possibility that anyone else is involved," Sheriff Kidd stated matter-of-factly. "These are our killers."

"What about the couple that had dinner with the al-Nassers the other night? Have we learned who they are?" Ryker inquired.

"Turns out it was Fadillah and his wife," Chief Bond replied.

"What about his wife? Is she involved?"

"We don't believe so," Roland answered.

"Why not?"

"Because none of the others have spoken to her concerning their involvement in the attacks or mentioned her in their conversations about them. Nor has she said anything that would indicate she knew."

"Still…"

"Besides, she isn't Arab and all indications tell us she is a practicing Scientologist."

"That Omar is one slick operator. How in the world has he managed to keep all of this from her?" Kidd pondered.

"Still…do we know where she is, or will be this evening?" Ryker asked.

"As far as we know, she should be home," Roland answered.

"Okay. When we take down the others tonight, I want officers to take Mrs. Fadillah into custody. I'd still like to have a few words with her anyway." Ryker looked down at his page of notes. "So, everybody agrees…these are the ones we're looking for?" A round of head nods and grunts in the affirmative was his response

"Okay, how do we get all the neighbors safely out of their homes without alerting the suspects to our presence?" Chief Bond asked.

Daniels was the one to answer. "We'll have an officer posing as a gas company employee going door to door directing them to leave the area."

"Do we really need to alert the neighbors?" one agent asked. "What I mean is, surely HRT can be in and have it over with pretty quickly. The neighbors shouldn't be in any danger."

"You're right, my men will go in quickly," Agent Daniels, responded. "However, we have no way of knowing if they have explosives in the house and no guarantees we will be able to prevent them from being detonated. No…we will need evacuate the neighbors, it's the only safe way and I think enough innocent people have been hurt already."

"What about the officer, isn't it possible they'll see him and get suspicious?"

"Sure it's possible, but we'll have him go to the suspect house as well. He'll ask them if they've smelled any gas; that we have reports of a leak in the neighborhood and we're trying to locate it. That will also give the officer a chance to get a general layout of the interior of the house before we go in."

"The terrorists could still be alerted when they see their neighbors rushing to get in their cars and leave," Sheriff Kidd said. "These people are not stupid. Evil yes, but not stupid."

"No, we'll give each resident a specific time to leave and stress to them to adhere to it. Besides we only need to alert those nearest the suspect house," Daniels answered. "We'll also send plainclothes officers to the other homes in the surrounding area and instruct the residents to stay inside until telephoned by police dispatchers that it is safe to return to normal."

"What about people that haven't returned home yet?" Sheriff Kidd asked.

"Well, most people have chosen to stay home as much as possible and avoid the chaos," Chief Bond answered. "Those that do elect to go out are taking care of their business and returning home as fast as they can. Seems no one wants to be anyplace where there are a lot of people gathered. So there shouldn't be a tremendous amount of traffic in or out of the area. Besides, the apprehension won't take place until after dark and most should already be home under curfew."

"We'll have to put up roadblocks to prevent bystanders from getting in the way, but we can't do that until we're positive all the suspects are in the house," Roland said.

"As soon as we know unequivocally that all the terrorists are in the house we shut down the roads to all traffic," Searcy explained.

"What about the breach and takedown itself?" the Sheriff asked.

"HRT will be handling all elements of that. We've managed to get a set of blueprints to the house from the building contractor so HRT will have a firm plan in which to proceed," Ryker explained. "Agent Daniels' team will handle the actual takedown. The rest of us will be there as observers and in support roles, nothing more, until after the suspects are in custody or neutralized and the house is declared secured."

Everyone in the room could tell by the Chief's body language and the expression on his face he didn't like that one bit. It was obvious on behalf of the Bakers, he wanted his department in on the action; any of them would no doubt feel the exact same way if they found themselves in a similar situation. He started to speak but Ryker raised his hand cutting him off. "Chief, I know what you're going to say and I understand, believe me I do. But if you are honest with yourself you'll admit that HRT is not only the best, but also the obvious choice to execute this operation."

The Chief again started to speak and then decided not to, evidently the ring of truth in Ryker's words having had their effect.

The group proceeded to discuss every fine little detail of the plan: points of entry, cutting power, the order of entry, angles of approach and time of entry. It was made very clear none of the terrorists could be allowed to escape, no matter what the cost. The planning was going along smoothly and the last particulars were discussed. The meeting was just about to adjourn when the stenographer, who had been typing away, stopped and looked up.

"Gentlemen?" she said in a mousy little voice.

They all turned to her as one. It was the first female voice any of them had heard in more than an hour. And not only that, it was not customary for the stenographer to speak during these meetings unless spoken to first. She was there to take dictation and nothing else.

"Yes?" Ryker asked.

"Well…um, obviously I've heard everything you gentlemen discussed, but I was just wondering, won't there be children in there? I heard it mentioned as one of the points that needed to be covered earlier, however, I haven't heard anyone discuss it since," she said softly, looking down at her steno machine.

The men sat there stunned, not from the interruption to their conversation, but because they had all failed to remember to cover that particular 'little' issue. Somehow, in all their excitement to be finally getting the terrorists, they had all overlooked that one very important element, no doubt, the most important one of all.

Ryker finally spoke, "What is your name?"

"Becky," she responded, sheepishly.

"Well Becky, from now on, whenever you have a question you make sure you ask it and I don't care who doesn't like it. You may have just saved this whole operation from going straight down the toilet. Good job." The other men all grunted in agreement.

"Alright gentlemen, I hope we all enjoyed our eggs," Ryker said, jokingly wiping his face with a handkerchief. "Now, what do we do about the children?"

The lawmen again huddled up to discuss this little chink in their well-made plans. In the end it was decided to move the assault back until just before 10:00 PM, by then the children should be in bed. Agents would be assigned to keep an eye on the bedroom windows watching for the usual bedtime activity, bathroom and bedroom lights going on and off at the expected intervals. This, in conjunction with the listening devices, they all agreed would tell them when the kids were in bed. And when it would be safe to proceed. In addition, as a safety precaution, the first commandos into the house would enter through the children's bedroom window and place them under immediate FBI protection.

"Anything else?" Ryker asked. No one said anything. He turned toward the stenographer, "Becky?"

"Yes sir?" she said meekly

"Have we missed anything else important?"

"No sir…I don't think so…I…" she stammered, uncomfortably looking around at all of the faces looking back at her.

Everyone started laughing. The meeting was adjourned and they all dispersed to carry out their respective assignments.

CHAPTER 22

▼

Raissa was starting to get a little concerned; the others should have been here already. She telephoned Rashiid, who informed her they had run into some unexpected delays, but would be there shortly. She only hoped they got here before dark; they couldn't risk getting caught for violating curfew.

Raissa had ordered dinner from a local pizza parlor. She looked at the clock on the wall and figured the others should start arriving anytime now, followed shortly thereafter by the food. Ironically enough, pizza parlors offering delivery service were among the few businesses the authorities deemed worthy of staying open after curfew.

This would, in all likelihood, be the last time all would be together in one place, at least for awhile. Things had gotten far too dicey to continue to take chances. Security in town was extremely tight and even with the current state of martial law, random attacks against Middle-Eastern people were occurring all too frequently. Everywhere she went people were watching every move she made, or so it seemed. It made her feel like a fish in a tank. She was hesitant to take her children out of the house for fear something bad would happen to them. *Ironic,* she thought, *we're becoming victims of our own actions.* After the next operation, they would all go inactive for a time and wait for things to calm down a bit. All would blend back into their 'normal' lives and pray they would not be found out, for there were still other, more vital missions to carry out in the near future. *We have been blessed so far and Allah has surely smiled on our efforts,* she thought.

Mustafa and Rashiid were the first to arrive and were greeted at the door by Mikal, who offered them a cold glass of tea. They both politely accepted and took a seat on the sofa in the living room. No sooner had they sat down than Abdul arrived followed closely by Omar. Mikal repeated the welcome. A few minutes later Raissa joined them.

They sat for several minutes discussing what they had already accomplished and all were quite satisfied with the results. Mustafa explained why they were late and how their plans to hit the power station south of town would have to be canceled. He added that after several additional hours reconnoitering other water treatment and power plants, those too would have to be scratched from the list of possible targets. All agreed it was an acceptable setback and inconsequential in the grand scheme of things. They knew Redding was nothing more than a trial run to see how America would react, in the face of bigger things to come. The little town would soon be forgotten once America saw what happened next; at least for a while.

*   *   *   *

On the sidewalk outside of the al-Nasser's house, an undercover police officer was walking door-to-door advising those residents living closest to the al-Nasser's to leave their homes for the evening. He found two families had already departed to stay with out-of-town relatives; another home was for sale and had been vacant for several months, thankfully leaving only a couple of houses requiring evacuation.

Officer Mike Stone, dressed in gas company attire, was nearing the front gate to the terrorists' house when a voice in his earpiece instructed him to terminate that step of the operation. The house was being closely monitored and as yet no one inside had looked out any of the windows facing the street. Surveillance reported no one inside had even said anything indicating they were aware of Stone's presence. It was decided it would be an unnecessary risk to approach the house and alert the killers that anything was going on outside. Stone stopped, glanced down at his clipboard, looked around curiously and then veered abruptly away and proceeded to the next house on his list.

*   *   *   *

Once it was verified all six suspects were present inside the house, police officers, deputy sheriffs and National Guard troops hastily set up roadblocks on every street into the neighborhood.

When the pizza deliveryman turned onto the street leading to his delivery address, several serious looking armed men greeted him. He was questioned by a very large deputy who sternly informed him that he would not be allowed to pass and should return to his store. When he insisted someone pay for the three pizzas, he was told to send a bill to the local FBI office. It didn't occur to anyone to ask him what address he was to make his delivery to; there were other more important things to worry about.

*   *   *   *

Inside the house the six zealots were finalizing their plans. As Mikal was typing them up on his laptop, the others complemented one another over its ingenuity. Although it would be left up to others to implement it, they had already taken care of their part and could now sit back and comfortably wait to see it carried out.

Mikal finished his typing, which included directions to five different storage units between Redding and Seattle, Washington. He then scrambled it and emailed it to an address in Paris. From there it would be forwarded to Brussels, Belgium, then Iwakuni, Japan and on to Khartoum in the Sudan and before arriving at its final destination in Calgary, Canada, it would pass through twelve other countries in total.

A young woman sat waiting for the encoded e-mail to arrive. After seven hours, it finally did. She promptly downloaded the information onto a disk, gathered her things and checked out of the motel she had registered in under a fictitious name two days before. Within fifteen minutes of receiving the information, Mariska Jabril was in her Toyota Camry and starting the long journey to Vancouver, British Columbia.

*   *   *   *

After sending the email, Mikal erased the hard drive. Since this was the only time this particular computer was used the task was accomplished very quickly. He placed the entire computer in the fireplace and lit the logs. Although it was still possible for a computer forensic expert to recover some of the data, there was no way the encryption could be broken. If by chance the police did somehow get their hands on it, and decipher it, it would already be too late.

Raissa excused herself and went to feed her children dinner. After finishing their chicken fingers and french fries, she bathed and put them to bed. They were fast asleep by the time the six terrorists gathered to pray.

*   *   *   *

The skies had opened up and a steady rain was again falling. Through an infrared lens, Ryker observed ten HRT commandos stealthily approach the house under the cover of darkness. Lucky for them, none of the exterior lights on the house were on. Five of them hunkered down in the shadows and bushes near the front door while the others quietly made their way around to the rear of the house.

After waiting a full sixty seconds, each team carefully began placing explosive charges on the door hinges. Other agents watched the windows of the house from a distance, ready to alert the commandos at the first sign of trouble. Finishing their delicate work in less than thirty seconds they sat back and waited for the signal to breach.

The FBI agents were dressed in black from head to toe and armed with 9mm H&K MP-10 machine guns loaded with thirty-round magazines. Their weapons load-out also included sidearms, tear gas and flash-bang grenades. On their heads they wore Kevlar helmets, each man was equipped with night vision goggles and their torsos were covered with state-of-the-art body armor. The commandos were highly trained, in top physical condition and ready for action.

Their instructions were to take those inside the house alive, if possible, but under no circumstances was anyone to be allowed to escape. Even though the agents were all supposed to be completely professional, each was aware and enraged that Chief Baker and his family had been slaughtered. The evil people responsible for their murders were, right now, lurking within the walls the commandos were now only moments away from breaching. They couldn't help but take it all a little bit personally.

*   *   *   *

The MH-6 Little Birds, designated Viper One and Two, sat with their rotors turning at the airport five miles away. Ready to take off at a moment's notice and ferry their commandos into combat, each were carrying four heavily armed and trained FBI agents. Although two of the helicopters had been brought in, it was determined that just one would be needed for tonight's mission. Viper Two was turned up and loaded, just in case something went wrong with Viper One.

The pilots received the 'go' signal and within fifteen seconds both lifted off and were racing toward the target zone at close to a hundred and thirty miles per hour.

*   *   *   *

As a concession to local law enforcement, HRT commander, Agent Mike Daniels was allowing Redding Police Officer Mike Stone to be the one to cut power to the house. In fact, he was at that moment crouching next to the power box at the side of the house. Stone knew his actions didn't amount to much, however, it was better than nothing and at least his department would be involved in the takedown in some small way.

*   *   *   *

Viper One and Two reached their holding area and were now hovering fifteen hundred feet above I-5, waiting for the green light. The darkly dressed men squeezed inside Viper One performed one last check of their weapons, hooked the rappelling ropes to their harnesses, and took a few deep breaths. *No matter how much you trained, the only thing that really settles your nerves is going active*, Agent Ray Warner thought. It was like a light switch; one moment your stomach was in your throat, the next moment the 'go' was given and all your worries disappeared with every thought focused on the mission. Warner had been on dozens of these missions and each was always the same; hours of nerves, stress and anxiety followed by a roller coaster ride of pure adrenaline.

The pilot informed them they had thirty seconds. The four warriors stepped out onto the catwalks on either side of the Little Bird and stood ready for action.

*   *   *   *

A soaking wet Dalton Ryker stood alone under an oak tree in the yard of a house two doors down from the al-Nasser's. He was waiting for everyone to get into position and hoping that nothing would go wrong. Even though their planning had been meticulous he couldn't shake the feeling that they were missing something important; something fleeting, elusive, in the back of his mind that he just couldn't get a grasp on.

As overall commander of the operation, it was up to him to give the signal to assault the house. While he would get the credit if things went well, he would also take full blame if things went horribly wrong. It wouldn't matter that he would never fire a shot or that he would be over one hundred feet from the house when the assault began.

Ryker listened to the radio as one by one the members of the tactical team checked in with Agent Daniels; informing him they were in position and ready for action. The wait was almost over.

*   *   *   *

Inside the house the six killers had just finished praying when the telephone rang. Raissa rushed to answer it before it awoke her sleeping children. She snatched the receiver by the second ring and said, "Hello?"

"Mrs. Nasser?" the caller asked.

"That's al-Nasser," she corrected him. *Why can't people get that straight?*

"I'm sorry, Mrs. *al*-Nasser."

"Yes," she replied.

"This is Ken from Mario's Pizza and Things. I'm sorry ma'am, but my driver was unable to deliver your order this evening."

"Why, did he have the wrong address?" she inquired.

"Oh no, nothing like that. The driver attempted to make the delivery but was turned away by the police."

"The police? Why would they refuse to allow a guy deliver a pizza?" she snapped her fingers in the air to get the others' attention.

"He attempted to deliver your order two times. When he was turned back on Idlewild Avenue, he tried again from the other direction on Morris Chapel. Both times he ran into roadblocks and was ordered to leave."

"Did he tell you what was going on?" Raissa asked, the concern readily apparent in her voice.

"He didn't know. He did say that there were cops and army troops all over the place."

"Thanks for calling..."

"Mrs. *al*-Nasser, the driver said it looked to him as if they were preparing to go to war. If I were you I'd stay inside and lock my doors. They're obviously looking for someone and it appears as if they want to catch them pretty badly," he cautioned.

A heavy feeling of dread washed eerily over Raissa. "Thank you again," she mumbled, as she hung up the phone. She stood there blankly staring at the wall, not speaking.

Mikal saw the look on her face and asked her what was wrong. Raissa quickly told him, then walked to the window and peeked through the blinds.

*   *   *   *

Outside, Agent Daniels, looking through his binoculars saw the blinds part. He whispered in his radio for the commandos near the window to hold very still. They all sunk down into the bushes, their black clothing blending in with the dark green foliage.

*   *   *   *

Rashiid and Mustafa joined Raissa at the window but none of them could see anything was amiss. They stood there studying the street and the surrounding houses; it was peaceably quiet. They glanced up and down the street and it was several minutes before they finally decided everything appeared to be normal outside. They had taken no more than a few steps away from the window when Raissa stopped dead in her tracks. "That's it!" she exclaimed.

*   *   *   *

Ryker saw the blinds close and decided it was time to go. "Green light, green light, go, go, go!" It was now out of his hands, whatever happened, happened. In a few minutes it would be over. Still, there was something nagging at him...*something...?*

*   *   *   *

"What?" Abdul cried.

"There is nothing going on. Not even old lady Webster sitting on her front porch across the street reading her book with the neighbors dog yapping at her."

"What are you talking about?" Mustafa asked.

"Every evening for the past six years, Mrs. Webster has sat on her porch reading a book from eight thirty until ten o'clock. And every night during those six years, the neighbor's dog has stood at the fence yelping its fool head off at her the entire time. You'd think she'd get tired of listening to him and would complain to the neighbors or find someplace else to read, but she doesn't," Mikal answered, walking over to look out of the window himself.

Outside the agents were again ordered to freeze.

"So what?" Omar said. "Perhaps she isn't feeling well this evening, or was tired and went to bed early?"

"No, and no!" Raissa replied vigorously shaking her head, the concern in her voice sounding more and more like real fear. "Sick or not, rain or shine, she's out there."

"It could be nothing," Abdul said.

"Don't you all think it's a bit too coincidental that the one night she misses, the police just happen to have roadblocks all around our house?" She looked at her husband, "Mikal, I don't like this, something's wrong!"

"You think they may have found us?" Omar asked.

"How could they? We've been very careful and left nothing behind that can connect the attacks to us." Abdul answered. "Besides, there's no one outside, you looked yourself."

"Yeah, but what if they…"

Suddenly, Mikal froze and indicated to everyone to be quiet by putting a finger to his lips. In the distance was the faint thump, thump, thumping of a helicopter and it sounded as if it was steadily getting closer. "Do you all hear that?"

"They're coming for us. What now?" cried Abdul, fear causing his voice to rise by three octaves.

The helicopter was indeed coming closer and Mikal didn't wait any longer; he bolted toward the hallway motioning for the others to follow. Jerking open a door he slid a giant trunk from out of the back of a large closet. Yanking it open he started handing out M-10 machine guns and extra magazines to the others.

Raissa grabbed a gun, spare magazines and a knife, turned and rushed toward the stairs with Omar following closely on her heels.

Mikal distributed earplugs and sunglasses to his remaining comrades. They knew this had always been a real possibility and had prepared for it as best they could. Mikal and Abdul moved a couch to block the hallway and quickly took up positions behind it. Though it wouldn't offer much cover, it would give them some protection from anyone coming through the front door.

Mustafa and Rashiid flipped over the solid oak kitchen table and placed it at the other end of the hall. From this position the terrorists could cover the back door quite well. There were no windows to their sides to worry about. Each man knew their fate but were all determined to take as many of the infidels with them as they could. They would soon be in Paradise and Allah would welcome them.

*   *   *   *

Upstairs Raissa and Omar were just reaching the children's room when the lights went out.

*   *   *   *

A deputy sheriff ran up to Ryker and handed him a note. It detailed the phone call Raissa had made to the pizza parlor and the one the pizza parlor had made to her.

"Why am I just hearing about this?" He thundered at the deputy, his face turning three shades of red. Not waiting for an answer he turned back toward the house, reaching for his radio. Just as he was pushing the button to warn the HRT members to abort, the explosive charges on the doors went off.

*   *   *   *

At the side of the house Officer Stone tripped the breaker plunging the house into darkness. He moved quickly to take cover behind a car in the neighbor's driveway. Overhead he heard and could faintly see the outline of the helicopter dart in and hover over the target house. From both sides of the Little Bird he saw four dark figures rappel smoothly down and come to a rest with their boots on either side of the upstairs windows. Stone heard glass shatter, followed by two loud bangs upstairs, followed by more at the front and the rear of the house. With a loud crash the four warriors swung inside and disappeared from view. Rapid gunfire quickly followed and though he couldn't tell who was doing the shooting, Stone was privately glad that he wasn't involved.

*   *   *   *

Moments after Stone cut the power; the ten HRT members on the ground triggered the explosives on the doors, blowing both of them off their hinges. Flash-bang grenades were thrown in, creating a tremendously loud noise and an excruciatingly bright light. Flash-bangs are designed to temporarily blind and stun barricaded suspects. The commandos counted to three and as they rushed into the house, their earpieces squawked, "They know we're coming!" Ryker screamed, "Abort! Abort! Abort!" The warning came too late and they were instantly met with gunfire, two HRT members dropped.

*   *   *   *

The terrorists, even though prepared for it, were surprised when the lights went out. They all looked away from the doors when they were blown and waited for the flash bangs to go off before looking up. The earplugs saved their hearing and they all ripped away their sunglasses and immediately began searching for something to shoot at.

Mikal and Abdul were the first to start firing. Through the smoke, Mikal saw one of the commandos thrown to the ground outside. The terrorists' biggest disadvantage was that they didn't have night vision goggles and their attackers did. Mikal held down the trigger, firing off thirty rounds in just seconds. He stooped down to reload and watched as Abdul was flung backwards to the floor, two perfectly round red holes tightly grouped in the center of his forehead. His eyes were staring straight ahead with a stunned expression on his face. Angrily, Mikal rose to continue firing only to be met by a hail of bullets himself. The HRT shooters were pulling no punches and Mikal was riddled with 9mm missiles. He too was hurled backwards and flipped over onto his face, his right leg shuddering, a crimson pool already forming around his body.

*   *   *   *

Ryker heard the gunfire erupt, and saw an agent stagger and fall to the ground. *Oh God, no!*

*   *   *   *

Rashiid and Mustafa heard their fellow warriors open fire behind them and quickly started firing themselves; it was too dark to see anything to shoot at so they just shot at the door, hoping for the best.

As they fired high, the crouching commandos came in low firing steady controlled bursts at the barricaded terrorists. The Baraka brothers emptied their weapons and ducked behind the table just as HRT bullets savagely splintered it.

They reloaded and rose again to return fire. That was their last brave act in the name of the all-loving Allah.

Neither stood a chance; as soon as their heads came up, the HRT shooters riddled them with a stream of screaming-hot lead. The terrorists were dead before they hit the floor, their souls already on the way to Paradise and their seventy-two virgins.

*   *   *   *

Upstairs, Raissa had taken up position in the children's bedroom. Holding the weapon tightly in her left hand she noticed that both her hands were sweating and shaking uncontrollably. The fear she felt was worse than anything she had ever known. Her mind traveled back several days to all of the people she had killed. She wondered if they had felt the way she did at this very moment: afraid, helpless, and all alone. She looked at her children in their warm beds, a tear rolled down her cheek. For a fleeting instant she questioned her beliefs and her commitment to this war. *Has everything I believe in been a lie? No, it can't be!*

When the HRT warriors came crashing through the windows, preceded by flash bangs, she knew without a doubt that her part in this war was at an end. Even though she couldn't see and her eardrums were blown, she attempted to raise her weapon to fire, but that was as far as she got. Agent Warner fired a double tap into her forehead sending her crashing against the wall and into eternity.

Warner swept the room for additional threats. He looked over at the sleeping children and wondered why they had not been awakened by all the noise. The answer jolted him to his soul. *My Holy God!* Both of their throats had been neatly sliced from ear to ear. He looked over at Raissa's body and saw a large bloody knife still clutched in her dead right hand.

*   *   *   *

Omar stood behind a large potted plant in the upstairs hallway. He heard the earsplitting gunfire from downstairs and then glass breaking, followed by more shots from the bedroom. He knew he didn't stand a chance if he stayed in the house. He ran to the end of the hall and looked down from the window into the side yard, he didn't see anyone outside. Hastily making his decision he opened the window and shoved the screen out of his way, slinging the machine gun around his neck, he crawled out feet first.

Hanging from his fingertips he lowered his body as far as it would go and dropped to the ground, landing in a rose bush and twisting his ankle. He ignored the pain and grabbed his weapon, prepared for the challenge that never came. He didn't pause to wonder why; he quickly turned and climbed the fence into the neighbor's yard. Standing in the dark, he listened, hearing nothing, he moved toward the rear of the house.

Moving as quietly as he could across the backyard, his ears were tuned to any sound that might alert him to someone's presence. The shooting had stopped back at the house and he knew it wouldn't be long before his absence was noticed. *Do they even know about me?* He wondered. *Maybe I still have a chance.*

The sound of cars screeching to a stop in front of the house he'd just escaped motivated him to pick up the pace. His thumping heart felt like it was going to burst through the wall of his chest. He hopped a short chain-link fence into the next yard. Stopping to listen once more, he ran on, starting to believe he just might get away.

He came to a six-foot high cedar fence and strained to see over the top. On the other side was a street and still more houses. No cars were moving along the road and no one was in sight. At the far end of the street were some heavy woods. *If I can get to those, I'm free!* He listened again for anyone approaching; satisfying himself that it was safe. He took a firm grip and raised his body toward the top.

"Freeze! Don't move another inch or you're heads a canoe!"

Omar was caught in a very vulnerable position, with one leg dangling on the other side of the fence. He thought about trying to make it over but knew he would fail.

"Very slowly, get down off the fence, real careful like!"

Omar thought for a few seconds and then carefully dropped back into the yard with his back to his would-be capturer.

"Place your hands behind your head, interlock your fingers and then get down on your knees and cross your ankles!" the voice commanded.

Omar was scared. He knew he must not allow himself to be caught, but he suddenly realized he wasn't quite ready to die as he thought he was. The infidel behind him couldn't have seen the small machine pistol hanging from the sling across his chest. He turned his head slightly to the left, trying to get a better idea of exactly where the man behind him was located.

"I said get on your knees! I won't tell you again!"

In one quick motion Omar grabbed for the weapon and pivoted toward the voice. He fired, holding down the trigger, but he had aimed too high.

The crouching Officer Mike Stone didn't. He squeezed off four quick rounds from his .40 Smith and Wesson semi-automatic. The first two rounds missed the terrorist completely; the third round caught him in the right shoulder and the fourth one ripped into his throat shattering his spinal column, nearly removing his head entirely from his body.

Omar's gun hand clinched tight and the remaining bullets in his weapon went into the cloudy sky. He struck the ground, his life's blood pumping out onto the neatly manicured lawn. Stone walked cautiously over to the body and kicked the weapon from Omar's spasming hand. He checked the dead terrorist for other weapons and noted how blood looked eerily black in the pale moonlight.

Stone stood there staring at the body. Tears welled up in his eyes as he remembered the Chief's family and wondered if this was one of the animals that had killed them. "Well, hero, I guess you got what you wanted!" Stone said. He then cleared his throat, bent over and spit on the corpse and kicked it in the head. "Go to hell!"

Stone turned back toward the street and reached for his radio.

*   *   *   *

The Hostage Rescue Team quickly checked the rest of the house and within ninety seconds of entering, it was declared secured. Two HRT members had been shot, but the bullets had struck their vests. With the exception of some severe bruising in the morning to remind them of their good fortune, they would be fine. Agent Daniels radioed Ryker and informed him it was safe to enter the house. All of the terrorists had been neutralized.

Local and cable news services, having been alerted something big had happened descended on the once-quiet neighborhood. They were all sorely disappointed when they were stopped in their tracks at the roadblocks. Their disappointment deepened when the only thing they were told was 'no comment'. Ryker had been directed from on high to leave all announcements to the White House in the morning. Though he didn't like it, at this point he really didn't care. He was just happy it was all over.

The rain had finally stopped and tomorrow's forecast was bright and sunny. Ryker stood watching the Coroner and his helpers as they began the laborious task of removing the bodies from the house and the one from the neighbor's back yard. He made a mental note to give a 'well done' to Officer Stone.

So much death, he thought. *When will it all end and what is truly being accomplished by it all?* To him it was a great big senseless mystery. It was impossible to understand why so many people were so eager and willing to kill and die in the name of their god. If this was what God sincerely wanted, then Ryker didn't want anything to do with Him. He watched as two small body bags were loaded into the back of the Coroner's van. He shook his head, then got into his car and drove away. He had paperwork to do.

CHAPTER 23

▼

Day Ten

Sunday

President Nicholson was awakened by a White House staffer at 0430 and given the good news. He let out a sigh of relief and thanked the aide for waking him. Nicholson stood up, stretched the sleepiness away and walked into the bathroom. He washed his faced, brushed his teeth, combed his hair and got dressed. By the time he entered the Oval Office at 0455 the White House Chief of Staff, the National Security Advisor, the White House Press Secretary, the Chairman of the Joint Chiefs of Staff as well as the directors of the FBI, CIA and Homeland Security were already waiting for him. Two secret service agents were alertly standing guard at the door.

The president walked behind his desk and sat down, barely able to control the grin that was threatening to spread across his face. He was very aware of the seven sets of eyes watching him, as he reached for the piping hot cup of coffee already waiting for him on his desk. He took a slow sip from the blue porcelain cup and set it aside. He turned toward Mark Gooden and motioned for him to proceed.

"Mr. President, we got them!" Gooden cheerfully exclaimed.

"Are we sure we got them all?" the President questioned.

"As sure as we can be. By all the intelligence we've been able to gather there are absolutely no indications anyone else was involved. The FBI, CIA, NSA and Homeland Security have been working through the night checking phone, banking and computer records of all seven terrorists. They found nothing that led them to believe they missed anyone," Gooden explained.

"You said seven?"

"Yeah, remember the suicide bomber that hit the hospital?"

"That's right," Nicholson said, seeming a bit embarrassed that he had forgotten.

"There doesn't appear to be any connection between the suicide bomber and the other six terrorists. It looks as if he was working alone," FBI Director Chuck Alexander said.

"No connection at all?" the President asked.

"Not one that we have been able to uncover. Of course, that doesn't mean there's not one. I'm sure he's got a handler somewhere but for now, as far as the actual operation goes, it looks like he carried out the attack on the hospital by himself," Alexander explained.

"So we potentially have two different cells operating in Redding at the same time?" Nicholson asked.

"Had, Mr. President, had," Gooden clarified.

"Right. So we've got two cells, operating independently from one another but they both go active at the same time? How were they contacted?"

"We're still working on that, Mr. President," Alexander said. "We're pretty sure that the cell taken out last night, at least to some degree, was contacted through a series of encrypted emails."

"Why do you think that?"

"Our agents on the scene found a laptop computer burned up in the fireplace after the house was secured. We think they were trying to cover their tracks. They did a pretty good job too, the thing was almost completely destroyed."

"What do you mean, almost?"

"Apparently hard drives are quite difficult to destroy, even in a fire. It is possible, however unlikely, that if they failed to adequately delete all of the data, FBI technicians may be able to recover some useful information."

"What about the lone bomber?" Nicholson asked, checking his notes. "Yasim, how was he activated?"

"We're not sure just yet. We searched his home, his locker at work and all the usual records and found no evidence that he ever used a computer. We also showed his picture to the staff of those little coffee shops that provide Internet access, no one recognized him," Alexander explained.

"You mean internet cafés?" Minetti inquired, smiling sarcastically.

"Yeah, those, smart aleck."

"How about cell phone records?" Gooden asked, "Did he have one?"

"We didn't find anything there either. We've checked all the local cellular providers but so far nothing has popped up. We couldn't find a post office box and we even woke up his mailman and got him on the phone, he couldn't remember delivering anything of a personal nature to Yasim's home. From all appearances this guy had no family, no friends and no interests aside from work. For all intents and purposes, he lived in a vacuum."

Nicholson scratched his head. "How did you manage to contact all of these people in the middle of the night?"

"Well, some *internet cafes* are open twenty-four hours," Alexander said smirking at Minetti. "Other than that, we used eight hundred numbers and coerced customer service supervisors to aid their government for the rest. In a few hours agents will be checking the local libraries when they open."

"So how was this Yasim contacted?" the President asked again, looking around the room. "Anyone?" They all sat quietly for several moments wracking their brains for an answer.

"Anyone, sir?" one of the secret service agents asked.

They all turned toward the agent. "Yes," he said, "Anyone."

"Well sir, I was thinking, from everything we know, these terrorists have been here for quite a long while and have managed to stay effectively hidden all of that time. With all the new security we have in place they would have to keep any communication to the barest minimum, right?"

"Go on, I'm listening," Nicholson encouraged him.

"Well what if he wasn't waiting for a message but a signal?"

"What sort of signal?" Gooden asked.

"Perhaps his instructions were to sit back and wait until he saw other attacks taking place; then, and only then, was he to go active. That would eliminate any unnecessary communications while at the same time allow both cells to operate independently of one another." Once again it got real quiet in the Oval Office. "Anyway, it was just a thought," the agent said, returning to his post.

Stuart Minetti spoke up for the first time, "I would say that was a pretty good observation, agent, good thinking. If what the agent suggested turns out to be accurate the next question is, what's next? Were these two cells just the first two dominos to fall?"

"Well let's hope not!" the President said. "Until we have something concrete to tell us otherwise, let sleeping dogs lie. The public doesn't know all seven were not working together and I don't see any reason to tell them differently. Our official stand will be that one cell carried out these attacks, let's pray to God we're right." Nicholson glanced around at some of the most powerful men in the world, waiting for someone to disagree. No one did.

"Does anyone care to venture a guess as to why they would put two cells in Redding, California, of all places?" Director Minetti asked. "I mean, Redding has no industry to speak of, it's not a financial hub, I don't understand, why there?"

"Unless that's not the only place they are," General Slade offered. "Why would they select Redding unless it was nothing more than a springboard for something else? I mean sure, they did scare a lot of people and even killed a bunch, but what was their goal? They could have accomplished the same thing in a lot of other places, bigger places."

"And so far we have not been able to connect any of the dead terrorists to anyone else that looks suspicious. From everything we've found so far they were working entirely on their own," Director Alexander said.

"But that's not the way they operate. Every cell we've ever broken up has been connected to another in some way. We just have to find out how," Gooden stated.

"And what if no connection exists?"

"Then maybe they were working alone or the terrorists have changed strategies," Slade said.

"Changed how?" Gooden asked.

"Perhaps all the cells are now working independently of one another. That way, by discovering one, it doesn't lead us to the others."

"That's preposterous, they're just not that well organized!" Gooden cried.

"You hope, young fella', you hope."

"I've had about enough of you…"

"That's enough!" the President ordered. "All we're doing here is speculating. General, do you have any evidence to support your suspicions?"

"No sir, just a hunch. And the fact it would make great tactical sense."

"Well, until you do, let's stick to what we know. There were seven terrorists in Redding and now they're all dead. We have no evidence pointing to any others and until we do, I will not tell the American people anything to the contrary. So for now we have one cell working alone, period!" Nicholson waited for any rebuttal. "Fine, now what's next?"

"Agents have completed their search of the other terrorists' homes." Minetti looked down at his notes, "The one named Omar Fadillah was a mailman. Agents found more than five thousand letters, all stamped and addressed, laced with Anthrax spores."

"Anthrax?"

"Yes sir, it looks as if we nailed them with very little time to spare."

"If those had gone out we would have been facing a catastrophe," Slade announced.

"Do we know if he managed to mail any of them?" Nicholson asked Director Alexander.

"We don't believe so. Although we can't be certain, of course, it appears as if he was holding them back for a more dramatic event."

"You hope!"

"Correct sir, we hope."

"Has the media got a whiff of that one yet?" Gooden inquired.

"Not yet, we're holding this one real close to the vest. In fact, local law enforcement is not aware of it either," Alexander, said.

"Good," the President said, "let's keep it that way. Things are bad enough as it is, we don't need to fan the flames anymore. Agreed gentlemen?" He received several nods from around the table. "Good. Next?"

White House Chief of Staff, Cornelius Bennett, spoke next. "Mr. President, Special Agent Ryker was informed not to make any statements concerning last night's events to the press and that order was passed on to local law enforcement as well. Some details have begun to leak out but most information has been withheld, pending your press conference at 1100 this morning."

"Who gave the order to hold off on the media?" the President asked.

"We...I...I thought it would be a good public relations move if the nation heard the good news directly from you, sir," Bennett answered.

Nicholson smiled, "Good call, that's what I pay you for. Anything else?" It was seemingly lost on the President that the taxpayers footed that particular monthly financial obligation.

Director of Homeland Security, Iverson James, spoke up. "Sir, we will continue to investigate all leads to try and determine who was financing these attacks. Obviously they were well-planned, well-funded, and the terrorists have been in place for far too long to not have some serious players backing them."

"I see your point."

"Mr. President?" Minetti asked. "Have you considered the possibility that a Nation State was behind the attacks?'

"Yes I have, and no, I don't believe they were. I think this was simply an al-Qaeda cell that slipped through the cracks and got missed, and that's the way I want it played."

"Yes...sir." Minetti, said hesitantly.

"What about the state of martial law that has been imposed out there, when do you want it lifted?" Gooden asked.

"We'll leave that up to California's Governor, but I'm sure it won't be necessary after a couple more days. Has my speech writer got my statement ready to go?" the President asked abruptly changing the subject. Very rarely did a president write the words he delivered to the nation. That particular privilege was always saved for someone else. All the president did was to give them a-thumbs-up, or down to the final draft.

"She's been up all night. Of course, after this meeting I'm sure there'll be a few adjustments to make but I believe she's about finished," Bennett said.

"Good. Then if there's nothing else, I'll see you all in a little while," the President said, politely dismissing them. He again reached for his coffee, thinking how good it was that this terrifying chapter in US history had been closed.

✳   ✳   ✳   ✳

The White House Press Secretary stepped in front of the Podium at 1108 Eastern Time, "Ladies and gentlemen, the President of the United States."

The President stepped behind the podium and paused, giving photographers a few moments to snap some pictures before he started.

Nodding at the members of the press seated before him, "Good morning. Ten days ago our Nation was once again the target of several heinous and cowardly terrorist attacks. The number of murdered Americans now exceeds thirteen hundred and continues to climb as more of our countrymen are removed from the rubble in California. The terrorists, through their atrocious attacks have attempted to break our will, to change our way of life, to take away our freedom and to rob us of our national identity. Once again they have failed as they have in the past and will continue to do so, because this is the greatest nation on the face of the planet and we will not succumb to the evil that threatens us.

"Last night, through the combined efforts of the FBI, CIA, Department of Homeland Security and local and state law enforcement agencies, the remaining despicable human beings responsible for these attacks were introduced to American Justice. While attempting to apprehend the terrorists, they resisted, using deadly force; two FBI agents were injured during the operation. Having no other choice, members of the FBI's Hostage Rescue Team shot and killed six Islamic radicals. Unfortunately, two of the terrorist's children were present in the house and their own mother slew them before government agents could come to their rescue. We, as a nation, send our prayers toward heaven on their behalf.

"Our Nation has indeed been wounded, but through our commitment to helping one another and our persistence in assuring this Nation remains the greatest in the world, we will heal and continue to prevail. Thank you. I will now take a few questions," he said, pointing to Sam from ABC.

"Mr. President, are we to assume that these attacks are over?"

"From all the information we have at this time, there were only seven terrorists operating in the Redding area, and they are now all dead. With that in mind, we are confident the attacks are over."

"You have stated in the past you believe the war on terrorism had practically been won, that al-Qaeda was defeated and on the run. In light of recent events, how accurate do you believe those statements to be now?" CBS asked.

"I still stand by them. US forces have tracked down and captured or eliminated over twenty thousand terrorists since 9/11. We have worked hard to establish democracy in the Middle East and I'm proud to say it's succeeding. Arab governments are cooperating with the United States and our allies to ensure terrorists no longer have safe harbor in any civilized country. I believe the battle is virtually won. But like fighting a major forest fire, even when the bulk of the fighting is over, there are still little hotspots that pop up here and there that require some further attention. That is what happened in California, and as you can see last night it was extinguished."

"But, how are we to know there won't be more *hotspots* popping up somewhere else?"

"We don't. However, our best intelligence indicates this was nothing more than a cell that got missed, and now it has been dealt with." Nicholson turned to a friendly face and pointed, "Maggie?"

The NPR reporter smiled, "Mr. President, what is the Government doing to find out how these terrorists got here and what is your Administration doing to prevent any more from getting in?"

"Now that we know who they are, federal agencies will begin investigating their backgrounds and try to determine their countries of origin. I have no doubts once they have completed the investigation we will learn how they arrived here and adopt new measures to stop it from reoccurring," he acknowledged the FOX reporter next.

"Sir, my sources tell me it's believed that a nation state may be behind the attacks. Is there any truth to this, and if so, what will the United States' response be?"

The President knew he had to tread carefully. "All resources are being utilized in an attempt to find out who financed these attacks. There is no, I repeat no, verifiable evidence at this time that a foreign power is behind these incidents. If we find through the course of the investigation that another nation is in some way involved, then we will consult with our allies and determine the best course of action to take at that time."

"Mr. President, my sources tell me that Anthrax may have been discovered at one of the terrorist's homes. Have you heard this or can you verify that is true? *The Washington Post* asked.

Nicholson thought quickly. *How in the world had she heard about that? Someone's head is going to roll!* "I have heard there is a rumor to that effect making its way around. I would caution everyone to be careful in spreading unsubstantiated gossip. We have certainly seen enough these past days to twist our stomachs into knots, so let's deal with what we do know and leave the rumors to the tabloids, okay? Thank you." The President turned and walked from the room, paying no mind to the slew of questions being hurled at his back.

It was not lost on a single reporter that the president did not even come close to answering the last question.

✳   ✳   ✳   ✳

Mariska Jabril arrived in Vancouver and drove to a large home in the northern part of the city arriving just before midday. She parked her car and walked straight into the house. There she found five men sitting in the living room, quietly waiting for her.

"Did you get it?" one of them asked.

"Yes, I have it."

"And...?"

A huge grin spread across her face, "And...you're not going to believe it."

PART II

▼

CHAPTER 24

▼

"If you strike their cities, their strength will be exhausted and their spirits will break"-Sun-tzu, The Art of War.

May 1988

The island was tiny and privately owned by a very wealthy Arab whose identity is a closely held secret. Although it covered only four and a half square miles, it was still quite a sight to behold. Located in the Aegean Sea, just north of the Mediterranean, it lay approximately one hundred miles southeast of Athens Greece. The island had a varied landscape, dotted with small hills, shallow valleys and rich, tropical forests. Near the eastern shore was a small lake, fed by an artesian well, which provided the inhabitants with a continuous supply of fresh cool water. The circumference of the island was fringed with coral reefs, golden sandy beaches and huge rocks jutting up out of the crashing surf.

Near its center was a huge fifty-seven thousand square foot mansion that had all the amenities one could ever want or imagine. An Olympic-sized pool was built in the very center of the structure diving board's of varying heights included. The house contained a hundred-seat movie theater, full gymnasium with sauna and Jacuzzis, and additionally twenty bedrooms, twenty-seven bathrooms, a full arcade, a three-lane bowling alley and a world-class caliber library containing more than a hundred thousand volumes on its numerous shelves. The huge swimming pool was even equipped for conversion to an ice skating rink, if one so desired.

On the grounds outside were a regulation basketball court, tennis courts, and a half-mile paved running course snaking through the woods. Several man-made waterfalls were dotted throughout the compound, as well as a number of ponds stocked with exotic fish. The huge garden was equipped with numerous misters to provide an Amazon rain forest type of atmosphere. If one wished, one could sit in a gazebo and enjoy the ambiance of rainstorms fabricated by a state-of-the-art sound system, all with the simple flip of a switch.

A quarter mile to the south of the main complex was a mammoth lagoon that served as a marina, which could accommodate up to ten large yachts at any given time. To the north a concrete runway was laid, able to handle the take off and landings of a gulf-stream jet or small cargo planes.

Security was the finest and more advanced than any other in the world. Surrounding the main house was a twelve-foot high concrete wall with high voltage electricity coursing through wires running along its top. Thirty heavily armed guards roamed the grounds outside the walls at all times and more were randomly stationed across the island. Another twenty patrolled the inside of the walled perimeter and were ever alert to anything posing a threat to the all but impregnable fortress. The main house could also be locked down on a moment's notice, by utilizing solid steel reinforced doors and bullet and blast resistant shutters on the windows.

Beneath the house was an immense, concrete reinforced bunker, equipped to house and feed up to thirty people for two weeks. Additionally, there were two escape tunnels leading from the bunker connecting to two hidden caves two hundred yards away. Inside those caves speedboats were moored that could be used in the event an escape was the only remaining option when faced with an overwhelming invading force.

Guards patrolled in two-man units, each attached to highly trained German Shepherds for added security. The armed men were rotated every four hours to prevent boredom and were never paired with the same person more than once a week. To avert temptation for bribery, all were paid extremely well. In addition to the armed guards, motion detectors, sound sensors, pressure plates and surveillance cameras were located all over the island. Essentially no one could get on or off the island without someone knowing about it. All of this made it the perfect location for the clandestine meeting.

Men of great wealth and influence arrived in ones and twos over a six-hour period by plane, helicopter, and boat; each was allowed only two bodyguards, a personal assistant and an interpreter. These men were the most powerful in the Muslim world. Khaddafi from Libya, Saddam from Iraq, the Ayatollah from Iran, the Palestinian leader Yassar Arafat, as well as leaders or delegates from Afghanistan, Syria, Indonesia, Sudan, Ethiopia, Yemen, Jordan, and seven other countries from the Arab and Muslim world. While many of these countries had personal issues with one another, like the nearly-decade-long war going on between Iraq and Iran, these differences were being temporarily laid aside for a greater cause. These powerful and violent men had gathered to discuss the destruction of the Great Satan, the United States, and the Little Satan, Israel.

The billionaire had covertly contacted each of them through intermediaries over a period of several months, communicating his wishes to them. He explained that for years he had watched the on going meddling of the US in world affairs and her sickening support of the godless country of Israel. He had witnessed his Muslim brothers wage a disunified and ineffective war against both countries for more than two decades, accomplishing very little. He told them the time had arrived to bring all Muslim nations together to fight their common enemies. Each leader was promised safe passage to and from the island and when the time to assemble was announced, they would have no more than twelve hours to respond. Without fail, each one agreed to his terms.

All were gathered in a great hall and seated around an exquisitely hand-carved round table. Much like King Arthur's Knights of the Round Table, everyone here would be considered an equal and have an equal voice. A great feast was laid out; the men had all had their fill of food and drink, now it was time for business.

The billionaire rose, tapping his solid gold goblet with his knife, "A toast," he said, "to unity and victory!" The men all raised their glasses and returned his toast.

"For years," he began "I have watched all the great Muslim nations fight the godless Americans and Abraham's bastard children the Jews. *You*, my brothers fight, bleed, and die for a most worthy cause, but *you* accomplish very little. Our children suffer, starve and die for lack of proper food and medical treatment. Yes, *you* wage war with courage and determination, but I have also watched *you* suffer bloody defeats time and again. *You* fail not because *you* lack commitment, or bravery, or faith in the cause. *You* fail because you are not united in that cause as one power. *You* repeatedly fight disorganized skirmishes, while your enemies have united and grown stronger. *You* fight amongst yourselves," he glanced at Saddam and the Ayatollah, "while the Great Satan provides each side with arms to continue the killing. The time has come for all of that to end," he picked up his goblet of wine and drank, while listening as the shock of his words worked their way around the table.

"But how do you change that, you might ask? How do you battle an enemy who has every resource the world possesses at its fingertips?" he paused for a brief second before continuing. "Starting this very day, if you all agree, *we* will covertly unite our countries in this single cause, the incremental and systematic destruction of the United States of America." He paused again to allow the impact of his words to sink in. "No longer will *we* fight amongst ourselves. No longer will *we* be puppets controlled by the evil puppet masters in Washington. No longer will *we* waste our resources on ineffective battles, while our enemies laugh at us and grow stronger, all the while plotting our demise. No, *we* will unite, *we* will pool our resources, and *we* will take this war to American shores!" The men around the table all applauded, while laughing and encouraging those around them.

"Today, each of you will be given a numbered bank account. In those accounts you will authorize the deposit of five hundred million dollars." That piece of information instantly removed the smiles and replaced them with muttering growls of discontent. "Gentlemen...gentlemen, please...please, all will be explained. I assure you, when you hear what I have to say, you will gladly contribute double what I have asked." The grumbling gradually subsided and the billionaire once again had their undivided attention.

"I propose we begin infiltrating America with our most faithful followers. They will have passports, social security numbers, birth certificates, homes, jobs, businesses; whatever they need to fit seamlessly into American society. I even want them to pay their taxes to the great Uncle Sam," he said sarcastically. "They are to draw no attention whatsoever to themselves and are to keep their faith in the one true god a secret."

"What are they to do during that time?" the Sudanese leader inquired.

"They will procure weapons, explosives and intelligence to carry out their mission. They will conduct surveillance on power plants, banks, military installations and government buildings. These faithful servants of Allah will do all of this and wait for the day when the go-ahead is given, but until that order comes they are to lead normal American lives. When all is in place, then we will strike. Not at the limbs of the beast, for they will only grow back, but at its black rancid heart."

"That could take years, decades even to accomplish." Arafat said.

"It may," the billionaire said simply. "But what if it does? This is not a war measured against the days and months of a calendar, but against the sands of time itself. Before it is over, many will die on both sides, but in the end Allah will claim the final victory."

"How many warriors would we have to get into the United States to have any hope of destroying her as an international threat?" the Pakistani Prime Minister wished to know.

"I would say no less than twenty thousand, perhaps more. We won't know until the day to strike arrives."

"Sure, getting twenty thousand warriors in will be easy, their borders are wide open and they believe themselves to be invulnerable. But hiding them effectively for so long seems impossible," Khadaffi, exclaimed.

"Not impossible. Difficult, yes, but not impossible."

"A plan so grand will take literally years to set up," the representative from Bahrain gasped.

"True, it will take many years, perhaps decades to ensure everything is in its proper place before we strike. In fact, some of us here today may have long gone on to be with Allah before the mission is completed. However, the reward and victory will be well worth it."

The men began to again mumble amongst themselves, expressing doubts and concern with the elaborate venture.

The billionaire allowed this to go on for several minutes before once again seizing control of the meeting. "My friends, America's power comes from her belief that no one can or will stand up to her. She believes no matter what happens, she can simply open her big coffers and buy her way out of whatever trouble she finds herself in. We must attack and destroy that confidence. We must take away the huge wallet Uncle Sam carries around in his hip pocket like a giant sledgehammer. When we do, and rest assured gentlemen we will, America will fall, and so will Israel."

"How exactly are twenty thousand of our faithful brothers and sisters going to manage that Herculean task?" Saddam asked. "America is a land of over two hundred million people. The Japanese, the Germans and the Russians were much more powerful than we and they failed miserably. What makes you think our cause will fare any better?"

"That's the beauty of it," the billionaire smiled. "My plan is so simple." He then explained in detail how it would all work. When he was finished, every man at the table deposited the money as requested.

Three months after the meeting, Iran and Iraq agreed to a cease-fire.

CHAPTER 25

▼

More than ninety-five percent of all US overseas trade is conducted from the nation's three hundred and sixty-one seaports. All in-bound cargo vessels are required by US maritime law to provide a complete and detailed report about their crew, their cargo and their ship a minimum of four days prior to arriving in port. At this time all crew and passengers are checked against terrorist watch lists and with the USCIS, United States Citizenship and Immigration Service, to ensure no one is in violation of US immigration law. Once the ships are allowed into port they are again subject to physical inspection by customs agents, although it is rare that one is actually conducted.

Each day close to six hundred thousand truck-sized shipping containers arrive in the United States by sea. Even after the events of 9/11, the number of containers that are actually inspected still hovers around five percent. That leaves approximately five hundred and fifty thousand containers a day that pass through the ports without being searched, or to place it into better perspective, two hundred thirty-seven million each year.

Prior to the events of 9/11, the number of containers inspected was less than two percent. The probability of terrorists smuggling weapons into the country is simply staggering. The sheer volume of conventional weapons alone is impossible to estimate; add in the very real possibility that nuclear, biological and chemical weapons could have also been smuggled in and you have a recipe for disaster.

For years the United States Government turned a blind eye to the grave security shortcomings present at all US ports. To think that terrorists will not, or have not already, taken full advantage of this gaping maw in America's defenses is completely irresponsible and foolish. A London Times report stated that Osama bin Laden has had access to as many as twenty cargo ships over the years, and that's just the ones they know about. According to some NATO sources, several of the ships were even used to deliver explosives to the terrorists that later bombed the US embassies in Kenya and Tanzania in 1998. In fact, even the explosives used in the bombing of the nightclub in Bali, Indonesia back in October 2002 were brought into the country by ships reportedly under the influence of bin-Laden and his henchmen.

In 2003, the Director of Homeland Security announced a new policy was going into effect that would scrutinize one hundred percent of all ships coming from the twenty 'high risk' ports throughout the world from which roughly sixty-eight percent of imported goods are received. He did not elaborate on how the new policy would deal with vessels coming from ports not on the watch-list.

Government claims aside, no one really knows what is coming into the United States through various ports of entry. Perhaps the terrorists have never chosen to utilize this simple and practically risk-free method of getting weapons across US borders. Perhaps they never seized the open opportunity that has been virtually handed to them on a silver platter. Perhaps if they made the attempt, then the two to five percent of the containers that are actually inspected, are the very ones they used. And the weapons were intercepted before they were put to some despicable use. Perhaps, but not likely. It is also possible that the sky will fall, but not likely.

One Homeland Security source said they have asked commercial shipping companies to 'know' their customers. This is simply not enough; it still doesn't explain what they know or will admit to knowing is really in the containers. The erroneous belief they could somehow know what is in each and every container is preposterous. Believing this policy will eliminate the very real possibility that something inherently dangerous to America is in these ships is foolish. The fact remains the US is blind to what is coming in and completely ignorant to what has no doubt already arrived.

According to a 2001 report by New York Senator Chuck Schumer, ports across the nation are extremely vulnerable to terrorists. The report states US ports lack vital security equipment such as small boats, cameras and vessel tracking devices. Poor intelligence sharing between local and federal agencies is partially at fault. There is such a severe shortage of inspectors and custom's agents, even if we wanted to search all the containers, we couldn't; at least, not without bringing the economy to a crashing halt. The longshoreman strike on the West Coast ports back in 2002, sent fear rippling through the stock market and the economy for weeks. By the time the strike ended, many manufacturers had used up their back stock of supplies and some were nearly forced to shut down production. If an attempt was made to search every container using the current staffing levels, cargo ships could very well sit offshore for weeks before being unloaded, and that will never be allowed to happen. By the government, corporate leaders or the every-day consumer for that matter.

While security at US ports has been incrementally increased, and there are plans to *improve* it even more, it's still not enough. If tomorrow a search started of each and every container, it may already be too late. It's like closing the barn door after the horse has already bolted. The threat is most likely already here. The really troubling thing, is that nobody truly knows, and even if they did, they have absolutely no idea where to start looking and for what. The federal government knows a highly publicized search would also be a public admission the danger is here and they will not risk the increased fear and panic that would likely result. All of this leaves only one real politically correct choice, wait…for an attack that could come from anywhere, at anytime, and most likely will.

CHAPTER 26

▼

Day Fifteen

Friday

Pineville is a small but rapidly growing town just southeast of Charlotte, North Carolina. In fact, the two cities are so close together they may as well be one. Pineville, like Charlotte, is a city whose population has been steadily increasing for the last twenty-five years. The tiny community has seen the building of a very nice mall, numerous shopping centers, and housing developments. One of the biggest benefits to the small city is that it lies directly on I-485. I-485 is a sixty-mile interstate that encircles Mecklenburg County, connecting Charlotte with the much smaller towns of Huntersville, Cornelius, Concord, Gastonia, Pineville and all the other little communities in between. This outer belt is probably the biggest contributing factor of Pineville's growth and renewed prosperity.

Grand Empire Cinemas is one of the newest major businesses opened in the community. Standing just a few miles south of the Piper Glen Country Club, it is where the Home Depot PGA Invitational Golf Tournament is played each year. It's twenty-four silver screens provide the local inhabitants with a great source of entertainment in which to waste away their Friday nights.

This was to be the gala opening night for Star Wars: Episode VII: Dark Betrayal. Its creator, George Lucas, had said several times that the Revenge of the Sith would be his last Star Wars film, and technically it was. However, after the great success of the sixth film in the series, the aging director's close friend, now in charge at Lucasfilm, had authorized another group of filmmakers to finance and produce the seventh film, under tight supervision by Lucasfilm of course. The previous six movies were all released in the month of May, but due to unforeseen delays the seventh was postponed for release in late summer, although many in the industry believed this to be a poor business move. The hype around Dark Betrayal ensured theaters would be bursting at the seams with fans.

Indeed, Grand Empire Cinemas was filled to capacity with eager moviegoers waiting to see the film extravaganza. Lines stretched out the doors and down long sidewalks. In this large mass of people were four couples; they were all pushing baby strollers with newborns in them. Having purchased tickets to the nine-forty showing, they had just sat down in auditorium seventeen waiting for the film to begin.

Minutes passed by agonizingly slow, but finally, at nine fifty-five the lights dimmed and everyone sat impatiently, suffering through several commercials by Coke, Toyota, Kodak and an anti-drug abuse tutorial. One man could be heard grumbling that he didn't pay twenty dollars just to sit and be sold something. "If I wanted a car, I would have gone to a blasted car lot," he muttered angrily, followed by his wife quietly pleading with him to be quiet and stop embarrassing her. Several trailers were shown for upcoming movies and then with a drum roll the familiar jingle of Twentieth Century Fox Films began playing. At last, 'a long time ago in a galaxy far far away' appeared on the huge screen in hazy blue lettering, followed by clamorous applause from the audience. The four couples would give the movie a few minutes to get going.

Shortly after a huge noisy battle of flashing laser beams and sonic pulse weapons centering on the Cloud City of Bespin was concluding, the couples stood up and walked to the back. First one man, then the other reached into a stroller and removed one of the two diaper bags there in. One by one each exited the theater and strolled casually down the corridor, passing other jovial moviegoers along the way; some holding hands, others clutching overfilled bags of freshly popped 'butter' lathered popcorn, spilling it faster than the poor employee following them around could sweep it up. The four men walked into separate dimly lit theaters and took seats as near to the middle of each auditorium as possible.

The women waited a few minutes before following their husbands out into the hallways. They also walked to separate theaters and pushed the strollers off to the side leaving them in the back. Reaching in and removing the remaining diaper bags, they too took seats in the middle of the mass of movie watchers. At ten twenty-five all eight people casually reached into their bags and then closed them. They then waited two full minutes before standing up and placing the parcels on the top of the now retracted seat cushions. Satisfied, they walked out the door, stopping to retrieve the strollers and the life-like dolls in them as they left. Exiting through side doors, they hurriedly walked to their cars and drove away. The four vehicles were nearing the interchange of I-485 and I-85, more than twelve miles away, when the eight bombs detonated.

Each bomb was constructed with two pounds of Semtex high explosives, a two-liter bottle of gasoline, two pounds of roofing tacks and a small baggy of rat poison. Explosions ripped through the tightly packed theaters, shredding flesh from bones and violently separating movie-watchers from their appendages. Limbless torsos, seats, popcorn, candy, sodas and toy light sabers were blasted in all directions while seat cushions, curtains, victims' clothing and hair caught fire. By placing the bombs on the seats rather than under them, the killers had ensured the blast radius would be much wider and more deadly. In eight theaters, one hundred seventy-eight people were killed by the initial blasts alone. Another sixty-eight died from the raging fires, six were trampled and killed in the ensuing panic, and forty-seven died within twenty-four hours of arriving at the hospital. This was only the beginning.

The bombings were not limited to the Grand Empire Cinemas in Pineville. Similar diabolical attacks were duplicated at theaters in Lubbock, Texas, Kalamazoo, Michigan, Savannah, Georgia, Tupelo, Mississippi, Salem, Oregon, Johnson City, Tennessee, Tallahassee, Florida, Sacramento, Albuquerque, New Mexico and twenty other cities and communities across the country. In all, over nine thousand five hundred people died from the more than two hundred, five-pound bombs alone.

Television news stations scrambled to broadcast the destruction on a mass scale across the globe. Late newscasts were dominated by the carnage that had been wreaked across the country. Smoldering buildings with brackish smoke escaping into the night skies were visible on every T.V. screen in the United States and the world. If not for the huge marquees outside announcing currently playing films, most of the gutted buildings would be unrecognizable as movie theaters.

Stacks of filled body bags were piled in nearby parking lots; grief-stricken survivors, friends and family members were being held at bay by city and state police officers. Hours later firemen could be seen in the background beginning the time consuming job of rolling up their hoses and collecting other gear from around the obliterated shells.

Reporters were everywhere *politely* shoving microphones in witness' faces, trying to get the exclusive that would make their career. Here and there people thanked God for saving them. Perhaps unconsciously believing they had been selected for special treatment by the Creator of the universe because he hadn't seen fit to step in and save those who died. Survivors relayed in detail the sounds of screaming and gnashing of teeth they heard from the less fortunate who never made it out alive.

Hundreds of people gathered around each of the 'theater complexes' in all thirty cities, everyone trying to feed their 'ogrish' and morbidly hungry curiosities. Not one of them took any notice of the taxicabs being quietly driven up and parked near the largest gatherings of onlookers.

When the taxis, each packed with more than five hundred pounds of explosives were detonated, the results were again horrendous. Thunderous blasts ripped into unsuspecting bystanders, shredding them like cheese. The lives of another thirteen hundred American citizens were instantly snuffed out.

Before any additional rescue people were allowed into the area to help potential survivors, police bomb squads and US Army explosive ordnance disposal teams would have to be sent in to ensure no additional bombs were present.

Remote news cameras captured the images of bloody survivors struggling to drag their broken bodies out of the blast zone toward help. Even though the police forbade anyone from entering the area, for their own safety, many ignored the orders and rushed in to help the injured.

While some lives were saved, hundreds more died. Allah's faithful had snatched away the lives of more than eleven thousand innocent people in less than three hours. They were just getting started. Unlike on 9/11, this time the infidels would not have the luxury of years to recover, heal and forget.

CHAPTER 27

▼

Day Sixteen

Saturday

"What in the name of all that's holy is going on!" the president yelled at his entire National Security Council as he stormed into the White House Situation Room. "Come on people, I need answers! I need solutions!"

"We're looking into it sir," CIA Director Stuart Minetti said, regretting it the moment the last syllable left his lips.

"You're looking into it!" the president raged. "We've got roughly thirteen thousand dead US citizens in less than three weeks, and all you can say is that you're looking into it? I don't want you to look into it, I want it stopped, now!"

"Mr. President, we all do, but you have to admit this caught us all a bit by surprise," FBI Director Chuck Alexander responded, slightly taken aback by the president's uncharacteristically harsh attitude.

"Well it shouldn't have! This is 9/11 all over again, only quadrupled and it doesn't look as if it's going to end this time. I thought we already stopped this newest terrorist threat?"

"The ones in Redding yes," Gooden said, "but we plainly misjudged their numbers and capabilities. There are obviously a lot more of them out there, and I'm convinced that everyone in this room knew it, or they should have."

"Well thank you for stating the obvious Mark, that's a big help. Of course there are more of them out there. What I demand to know is where are they and why did we again get caught with our pants down?" Nicholson glanced around the room, "Anyone?"

The men all sat there looking at one another, no one daring to be the first to speak. Finally, Homeland Security Director, Iverson James spoke up, "Sir, it would appear as if they are everywhere and nowhere."

"Well, that sure cleared up the mystery, thank you very much!" Nicholson snapped.

"What I mean sir, is that they struck in thirty cities last night alone. We had absolutely no indications or forewarning that they were going to. Nor did we believe they were so well equipped and organized to pull off something this grand in scale."

"How is that possible? You should have known! That's what America pays you for. Every single person in this room has failed their country!" the president railed. "Including myself! We've got several thousand suspected terrorists under around-the-clock surveillance, and you're telling me that none of our operatives saw these hyenas so much as fart in the wind last night?"

Director Alexander leaned forward in his chair, "Mr. President, the terrorists didn't hit any of the obvious targets. We have more than one hundred and fifty cities and installations listed as most likely targets. The *hyenas* didn't hit any of them." Alexander paused for a moment, "And no, evidently nobody we had under surveillance last night had any gastrointestinal issues, at least none that were readily apparent, sir." A round of suppressed laughter momentarily interrupted Alexander. "The cockroaches that hit last night came out of nowhere and then quickly vanished."

Nicholson ignored the humor, "Well obviously your list of *most likely targets* is incomplete. Now, am I to believe that with all of the intelligence resources at our disposal we have absolutely no idea who these people are or where they might strike next and when?"

"To answer your first question, specifically, no. Generally, yes." General Slade commented.

"And what in the world is that supposed to mean?" Nicholson asked.

"Only that we don't know individually who they are, but I think everyone in this room, and the country, know they're religious Muslim fanatics."

"So, what will they do next?" Nicholson repeated, ignoring the general's comment.

"That's anybody's guess, sir," NSA Director Mims answered. "So far they have struck pretty much wherever and whenever they want to. The simple answer is, they don't appear to be following any kind of logical target selection, and so the odds of us accurately predicting where they will strike next are quite remote."

"Why? Tell me why we can't." Nicholson pleaded.

"They're hitting Middle America, which leaves far too many possible targets to adequately protect. Up 'til now they've only been going after soft targets and there is no discernible pattern that we can see," Minetti explained.

"So...?"

"Simply put, we're at their mercy for now."

Nicholson frowned and grabbed a can of Coke off the table, downing the entire thing in one shot and then lit a cigarette. Taking a long draw into his lungs, he sat back in his chair and allowed the nicotine to perform its magic. He looked up and blew smoke toward the ceiling. "So, if we don't know who they are, then how do we find them? More importantly, how do we stop them?"

"They don't have an organized military for us to hit back at, so the way I see it we need to identify who is calling the shots," Iverson James answered.

"That's easy, the answer's as clear as the nose on your face," Slade scoffed.

Gooden looked surprised, "You mean you know?" he asked expectantly.

"Of course, the all lovin', all powerful and merciful Allah," Slade answered with a low-wattage grin. "Didn't you know that?"

"Oh for the love of Pete…we're trying to have a serious discussion here," Gooden snapped," Why do you insist on being such a wise a…"

"That'll be enough gentlemen," the president intervened. He turned his attention toward Barclay Mims, "Has NSA come up with anything that might indicate who is issuing these savages their marching orders?"

"No sir. We have stepped up monitoring of all communications worldwide to include phone and Internet traffic. We got a big fat zero!" It would probably surprise most Americans to learn that the NSA had satellites monitoring every phone conversation they made. Huge Cray IV computers in the basement of NSA headquarters in Fort Meade, Maryland were programmed to scan for a predetermined list of trigger words such as assassination, president, White House and a long list of others. When one of these words was encountered, NSA analysts kept a transcript of the conversation for a later, more thorough scrutiny.

Most of the time the discourse was discovered to be nothing more than someone relaying tidbits of a recent movie they'd watched or the plot of the book they were reading to a friend. But, from time to time, something of a more tangible nature was discovered. When that happened, federal agents were assigned to take a more thorough look at it, and take whatever action was deemed appropriate.

"Anything else?"

"We've also been monitoring Internet chat-rooms for suspicious activity, so far nothing there either, sorry."

"All right, let me get this straight. We don't know who they are. We don't know where they are. We don't know who is in charge of them. And we don't know where they will strike next. Basically, we don't know a blessed thing. Does that about sum it up?" Nicholson asked, looking around the room and taking another drag on his cigarette. He received a few nods, but nothing more promising would be forthcoming.

"Next question," he continued, "How do we stop them? Because gentlemen, I refuse to accept there is absolutely nothing we can do."

General Slade stood up, "Sir, where they are, what's next, and who is in charge is anybody's guess. What to do about it is something else."

"Here he goes again," Gooden scoffed.

Slade turned his head toward Gooden preparing to deliver a scathing comment about his genetic makeup, but Nicholson spoke first, "Mark, that's enough! We don't have time for this pointless bickering. Donovan, what do you suggest? At this point, I'm all ears."

Slade cleared his throat before speaking to give himself a second more to consider what he was about to suggest. "Sir, there are two things ninety-eight percent of the terrorists in the world have in common. The first is that they are all Arab; the second is they are Muslim. I submit that the time for political correctness has indeed come to an end. It's time we start rounding them up and shipping them back to their own countries," Slade braced himself for the tirade that was to surely come his way.

A dead silence filled the room as everyone, including the president, stared at Slade. "Have you lost your ever-lovin' mind, Donovan?" Nicholson thundered. "Do you think the American people would sit still for that for one minute? They'd demand my head on a chopping block by day's end!"

"Maybe before all of this madness started," Slade said, "But I'm not so sure they would now."

"You're nuts, Slade. You always have been!" Gooden said, half rising from his chair."

"Young man, sit down and shut up!" Slade roared, squaring his shoulders toward the NSA, clearly ready for any confrontation. Gooden sank back into his chair noticeably shaken by the large General's combative stance. Slade scanned the room; "You can all take your sanctimonious attitudes and shove 'em for that matter. I haven't said a thing that every one of you cowardly hypocrites hasn't already thought about. You're just more afraid that someone may think poorly of you or tag you with a career-wrecking label like *politically incorrect* if you dare exercise enough courage to say what you truly believe out loud. Well gentlemen, I for one am not afraid to speak the truth…"

"Calm down, General," Nicholson calmly ordered.

"Sir, if we try to fight this war, while trying to be sensitive to our enemies' feelings, then we've already lost. We just don't know it yet. You can't allow that to happen, Mr. President."

"I don't intend to, but I'm just not certain that mass deportations are the answer either."

"I understand your concern, sir. However, a president cannot allow himself to do what is considered popular. He must do what is best for the country."

Nicholson exploded, "Don't you portend to tell me how to do my job! I know what my responsibilities are!"

"Mr. President, I wasn't suggesting that you…"

"Whose next, Donovan?" Nicholson shouted, cutting him off. "All the Nazi lovers because they love Adolf Hitler? Perhaps African Americans, who question the government, conduct rallies and organize million man marches? We could send all of the blacks back to Africa, would that be okay too?"

"Sir, that's not the same and you know it," Iverson James said, coming to Slade's defense.

"It is the same! We can't solve the problem by rounding up a group of people just because of their skin color or religious beliefs. Or kick them out of the country because we hope the ones we're looking for are in that group. Following that logic, if we have a serial killer we know to be a French citizen, but not who he is, we just round up all the French and send them packing as well. Then, when another group commits an unacceptable offense, we kick them out too. Where does it end? We cannot allow ourselves to sink to that level. Hell…we don't even know if Muslims carried out the theater bombings. It could have been any number of different groups." Nicholson really didn't believe that last part and neither did anyone else in the room. "There must be another way, another answer. Think gentlemen."

White House Chief of Staff Cornelius Bennitt spoke up, "Sir, all of these latest attacks were meticulously coordinated. All the bombs went off within forty-five minutes of one another. I'd really like to know how they managed to do it. Once we figure out their means of communication we'll catch them."

The President turned his attention to the Director of the National Security Agency Barclay Mims. "Bark…what can you tell me?"

"Not much. Like I said before, since the first attacks in Redding, we've stepped up our ELINT coverage worldwide." Mims explained, referring to electronic intelligence. "So far nothing's surfaced. We're pretty stumped how they managed that kind of coordination without us finding out about it, or at least catching a sniff something was in the works."

"Chuck? How about surveillance on suspected terrorists? Anything out of the ordinary?"

"Nothing sir. We've been vigilant to bring in all the most likely suspects and have conducted intensive interrogations…so far nothing worth talking about."

"*Intense*? Perhaps they haven't been nearly intense enough."

"Yes sir," Alexander replied.

Minetti leaned forward. "We are exploring all investigative leads sir, but so far…"

"Are you telling me that with all the money and manpower we throw at our intelligence services, we don't have a single lead?"

"Just what are they supposed to do to get the information we need?" Slade asked.

"Interrogate suspected terrorists," Gooden answered.

"You've got to be joking! How are they supposed to go about it?"

"I'm no spook, how would I know?"

"Dunno, but I will tell you one thing, they can't *effectively* interrogate them even if they want too."

"Why not? That's their job!"

"I realize that, but the Sensitive Sallys in the government have declared that all of the most effective techniques are off-limits."

"You're talkin' torture, General."

Slade smiled.

Gooden leaned forward, "General, these people do have the right to be treated humanely."

"Why? They don't serve in any organized military or wear a uniform. They serve no recognized government. They are not American citizens and they are not signatories of the Geneva Convention."

"But still…"

"No Mark. Even if the Geneva Convention applied here, they have refused to abide by it. If they won't adhere to its provisions, why should we? These people do not follow any rules of decency and they would gladly walk in here right now and carve out each of our spleens with a soupspoon if they could. They're fanatical about what they believe and if they are not well *motivated* to spill the beans, they won't."

"I believe you're point has been clearly made, General, thank you," Nicholson said. "Now, how about internationally? Have any foreign powers taken the kind of actions that might indicate they may have had any forewarning that all of this was about to go down?"

"Such as?" Mims asked.

"Did any of them place their military forces on alert, or deploy them in ways inconsistent with their normal routines?"

"Not that we've seen," Slade answered. "Many have gone to increased alert levels, but that was only after the attacks began."

"I have an idea," Minetti said. "I accept that we can't conduct a mass deportation of a specific population due to the complete unfairness of it. I also agree that not all Muslims are terrorists; in fact, the great majority of them are not. So how do we isolate the ones who are guilty without knowing who they are or treating the innocent like criminals?"

"Great question, now answer it," Nicholson stated.

"We have designed new security technology that I think will be beneficial to solving our dilemma. We've inserted a GPS locator inside a titanium bracelet and I think we need to find a legal way to compel all known Arab Muslims in the country to wear one. Temporarily of course."

"Have you lost your ever lovin' mind?" Gooden, blurted out. "You're as crazy as he is," pointing toward Slade, who just scowled and slyly grinned.

Minetti spun toward him, "You got any better ideas? Does anyone? If we can get this done, it would accomplish three things. First, those that are innocent would be above suspicion, at least from being the ones that are actually carrying out the attacks. And second, as soon as another attack occurs, and it will, we'll know within a very short time if any of the bracelet-wearing individuals was near the incident. Number three, it will drastically reduce the number of potential suspects."

"Depending on how many actually submit to wearing one," James said.

"Correct."

"Why titanium?" Bennett asked.

"Those wearing it aren't going to be able to cut it off with a hacksaw in their back-yard tool shed; at least not easily. Titanium is three times stronger than steel and forty-two percent lighter. It's bend, dent, scratch resistant and corrosion proof. It's the strongest metal in the world. Basically whomever we put it on, keeps it on. It also emits a signal to the National Security Agency if it's tampered with." Minetti smiled, "We can even offer it in a multitude of vibrant colors for those that are more fashion conscious among us, if that helps." Soft snickers rolled in from around the table.

"How do we ask people to submit to this? Talk about stirring up a hornet's nest," Alexander said. "I mean, I personally like the idea, but to convince people to give up their right of freedom of movement will be quite the undertaking."

"We're not taking away their freedom of movement, only monitoring it. If they're not up to anything bad, what does it hurt? What we will do is appeal to their sense of patriotism and their deep-seated love of their fellow man, or their fears, whichever approach works," Minetti replied.

"Find out if any of the nearly thirteen thousand plus dead are Muslim. Hopefully, when they see that their own people are just as vulnerable as the rest of us, it will help some in the convincing," Nicholson said.

"Will do sir," Alexander replied.

Nicholson extinguished his cigarette in an ashtray, "I'm not sure I like this idea. However, I don't see a whole lot of options. And so far our best efforts have accomplished absolutely nothing except make us all look impotent to adequately protecting our people. What if we can't legally compel them to wear the bracelets?"

"You may have to sign an executive order in the interest of national security," Minetti said.

"That will put us precariously close to having a police state."

"I know it will sir, but from where I'm sitting you don't seem to have a lot of workable options."

Nicholson sighed, "This is really getting out of hand. Gentlemen, check into it and get back to me with some options, if there are any. Other business?"

"Sir, the economy is already in poor shape with the fuel crisis being as it is. And without a doubt it's going to take another tremendous hit due to what just happened. When the markets open Monday…we'll we don't think it's going to be pretty," Gooden said.

"How bad?"

"Treasury anticipates a drop in the Dow by as much as five hundred points and T-bills are going to take a hit as well. Consumer confidence is anemic, and people are not going shopping, to dinner, and definitely not to the movies. This is far worse than what happened after 9/11."

"Worst case scenario?"

"If we don't get a grip on this thing quickly, it will make the Great Depression look like a bad April Fool's joke."

"This day just keeps getting brighter and brighter. Does anyone have any good news to report?"

"Yes sir," Bennett answered. "Rescue workers at the hospital in Redding found a seven year old girl alive this morning. They were just about to stop looking for survivors when they found her trapped in an elevator car that smashed through the floor and into the basement."

"How did she live so long? Her survival seems unlikely after so many days," Nicholson asked.

"Seems a slow trickle of water was seeping into the car from somewhere, maybe a broken water line, anyway she drank from it and fed on packs of ketchup she found in a box in the elevator. Doctors are still not convinced she's going to make it just yet. She's lost a lot of weight, but they are hopeful."

"Let's pray she does, this country could use some good news."

The President directed his attention to General Slade, "Donovan, I want all our military forces worldwide placed immediately on the highest alert level. Also, notify our National Guard Commanders to prepare their personnel for full deployment."

"All of them, sir?"

"Yes, all of them. Gentlemen?" Nicholson said, looking around the table, "Does anyone in this room sincerely believe that these attacks are over or that we've seen the worst of them?" No one answered. "I didn't think so, we've already made that erroneous judgment once. If that is all, you're dismissed."

Everyone stood and walked out of the room, leaving the president alone with his thoughts. Nicholson sat there amazed that in just over two weeks, he was beginning to question his entire belief system. To think that he was actually entertaining the notion of infringing on the rights of a group of his fellow Americans shook him to the core. There had to be another way, but for the life of him he couldn't see what it might possibly be short of giving in to standing terrorist demands.

CHAPTER 28

▼

In late December, nineteen seventy-nine, the former Soviet Union without warning and without provocation, invaded the much smaller country of Afghanistan. Their reasons for doing so were the perceived benefits of having the third world nation under Soviet military control. It would provide the Soviets easier overland access to the mouth of the Persian Gulf and most of the world's oil fields. Believing the task would be easily accomplished, the Russian Politburo failed to clearly think things through and were completely surprised by the ferocity with which the Afghanis fought for their freedom.

Even more surprising was the vast amount of financial and military support the freedom fighters would receive from the United States Government. That aid would ultimately lead to the Soviet Union losing the war and retreating from the rugged underdeveloped country ten years later in failure and disgrace. Over the course of the war, America provided in excess of three billion dollars in war aid, and the Soviet armed forces suffered more than twenty-two thousand deaths and at least three times that number wounded, many maimed for life.

Shortly after the Soviets invaded, a young Saudi named Osama bin Laden rushed to the mountains of Afghanistan. There he eagerly gave his support to the besieged warriors and waged war with them against the godless communist aggressors. With over thirty million dollars he had inherited from his father's construction business, Osama was able to provide vital financial support. Osama's intent was more to fan the flames of Jihad (holy war) with the west than to simply expel the invaders and believed a war with the Soviets would eventually aid him in his global endeavors. Even though it would take many years to come to pass, bin Laden never wavered and stayed the course.

Although the US provided numerous arms to the Afghanis, the most significant portion of that aid was the more than one thousand FIM-92A Stinger Missiles. The Stinger is a man portable, shoulder-fired, surface to air missile utilizing a passive infrared seeker head, a high explosive warhead and is capable of engaging any aircraft flying under ten thousand feet elevation. Weighing less than forty-five pounds the Stinger is very easy to operate in any combat environment.

The Afghanis quickly employed the high-tech weapon against the Soviet Hind Attack Helicopters and found that it helped to significantly level the playing field with their much better armed enemies. No longer would Soviet forces have air supremacy over the poorly equipped and ill-trained Mujahideen warriors, literally translated from Arabic to mean 'struggler'.

During the war America's political leaders grew very troubled, not only with the transfer of the missile, but more so because of numerous reports indicating Afghan rebels were passing many of the missiles off to Iranian terrorist groups in the region. Due to these concerns shortly after the war ended, and the Soviet military machine's withdrawal of forces, the United States attempted to buy back the remaining missiles at a cost of between fifty and one hundred thousand dollars per unit. Even though a premium price was offered, less than two hundred of the dangerous weapons were ever recovered.

In the halls of political power in Washington DC, it was hoped that the unaccounted-for missiles may have degraded over time and would not work properly. However, many of the recovered weapons were taken to military test ranges and fired. Even though the Stingers were over thirteen years old at the time, each weapon worked perfectly as advertised and quickly eliminated any doubt the remaining ones could continue to present a clear and viable threat to anyone they were employed against for many years to come.

To this day, no one knows exactly how many of those unaccounted-for missiles were employed in the Soviet/Afghan war. More importantly, nobody knows how many of them found their way into the hands of terrorist organizations throughout the Middle East. The Afghan leadership, the Taliban, vowed none of them were given to terrorists, however, it is feared, in some circles, that a great number were either stolen or purchased by Osama bin-Laden and his followers.

American intelligence agencies stand ever-vigilant waiting for the day they are finally put to some heinous use. It is speculated that in excess of two hundred Stingers actually found their way into the hands of radical Islamic fundamentalists. The question is not if they will ever be used, but when and against whom?

CHAPTER 29

▼

Day Seventeen

Sunday

Paranoia is the term used by mental health care professionals to describe suspiciousness, or mistrust, that is either highly exaggerated or simply not warranted at all. In the case of the American people, their paranoia was highly justified. While the percentage of the population directly effected by the terrorist's attacks was minuscule in the grand scope of things, the terrified citizens had heard and seen enough to send large numbers of otherwise law-abiding people over the edge of reason. However, some groups did not necessarily need to be pushed. They were simply waiting for the right opportunity to strike.

Over the past several decades neo-Nazi skinheads have been responsible for more than seventy-five murders. While some of those killings resulted from skinhead-on-skinhead violence, the great majority were perpetrated upon Hispanics and African-Americans. But their scourge on society was not limited to just murders. These animals committed thousands of other less 'offensive' crimes as well; synagogue desecrations, stabbings, beatings, rapes, armed robberies and burglaries were also among their long list of accomplishments.

Throughout the late nineties skinhead gangs saw their numbers steadily dwindle, however, that downward trend corrected itself after the events of 9/11 and recruitment has been on the rise ever since. They tend to target young white males between the age of twelve and twenty-five; although, the number of female followers had also seen dramatic growth.

For decades white supremacist skinheads waited for the opportunity to take out their venomous hatred on ethnic, social, minority and religious groups with which they had differing opinions and *values*; or simply hate for no rational reason. That opportunity they had been waiting for was now a reality and their hungry black hearts would now have a bountiful supply in which to feed upon.

Survivalists and militia groups had also been patiently anticipating the day when they could step forward and 'come to the defense of their country'. For decades they had stockpiled weapons and supplies. Days, weeks and sometimes months have been dedicated to training for the day many hoped would eventually arrive. These groups were organized and now prepared to take justice into their own hands.

*   *   *   *

Ali Hassan could not believe his good fortune. Here he was strolling down the boardwalk in Myrtle Beach, South Carolina, hand in hand with the most beautiful girl in the world. The moon was shining brightly, the crashing surf was breaking beneath their feet, and the scent of her perfume was intoxicating in the cool salty air. The closeness of her body to his was electrifying and had his heart racing. He struggled to keep his breathing under control and hoped she did not notice that his palms were sweating.

He could feel the lump of the felt-covered ring box in his left front pocket. It had taken him more than four hours to decide on just the right one but finally he had made his choice. The helpful clerk assured him that it was a marvelous selection and that any woman would be proud to wear it. He placed the seven hundred dollars he had labored to save for the past eleven months on the countertop, and the ring was his.

Ali looked over at Kira, his heart swelling with love…and fear. Fear that she would tell him no, and a love so powerful he had no choice but to take the risk. He led her to the end of the boardwalk overlooking the Atlantic Ocean, stopping in the faint illumination from a fluorescent light swinging gently in the breeze from a pole overhead. It was past midnight and the beach was deserted for hundreds of yards in either direction. Ali turned to face her, reached into his pocket and slowly knelt down on his right knee.

"Kira?" he said, his hands shaking uncontrollably, his stomach in knots, "you know that I love you more than anything. I've reached a point where I can no longer imagine my life without you in it and I can barely remember what it was like before I knew you. All I know is that now, colors are brighter and birds sing more beautifully. Whenever you're not with me I spend my every waking moment wishing that you were. Thoughts of you pervade my mind to the point I can't think of anything else." He opened the box and offered it to her. "Kira, would you do me the honor of becoming my wife?"

Ali could see a wide smile spread across her face and what he hoped was tears of joy rolling gently down her soft cheeks.

"Ali…I love you too…"

"Well…isn't that special!"

Startled, Ali and Kira spun toward the sound of the ominous voice. They saw three of the largest and most terrifying looking men that either of them had ever seen before walking threateningly toward them from out of the darkness.

"It looks like something out of a romance novel, don't you think, Mikey?" one of them said.

Ali stood up, grabbed Kira by the hand and attempted to walk around the hulking figures. One of them moved into their path. "Where you going in such a hurry? She hasn't gave you an answer yet," he said nodding toward Kira. "Don't ya want to hear what she has to say?"

Again Ali attempted to sprint passed the men, but the largest of the three grabbed him and quickly placed him in a savage Bear Hug that he couldn't escape no matter how hard he tried. The man's face was mere inches from his own and the over-powering smell of booze nearly caused him to wretch. The huge arms wrapped around his body began constricting even tighter and Ali's head began to swim from lack of oxygen. He fought with every ounce of strength he possessed, but the harder he struggled the tighter the arms became. His vision grew blurry and just as he blacked out he heard the terrified screams of Kira behind him.

Seven hours later, the bound, gagged and brutally tortured bodies of the young lovers washed up on the wet sands of Atlantic Beach. The killers were never identified. Their motives were never officially determined. But, everyone knew what had happened, and why.

*   *   *   *

In Shreveport Louisiana, four young Muslim-American males were playing basketball in an abandoned park. The sun was setting over the top of the trees and the lights around the court had just come on. Eight men dressed in black and carrying baseball bats, stepped out of the woods and rushed toward the athletes. Before any of the boys were aware they were in any danger, it was already too late. The skinheads launched themselves, pouncing upon their unsuspecting prey, viciously swinging their lethal clubs with deadly precision. The attack was quick, brutal and delivered without the slightest measure of mercy.

By the time an evening jogger passed by an hour later, three of the young men were already dead. The fourth, his skull fractured in several places, died in the back of an ambulance racing toward the hospital. He never opened his eyes nor uttered a word to identify his murderers.

*   *   *   *

As Muslims were gathering for evening prayer in San Antonio, Texas, a dark van was pulling up to the rear of the Mosque. Five men, dressed in camouflage fatigues, got out with ski masks covering their faces. One of the men used a large set of bolt-cutters to clip the knob off the door gaining access to the basement. Three men followed him inside and down the creaky, dimly lit staircase.

At nine-thirty exactly, the man left outside cut electrical power to the building, plunging it into darkness. The intruders inside, lurking just outside the worship hall, jerked open the doors and began throwing lit Molotov cocktails into the midst of Allah's kneeling faithful. In all, ten crude bombs were hurled before the maniacal killers turned and rushed back through the basement to the waiting van.

The fires inside raged swiftly through the holy place, rapidly overtaking the fleeing masses. Clothes and hair ignited, shrieking screams of burning people could be heard blocks away.

The inferno rapidly expanded to engulf the entire room and panicked people were madly racing death to the freedom of the open door. The wrathful blaze was sucked toward the exit and the bountiful source of oxygen it supplied. In the end, many lost the race, for there were simply too many to get through the single door fast enough. People fell and were trampled. Others collapsed, overcome by the suffocating smoke that had already blanketed the worship hall.

Hours later, when police began their investigation, no one was able to identify or even offer a description of the five men who were responsible for the deaths of thirty-eight people and the injury of more than fifty others. Among the dead and injured were seventeen African-Americans.

By morning, the Reverends Jessie Jackson, Al Sharpton and Minister Louis Farrakhan, were all demanding the guilty be found and punished.

*   *   *   *

Maria and Joseph Olarte had already experienced a long day at their primary jobs and were now laboring late at a carwash in Tucson, Arizona. The couple had only purchased the self-service business three months earlier, after finally gaining citizenship, having waited more than five and a half years for approval.

They were in the process of restocking vending machines with Windex and Armour-All wipes, when an older Chevy pickup truck pulled into a nearby wash bay. The Olartes, other than nodding to them, paid no attention to the man and woman who got out, slipped several coins into the control box and began washing their vehicle. The Olartes only concern at the time was finishing up their task and going to pick up their three children from the babysitter.

They were just finishing the restocking when they turned to see the couple standing directly behind them. Before either of the Olartes could even ask if they needed help, the couple drew pistols from their waistbands and fired.

In the course of the investigation, detectives discovered racial slurs spray painted on the walls of one of the wash bays. The slurs demanded that all rag heads and camel jockeys go home.

*   *   *   *

The angry young man crept through the sewers, his feet sloshing in the gray muck and offal of New York City. He had walked these dark, dank tunnels several times over the past few days, memorizing the route to the point he could traverse it blindfolded. He jumped when several huge rats scurried past only inches from his feet. Just a couple more turns and he would be in position.

*   *   *   *

Malook Malmoud was halfway through the laborious task of polishing the stainless steel on his hot dog cart to a blinding finish before calling it a day. It had taken several months of appeals, *begging* really, but he had finally managed to get a vending license that allowed him to operate his cart near Times Square. After years of struggling, his small business was finally starting to turn a nice profit and hopefully he and his wife could move their family to a nicer home.

A garbage truck was dumping a trash bin in the alley nearby, preventing Malook from hearing the heavy iron manhole cover scraping softly across the pavement ten feet behind him.

Bryce Wagner peeked out from the darkness of the sewer through the tiny crack around the heavy iron lid and watched the filthy Arab cleaning his cart. Though it was shadowy outside, the street was dimly lit and he could see no one else nearby. He pushed the heavy lid another eighteen inches out of the way and rose slowly up through the murky hole in the street.

The 'hot dog man' did not see him. Bryce took another look around and then raised a sawed off double-barreled twelve gauge shotgun, pointing it at the vendor's back. Taking a deep breath to steady his nerves, he carefully aimed the weapon and squeezed both triggers.

The gun kicked back violently as eighteen thirty-two-caliber lead balls exploded from the end of the barrel and took Malook full in the center of the back, virtually severing him in half. His ravaged body was thrown over the cart and he was dead before his brain could register the ghastly pain that ended his life.

Bryce did not hesitate to observe his deed. He immediately dropped the gun into the sewer, grabbed the manhole cover and pulled it back into position and with a solid metallic thump removed himself from the horror he had just created. The noisy truck helped mask the sound of the shots and no one saw the killer of Malook Malmoud the hard-working hot dog man.

It serves him right! Bryce thought, as he climbed down the ladder and retrieved the gun from the gooey muck. *Someone had to pay for Uncle Mitch's death!* His heart still ached when he thought of his uncle and family, now lying in the cold ground in Redding. *It was so easy! Next time will go even smoother!*

*   *   *   *

Incidents like these were occurring all over the country. Muslim-Americans were being assaulted, robbed and killed in mass numbers without the slightest bit of provocation. These attacks did not surprise most law enforcement officers in the least. In fact, they were somewhat amazed that it had taken so long for the retaliatory attacks to begin in earnest. What was surprising was the high number of Hispanic Americans, both legal and illegal, that were being targeted. After a prolonged debate, it was determined that the perpetrators of the crimes seemed to be having trouble making a distinction between Hispanics and Arabs.

Within the last forty-eight hours, close to five hundred Hispanics and Arabs had been murdered by vicious vigilantes throughout the country. Ten times that number had also been attacked, injured or maimed during the same period. As if they didn't have enough trouble on their plates to worry about, police departments were now being inundated with calls reporting suspicious behavior from just about everybody. Police officers had their fingers in the dam and the thing was crumbling down around them.

The terrified populace was quickly losing faith in their elected officials and law enforcement's ability to protect them. Many had decided their only recourse was to take matters into their own hands and that was exactly what they were doing.

Order was not being restored and vigilante justice, reminiscent of the old west, was rapidly becoming the favored alternative embraced by many in the country.

CHAPTER 30

▼

Day Eighteen

Monday

US Airways flight 1135 was inbound from Salt Lake City, Utah to Charlotte, North Carolina. On board the Boeing 757 were two hundred and eighteen passengers and crew, forty of them husbands and fathers on their way to the annual Promise Keepers Convention, a Christian evangelical ministry dedicated to uniting men to become godly influences in the world, their communities, and most of all their families.

Captain Michael Vitte was eager to complete this flight for two reasons. The first was that it would represent his ten thousandth accident-free flight-hour. And while that was a career milestone for him, it was not the more important of the two. At least not right now. The other reason was that he and his wife would get to begin the long thirty-day European vacation they had been planning for more than a year and a half.

The flight had gone like clockwork. It had encountered very little turbulence and had even caught the jet stream, which would allow them to arrive fifteen minutes ahead of schedule. Vitte had received final clearance to land ten minutes earlier and was now on final approach, having already descended the aircraft to under fifteen hundred feet and cut his airspeed to less than a hundred sixty miles per hour. With the exception of a twenty-knot right to left crosswind, everything was going smoothly.

The starboard engine exploded and the huge flying machine bounced violently, red-hot shredded metal ripped into the wing igniting the fuel. Vitte shoved the throttles all the way forward and pulled back on the controls in an attempt to regain control of the floundering aircraft. While doing this, he reached over and hit the fuel-dump switch for the right wing. If he only had more time, more airspeed and more elevation, he might have been able to save the plane with its one remaining engine. Unfortunately, he didn't. The wounded aircraft tipped over to the right, unable to adjust quickly enough to the sudden loss of power and hurled toward the earth at over one hundred-thirty miles per hour.

The plane slammed into the end of the runway, exploded and shattered into millions of pieces before erupting into a huge fireball that stretched hundreds of feet into the air, the smoke visible for miles around. There were no survivors. Many bodies were completely consumed by the searing flames and those that weren't would have to be identified using dental records and DNA.

A spokesperson for the National Transportation and Safety Board would later report that the crash was so monumental two recovery workers picked up the biggest piece of recovered wreckage and loaded it by hand onto a waiting truck.

*   *   *   *

Senior air traffic controller, Patricia Clark, was standing behind the newest employee on her shift. He was in the process of guiding in his first flight unassisted. The *Airbus 330*, with three hundred and thirty-seven passengers and crew, was inbound from Paris, France to Atlanta, Georgia. For a new employee, Brad was doing a good job and seemed uncharacteristically comfortable with his critical duties; so far he had done everything properly.

She looked away for only a moment, to retrieve a cup of coffee from the counter behind her, when Brad came half out of his seat and started yelling excitedly that something had hit the plane.

Clark wheeled around and quickly located the *Airbus* less than a half-mile from the end of the runway. Grabbing the binoculars from around her neck, she saw black smoke and bright orange flames shooting out the back of the portside engine. The aircraft was shuddering violently, but after several tense moments it seemed to stabilize.

Clark had just let out a huge sigh of relief when she saw a streak of faint white smoke erupt from the tree line beyond the runway and shoot toward the damaged aircraft. The starboard engine disintegrated, the plane lost all power and nose-dived into the end of the runway, plowing twenty feet into the concrete, instantly killing everyone on board.

*   *   *   *

In Detroit, Michigan, another 757 struck the runway, bounced several times before yawing to the right, skidded sideways down the tarmac and off the runway into the grass. The left wing dipped down and dug deep into the soft soil, causing the huge plane to begin cartwheeling wing tip over wing tip. The *Boeing* fragmented into huge pieces and burst into a roaring fireball. Pillars of filthy black smoke churning upward, carrying with it debris from the wreckage and the souls of the dead into the heavens.

*   *   *   *

"Mr. President!" Mark Gooden yelled as he stormed into the Oval Office. "The vermin are blowing planes out of the skies!"

"What are you talking about?" a startled Nicholson asked.

"Just what I said sir! They're using missiles to shoot down planes!" Gooden explained.

"Where? How?" Nicholson stammered.

"Last count, seven!"

"Seven? Oh my god! Where?"

"Everywhere!"

"What do you mean everywhere? Nicholson cried.

"The first was a 757 on final approach in Charlotte. Followed by an Airbus 330 in Atlanta. Then quickly, almost on top of each other, 757's in Detroit, Las Vegas, Dallas-Fort Worth and MD-80's in Portland, Oregon and Bangor, Maine!"

"Survivors?"

"Too early to tell sir, the crashes are pretty horrific and it doesn't look good. Those poor people didn't stand a chance!"

"Have we grounded all commercial aircraft?"

"Yes sir, the order just went out, however, there are still a lot of planes in the air." Gooden elaborated. "Understandably, many of the pilots are refusing to land."

"What do you mean they're refusing to land?"

"Sir, all of the planes that have been shot down were either taking off or landing at the time. The remaining pilots are refusing to land until they are assured the area around the airports is secured, or they're forced to land from lack of fuel. Some have even taken it upon themselves to divert to military bases."

"That's just great!"

The President turned on the television just as Gooden's cell phone rang. He flipped it open and answered. While listening, his face grew paler, if that was possible. Clicking off the phone, he turned toward the president. "Three more down sir, Memphis, Des Moines, Iowa and Green Bay!"

"What in the hell are we doing to stop this?" Nicholson demanded to know as he looked at the television."

Gooden noted that Nicholson was no longer watching CNN, *interesting.* FOX News had split its screen into four pictures and yet, was still unable to cover all the carnage that was taking place. Every screen was filled with smoke, flames and the wreckage of broken airplanes. Valiant rescue workers were visible darting about the killing-fields doing their best to save someone, anyone. Injured, maimed and bloody people were staggering around dazed and confused. Bodies lay everywhere.

In the bottom left screen, Nicholson saw firefighters abruptly drop their hoses and begin running frantically away from a burning *7E7 Dreamliner.* Moments later, Boeing's newest luxury liner exploded, blasting hot rubber, plastic and composite shrapnel in all directions. Several of the fleeing rescuers could be heard screaming as they were enveloped by the fireball and disappeared from view.

Gooden and Nicholson stood there quietly trying to process what they just witnessed, as the news commentator attempted to explain it to them. However, even she quickly determined no words were necessary and stopped talking, letting the horrible pictures explain it for her.

After a long moment, Gooden broke the silence, "As I said, we've grounded all commercial flights. We're scrambling fighter jets from all our bases but I don't know what good it will do. The terrorists are hitting the planes with surface-to-air missiles."

"Where did they get those?"

"We're not sure. But wherever they got them, it would appear they have plenty."

"Can't we stop them?"

"We're trying, sir. But we have to locate the shooters first and that's not easy."

"How hard can it be to find a guy firing a missile, for pity's sake?"

"Mr. President, MANPADS are easy to…"

"What in the world are MANPADS?"

"Man Portable Air Defense Systems…as I was saying, they are very easy to use. The operator can come out of hiding, acquire the target, fire and be back in hiding in under thirty seconds."

"Our fighter planes are equipped with machine guns, aren't they?"

"I assume so, sir."

"Well, instruct our pilots if they see someone fire a missile to smoke the bastard!"

That goes without saying. "Yes, sir!" Gooden responded once again flipping open his phone. He passed on the president's orders and then listened for a moment then hung up. "Sir? Sacramento, Pittsburgh, Wilmington, Delaware and Oklahoma City are reporting planes down. Charleston, South Carolina, Raleigh North Carolina, and Seattle are also reporting planes hit, but thank God those have landed safely."

"What in the name of Mother Mary are the Police Departments doing? Can't they stop this?

"Sir, they're blanketing the area but there's a lot of ground to cover. There is a tremendous amount of trees, brush and industrial buildings around airports that give the terrorists plenty of places to hide. And remember, this has all happened within the past twenty minutes, give them time," Gooden immediately regretted that last part.

"Give'm time? They're knocking planes down like bowling pins! We don't have time!" Nicholson reached for the remote and turned up the volume. The two men stood there quietly watching for several minutes neither wanting to speak due to some irrational fear that somehow it might make things worse. Finally, Nicholson broke the silence, "Are we a target?"

Gooden seemed a bit confused, "Yes sir. We all are."

"I mean right here, at the White House, Mark!"

"We don't know yet, but I would say it's a strong possibility. The Air Force has four F-15's flying combat air patrol over the DC area and we have significantly increased our perimeter security as well. We should be relatively safe."

"Safe? I'm not even sure I know what that word means anymore."

They both looked back toward the television. The news commentator was holding a hand over the earpiece on her left ear and looking down and away from the camera. Apparently getting the information she wanted she looked up. "Ladies and Gentlemen, we're getting reports that police officers have cornered two persons of interest in the woods outside of Charlotte Douglas International Airport in Charlotte, North Carolina. We're going to a live feed from an affiliate news chopper on the scene."

The picture changed to an overhead shot of some thick woods at the end of a nearby runway. The cameraman zoomed in on what appeared to be two men hunched down behind a fallen tree. They were firing, what were obviously automatic rifles in the direction of several police officers. The officers had also taken cover and were returning fire as best they could. It was glaringly evident to Nicholson, Gooden, and anyone else watching that the police handguns were no match for the terrorists' high-powered rifles.

The camera shifted angles to show several more officers cautiously working their way toward the terrorists from behind; each carried a shotgun

Trying to distract the terrorists' attention from the newly arriving officers edging ever closer to them, one of the handgun shooting officers stuck his head out a little too far. His body was flung backwards over a boulder by a shower of rapid gunfire from an AK-47.

The approaching officers opened fire and the gunmen slumped to the ground. Their firing appeared to stop but no one was immediately willing to risk coming out from behind his or her cover. Several minutes passed before the officers moved in to secure the scene. One patrolman could clearly be seen kicking a rifle out of the reach of an apparently dead zealot.

One of the terrorists abruptly moved, followed by an explosion. To avoid being taken alive he had pulled the pin on a hand grenade. Both terrorists and three police officers were instantly reduced to shreds by a volatile cloud of hot shrapnel.

Nicholson lowered the volume. "These people have absolutely no problem with dying or killing as many of us as they can to further their cause do they?"

"No sir, they don't." Gooden replied.

"How do you stop someone who is not afraid of jail or death? There has got to be a way of stopping these monsters, but I'll be damned if I know what it is. None of our laws allow for this. Nothing in our system of justice enables us to hunt these people down using whatever means necessary to stop them."

"That's true sir."

"Then maybe we need to re-evaluate how we're going about this whole thing. I never thought I would hear myself say this, but maybe it's time to step on some people's rights for the good of the whole. I hate the whole idea but I just don't see any way to avoid it. These terrorists are using our laws, our justice system and our own decency against us. That's got to stop!"

"I know, sir."

"I do believe we have finally reached the point where the advantage of the law has tipped significantly in the favor of the evildoers. That is not how it's supposed to be nor will it be any longer. We must find a way to stop these fanatics."

"How sir? How do we stop them without trampling all over people's civil rights?"

"As I said, Mark, I don't know if we can avoid infringing on some rights anymore. But I do know that life in this country has, this day, been forever changed. It will never be the same again. Get the National Security Council together. Include the Speaker of the House and both the Majority and Minority leaders of the Senate, as well as the Chief Justice of the Supreme Court. We need to have a powwow and come up with some answers."

"Right away sir!" Gooden left to make it happen.

Nicholson turned back to the television to see a report of three more planes down, one in Little Rock, Arkansas, one in Fresno, California and a second now in Portland, Oregon.

Video of airport after airport, and city after city was being flashed across the television on all channels. Each was a virtual mirror image of the others; twisted metal, burning wreckage and suffocating black acrid smoke as far as the eye could see. He sat down, heartbroken that he, supposedly the most powerful man on the planet, was himself an observer as the most vicious attacks his country and perhaps the world had ever suffered were taking place.

CHAPTER 31

▼

Day Nineteen

Tuesday

As recovery operations continued, emergency workers could only confirm the number of dead would significantly rise; by how much was anybody's guess. Many houses and businesses had been crushed under the weight of the stricken airliners. There was just no way, so soon after the attacks, to accurately calculate the dead. It would likely take days, even weeks before anyone knew for sure, perhaps not even then.

Emergency rooms were packed with crippled, mangled and mutilated bodies of survivors. Many doctors believed it would have been better if some of them had perished in the planes; knowing full well that their quality of life, if they survived, would be about a minus three on a scale of one to ten.

Waiting areas were bursting at the seams with frantic friends and family members hoping, praying for any confirmation that their loved ones were okay. Very few would hear anything that even came close to resembling happy news. Most of the victims that had made it as far as the hospitals still had a long road ahead. Many would be scarred for life having lost arms, legs and even their sight.

Burn units were filled to capacity. Morgue attendants stood nearby with gurneys, having no doubt that their services would soon be needed.

Civilian volunteers were walking back and forth in front of the hospitals armed with rifles, shotguns and even baseball bats, daring anyone to threaten the sacred places of healing.

Sales of caskets and funeral plots were astronomical. Coffin manufacturers were forced to hire more workers. Running three shifts around the clock, one worker commented that it was a macabre way to create new jobs.

*   *   *   *

Muslims, Hispanics and anyone else with an ax to grind were gathering in large numbers outside police departments and city halls all over the nation. All were demanding the authorities protect them. While their pleas were not falling on deaf ears, there was not a whole lot that could be done to accommodate their supplications. Police departments were working their officers overtime, around the clock, in an attempt to head off any more terrorist attacks. The retaliatory acts that were taking place were doing nothing more than complicating things even further. There were simply no available resources to throw at this new problem. Authorities had nearly reached their breaking point and there was nothing more that they could do to restore order.

In Washington DC, things were even worse. Mobs of angry and frightened people marched outside the capitol building and the White House, all making application for the same thing. Bottles, trash and rocks were being thrown over the fence onto the south lawn of the White House, as angry citizens cried out for the government to take action and stop the attacks.

The Secret Service and Capitol Police were willing to stand back and allow trash to be thrown, hoping it would help to disburse the irate crowd's hostility. That all changed when a man started waving a pistol over the heads of the crowd and then pointed it toward the White House. He was quickly taken to the ground and handcuffed by uniformed secret service agents entrusted with protecting the President's home.

The incident prompted the DC police to field riot control squads to break up the unruly mobs. While they failed to disperse the crowds, they did manage to push them back across Constitution Avenue and into the National Mall. Although they continued to rail and wave their fists violently in the air, the only threat they presented now was to one another. And that was an acceptable risk.

In cities across the country terrified people were descending on grocery, sporting and gun stores in greater and greater numbers. Widespread panic had taken a firm hold and citizens were preparing for the worse. As cable news networks televised the hysteria, more and more people joined the rush to stock up. Within a few short hours a mirror image of what had taken place in Redding a little more than a week before, was being duplicated in cities and communities all across the nation.

What was once a peaceful and civilized society was steadfastly deteriorating into one of mass lawlessness. Terrified people were doing whatever they could dream up to protect themselves and their families. County Sheriff's began swearing in new deputies as fast as they could find willing and qualified candidates. Former and retired police officers were walking into local police departments offering their services free of charge. Even with the countless volunteers, the police, for the most part, could barely knock a dent in the madness. In most cases they had no choice but to sit back and watch the unrest continue to spread like the Black Plague, vainly hoping it would soon burn itself out.

CHAPTER 32

▼

Tuesday

President Nicholson was pacing back and forth, wearing a path in the plush blue rug behind his desk in the Oval Office, glancing occasionally at unfolding events on the television. He was dumbfounded that even though the United States was the most powerful nation in the world, he found he could receive more accurate and timely updates through the cable news networks than he could through his own intelligence services.

Scanning through the reports he had been given just moments ago, he learned that thirty-four commercial aircraft had been attacked the day before. Of those, only eight had managed to land safely. The last aircraft to be fired upon went down in a flaming fireball just outside of Springfield, Massachusetts, killing more than one hundred seventy-five, but somehow, God only knows how, thirty-one survived although severely burned. The three remaining aircraft to land safely, and relatively intact, were in Kansas City, Missouri, Syracuse, New York and Peoria, Illinois.

Nicholson turned up the volume so he could hear the reporter, *"Early figures indicate more than four thousand seven hundred have already been confirmed dead from yesterday's attacks. That estimate includes a little over forty-one hundred that were on the planes and close to five hundred others on the ground when the planes were brought down. Those figures do not include unknown thousands that have sustained life-altering injuries or the countless others still missing and presumed dead.*

"Government officials have been very tight lipped concerning where they believe the terrorists may have appropriated the more than fifty missiles they used to target the nearly three-dozen passenger aircraft. Our military advisors have stated emphatically the weapons are Stinger missiles and are equally convinced they must be part of the allotment the United States gave to Afghan freedom-fighters during their war with the Soviets back in the eighties. How they managed to smuggle those weapons onto the US mainland is still a mystery. What is most frightening is what if they have more? And what else do the terrorists have in store for us?"

You said a mouthfull there young lady! Nicholson thought as he lowered the volume. He turned back to his notes and continued to read. The 757 that was brought down in Des Moines had flipped over and went belly up on top of a day-care center and several residential homes, killing fifty-three at last count, not including those on the plane.

All commercial air traffic in the Continental United States (CONUS) had been suspended, indefinitely. Airports were overflowing with stranded travelers, local hotels and motels were filled to capacity and all rental cars had already been snatched up.

Airport personnel, coping as best they could, were scrambling to find ways to get people home. Until then, they were providing those stranded with blankets, pillows and the boxed meals that were no longer needed on the thousands of cancelled flights.

In short order, airport concourses were so completely packed with weary travelers it looked like Wall Street on a busy workday. Frustrated people were bumping and elbowing their way through the disorganized throng looking for someplace that wasn't already congested. The lucky ones found a corner or a service hallway to sleep in, affording them some modicum of privacy.

The wait to get into the restrooms, men's as well as women's, was excruciatingly long. Those that were more opportunistic realized it was indeed the only place they could have some solitude and elected to stay in their stall longer than necessary reading, talking on the phone, and working on laptops until the batteries went dead; all while ignoring the repeated pounding on the door to hurry up. Several violent confrontations ensued as a result.

Power outlets in airports are also limited and this led to more outbreaks of violence as impatient travelers stood in line with dead cell phones and laptops waiting for a charge. Eventually, airport custodians showed up with power strips with multiple outlets; this helped greatly to calm people down.

In many airports, agitated people were taking out their hostility on unfortunate Arab-Americans stranded among them. Although airport security stormed in and quickly restored order, it was decided that it would be better for everyone if Arabs could wait in a segregated area, for their own safety, of course.

City governments and the Red Cross were frantically working to set up shelters to help relieve the overcrowded airports. School buses were ferrying stranded travelers to area schools where they would be temporarily housed until other arrangements could be made.

This all worked for a time, that was until homicide bombers began walking into shelters across the country and blowing themselves up. The result was hundreds more dead and thousands of people taking to the streets, electing to fend for themselves.

As on 9/11, commerce was slowing to a virtual standstill. Americans were choosing to stay home, most glued to their televisions anxiously awaiting the next update, all hoping and praying there was some end to this madness in sight.

Newspaper headlines said it all. The front page of the *Charlotte Observer* proclaimed in big bold red lettering, 'ARMEGEDDON AMERICA!!!' The *Los Angeles Times* declared, 'MELTING POT BOILS OVER!', The *San Francisco Chronicle* announced 'CHICKEN LITTLE'S PROPHESY COMES TRUE', while the *Atlanta Journal Constitution* went to great lengths to lay it all at the feet of the Republicans' continual meddling in the Middle East. One left-wing columnist with the *St. Petersburg Times* in Florida wrote that the vultures of US foreign policy had finally come home to roost, enflaming millions of conservatives.

Through it all, America was hoping to learn their government had a solution to the crisis. That was something even their president would like to know. At present there did not seem to be an answer. Emergency services were being stretched to the breaking point. Even FEMA, the Federal Emergency Management Agency, found they were completely unprepared for the magnitude of the emergency. The number of reprisal attacks against Muslim-Americans, and anyone mistaken for being one, had multiplied ten fold in the past twelve hours. The nation was on the verge of total anarchy; any semblance of order was rapidly disappearing.

Near riots were breaking out nationwide at grocery stores as panicked people scrambled to get their fair share of what was perceived to be a limited supply of food. While this was not the case, try telling that to someone who believed it and was concerned with how they were going to feed their families.

Nicholson had also received reports that in countries throughout the Middle East, Africa, Southeast Asia and Southeastern Europe, angry Muslims were gathered outside US Embassies. The deaths of innocent Muslims in the States from vigilante justice had kindled their anger. Enraged people were hurling rocks, bottles and anything else they could find over the security fences, demanding the US leave their country. Random incidents of gunfire had even taken place.

Rioters were burning American flags in full view of Marines tasked with the responsibility of guarding the American diplomats inside. They had been ordered to exercise restraint and not return fire until told otherwise. Furthermore, if any of the hostiles managed to get through the fence, then they were to be taken into custody and peacefully turned over to the local authorities. There was to be absolutely no use of deadly force.

What's going on? Has the entire world suddenly gone mad? Nicholson pondered. With total anarchy looming on the horizon, and the complete evaporation of American society not far behind it, Nicholson made a decision. He pressed the intercom on his desk, "Get me General Slade on the phone...ASAP!"

A few minutes passed before the intercom buzzed, "General Slade on three sir."

Nicholson snatched the receiver off its cradle, "General?"

"Yes Mr. President?"

"Donovan, where are our carriers?"

"Which ones, sir?"

"All of them."

"Very well, sir. Give me a moment to get that information." A minute later Slade was back on the line. "Are you still there, Mr. President?"

"Yes, proceed."

"The Roosevelt Battle Group is in the Med, the Truman is in the Persian Gulf and the Reagan is currently steaming north from Diego Garcia toward the Indian Ocean. The Enterprise is approaching the Straights of Gibraltar to relieve the Roosevelt in two weeks, and the John Stennis," which is nicknamed Johnnie Reb, "is on station in the South China Sea," Slade paused for a moment, "Oh, and the Carl Vinson is making a port call in Japan."

"What about the ones not on patrol?"

"The Nimitz is conducting workups off the coast of California. The Lincoln is in Pearl Harbor; the Eisenhower is in Newport News on leave while she has a new waist catapult installed. The Washington is in Norfolk preparing to leave in two weeks to relieve the Truman in the Gulf."

"Is that all of them?" Nicholson asked, furiously scribbling down the information.

"No sir, the Kennedy is in Mayport, Florida on leave, Kitty Hawk is about three months from finishing up with her extended refueling and refit, and the George Bush is about eighty percent done with sea trials."

"Okay, I want you to send the Lincoln to the Arabian Sea and direct the Stennis to take up position off the east coast of Africa. Also redeploy the Reagan to the Atlantic off the coast of Morocco. Terminate the Vinson's port call and direct them to stand in relief of the Stennis in the South China Sea." Nicholson thought for a moment, "Instruct the Washington to expedite her transit to the Med and have the Roosevelt remain on station there with the Enterprise."

"Mr. President...that puts seven battle groups within striking distance of the Middle East and North Africa." In fact, that placed more than five hundred combat aircraft in very strategic locations if and when they were needed. The air-power from one carrier, in most cases, exceeded that of most any other countries air force in the world. "That's a lot of punch, sir. What do you have in mind?"

"I don't know just yet. I've got a sneaking suspicion that we're going to need them and I don't want to be sucking hind tit when the time comes. And make sure they have a full war load of weapons and their fuel bunkers are topped off."

"Aye, sir."

"Also, make sure all replenishment ships are fully loaded with Tomahawk missiles so our warships can quickly reload."

"Sir, may I suggest that we allow the Roosevelt to make a port call in Tarragona, Spain when the Enterprise arrives?"

"Why?"

"Well, they've been deployed for more than six months, and if your suspicions are correct, some much needed R&R will definitely help those sailors perform their duties better when the time comes," he explained.

"Very well."

"Anything else, sir?"

"Yes, alert all National Guard Commanders to initiate full call-ups."

"All of them, sir?" Slade asked. *Could he finally be ready to take some serious action?*

"You heard me correctly, General. Things are going to get worse, and it's going to be awhile before it gets any better, if it ever does. Police departments can no longer keep up with the demands put on them. We've got to get them some help. As much as I detest the idea of giving federal troops authority over our people, I don't see as we have a choice any longer."

"Are you going to invoke martial law?"

"I'm still wrestling with that. But I do want all of the pieces in place if it becomes necessary, and that is what I want you to make clear to all commanders to be prepared for.

"Aye, sir."

"Also, instruct all carrier battle groups to be prepared to evacuate our embassies in the entire Middle-Eastern region. All hell is starting to break out over there too and we need to be prepared to get our people to safety."

"Is that all sir?"

"Yes…thank you General."

"You're welcome, Mr. President." Both men hung up the phone at the same time. Slade sat there thinking over the orders he had just received and what they could indicate that the president had in mind. He knew he was not supposed to second-guess his superiors' orders but this was not exactly a wartime president. Everything he knew of Nicholson's past told him the man was a pacifier. He was like water, always taking the path of least resistance, until now, it would seem. The orders he had just received seemed to indicate, on the surface, that the man may have finally grown a pair, if he wasn't just posturing as the last Democratic President had done so many times before.

What's more, he should have taken drastic steps days ago. The foundation of our society is crumbling down around us and he's still trying to negotiate and investigate our way out of the crisis. When will the liberals realize that the only way to ensure a strong America is with a strong military and the political will to employ it when the need arises? Why can't they see that every freedom we hold dear we have because our forerunners fought and died for them? Political correctness is gutting the heart out of this land like a fish and no one seems to have the character or the will to stop it.

Slade believed the president had failed to act decisively because he feared upsetting his voting base. Though he had looked, Slade was unable to locate where it was written in any of the founding documents, or any of the amendments that followed, that American's had a right to not be offended. We have become a nation of childish spineless whiners, where every blame must be assigned, every wrong addressed, and every slight to inflated egos be dealt with. *What ever happened to the saying, 'sometimes stuff just happens?'*

Slade picked up the phone and made the necessary calls to put the President's naval deployments into action. He then summoned one of his aides. "I want all of the tactical plans we have that deal with massive military strikes throughout the Middle East. Include everything from Morocco to Pakistan. The plans should include all strategic targets, and what will be required to take them out, whether that is by sea, air or land attacks. Include what assets we need to move into place to achieve those objectives, as well as the time it will take to get them there."

"Yes sir, right away sir."

"William?"

"Yes sir?"

"Do this all on the QT. I don't want a word of this to get out or you'll be studying the migratory patterns of penguins in the Aleutian Islands...understand?"

"Aye sir!"

"Dismissed."

Slade was not too sure what goals the president really had in mind, but if his suspicions were correct, he was going to do all he could to see that the man achieved them. He reached for the phone and made the necessary calls to alert National Guard commands to mobilize. All that was left to do now was to wait until the president issued the order to institute martial law. *I hope he doesn't wait too much longer,* he thought. A decision had to be made quickly, good or bad, to get things under control. He remembered a quote from General George Patton years ago, "In case of doubt, attack!" The time had now come. *The longer we sit back and do nothing, the more damage will be done and the longer it will take to recover.* He knew the proper course of action would not be popular in some circles, but that was too bad. *It sure beats standing around, arm in arm, singing Kumbaya!*

✳   ✳   ✳   ✳

"Barb, have you spoken with the leaders of the countries where our embassies are under assault?" Nicholson asked the Secretary of State, Barbara Duncan.

"Yes, sir I have,"

"What was their response when you made it clear to them that if our embassies, or our citizens working in their countries were harmed in any way by this mob violence, then the United States Government will be very displeased?"

"Most of them understood and promised to help in any way they could. However, a few wished to know why we are not affording their Arab citizens the same courtesy here in the States."

And what did you tell them?" Nicholson asked.

"I said the two situations are completely different. I reminded them that radical Islamists have attacked our country and we're at war and that sometimes, while unfortunate, innocent people are hurt in times of war."

"And?"

"They still insist that we are just as duty-bound as they are to protect the innocent."

"Fine…if that is their position, ask them if they are comparing the assaults on our embassies in their countries, to the current state of war in our own. And if that is the case, should we instruct our Marine embassy guards and our carrier battle groups to treat their rioting citizens as enemy combatants?"

"Are you sure you want me to get that forceful?"

"You better believe it. We've got enough to worry about without having to deal with a bunch of Mickey Mouse nonsense over there," Nicholson considered his instructions briefly. "Make sure they also understand that if they protect our

people, the United States will take it as a personal favor and will be very grateful."
Diplomatic language for 'you scratch our backs, then we'll scratch yours.'

"Anything else, sir?"

"Yeah, I think we need to advise US citizens living in hostile countries to consider leaving them."

"And where are they to go?"

Nicholson thought for a moment, "Contact the British Prime Minister and see if they can help. Other than that, notify base commanders around the world to expect possibly large numbers of civilian refugees."

"Are you sure, Mr. President?"

"Barbara, we have absolutely no idea what is going on here, and we sure haven't got the foggiest clue of what will happen next. Those people could be in mortal danger. If we don't at least warn them and something happens, their blood will be on our hands."

"I'll see that it's done."

"Also, advise our embassies to be prepared to evacuate on a moments notice. If it becomes necessary, they're not likely to get much of a warning."

"Very well, sir."

"Also, let them know that we have redeployed several carrier battle groups to help aid in any possible evacuations. If they receive any inquiries from their host governments concerning their presence, then that is what they are to say."

"Yes, sir," she said, and then left to carry out her orders.

Nicholson stood there looking out the window. In the distance he could see the angry mobs in the National Mall screaming for justice. Begging for help. Nicholson had to admit that from the beginning of this whole mess he was just not prepared to handle it. He had worked hard to perform his duties to the best of his abilities and had done what he sincerely thought was in the country's best interest. He now knew that he had waited too long to act and thousands were dead as a result. If he had acted sooner could lives have been saved? Possibly. But, now he'd never know.

His advisors kept telling him no one could have predicted what was taking place; that there was noting he could have done. He believed they were just trying to cover their butts. The truth of the matter is it should have been predicted. That is what the American people who sacrifice over forty percent of their income in taxes expect to happen. Nicholson believed that if someone could plan these attacks, then surely someone in the government should have seen it coming. But that was now all water under the bridge.

Regardless of what could have or should have been done, the reality was that the terrorists were hitting everywhere and it was simply overwhelming. Homes, hospitals, churches, airplanes and theaters. Now even emergency shelters were being targeted. It was plainly clear that whoever had orchestrated these attacks was intent on leaving the American people with no safe harbor, and none of the conventional methods for dealing with terrorists was proving effective.

Well that was going to change. It had to. *If conventional means won't work, then we'll try something unconventional. One way or the other I'm going to put a stop to this crap!* The phone rang and Nicholson sat down to answer it.

"Sir, the construction company CEOs are gathered in the conference room."

"Very well, inform them I'll be there in a couple minutes," Nicholson said and hung up. *Well, Mr. O'reilly let's see if you're as smart as you think you are!*

CHAPTER 33

▼

Tuesday

Mariska Jabril and her compatriots in the Washington State-registered Chevy Suburban were driving south from Vancouver. They crossed the US/Canadian border using fake identifications and the cover-story they were all returning from a two week camping expedition in the Canadian wilderness; hopefully a week of no shaving, on the men's part, would help to sell their lie. The border patrol agent took their ID's and went to check them against a terrorist watch list. Several minutes later he returned, looked in the back of the Suburban and then inspected the luggage rack on top. The tremendous amount of camping gear, carefully soiled with leaves and twigs, evidently convinced him to let them proceed. *It's still all so easy,* Mariska thought.

Maintaining sixty-five miles per hour on Interstate Five, they arrived in Seattle in a little under three hours. Mariska had taken her time to ensure that they were not stopped for any traffic violations. They made their way past the turnoff for the Seattle/Tacoma International Airport and a short while later stopped in Star Lake, easily locating the first storage facility on the list.

Checking the notes Mariska had made, they easily found Section T, row H and unit X-1138. Opening the combination lock, they inspected the Suburban and trailer inside the large storage unit. They could detect no signs of any tampering and the vehicle started easily. The group carefully inspected the contents of the trailer and within thirty minutes they were satisfied all was in order and were again heading south on the interstate.

They drove for another two hours before arriving in Long View, Washington where they ate a quick meal at the Burger King, fueled up at a nearby convenience store, grabbed drinks and snacks, and then made the short trip to the next storage facility on the list.

Forty-five minutes later they were again on the road driving south, this time in three vehicles, two of them pulling trailers.

*   *   *   *

In Johnson City, Tennessee, a man and his wife walked into the hospital emergency room complaining of severe flu-like symptoms and high fever. They had been convinced that it was nothing worse than a bad case of the flu, until the man's wife noticed sores on her stomach. When she went to show them to her husband she found a similar one on his forehead near the hairline. Twenty minutes later they arrived at the medical center.

Shortly thereafter, a young doctor tentatively diagnosed them as being infected with anthrax. He elected to not immediately tell them what he suspected was wrong, only that he'd like to admit them for further testing. He didn't see the sense in starting an unnecessary panic. The country already had enough to be worried about. The patients were placed in a private room and immediately started on a round of the antibiotic, ciprofloxacin (Cipro), for what was described to them as a mild seasonal viral infection.

The young Algerian doctor immediately reported his findings to the Center for Disease Control in Atlanta. He hoped his diagnosis was incorrect, but the symptoms told him it wasn't. He had done what he could for the unfortunate patients; the rest was up to Allah. Surely he would show them mercy; they seemed like very nice people.

The doctor sat down in the physicians lounge to start filling out the necessary paperwork. Although he was quite concerned for his patients, he was more concerned with how they had come to be infected in the first place. One does not catch Anthrax through casual contact with others and there is no 'Anthrax Season'. Someone had intentionally infected these people and he hoped he was wrong about who was responsible. He prayed that it was not another of his misguided Muslim brothers who had perpetrated this terrible deed. His people had already suffered enough persecution for the acts of a few radicals and this would no doubt amplify it even more.

*   *   *   *

The Centers for Disease Control, more affectionately known as the CDC, is an agency of the United States Department of Health and Human Services. The CDC, founded in 1946, was originally tasked with the responsibility of fighting malaria and other contagious diseases. As time went by its scope changed to include smallpox, polio and a wealth of other maladies.

Today it is recognized as one of the top health research institutes in the world, dealing with everything from flu epidemics and heart disease, to infectious diseases like Ebola, Dengue Fever and bioterrorism agents. When a severe health crisis develops anywhere in the world, the CDC is one of the first places troubled doctors call for help.

The Director of the CDC, Doctor Samantha L. Murphy was receiving reports of anthrax cases from several different cities across the country. In ones and twos, they were being reported in Salem, Oregon, Savannah, Georgia and Tallahassee, Florida. By four o'clock she already had confirmations of thirty-seven cases, including five from Tupelo, Mississippi. Something about the locations was tickling her memory but she couldn't seem to place her finger on it.

An aide walked in at 5:30 and handed her a report detailing seven more cases in Kalamazoo, Michigan and Albuquerque and four in Tallahassee. It took another forty minutes before the answer came to her. "That's it!" she exclaimed.

Her secretary peeked his head into the office; "Doctor Murphy…is everything okay?"

"Yes, and no, Matthew," she replied. "Get me a list of the cities where the theater bombings took place, will you please?"

"Sure, I think I still have a copy of yesterday's newspaper." Matthew stepped out to his desk and returned seconds later with the front section of the *USA Today*. "Here you are."

"Thank you." Dr. Murphy spread the periodical out on her desk and started scanning through articles, quickly finding one re-telling the events of the past Friday. It took only a moment to verify that so far all of the cities that were reporting anthrax cases were also on the list of theater bombings. *Coincidence? Not likely! Those bastards put anthrax in the bombs!* Murphy thought. *What will they do next? This has got to stop, no matter what it takes.* She looked up to see Matthew place a document on her desk alerting her to twenty-six more cases, and the first ones in Lexington, Kentucky, Omaha, Nebraska and Norfolk, Virginia.

Thirty minutes later an alert was put out to all of the hospitals in and around the affected cities to expect new cases of anthrax poisoning. Within the hour, the CDC was receiving updates of dozens of cases in smaller towns surrounding those that had already been alerted.

*   *   *   *

By six-thirty in the afternoon the caravan of three Suburbans had traveled as far as Portland, Oregon. They took exit 299-A, turned left on Powell Blvd. and arrived at the Motel Six, near Thirty-Second Street. They parked the vehicles in the back, as far away from the front entrance and the street as possible. Mariska went in and paid cash for three rooms, requesting that they be at the back of the building on the first floor if at all possible.

Mariska verified the directions to the next storage facility and they all piled into one of the vehicles. When they arrived, they found the gates locked and the office closed for business until the next morning.

Dinner was purchased from a nearby Kentucky Fried Chicken and Mariska asked the cashier for directions to a local park. They easily located Kenilworth Park, found a table and sat down to eat their dinner. Under the faint light from a nearby pole they discussed the remainder of their mission. Only Mariska and one of the other men had so far been allowed to know all the details, just in case by some chance one of them were captured by the authorities.

"How many more stops do we have to make?" asked Qasim, impatiently.

"Four more before we have what we need to complete our mission," Najjar replied.

"And how much further do we have to go?" asked Hassan.

Mariska set down her chicken and wiped her mouth with a napkin, "Several hundred miles; we should be there and ready to go sometime the day after tomorrow," she answered.

"I want to know exactly what we will be doing?" demanded Mansur. "I think we all have a right to know."

Mariska looked at him coldly, "Mansur, when it is time for you to know, then I will tell you, and not until then. Rest assured that you will be part of a glorious event and Allah will richly reward you for your sacrifice. After we have completed our mission, these infidels will cower under their blankets at night, shaking and begging Allah for his mercy. For now that is all you need to know."

*   *   *   *

Dr. Murphy was still at her desk at ten-thirty that night. There were now two hundred and seventy-eight cases and the first confirmed fatality. An eleven-year old boy went into respiratory arrest in Kalamazoo, within the hour he was dead.

While anthrax could not normally be spread from one person to the next, this is not the case if a weaponized version of the bacteria was employed. Therefore, an alert was just about to be released directing everyone within a hundred-mile radius of the affected cities to stay home. This directive would stay in effect until it was determined exactly what form of the deadly bacteria was actually utilized, and what could be done to halt the rapidly spreading epidemic.

*   *   *   *

The marvel of satellite television is that information travels around the world so quickly, nearly everyone hears the latest breaking news at the same time world-wide. That was even the case on a small island in the Aegean Sea.

The billionaire sat watching the report that a medical quarantine had just been put into effect in several of America's cities. He smiled and set aside the bowl of popcorn he had been munching on while watching. His chest swelled with pride, the plan he had initiated so many years ago was working out perfectly.

For years he had been plotting the demise of the United States and Israel, even before his clandestine meeting with other Arab leaders back in 1988. He had to admit that even he had gotten a little nervous when his brothers, who had carried out the attacks in Munich in 1972, started turning up dead. For a while there he was concerned that Golda Meir's tenacious assassins may one day come knocking on the door to his little island paradise here in the Aegean Sea. Luckily the Israel-ites had never connected the vicious attacks to their mastermind.

He had no real concerns about dying. Everyone started to die from the moment they drew their first breath. Death was the one known absolute in this life. What wasn't known was the manner in which one would meet that death. He knew that when the fateful day arrived, he would finally be in Paradise. What did frighten him was that he might meet his end before accomplishing what Allah had put him on this planet to do.

He had inherited his money from his rich father who was one of the wealthiest oil sheiks in the world, before his untimely death. The fact that his father had willed him more than twenty-five billion dollars was a complete mystery to the world. Equally mysterious was his very existence at all.

He was born to one of his father's many mistresses in secrecy and then whisked away in the dark of night to begin the long and arduous journey to where he was now. He never saw his mother again. He was never allowed to play or interact with other children. To this day he couldn't even ride a bike. His every waking moment had been devoted to molding him into what he was to become; Allah's perfect weapon. He was schooled and trained to accomplish one very important purpose with his life, destroy America. In fact, he would later learn that his birth itself was deliberately and carefully orchestrated for this very reason.

Fluent in seven languages, he spent years working in the shadows. Using his financial power, he coerced and manipulated terrorist groups and even heads of state to do his bidding. He invested his money wisely and his fortune had more than doubled.

If the Western world knew what he had orchestrated through the years, he had no doubt that his little island would have been swept from the face of the earth by America's most powerful weapons. In fact, the great leaders of the Muslim world knew nothing of his existence until he greeted them at his island fortress more than twenty years ago. Even now they only knew what he told them, or allowed them to find out. They could never know that the man behind their covert coalition was a bastard.

To protect the sanctity of the family the Koran forbids premarital sex. Not only to ensure proper lineage is clearly defined, but also so no one unknowingly marries his or her half-sibling somewhere down the road corrupting the bloodline. According to the Koran anyone found guilty of fornication must receive one hundred public lashes for their sin; although proving fornication is quite difficult. Four eyewitnesses must testify to having witnessed the actual deed before punishment can be administered. Therefore the lashes served more as a deterrent than as likely punishment. No, it would be better to keep his origins private. All they needed to know was that he was placed here by Allah to lead them in this most wonderful undertaking.

Through the years, the billionaire had masterminded many of the most well known terrorists attacks carried out in the modern world. He had provided financial might to the terrorist group Black September so they could carry out numerous attacks around the world. He had aided, on numerous occasions, Ilich Ramirez Sanchez, better known as Carlos the Jackal. He even pulled the strings of the German terrorist unit the Baader-Meinhoff Gang, a front group for the liberation of Palestine and had collaborated in the bombing of Pan AM flight 103 over Lockerbie, Scotland in nineteen eighty-eight which killed two hundred and seventy people.

His scheming knew no bounds. He knew that to ultimately bring down America, her forces would have to be so spread out that she could not effectively deal with a serious threat to her homeland. Americans knew that Osama bin-Laden was responsible for the attacks of 9/11. What they didn't know was how that information had found its way so quickly into the hands of the American authorities. He wasn't proud of the fact that he had set nearly the entire world after his loyal brother, Osama, but it was a necessary evil if the US was to be coerced into a war with the Taliban.

Then came Saddam Hussein. The world still didn't know his true reason for invading Kuwait and they had no idea that he had long ago complied with the UN resolutions and disposed of his WMD's, and that was the plan all along. He had to keep America, and the world, believing he still had them or they might not have invaded Iraq; and that had to happen as well. To ignite true Jihad with the West, the Islamic world needed an effective catalyst to stir up believers in every Muslim country and bring them against the US with all their fury. But after the US invaded, they couldn't be allowed to find what they came looking for. What better way to sew discord amongst the American people than to have them believe their own leaders had misled them into war?

As a result, the United States was now engaged in a war in three Arab countries and she had more than half a million troops and support personnel on the ground in those countries. America was politically split down the middle and the waters had been so muddied that no one knew the truth. Every day more and more faithful Muslims were flooding into Syria and Iraq with one clear purpose in mind; keep the Americans in the Middle East and thereby weaken her capabilities at home.

The plan had worked perfectly. Well almost perfectly. The one glaring exception was the unexpected capture of Saddam. Who knew that the Americans would take Baghdad so quickly? Saddam was supposed to have had more time to escape. The billionaire's agreement with the dictator, hatched back in 1988 in a private meeting, was to eventually bring him here to the island where he would live out his days in luxury. Unfortunately that didn't work out so well. *How humiliating to be found cowering in a hole,* he thought.

The American government had no idea that she had been manipulated so slyly. Like a game of chess, every move had several possible counter-moves. What an unfair advantage to be able to anticipate the moves your opponent will make before he makes them.

The billionaire was a dangerous man to have as a friend and even more fearsome as an enemy. His planning had been meticulous. He had taken into account every contingency, even making it possible for the US authorities and her allies to break up specifically designated cells, from time to time, so they would continue to believe their pathetic war against terrorism was working.

Sure, some points or elements of the operation had to be adjusted occasionally, or even completely altered to maintain overall success and secrecy, but the heart of his scheme had held strong. Soon the fat and spoiled American infidels would learn what it truly meant to live in fear.

Throughout the ages kingdoms have risen and fallen, and the rise to power always takes longer than the collapse. Over time those within the empire begin to believe that they are special; that their *goodness* will protect them. When one is king of the hill for so long, one starts to believe they cannot be knocked down. But every dog would have his day. And so shall the Americans.

CHAPTER 34

▼

Day Twenty

Wednesday

The United States Border Patrol is nothing more than a relatively small number of valiant people tasked with protecting America's vast borders. They vainly attempt to do their job with far fewer government-funded resources than any other comparable service in the entire world. Yet, even with this, they are expected to guard both the northern and southern borders of the United States, which covers more than seven thousand land miles and two thousand coastal miles. Whether in scorching desert heat, freezing artic weather or on the high seas, they stand at the ready, courageously protecting the country, America's homes, and America's families from those that would do the US harm.

Each and every day, border agents battle to stem the ongoing flow of illegal immigrants, over eight thousand per day, and drugs making their way onto US soil. And everyday that challenge gets more difficult. From the *coyotes* sneaking in the illegals, to the traffickers smuggling in tons of heroin and cocaine by whatever means they can dream up, the Border Patrol is slowly but surely losing the war; contrary to what the government spin machine may claim.

Although they are undermanned and underpaid, they still fight the good fight. Each day they come to work and make sacrifices that may one day cost them their lives. In the history of the US Border Patrol, more than one thousand agents have been either killed or wounded in their gallant attempt to protect America.

Officer Brad Oliver had been with the United States Border Patrol going on sixteen years. During that time he saw the massive numbers of illegal aliens pouring across the southern border of the United States virtually unchecked. Oh sure, the government and the media were very good at telling the American people the problem was not nearly as bleak as some reported it to be. In fact, the government had even boosted the number of border patrol agents in the years following the events of 9/11. However, that had been nothing more than window-dressing for a weary and frightened American public.

Added agents had definitely helped with controlling border crossings in and around official border checkpoints, but it did little to curb the inflow of illegals electing to circumvent the checkpoints and cross over by making their way through the deserts.

Oliver knew the Director of the Border Patrol personally and he had firsthand knowledge that the Director had requested, a number of times, the military be used to fortify the borders. His requests were met with a resounding 'no' each and every time. No one in Washington was willing to risk the political ramifications they would suffer from all the special interest groups as a result. Not a single politician was willing to sacrifice a single Hispanic vote just to stop 'a few migrant workers' from coming into the country.

If it were just migrant workers, then that would be perfectly fine, Oliver thought. Even though officially it was his job to prevent them from getting in, he knew they served a vital role in the economy. Many of his fellow Americans spoke out loudly against them being here, but he knew without them the financial stability would rapidly stagnate and crumble, worse than it already was.

But migrant workers were not the only ones coming across. Illegal drugs were coming in by the thousands of tons and that was only one of the problems. Who really knew how many terrorists had been able to gain access through porous borders? Worse yet, who was to know what they were bringing with them? Oliver was convinced that if America did not close the gaping holes in her borders immediately and exercise more control over who was allowed to enter, then America was in for more trouble than she had seen so far, a lot more.

Oliver's shift started at 0800 and what he saw when he arrived at headquarters in San Ysidro left him stunned. The sheer number of people crossing the border this morning topped anything he had seen so far in his career. Cars and pedestrians were backed up as far as the eye could see. Vehicles were packed so tightly that people were actually riding on top of them, evidently so that they could cram as many of their worldly possessions as possible inside them. Beds of pickups were so full that people were standing on the rear bumpers. People without cars were pulling wagons, pushing shopping carts and using whatever conveyance they could find to take along their belongings. However, the most amazing thing was that they weren't coming into the United States; they were all crossing the border back into Mexico. The great escape was under way.

Oliver approached another agent and asked what was going on.

"Morning Brad," Officer Libby King, said. "Best we can determine is they're all scared to death."

"Sure...I understand that. But surely not everyone is running away."

"Apparently six Mexicans were killed while they slept in their beds last night in Riverside, as well as a slew of others across the country. Vigilantes are striking out at anyone they think might be a terrorist and it would seem that the common denominator is skin color."

"Yeah, I heard that was happening. Not only have quite a few been killed, but scores more have also been viciously attacked." Pointing toward the checkpoint, "Evidently those people truly believe they're running for their lives."

"Can you blame them?" King asked.

"Not one bit. Things have gone absolutely crazy. These terrorists are sure giving this country a bloody nose. The problem is, from what I'm hearing through a friend of mine at Homeland Security, the government is clueless about what to do about it."

"I've got an idea…let's round them all up and send them back home."

"That's not likely to happen, Libby. The American people wouldn't stand for that."

"Three weeks ago I would have agreed with you…now I'm not so sure. When you scare people like our people are scared right now, you'd be surprised what they'd agree to."

"You just may have a point there," Oliver said.

"Tell you what…if we did send them all packing, it would sure eliminate the problem of trying to figure out which ones are bad and which ones are not."

"So…how long have they been lined up like this?" Oliver asked, abruptly changing the subject.

"Since just before sun up. What's more, they're lined up at every border crossing between here and Brownsville, and more are on the way."

They both stood there for a couple minutes watching thousands of Mexicans, many of them American citizens, pushing their way across the border to 'safety'.

"The Mexican authorities tried to stop them from coming home at first," Libby said.

"What?"

"Kept claiming they couldn't absorb that many people at one time."

"Poor babies. I see they changed their mind."

"You bet they did! The State Department actually proved they could get things done when they want to."

"I never thought I'd see the day Mexico would have an immigration problem."

"Ironic, isn't it? After years of refusing to help us manage the problem, now their indifference is biting them in the butt!" Libby snickered. "Let's see how they like it now that the shoe is on the other foot!"

"You know, even after 9/11, I always imagined when we were attacked again it would be in the big cities," Oliver said.

"I'm pretty sure that is what most people believed. We all thought New York, Los Angeles or Chicago were the most obvious targets"

"There also seemed to be a mindset, almost a sort of comfort, that if the big cities became unsafe we could just leave them and go where it was safe."

"Yeah, Middle America. The problem is that's just where the terrorists are striking," King said. "So where do people go now? There doesn't seem to be any place that's safe."

They both looked back toward the border and the long lines that seemed to grow with each passing minute. They saw the looks of fear, despair and utter hopelessness, both of them wondering if their country would ever be the beacon of freedom, opportunity and hope to the world that it had once been. Libby King's heart sank knowing that somehow it wouldn't.

Within days, America would awake to yet another threat to her once thriving economy. Officer Oliver's belief that migrant workers were vital to a healthy economy would be proven accurate. The mass exodus of Mexican workers back across the border left many US industries without sufficient labor to conduct business. Landscapers, painters and building contractors came to work to find they had few or no laborers. Restaurants found themselves short of cooks, dish-washers and busboys. Hotels and motels were attempting to do business without a full housecleaning staff and the farmers that were lucky enough to still be in business had no field hands to work their crops. The list went on and on. One thing was certain, people's sense of security had better be restored quickly or the United States would be looking at a fate worse than it had during the Great Depression.

*   *   *   *

After retrieving another vehicle from a storage unit in Portland, and grabbing breakfast at an IHOP, the growing caravan of four vehicles was once again travel-ing south on Interstate Five. Three of them were now pulling trailers and all were painted exactly the same. It was quite a sight to see them rolling single file down the interstate. *What better place to hide than in plain sight,* Mariska thought. Just two more stops and then on to the final objective.

*   *   *   *

Nearly four hundred miles away five men were surprised it had taken the better part of seven weeks to accomplish their task. It had taken so long because they couldn't take the risk of being spotted. At times an innocent bystander would walk by, no doubt unaware dangerous men were lurking in the shadows above them. Nevertheless, their mission was much too imperative to take any chances, so they would simply postpone what they were doing and wait for another opportunity.

Occasionally while they were working, a police car would happen by making it far too dangerous to proceed. In fact, one night an officer had even stopped and looked over their vehicle parked along the side of the road with a white rag hanging out of the window. He slipped a red tag under the windshield wiper and drove away. After he left, they waited several minutes ensuring he didn't return, and then they climbed down and read the tag informing them they had five days to remove the vehicle or it would be towed away at owner's expense.

In light of the repeated delays, tonight they had finally positioned the remaining package on the last of the six structures that been assigned to them. Although it had taken great effort to accomplish, each one now had more than three hundred pounds of C-4 plastic explosives attached to them at critical locations. They realized it was probably overkill, but success must be assured. When the time came to detonate the charges, the men knew that they had placed more than enough explosives on the structures to bring them down. They coiled up their ropes and other equipment and climbed into their van. Within an hour the men had all returned to their respective homes and families, who had no idea what their true identities were or what evil deeds they had been up to.

CHAPTER 35

▼

Wednesday

"Sir, there are now more than seven hundred confirmed cases of anthrax," Mark Gooden said, updating the president. "Seventeen people have already died and the CDC has informed us they believe the cases may have resulted from a weaponized version of the bacteria."

"What are they recommending?" Nicholson asked.

"They said the quarantines should remain in effect until they have a confirmation one way or the other."

"Very well. Do they have an estimate of about how long that may take?"

"Perhaps by noon tomorrow."

"Have they had any luck containing the spread of the virus?"

"Some…but it will be a couple more days before they know anything definitive. Until then, they are strongly considering expanding the quarantine zone around each contaminated area by another fifty miles."

"Tell the CDC to do whatever they have to do to contain this. On that note, do we have enough antibiotics on hand to treat everyone infected?"

"Yes…we believe so. Ever since the scares after 9/11 the CDC has kept a large supply on hand. Also the pharmaceutical companies are ramping up production just in case."

"So, it's a wait and see game?"

"Yes sir."

"What else?"

"We've taken the first steps toward getting Minetti's bracelet idea going forward."

"And?"

"Well…we've had several trusted senators and house members contact spiritual leaders within the Muslim community requesting their support during this crisis."

"And what was their response?" Nicholson asked, taking a drink of his Coke.

"Less than positive, just as we expected it would be. In fact, I would say, from what I was told, they were downright hostile to the entire idea. The Muslim clerics wouldn't even consider presenting the proposal to their people. They categorized it as downright discriminatory, hateful and strongly urged us to abandon the entire idea."

"Our people did make it clear to them that the bracelets may very well be the only way to defuse the situation, catch the bad guys and restore order?"

"Yes sir, they did."

"And it was explained to them it would also aid in the protection of innocent Muslims as well?"

"It was."

"I also assume it was made abundantly clear if they refused to help, it could very well leave us no other choice than to force them to submit?"

Gooden nodded.

"And even knowing it was the only method at our disposal to prevent further loss of innocent lives, they still refused?"

"Even then sir. They also said if we pursue this, they would have no choice but to implore their people to resist."

"They wouldn't dare!"

"I believe they would sir, it's a matter of principle to them."

"Principle? What could be more principled than saving human lives?"

"They asked why we were not advocating the entire population wear them, instead of just Arabs?"

"Because it's Arabs that are blowing the hell out of everything!" Nicholson thundered.

"They said they've been shown no proof to support that conclusion."

"Give me a break! If they don't believe it's Arabs doing all this, then they're the only people on the planet that don't."

"I understand that, sir. One cleric went as far as to inform us that we would just have to figure out another way and that if we insisted on this particular course of action, it would leave them no other recourse than to appeal to their home countries to request any further oil exports to America be suspended."

"That would destroy their economies even quicker than ours. They need our cash as much as we need their oil."

"Not likely sir, the Dow is in a nosedive. It's fallen more than thirty percent since the first attacks in Redding and doesn't show any signs of leveling out.

"Tell me something I don't already know! I'm quite aware of the current economic crisis, Mark!" What neither man bothered to mention was, in all likelihood Middle Eastern oil would soon find its way to China. Over the past twenty years the nation of nearly a billion and half people had been steadily relying more and more on petroleum. The Chinese consumer was gradually giving up their bicycles and replacing them with gas-guzzling automobiles. That, coupled with the huge demand by China's ever-increasing military machine left no doubt that OPEC would have little trouble finding buyers for its vast supplies of liquid gold.

Was the President starting to break under the pressure? Gooden took a deep breath before continuing, "Sir, I know you are, however, the economy is in the toilet and it's about to be flushed if we don't do something fast."

"I know…I know," Nicholson mumbled. "Have we got any leads? Any hopes of catching the terrorists before they strike again?" already knowing the answer.

"You know we don't sir, but if we tell that to the American people it's over, game, set and match. Our entire infrastructure, our society and what's left of our already anemic economy will collapse under the stress," Gooden cautioned.

Nicholson turned toward General Slade, who had been sitting quietly off to the side until he was spoken to, "What can we do to protect our airports, General?"

"Not much of anything sir."

"Don't tell me that, it's not what I want to hear! If we can't fly our planes, were finished!"

"Yes sir. But until we can root these maggots out, there's just not a whole lot we can do."

"What if we place troops around all of the airports?"

"Not feasible."

"What do you mean, not feasible? Don't tell me it's not feasible. It's you're job to make it feasible, for grief's sake!"

"Sir, to protect just the twenty-five largest airports alone would be a nightmare."

"Worse than the one we're already living through?"

Picking a random number out of thin air to make his point, "You're talking about a bare minimum of five thousand soldiers and Marines per airport."

"Why so many?" Gooden asked sounding shocked.

"The Stinger has a range of nearly two miles. We'd have to secure every home, business, outhouse and doghouse for two miles in every direction of each airport you want protected."

"It can be done, it's not impossible," Gooden insisted.

"Okay, now assume that the terrorists decide to change tactics and work outside the two mile range. They can sit four even five miles away and just wait for an unsuspecting plane to fly over."

"I thought you said they only had a range of two miles?" Nicholson asked.

"In every direction, sir. In every direction, including up."

"Can't we station those Patriot missiles at the airports? They have a lot further range, don't they?"

"Yes they do, but it still won't do any good."

"Why not? I thought they were supposed to be able to shoot down enemy missiles, they worked pretty well against Iraqi SCUDS in the first Gulf War back in '91?" Gooden questioned.

"They can shoot down missiles, but not the Stingers the terrorists have been using. The Patriot is designed to engage medium and long-range ballistic missiles, not short-range shoulder-fired ones."

"But still…why couldn't they work? Why can't we at least try?" the president asked, desperate to come up with something that might give them hope.

"Because the Patriot is designed to arm in approximately nine seconds…by that time the Stinger has already closed with the target and it's too late."

"Why *not*? Why did we spend billions of tax-payer dollars on the blessed things if we can't use them when needed?"

"Mr. President…the Stinger was designed to engage combat aircraft, not commercial airliners. Most military aircraft are equipped with some sort of countermeasure like chaff and flares to distract the missile, giving the endangered aircraft time to take evasive action and escape. When it was developed for the US military, I don't think the designers envisioned it would be used against civilian targets."

"What about radar guided machine guns like we have on our naval ships…why wouldn't those work?"

"Radar guided machine guns, sir?" Slade asked, a bit confused.

"You know…those little white dome-looking things that resemble R2-D2 from Star Wars," he clarified.

"Oh, you mean the Mark 15 Close in Weapons Systems." The CIWS, pronounced "sea-whiz", is a rapid-fire 20-millimeter gun system that provides US Navy ships with a final layer of defense designed to engage anti-ship cruise missiles and fixed-wing aircraft at short range, which have penetrated other fleet defenses. CIWS automatically performs search, detecting, tracking, threat evaluation, firing, and kill assessments of targets. The fire control assembly is composed of a search radar for surveillance and detection of hostile targets, and a separate radar for aiming the gun while tracking a target. The gun subsystem employs a Gatling Gun consisting of a rotating cluster of six barrels. The Gatling Gun fires 20mm ammunition at either 3,000 or 4,500 rounds-per-minute. CIWS has been one of the main self-defense systems aboard nearly every class of ship since the late 70's.

"Yeah, that one. Let's use it."

Slade was one salty soldier who was very close to losing his military bearing. For the life of him he couldn't figure out why the American people continually elected men as their Commander in Chief, who had absolutely no military background or at least some cursory knowledge of how the military operates and its capabilities. Would anyone consider letting Donald Trump perform his or her brain surgery? Not in a million years, but they'd put a guy with no military training in command of the most powerful military to ever exist on the face of the planet without a second thought. Each and every time the nation faced a crisis, the military wasted precious time explaining the most mundane of things to them because they wouldn't even take the time to educate themselves when they took office. *This guy's a train wreck looking for a place to happen!*

"First of all, there is just not enough time for the radar to locate, lock on, fire and strike the missile before it hits an aircraft. Secondly, these guns fire a twenty millimeter round, and hundreds of them would have to be fired to have any hope of successfully shooting down a missile. And that's only if by some act of God the radar can solve the first problem. Then the question is, where do all of the hundreds of rounds that miss end up? How much damage do we end up inflicting on innocents miles away as a result? Sir, they just won't work."

"So, we either continue to keep all commercial aircraft on the ground and watch the destruction of our economy, or we let them fly and hope to God above the terrorists don't have anymore missiles? Does that about sum it up, General?" Nicholson asked, sharply.

"Yes sir...that's about it."

"Well gee...why don't we just pull down the American flag flying over this building and run up a white one. Are you telling me the most powerful military in the world is impotent against a bunch of desert-trained, tent-dwelling savages?"

"No sir...I'm not!" Slade said, with an edge to his voice. "If the intelligence services can get us some viable targets we'll end this thing. The military has been advising all-knowing politicians for years that something like this could happen. We've been begging and pleading for the necessary resources to protect this country properly and have been ignored at every turn. We've been yelling that we're vulnerable…but the Washington elite are more concerned with getting reelected, investigating steroid use by athletes, going on fact-finding missions to Tahiti and attending five hundred dollar a plate dinners than they are about doing what's best for the country."

"Watch your tone, General," the president cautioned.

"No sir…this has to be said. There used to be a time that strong, loyal and patriotic men and women left their homes, jobs and businesses to come to Washington and serve for the good of the country, and after a time they'd return to their normal lives. But not anymore…now it's nothing more than a power grab. The framers of the Constitution never intended for political service to be a life-long appointment. But nowadays, once a politician gets to Washington, their butts grow roots so deep you can't dig them out with a backhoe. It's time you, and everyone like you, quit trying to do the politically correct thing and start doing the right thing. Quit pandering to special interest groups and start serving the people."

"General, you're treading on thin ice…"

"Then fire me…but some one has to stand up for what's right and proper! Most Americans could care less about the motivations of special interest groups. The great majority just wants to work and safely raise their families. If by some chance there's enough money at the end of the week, then maybe they'll all go to a movie and get a pizza. Now they can't even do that. And why…because we have all failed to do the job they pay us to do…"

"General…"

"We need to be reminded we don't work for the special interest groups, we work for the guy who pushes a hot dog cart down the streets of Manhattan every day, and the kid who mows your grass once a week in the summer," Slade paused for long moment. "Mr. President, I mean no disrespect, but you took an oath to protect and defend the Constitution of the United States; in other words, to protect the citizens of *this* country, not the citizens of *every* other country in the world. That responsibility lies with *their* leaders and if *their* leaders are failing in *their* jobs, then *those people* need to rise up like *our* forefathers did and demand things change."

The President looked at Slade for a long time before speaking, "What do you propose, General?"

"It's time to enforce the laws that are on the books. The people that are here killing our citizens are more than likely here illegally and they need to be removed."

"What do you mean, *removed?*" Gooden interjected.

Slade turned sharply toward Gooden. "I mean round them up and ship them home. There are legal ways to come to this country...so kick them out and let them start over...the right way."

"We can't just kick millions of people out of the country," Gooden said.

"And why not?" Slade responded. "We have laws that say we can, and what's more, we're supposed to."

"But the special interest groups would..."

"If you say the special interest groups would crucify us, I'm gonna' pop your head like a pimple...you hear me?" Slade warned Gooden. "That's the very attitude that's ruining this nation. The law says, with a few exceptions, if someone comes into the US illegally, then they're supposed to be deported...period...end of story, Mark!"

"Yeah, but..."

"That's just it, there is no *but*. There are no buts in the law. There's also nothing in the law about doing what's considered popular at the time. If you don't like the law then change it...until then, enforce it. That's our job...that's what we all took an oath to do, and that's what the American people believe they're paying us to do."

"And what about the ones who are here legally? Surely with the way they've managed to hide themselves, many of the terrorists have to be here legally," Nicholson observed.

"So what if they are here legally? Then they did so with less than honorable intentions."

"What's that supposed to mean?" Gooden asked.

"When they took the oath of citizenship, if that's what they did, they took an oath to denounce any loyalty to their countries of origin, and to even bear arms in the defense of the US, if asked to. The two common denominators that virtually all terrorists have worldwide, and I've said it before, is that they're Arab and they're Muslim. Those are the facts and simply because we're uncomfortable with it and don't want to say it publicly doesn't change it," Slade lectured. "If they're here on work or student visas, then lump them in with the illegals. We must start the entire immigration process all over from scratch, because there is no other way to be sure of who is here, and where they're at."

"But if they're here legally...how do we identify the ones who are less than loyal to the country? Okay sure...we kick out all the illegal Arabs..."

"Not just the Arabs, Mr. President...*all* illegals. If we're going to do this, then let's start over completely and do it right this time."

"I don't know if I would be comfortable going that far, General."

"This is not about your comfort level, or anyone else for that matter. It's about the survival of the country. This opportunity may never again repeat itself. Now is the time to completely overhaul and correct our immigration problems. I assure you the vast majority of the American citizens will support you. And not only can you put an end to the current calamity taking place, but you could also lay the groundwork to ensure the nation's security for decades to come."

"But back to my question…how do we identify the loyal Arabs from the others? It's not like they're running around with a sign on their heads saying 'kill all Americans'."

"Are you sure about that, Mr. President?" Slade asked.

"What do you mean?"

"Well, sir, we've asked the Muslim population to help us identify the terrorists by wearing a simple little bracelet. We've assured them it would only be used in the case of another terrorist incident, and then, only the GPS signatures in the vicinity of the attack would be investigated, they adamantly refused."

"That is their right, General," Gooden stated.

"Is it? Thousands of Americans are dying and you can rest assured more are on the way. The Muslim leadership has an opportunity to help us stop that, or at the very least, help us eliminate thousands of suspects so that we can concentrate on the bad guys. They refused."

"As I said, that's their right."

"Why?"

Gooden seemed a bit confused, "Well, they took the oath of citizenship. Therefore, they have a right to equal protection under the law. Why do I have to explain this to you?"

"When they took that sacred oath, they swore loyalty to this nation before God and everybody. If they are as loyal as they claim to be, then let them prove it. If they won't, then out they go, the time for Mr. Nice Guy is long passed."

"We can't do that Donovan, that's a major violation of their rights," Nicholson cautioned.

"Not only can we, but we must. We no longer have any choice, sir. I say they sacrificed their rights when they firmly refused to protect the innocent lives of their fellow citizens. The oath they took to become citizens of this country says they would protect America by bearing arms if necessary. I believe the spirit of the oath applies here."

"How so?" Nicholson asked.

"That basically we're to do whatever is necessary, reasonable or unreasonable, for the greater good of the country."

"That's a bit of a stretch, don't you think, General?" Gooden asked.

"Not at all. If we don't enforce the oath, then why have one? It doesn't mean anything and we might as well dispense with it and save the taxpayer some money from making people go through the process." Slade thought for a moment, "Look, our police officers, our servicemen, our judges, lawyers, doctors, politicians and even the boy scouts take oaths to maintain a certain level of moral conduct and to fulfill certain duties while they hold their positions. When they violate that oath, they are subject to disciplinary and punitive consequences. When someone lies on the witness stand in the courtroom they are charged with perjury and punished as well. Why?"

Gooden looked coldly as Slade, "To ensure they hold to an acceptable level of conduct demanded by our laws and our society."

"Exactly! So, why should every other person that takes an oath in this country be open to consequences, but not immigrants?"

"They are subject to legal repercussions if they break the law," Nicholson offered.

"You're right, but we're not talking about breaking the law here, we're talking about carrying out acts of war and aiding and abetting the enemy. Our laws don't give us much relief in those circumstances."

"You know, thousands of natural-born citizens violate the law every single day, do you propose we kick them out as well?" Gooden prodded.

"No, I don't"

"Why not, what's the difference?

"The difference is that they were born here, and as such, were not required to take an oath of citizenship. Like it or not that's the way the ball bounces. Any laws they break must be dealt with within the confines of the judicial system."

"Same question, what's the difference?"

"The difference is that naturalized citizens came here requesting the right to become Americans. We said okay, but first you must meet our stipulations and you must take an oath agreeing to certain requirements. The people we're talking about freely took that oath and now they must either fulfill it or suffer the consequences. And again, remember, we're not talking about breaking the law here. If we were, then *we* wouldn't be having this conversation in the first place. We're talking about *war*. We're talking about *treason*. We're talking about people who came here under less than honorable circumstances and are now using the very rights and freedoms we gave them, to wage war against us. I believe it's time they are finally held to the oath they so freely took."

"So, what you're saying is, if they refuse to wear the bracelet and they're not natural-born citizens, we deport them?" Gooden asked.

"Exactly. Although personally, I don't think we'll have to kick many out to show we're serious. Once we start with the illegals, then the rest of them will probably fall into line, albeit kicking and screaming."

"You really think so?" Nicholson asked, hopefully.

"Sure. When you get right down to it, they all know this is the best place to live on the face of the earth. I don't see many of them sacrificing that privilege and risk being sent back to a third-world backwater country. At least not the ones who are truly here for the right reasons." Slade explained. "When we start kicking people out, then I believe the good, law-abiding Muslims will start pointing fingers at the bad guys real quick."

"Okay...say I decide to follow your advice. How do we go about it?" Nicholson inquired.

"Mr. President, you're not really considering this horse cr...!"

Nicholson raised a hand, cutting Gooden off in mid-sentence. "Go ahead, General."

"Well sir, we've already got the National Guard on full alert nationwide. It will only take a phone call from you to institute martial law. In fact, I believe that not only are the American people expecting it, I think that it's long overdue and they're hoping for it."

"And then what?"

"You draft an executive order laying out the plan in detail and then initiate it in the interest of national security. You state the terrorists' attacks are a clear and present danger to the safety and security of the United States, and as such, these measures will be put into place forthwith."

"General...do you honestly think it will work? Do you really believe this will stop the attacks and order will be restored?" Nicholson asked.

"It better, Mr. President. Because if it doesn't...you'd better get out that white flag you were talking about."

*   *   *   *

Saddam Hussein sat quietly on the bunk in his small damp and dank prison cell just outside of Baghdad. If he stood on his tiptoes he could peer through the tiny window and see the very top of what had once been his presidential palace on the Tigris River.

He laughed at the weakness of the so-called civilized world that had spared his life, even though he was personally responsible for the deaths of virtually millions of people. After all of his heinous and barbaric acts they still could not bring themselves to order his execution. That weakness would ultimately be their downfall.

The amount of information he was allowed to hear regarding the events going on in the outside world was strictly limited. However, he had learned of the attacks now being carried out against that whore of a nation, America. He smiled each time he learned a tidbit about the latest round of chaos and carnage being exacted on the US.

Saddam was quite certain he would die in this hellhole, never again knowing the freedom and power he had once possessed. However, he gloriously basked in the knowledge that he had seen his part in the destruction of American had been financed so many years ago. And, even though he was locked in a cell twenty-three hours a day with very few privileges or comforts, he was still waging war against the Great Satan. If the next attack was carried out according to schedule, then America had yet to see the justice of Allah.

Saddam Hussein, former president and dictator of Iraq, settled back on his bunk and moments later had fallen fast asleep, a warmth filling his heart that he had not known in many years.

CHAPTER 36

▼

Wednesday

"This is an exclusive special news bulletin from CNN," the announcer said, interrupting regularly scheduled programming. "CNN only two hours ago received a video tape from what we believe to be a high-ranking member of al-Qaeda named Rahim al-Zarqawi. Zarqawi is believed to have stepped into the number two role in al-Qaeda after his cousin Abu Musab Zarqawi was killed by US forces raiding an al-Qaeda stronghold in Syria just three months ago. Until now it was only rumored Rahim had taken his cousin's place, we believe the following tape ends that speculation."

The screen shifted images to reveal what appeared to be the inside of a roughly hewn cave. A gaunt bearded man with dark deep-set eyes was seated center screen, an AK-47 rifle leaning against the wall just over his right shoulder. He was dressed quite similarly as Osama bin-Laden had been for his previous videos with a loose head-wrap and long flowing robes. He leaned forward and began speaking, the dark orbs of his eyes revealing the churning hatred within his heart.

"Allahu Akbar! The United Islamic People gave notice to the American Government many times that the war would be brought to your shores, your streets and your homes, if you did not stop meddling in our countries. You ignored our warnings. You continue to believe the illusion that you are safe, protected by your oceans. You thought we were weak, and that we could not touch you. You thought by waging an unjust and imperialistic war in Iraq, Afghanistan and Syria you could change our beliefs, our way of life, and we would break. You were wrong; the harder you push, the stronger our resolve.

"Our weeping widows, our orphaned children, our sick and infirm have begged you to leave us be. Yet, you dismiss us as one would a wailing child stomping his feet because he doesn't get his way. However, a child tends to be powerless and without the means to alter things in his favor; as you see we are not like a child.

Your stubborn belief that your way is the only way has brought the rage and justice of Allah to your land, just as we promised it would be. Still you ignore us, and more of your people, your children, continue to die. Is your desire to control the events of the entire world so strong that it is worth the further loss of American lives?"

"Do you honestly believe you are so much better than we are? Why don't you step back and take an honest look at yourselves. In your schools, children are slain everyday by other children when they are supposed to be learning to read and write. We do not have that problem. Millions of your people lay in the streets and gutters drunk and strung out on drugs. We do not have that problem. You have entire cities where the idea of men rooting around in the bed with other men like pigs is considered morally justified. We do not have that problem. Your people break into their neighbor's homes and steal their belongings. We do not have that problem. Your women, old and young, prance around publicly in garments even you once believed were better suited for the privacy of the bedroom. We do not have that problem. Is this the sort of debauched lifestyle you say we need to embrace in order to fit into your civilized twenty-first century? If it is, then please, keep it to yourselves.

"People of America, we do not wish to be at war with you. We too cry at the deaths of your innocent children, just as we cry each time an innocent Muslim child dies at the hands of an American soldier. We too hunger for peace the same as you, however, not wholly on the terms you dictate.

"Your government is no better than a schoolyard bully pushing and intimidating smaller children so they will bend to his unreasonable wishes. In time, a higher authority intervenes and stops the bully, or the one being bullied finally grows strong enough, and courageous enough to fight back. Those of you who were bullied when you were young will understand this."

"It is time you demand your government change its foreign policy and put your safety first. Your government must withdrawal all military forces from the Middle East and leave us to decide our own destiny. We are doing nothing more than what your own forefathers did more than two hundred years ago when they shook off the shackles of tyranny imposed upon it by another. You look back on their actions with respect, with pride, and with honor, will you not afford us the same courtesy? Must you control the entire world?"

"To the American President, understand this, if you do not take immediate and drastic steps to begin the withdrawal of your troops within the next thirty-six hours, the attacks will resume. We will show no mercy, we will not faint or falter and you will not find anyplace that is safe to hide. We have shown we can and will strike when we choose and where we choose. Believe me when I say there is nothing you can do to stop us. Adhere to our demands or suffer a violence that you can only imagine in your nightmares. Allahu Akbar!"

The screen changed to show a picture of a hooded figure standing in front of St. Jude's Children's Hospital in Memphis, Tennessee. The figure, obviously a woman from her stature, was holding an AK-47 rifle and had at least ten sticks of dynamite strapped to her chest. She was holding a copy of that day's *Memphis Daily Commercial*. The figure turned and began walking slowly toward the front door.

"That concludes the tape, we will return to discuss what we've just seen with our panel of guests, right after these messages."

*   *   *   *

In the White House Situation Room, the President sat at the head of a long table. Present with him were the Directors of CIA, FBI, Homeland Security, National Security Agency, Chairman of the Joint Chiefs and National Security Advisor. They had just spent the last twenty minutes repeatedly viewing the tape CNN had moments ago broadcast themselves. Only the copy they viewed had been delivered by special currier from FOX News a half-hour before. They had no knowledge that CNN had just broadcast it to the entire world.

"Has the hospital been attacked?" Nicholson asked worriedly.

"No sir, it's safe, for now," FBI answered. "We have agents on the way there as a precaution and all unauthorized personnel have been ordered off the premises as a precaution."

"What was she holding that newspaper for?" Gooden asked.

"They wanted us to know that they could have done it today if they'd wanted to. Couldn't have us thinking it was an old picture, could they?" Stuart Minetti explained.

"I guess not."

"This Zarqawi sounds like he's been educated in the west. Did you hear how he talked? He came off like an American, any chance it was a voice over?" Nicholson asked.

"Sure, it's a possibility, sir. However, it was probably authentic," Barclay Mims answered.

"You're sure?"

"No, I'm not positive. But what we do know is that he attended college at Oxford for a year and a half and spent another two at Berkley. So my best guess is that it was his voice on the recording; he would want all Muslims to know that it was him. He wants the entire world to know he is firmly in place as the number two man."

"What do you make of it Iverson, you think it's for real?" the president asked.

The Director of Homeland Security thought for a moment before answering. "I would tend to think it's authentic. Our intelligence indicates Zarqawi is the new number two man and there are some indications bin-Laden is suffering from severe health issues and Zarqawi may even be in charge now. If he is, then I agree with Bark, he'd want everyone to know it."

"That coincides with what we've come up with at CIA." Stuart Minetti said. "If it's true…then we're in far worse trouble than before."

"How so?" Nicholson asked, glancing over at Gooden as he answered a ringing phone.

"Rahim Zarqawi is reported to be far more brutal than bin-Laden ever dreamed of being. He had his own mother killed just so there would be no chance of her being used against him in the event he were ever captured. I believe there is no evil act he won't carry out to accomplish his goals. In addition to that he's supposed to have an IQ in the 150's and his mission planning is unparalleled."

"And the hits just keep on comin'." Nicholson said, sarcastically.

"That's an understatement, sir," Gooden said, snapping closed his phone, "You better turn on CNN."

Nicholson switched on the television and found he was once again viewing the video of Zarqawi, having his version of a fireside chat with America, 'asking' her to get out of the Middle East.

"Those traitorous bastards!" Director Mims, blurted out. "Don't they know what further violence they could be instigating? This tape may be nothing more than a coded message to terrorist operatives in the US to initiate further attacks."

"Is CNN the only network airing the tape?" Nicholson asked, directing his question to Gooden.

"At present, it appears to be, sir. Evidently all of the major news channels received a copy of the tape, but CNN is the only one to have run with it. I guess they wanted to break the story first."

"And cost how many more lives as a result?" General Slade asked.

"Anything for a story, the consequences be damned. All right gentlemen…it's out now. The question is what do we do about it?" Nicholson said.

"I think you need to put into effect the measures we discussed earlier today, sir," Slade replied, the other cabinet leaders turning to look curiously at the President.

"Not just yet, Donovan," Nicholson said. "What is this United Islamic People Zarqawi spoke of?"

"We really don't know much. It's only the second time we've heard of them, Mr. President." Minetti answered. "The only other time was in the notes we received after the first attacks in Redding. If they are for real, then it's a totally new group and it would appear as if al-Qaeda is in bed with them."

"Ideas…opinions as to what it means?" the president prodded.

"Sir, you know these terrorist organizations, their names rarely mean what they appear to," Gooden cautioned.

"I know that, Mark, but if it is accurate and does have some meaning, what is it?"

"It would appear, at face value, to indicate that Islamic countries, at least to some degree, have agreed to work together. To unite as the name would suggest, but I wouldn't place much weight on it," Mims said.

"Well, our track record so far at predicting what these people are thinking isn't too great, so I ask again, what if it's an accurate description, what does that tell us?'

"Then, Mr. President…it's a whole new ball game," Director Alexander said. "If by some chance foreign governments have thrown their hats into the ring and are working together against us…then this is an undeclared act of war. We would be well within our rights to strike back unilaterally against them."

"You're talking about World War Three," the president said.

"If foreign governments have directly or indirectly supported and aided in these attacks, then yes sir, that's exactly what may happen. Or we can tuck tail and buckle to their demands."

"On the other hand, it could also indicate that only major terrorist groups have come together. If that's the case, we're still looking at a very dangerous situation," Minetti said. "In any event, we still know there is no way groups like Islamic Jihad, Hezzbollah and al-Qaeda could operate so effectively without state sponsored support. In the end, it will come down to dealing with government bodies throughout the Middle East if these groups are to ever be stopped."

The president sat down in his chair, a look of deep despair washing across his face. Did he have the courage to see this through? Could he actually order military action that would result in starting the third world war? Perhaps this was to be the Battle of Armageddon itself, as the Holy Bible prophesied? *No…things had not gone that far, had they?* America just needed to stand strong as she had for over two hundred thirty years now.

Her president was now faced with some very difficult decisions. Decisions if his predecessors had the *cojones* to make earlier, he wouldn't be burdened with now.

He looked around the table at some of the most powerful and influential men in the entire world; all of them trusting, in the end, he would make the correct decisions. Sure, they could give him counsel and encourage him to do what is just, but in the end he would stand alone. History would not judge them nearly as harshly as it would him.

No matter what direction he chose to take the country, there would be those that would question his decisions and his sanity. Many would second-guess him at every turn; all believing they had a better way. The problem was that it was not their decision to make. The path of future generations would not be altered if they were wrong and lives would not be lost.

For some reason, the American people seemed to believe that with the oath of office, the president received a crystal ball. That somehow he was so much smarter than every other man on the planet and should always have the answers. That was simply not the case. He was just a man. He had the same fears and hopes as any other, as well as the same failings. When tired he sleeps, when pierced he bleeds and when hurt he cries. And right now he wanted to cry. Not because he was weak, but because he was hurting so deeply for his nation. For he now knew what he must do, and because of that the nation, and the world, would never be the same again.

"We will not give into their demands," he finally said. "The United States has never and will never negotiate with terrorists. If they want a fight, then by gosh they're going to get one. General...how goes the redeployment of our carriers?"

"I just spoke to the CNO before this meeting," the general said referring to the Chief of Naval Operations. "He assured me all orders have been sent out, but it would take as many as two weeks before everything is in place."

"Good enough," he looked over at Gooden. "I want a full meeting of the Congress and the National Security Council first thing tomorrow morning."

"That may not be possible on such short notice, sir."

"I don't want excuses...I want action. If they're out of town tell them to get here. Just make it happen. Everyone needs to do what is required of them to serve their nation. I don't say that with any animosity; however, I need some answers. Start shaking trees. Round up any and all suspected terrorists and hold them, question them...do what you need to do, but get them talking. Someone has some answers and we need to motivate them to talk. Chuck, have your field agents turn their informants upside down and shake them, let's see what falls out."

"You got it, sir."

"Stuart...I want you to personally make contact with your counterparts in friendly foreign intelligence services, compel them, I don't care how, and ask them to do the same with their sources as well."

"Aye, sir."

"Gentlemen, make it known, just as President Bush did a few years ago, foreign heads of state are either with us or against us. There is no middle ground. If they don't pull out all of the stops and help us in our most desperate hour, then to hell with them. They'll not receive another dime of US assistance and not one more American soldier will spill his or her blood in defense of their countries." He took a moment to look into the eyes of each and every man at the table. What he saw disturbed him. To the man they were just as scared as he was. In reality, no one had any idea how to fight a faceless enemy, at least not within the confines of the law. That was all about to change, there were other ways to deal with this predicament.

"General Slade?"

"Yes sir?"

"As quickly as possible, you're to get with the other joint chiefs and draw up plans to shuffle around our troops stationed overseas. Have General Peterson get the Military Airlift Command spun up and ready to go."

"What do you have in mind, sir? I'll need to tell him where to send his aircraft so he's properly prepared."

"I want fifteen thousand troops brought home and prepared to assist in closing our borders. I want another fifteen thousand deployed to Iraq, those men are going to need the help there."

"Where are they to come from?"

"Germany, South Korea, Japan, I really don't care, just get them."

"Are you sure about that, Mr. President?" Director Mims asked.

"Never more."

"Sir, that's going to take some time...a lot of time. Just the heavy equipment alone..."

"No General...just the men and their light equipment. We have all the heavy stuff we need in Iraq and here in the States. What we don't have is enough troops," Nicholson clarified. "I also want a full call up of reservists, all branches, Coast Guard too. If this thing goes where I think it may, we need to start preparing...now."

"Mr. President, the press and the Republicans are going to roast you," Gooden warned.

"You're right...at least about the press. However, I think you're wrong about the Republicans. This is the very kind of move they'll like, and I find it rather unsettling that I find myself agreeing with them. For years I thought they were nothing more than warmongers, to be honest, I'm still not sure, but at least in this situation I concur with them. There can be no peace without a strong military and a government with the will to employ it if necessary. I do think though my fellow Democrats are going to be a bit miffed, but oh well. I believe we have to do what is right, not what is popular," pausing to look at General Slade, "A friend told me that very thing just this morning, it took some time for his message to sink in, but I believe now that it has."

"Anything else sir?" Gooden asked.

"Yes...General, direct all National Guard units to be prepared for action on an hour's notice. Instruct them to begin prepositioning their equipment."

"Aye sir."

"Gentlemen, dismissed."

*   *   *   *

The caravan of vehicles made another stop at a storage unit in Medford, Oregon. Yet another vehicle and trailer as well as a fifth trailer for the Mariska's vehicle were retrieved. They grabbed a bite at a local Arby's, one of the few businesses still open and then were quickly back on the road heading south. Just one more stop to make.

*   *   *   *

In a secluded house in Shasta Lake City, a small town just a few miles north of Redding, California, nine men and a woman gathered in secrecy. Their leader sat them all down and began to explain in detail what their operation would entail. He assured them there would be no room for error and no cost was too great to ensure they accomplished their goals. He explained what the responsibilities of each person would be, including just how they were to go about achieving them. With the help of three of the men, he carried seven large crates into the room.

The leader bent down and opened the first one. Inside were several hand-held weapons, including 9mm pistols and Uzi submachine guns with numerous full magazines of ammunition. The other six were then opened. Each contained several hundred pounds of Semtex and C-4 plastic explosives with remote and time delay detonators. One thing was very obvious; someone was serious about taking down the target.

*   *   *   *

As they received the recall, tens of thousands of National Guard troops began flooding into their armories throughout the fifty states. At first it started slow, but as the word spread it was as if a dam had burst. Just as soon as they reported in and were checked 'present' they were issued weapons and ammunitions and given orders where they were to go. Thousands of huge trucks, buses and armored Humvees were loaded with troops at military bases across the country. One by one they drove out the gates, disappearing into the night, prepared to take back America's cities and pride.

CHAPTER 37

▼

Thursday

Day Twenty-One

As part of a massive nationwide effort, huge convoys ferried thousands of reserve and active duty military personnel throughout the night, ensuring they would be in position for when the Commander in Chief called upon them. By noon eastern time, they were dispersed around every major airport, government building and most major thoroughfares leading into the fifty largest American cities. They were not yet impeding anyone's freedom of movement; but no one was foolish enough to believe that it wasn't imminent. Armored personnel carriers and Humvees patrolled cities, making a show of force, allowing the population to get used to seeing them around. For most, their presence was comforting. However, a small segment of the country was opposed to the very thought of the nation being placed under military rule and the ACLU (American Civil Liberties Union) was leading the charge.

One very prominent attorney filed an appeal for an emergency injunction in federal court requesting the president be compelled to remove the troops and return citizen security back to civilian authorities. The request was quickly denied on the basis that martial law had not officially been invoked and the soldiers had not yet superseded civilian authority. The wording of the judge's written ruling made it very clear to those familiar with legal jargon, that she would not be very accommodating if the complaint was later re-filed. In other words, 'find another judge.'

*   *   *   *

The caravan approached the California/Oregon border a little after 9:00 AM Pacific Time. Rather than separating and staggering their crossing of the border, they had agreed it would be less likely to draw suspicion if they all crossed together. As instructed, the six vehicles lined up in single file and approached the 'fruit and vegetable' inspection gate farthest to the right. Mariska was in the lead vehicle and had elected herself to do the talking in the event there were any unexpected inquiries from the border officer.

There were four other vehicles in front of her and it took several minutes to reach the gate. When she did, she had already lowered the window and had a polite smile on her face. The pale skinned officer returned her smile. "Good morning," he said, and then looked back at the other vehicles behind her, seemed to think for a moment and then turned toward her. "Are you folks going to some sort of a convention or something?" he curiously asked.

"Yes sir, we are." Mariska answered. "There's a huge outdoor recreational vehicle and sports show this weekend in San Jose." In fact, there was a show. Part of her meticulous planning was to make certain if anyone were to doubt her cover story and decide to check it out, they would find she was telling the truth. They would also find that the show had been cancelled, but that was something that could be easily explained away as a last minute decision that Mariska had not yet been informed of.

The guard's radio squawked and he cocked his head to the side to listen. After a moment he excused himself and went inside the gatehouse. Mariska watched him pick up the phone receiver and dial a number. He looked back at her and smiled while waiting for the answering party to pick up. "Hey, it's Jack," he said, and reached over to slide the door to the guard shack closed.

Mariska's grimaced as her stomach twisted into knots. She began to sweat. Her hands started to shake. *Who could he be talking to and does it involve us,* were the questions that began to dart through her mind? She tried her best to appear relaxed and decided to look casually around the area, anything to force herself not to watch the officer and not appear as worried as she felt.

What she saw made her even more nervous than the untimely telephone call had. Sitting not fifty yards away, next to a large maintenance shed, were two heavily armored Bradley fighting vehicles. Placed atop each were .50 caliber machine guns with serious looking soldiers sitting behind them, their hands on the guns. The soldiers' posture made it quite clear they were very alert. The stern looks on their face left no doubt they were prepared for any trouble that might come their way. They were watching every single vehicle as it approached the checkpoint. She wondered how in the world she had missed them as she approached the inspection station. She was getting a little sloppy, she decided, and promised herself if they got through this it would not happen again.

She glanced back at the officer who continued looking at her while talking. In the rearview mirror she saw two soldiers carrying rifles at port-arms with a German Shepard between them coming in her direction. Further back, two California State Highway Patrol Interceptors pulled in and stopped back at the end of the line of cars. Her fear was getting the better of her and she almost resigned herself to gun the engine and just take her chances. But, just as she was easing her foot off the brake pedal toward the accelerator, and her right hand to the Beretta 9mm between the seats, the officer hung up the phone, slid open the door, and returned to her window.

"Sorry about that ma'am. That was an emergency at home and I had to take the call, sorry to keep you waiting for so long."

A quick glance back told her the soldiers had stopped to talk to one another, one of them lighting a cigarette. *Not exactly the behavior of two guys getting ready to shoot.* "Oh, that's all right…it happens to all of us from time to time," she said, the tension slowly ebbing away.

"Thank you for understanding. Do you have any produce in your vehicle that you purchased from out of state?" he asked.

"No sir, I don't." *That question is about as useful as asking someone at the airport if they packed their own bags and if they've had them with them the entire time. If only these bozos were in charge of security in Israel.*

He looked back at the other vehicles and then asked, "Do any of your companions that you know of?"

"No sir, I'm pretty sure they don't either."

"Very well ma'am. Due to recent events we will have to look inside your vehicles, as a precaution of course."

Mariska's skin went cold as the man directed the two soldiers to begin the inspection. They started with her vehicle walking along both sides looking at the under-carriage with mirrors on stainless steel rods. Satisfied that nothing was out of order they quickly looked in the cargo area of the SUV and then moved on to the trailer. Again, they looked underneath and then unfastened the tarp on the top.

Mariska watched the soldiers closely, her hand on the pistol, ready to act at the slightest indication they had been discovered. In the mirror she could see Mansur observing the soldiers as well. The GI's finished up, refastened the tarp in place and moved on to Mansur's vehicle. Mariska breathed a subtle sigh of relief and knew in her heart if that was as close as the soldiers intended to look, then they were safe. Several minutes passed as the privates worked their way to last vehicle in line and then waved back to the gate guard that all was okay.

"You have a nice day and you all enjoy your show," the guard said.

"Thank you very much," she answered.

"Welcome to California," he said. As she slowly drove away, she couldn't be sure but she thought she heard him utter, "Go with Allah." She started to pull to the side of the road and wait for the other drivers to be cleared, however, she looked in the rear view mirror and saw the officer was waving the others through behind her. She let out a huge sigh of relief as the others quickly closed the distance and they all cautiously drove away to the south and their destiny. Looking back, Mariska could still see the guard watching intently as they drove away.

They had one remaining stop to make and the final part of their mission could begin. So far things were going exactly as planned. With all that had taken place, the Americans still assumed everyone was harmless until they saw something to convince them otherwise. Allah's blessings were truly upon them and the chances of their success had just multiplied significantly. Crossing over the state line had been Mariska's biggest concern. She knew making it past the increased security would present the most risk. Now, they pretty much had free reign of the state, of course they would only need it for a couple more days.

*   *   *   *

What was surprising to many was that the Army Corps of Engineers, the Navy Seabees and private contractors were already in the process of pre-positioning hundreds of tons of construction equipment and fencing materials along both the northern and southern borders of the United States. Modular bunkhouses, cookhouses, and portable toilet and showering facilities were already set up and ready for use.

It was amazing what could be accomplished when the politicians cut through the red tape and decided to work together. So much more got done when contracts were simply awarded to the companies who could accomplish the job without first going through the time-eternal bidding process. Although during times of peace, bidding was the proper and fair way to do things, now was not the time.

At present, logging companies had already started work clearing a hundred-yard wide swath that would run the length of both borders. The majority of the work would begin on the southern border, as that was where the biggest security issues lie. After some strong political pressure from the US State Department on the Canadian Government, they had reluctantly agreed to assist with the work in the north.

It was sure to take many months to accomplish the installation of the three twenty-foot fences that were to be erected along the entire length of both borders and most of the work would have to be doled out to private contractors. The outer fences would be topped with razor wire and would have steel beams inserted ten feet into the ground every twelve inches to make it almost impossible for someone to tunnel under. The middle fence would be charged with high voltage electricity in the unlikely event anyone made it over the outer ones.

Until the fences could be erected, soldiers, Marines and armed helicopters would patrol the borders using infrared night vision equipment. Their orders were to detain anyone who attempted to cross the borders at any unauthorized point. If anyone resisted or attempted to flee, the troops were authorized to use whatever force they deemed necessary to prevent them from escaping. Alerts were put out nationwide in the United States, Mexico, and Canada on all radio and television stations, as well as Internet home pages concerning the new security measures being put into place. Bilingual signs were posted every hundred feet along the borders as well. The repercussions of what would befall anyone caught violating the new security measures were made quite clear.

The best-case scenario called for the borders to be sixty-five percent closed within ninety days and completely sealed off within six months. For the first time in American history, the United States government was finally taking the security of the homeland seriously. From now on, if someone wished to enter the country by land, they would have to access it through armed security checkpoints and pass a mandatory background screening first. By presidential executive order, there were to be no exceptions.

*   *   *   *

In Long Beach, California, Charleston, South Carolina, Houston, Texas and Pittsburgh, Pennsylvania, twenty men in groups of five, gathered up their diving equipment and inspected it one more time before packing it away in the back of their SUV's.

*   *   *   *

In the basement of a small two-bedroom house just north of Winston-Salem, North Carolina, Sayed Mirkalami knelt on his prayer rug mentally preparing himself for what would be his last act upon the earth. He had been waiting for many years for the moment that was rapidly approaching and had no doubts he possessed the courage to see it through.

*   *   *   *

Four men had checked into the cheap, fleabag motel two miles northeast of the nation's capitol the night before. The underpaid desk clerk had no problem when they asked to pay with cash after explaining they had no credit card, especially after they offered him an extra fifty for his trouble. They had spent the night carefully inspecting their equipment. Using a wireless Internet connection they had just received the green light to proceed. Gathering their things, they packed them in large duffel bags and left the room. While one of the men checked out, the others loaded the bags into the trunk of a sedan parked at the rear of the parking lot. It would take less then fifteen minutes to get to the warehouse, but they wanted to stop and get one last meal before they did.

*   *   *   *

In San Francisco, New York, Chicago, Atlanta, Dallas, Los Angeles, New Orleans, Boston, and a slew of other cities, wives and mothers kissed their husbands and children goodbye before going off to work.

CHAPTER 38

▼

Deputy Sheriff Greg 'Bam Bam' Davis had been with the Monongalia County Sheriff's Department in West Virginia going on eleven years. Prior to that he served four years in the United States Marine Corps as a military policeman where he'd received his nickname for being a crack shot with a sidearm. After his enlistment ended he decided that civilian law enforcement would be the best career move. Within two months of leaving the service he was offered a job with the Sheriff's Department. He thought it over, discussed it with his wife and then jumped at the opportunity. Since he lived in Morgantown, the county seat, it wasn't a difficult decision to make.

Like many Sheriff's employees across the nation, Bam Bam began his new career working in the jail. This was not exactly what he wanted to do, but figured he had to start somewhere. The fact that both he and his wife's families also lived in the Morgantown area made it a lot easier to take the lesser-appreciated position.

He worked hard at his new duties, took night courses in criminal justice at the local college and within two years had been reassigned to the Sheriff's fugitive apprehension unit. As part of the unit he took an active role in the arrests of many of the areas most dangerous criminals. Even though there were only about ninety thousand people in the entire county, there never seemed to be a shortage of bad guys.

*   *   *   *

Four men drove slowly down Chestnut Ridge Road in a silver Ford Crown Victoria, passing the school for the second time in the last half-hour. They had checked out several schools over the past few weeks before deciding this one best suited their needs. The location of the school provided easy access in and out to highway 705 just a short distance away, ensuring them a clean and speedy get-away.

Bari parked the car two hundred feet from the entrance to the school grounds, adjusted his seat back slightly and decided to just sit and watch for anything that might interfere with their mission, such as new or increased security measures.

Bari scanned the school grounds taking note that the playgrounds were empty and no staff members were visible roaming the campus. *Everyone bottled up nice and neatly inside. Perfect!*

*   *   *   *

Deputy Davis was off-duty and presently driving towards his son's school. It was only a few minutes past noon, but his son Isaac had an appointment with the dentist's drill at one o'clock. He hated pulling his boy from school early, especially this soon into the new school year, but this was the only appointment available for three weeks and his wife didn't want to miss it. Normally, Mrs. Bam Bam handled these little chores, but since it was his day off she had allowed him the honors. Bam Bam had tried his best to convince her to reschedule because he had things he had to get done around the house. No go. She'd dug in her heels and wouldn't budge. *Oh well, I guess the painting will have to wait.*

As he drove down Chestnut Ridge Road and drew near the school, he noticed four men sitting in a silver Ford on the far side of the driveway. He had been on too many stakeouts in his career to not recognize one when he saw it. But something about it just didn't sit right with him. *Why were they watching an elementary school?* Maybe it was nothing more than his nerves getting the better of him, what with everything that had been happening lately. Still, something just didn't seem right about it.

He made the left turn into the circular drive in front of the school office and was able to faintly make out the outlines of four occupants. There were two in the front seat and two in the back. He couldn't see their faces, but from the continuous movements of their heads it was obvious they were alertly watching for something, for what Bam Bam couldn't begin to imagine. The driver appeared to look directly at him and Bam Bam gave him a friendly nod and then slowly turned his head away. *I don't know who they are, but they're not cops!* As a precaution, he reached for his hand held radio and called the dispatcher. They sure weren't with the Sheriff's Department; he knew all of those guys.

"Four seventy-eight to dispatch."

"Go ahead, four seventy-eight."

"Can you tell me if there are any city officers currently present, or near, twenty-three eighty-seven Chestnut Ridge Road?"

"I'll have to contact MPD, be back with you in a moment."

"10-4."

*   *   *   *

They had been sitting there for more than an hour and still had not mustered enough nerve to get out and do it. Marwan, Bari, Mousa and Hossein were in their early twenties and had all been prepared for this mission in the same training camp back in Libya. They had been in the United States for less than three months, having crossed over the border near Brownsville, Texas in the middle of the night. They had orders to carry out three operations before attempting any contact for additional instructions. Their hesitation to begin was not from fear of failing, but from being unable to complete the other assignments with which they had been tasked. They had to make sure.

Bari's head came up when he saw the mini-van pull into the parking lot in front of him. The driver nodded politely but Bari ignored him. *Good, another target!*

*   *   *   *

"Dispatch to four seventy-eight," Bam Bam's radio squawked.

"Go ahead, dispatch."

"Greg, city is reporting that they have no officers working that area at present, and haven't all morning."

"Are they sure?"

"That's affirmative."

"Amanda, I've got four guys just sitting here in front of the school in a silver Crown Vic, looks like an unmarked, but there's something just not right about it, I can feel it."

"Can you give me a description?"

"Not really. The sun is directly behind me and their visors are down."

"Very well four seventy-eight. I see your location is a school, do you think they could just be waiting to pick up their kids?"

"Possibly, but not likely. School doesn't let out for at least another couple of hours," he thought for a second, trying to make sure he wasn't overreacting. "Dispatch, I have a bad feeling about this."

"Would you like me to send a couple units your way as a precaution?"

"I think that's a good idea, and make it quick, but real quiet like, 10-4?"

"10-4! I'll get them heading your way." The dispatcher was quiet for a few seconds and then the radio squawked. "Units five seventy-two, four ninety-six and three eleven, please assist off-duty officer at Briarwood Elementary at two, three, eight, seven Chestnut Ridge Road. He is reporting suspicious individuals on school grounds."

One by one the deputies quickly responded declaring that they were en route. Other deputies throughout the county, upon hearing the broadcast, began altering their patrol patterns, conveniently taking them closer to the school as well.

Bam Bam cut off the engine, reached into the glove compartment, grabbed his off-duty weapon and slipped it into his waistband, covering it with the tail of his favorite Hawaiian shirt. He slipped a couple of extra magazines into the back pocket of his Levis and opened the car door. Without looking toward the suspicious car, he walked briskly toward the building, passing the American flag flying at half-staff along the way.

*   *   *   *

Bari watched the big man enter the school building and finally decided it was safe to proceed. Telling the others it was time, he slipped the car into gear and drove slowly forward a hundred feet, bringing them closer to the entrance. Leaving the engine running, they got out and walked around to the rear of the vehicle and opened the trunk.

*   *   *   *

Inside the front door of the school, Bam Bam stood in the lobby watching the four men from behind a partially opened verticle blind. He saw them pull forward and then exit the vehicle, walk around to the back, look around and then open the trunk. *What are they...?*

"Mr. Davis…can I help you?"

A startled Bam Bam pivoted around to see the principal, Mrs. Templeton standing behind him. "I'm not sure just yet. There are four unsavory looking characters out there and I'm just watching to see what there up to," he answered.

A look of concern quickly replaced the polite expression on her face. "Should I be worried?" she asked, moving to her right and looking out the window in the direction Bam Bam was indicating.

"Again…I'm not sure." When he was finally able to return his attention to the men they were less than seventy-five feet away, walking quickly toward the entrance of the school. They were all carrying AK-47 assault rifles.

Bam Bam spun around, grabbed Mrs. Templeton above the elbow and shoved her toward her office. "Get in your office now and warn your teachers to get all their students in the classrooms and lock their doors!" he yelled.

"Mr. Davis, what's going on…?"

"Move!" he roared again. A now terrified Mrs. Templeton scrambled to carry out his demands.

Davis keyed his hand-held radio and screamed, "10-33…10-33, officer needs help at Briar Wood Elementary. Four armed gunmen on campus! Repeat…at least four armed gunmen on campus," all while reaching for his .40 Smith & Wesson side arm.

*   *   *   *

The terrorists walked quickly toward the front door and were pleased to see that so far it didn't appear as if they had attracted any unwanted attention. Each had several full magazines of ammunition and was confident this would turn out to be a glorious victory.

They started up the steps and raised their rifles in preparation to fire. Suddenly an alarm began blaring inside the building and at that same moment the door in front of them burst open. A huge bear of a man came charging out aiming a big black pistol directly at them.

"Police! Drop your guns!" Bam Bam shouted. The killers acted as if he hadn't spoken. They didn't even pause as they continued to raise the rifles to fire. Bam Bam, realizing he had no other choice, opened fire first.

CHAPTER 39

▼

President Nicholson strolled leisurely through the White House Rose Garden, trying to wrap his mind around the tragic events that had been taking place. He paused to bend over and sniff the sweet fragrance of a colorful flower that he didn't even know the name of. He enjoyed his walks through the garden, as this was the only place he could truly be alone with his thoughts. With a nod of his head, he acknowledged one of the secret service agents standing nearby. Although the agents never really let him out of their sight, they did their best to give him as much space and privacy as possible, while still carrying out their assigned duties.

The constant scrutiny of the Secret Service was one of the things that took the most effort to get used to. He understood it was a necessary evil; the leader of the free world had to be protected at all costs. There were numerous enemies out there who would love to see him dead. From the leaders of enemy foreign powers, to the CEO's of large corporations, whose bottom line may be adversely affected if the president didn't approve the legislation their lobbyists had fought for like rabid pit bulls. Of course, add in the individual nut jobs that believed it was their God-given duty to protect the country from that 'liberal black devil in the White House' and it made him quite appreciative to have the sunglass wearing Samurai close by.

The one thing he didn't understand, although he couldn't prove it, was why they had to watch him why he was in the bathroom. Were they so afraid he might actually fall in? Did the bathroom present such dire hazards that armed men needed to observe him? Although the commander of his Secret Service detail adamantly denied they were violating his most private moments, a former service agent, now retired, assured him he was being constantly scrutinized by way of pin-sized cameras hidden in the elaborate design of the floral wallpaper. Being watched was something he couldn't adjust to, so he either chose to use the staff bathrooms or simply took care of his business with the lights off. His friend had informed him those were safe options.

Since this crisis had begun, recent events had not permitted him to spend any time with his lady friend either. Most Americans would find it interesting to discover their president had a girlfriend, but he did. And he missed her terribly. That was just one more of the reasons why this whole nasty situation needed to be laid to rest. He, like the rest of the nation, wanted to resolve this calamity so that he could resume his 'normal', everyday, static life. *Well, as normal as life can be for the leader of the free world.*

He had only minutes ago received the latest casualty figures relating to the anthrax outbreak. So far there had been five hundred and thirty-two deaths from more than forty-seven hundred diagnosed cases. He'd just spoken on the telephone with Dr. Murphy in Atlanta, who told him the numbers of newly diagnosed cases were on a steady decline and the entire situation should be under control by the middle of next week; barring any new surprises of course. She assured him, as bad as it was, if he hadn't enforced the quarantine so quickly the results would have been truly devastating. While it wasn't the greatest of news, at least it was something somewhat positive to point to, he thought.

Although reports of anthrax poisonings were still trickling in, it had been nearly a week since the attacks. Nicholson wasn't naive enough to believe there would be no further such attacks; however, he hoped they would be delayed long enough to give everyone time to catch their breath and figure out some way to prevent them. Frankly, setting aside the most drastic of ideas, he didn't see how that impossible task could realistically be accomplished. People in this country have such freedom of movement it is inconceivable for the government to keep track of everyone at all times.

There are some that have lobbied for the implanting of small GPS computer microchips under the skin of the entire population. While this was an option that would no doubt greatly aid in the government's ability to account for most everyone around the clock, it was not something he could bring himself to condone.

First, America's civil liberties had already been dangerously eroded in the past few years in the interest of fighting terrorism. Congress had seen no other way to battle the enemy without giving broader powers to the FBI and the Department of Homeland Security to act in the interest of all Americans. The Patriot Act had supposedly given them that power, but from what Nicholson had seen take place these past weeks, it obviously hadn't done nearly enough. He viewed the 'chipping' of people as far too dangerous a power to give the government without a clearly laid out end game to retract that authority when the threat was eventually dealt with. Nicholson was all too aware that governments, this one included, rarely gave back power once they got a taste of it. *Absolute power absolutely corrupts!*

He had a more troubling and personal reason to resist giving sanction to the technological marking of people. While he was not a particularly religious man in the strictest definition of the word, he had gone to Sunday school as a boy and had heard about the Biblical events prophesied in the Book of Revelations. There it spoke of the Anti-Christ causing all to receive a mark in their right hand or forehead so that no one without the mark could buy or sell anything. One of the things supporters of the chip espoused was that once the chip was implanted people would no longer need money, debit or credit cards to make their purchases. The hand or forehead, where they recommend the chip be inserted, could be easily scanned. That was something that could not be allowed to happen, and would not happen as long as he had anything to say about it. Never in the history of man had there been available the technology for one being, the Anti-Christ, to control all men, until now. The chipping of human beings was a thought more frightening than terrorism. People could not allow their fears to overpower them to the point they allowed the government to have that kind of control. In life, bad things sometimes happened and that was the way it has been since the beginning of time. To give up one's freedoms out of fear was completely insane.

*   *   *   *

Bam Bam's first two bullets struck Hossein directly in the heart, throwing him backwards down the steps he had just run up. The third and fourth bullets missed completely and Bam Bam leapt back inside the door and dove behind a huge concrete planter just as the remaining terrorists opened fire. The 7.62 mm bullets from the fully automatic rifles shattered the windows and shredded the doors in the front of the building. Bam Bam hunkered his large frame behind the planter and prayed to God his backup would get here soon and that a lucky shot didn't get him in the meantime. As if answering his silent prayer, he heard sirens screaming in the distance as a shower of splintered glass rained down around him, slicing into his face and arms. *If only they can get here in time,* he thought.

Outside the killers stopped to reload and Bam Bam seized the moment. He leapt to his feet and fired several more rounds in their direction. He wasn't really trying to hit them, just give himself a chance to get to a nearby hallway before they came inside and cornered him.

Luck was on his side, one of his bullets struck pay-dirt. Marwan had just turned his head to look at the body of Hossein. The copper jacketed missile ripped into his head slightly forward of his left temple, tore through his skull and exited through his right ear taking with it bone, brain and a mist of pulverized tissue. Marwan's body jerked violently to the right, flipped over and landed with his head on Hossein's chest. The picture they created would have led one to believe they were two gay lovers taking a nap together in the warm afternoon sun, if it were not for their life's blood already coagulating in a pool on the hot concrete.

Bam Bam succeeded in reaching the hallway just as Mousa again opened fire. He could hear the distinct sound of bullets splintering the walls and ricocheting off the pipes within. Breathing heavily, he ejected the partially empty magazine, slipped it into his waistband and then slammed a fresh one in the pistol grip. He could hear Mrs. Templeton screaming inside her office. *I hope she shuts up before those two hear her and shut her up for good!*

The two remaining zealots could see the police cars tearing down the road toward them and they knew they would not escape. They looked briefly at one another and seeming to read each other's minds, both screamed "Allahu Akbar!" and charged through the doors. Bam Bam was waiting for them.

Peeking around the corner, Bam Bam saw two police cars screech to a stop outside as the two killers came charging through the doors firing their rifles, delivering a fusillade of bullets in his direction.

He jerked his head back just in time to hear the whistling lead scream past his ears. Switching his pistol to his left hand he took aim from around the corner and fired.

The first round caught Bari in the right thigh just above the knee, the bone cracked and he collapsed to the floor with his finger holding back the trigger, the rifle spraying bullets into the ceiling, ripping into the sprinkler system. With mangled pipes spewing water in all directions, Mousa let loose with an entire magazine in Bam Bam's direction. Again, he got out of the way just as the lethal projectiles tore into the cinder block wall mere inches from where his head had been only a split second before.

Mousa stopped to reload and Bam Bam again took advantage of the opportunity. He sprang out from his cover and fired three rounds directly at the killer. All three rounds struck Mousa in the throat and he was dead before his body hit the floor. They didn't call him Bam Bam for nothing. But in all of the confusion he almost forgot the injured terrorist lying on the floor. As he was pivoting toward him, Bari, having managed to stand up and now balancing on his good leg, raised his weapon and aimed it directly at Bam Bam's chest.

People say that when they're about to die their whole life flashes before their eyes in a matter of seconds and that's not entirely untrue. In the split second before the killer pulled the trigger Bam Bam thought about his son, his wife and practically every significant and good thing that had ever happened to him. He closed his eyes, a vision of his loving family in his mind's eye, as he heard the shots fired, bracing himself for their impact.

*   *   *   *

The women were mostly employed as maids, secretaries and housekeepers for many of the richest and powerful people in the country. The list included bankers, judges, high-ranking politicians and actors to name only a few. These women had worked tirelessly for many years to gain their most trusted of positions and had worked equally as hard to keep them. They saw to their duties with great attention to detail, taking no risk that an unhappy employer should wish to discharge them. The critical nature of their mission was just too important.

The time had finally arrived to fulfill their destinies.

Without hesitation, those working as nannies began slaying those in their care, either by knife, poisoning or some other equally lethal means.

Housekeepers set about preparing the evening meals for their 'families'. Having laced the food with lethal doses of cyanide, it was placed inside refrigerators to await its eventual consumption; each housekeeper left work early.

Secretaries had to be a little more patient and wait for just the right time to strike. When they did, they did so with the quickness and ferocity of a rattlesnake. In luxurious buildings across the country, the women strolled into their employer's offices under the auspices of some official purpose and showing no mercy, the felines pounced upon their prey.

A few utilized small silenced pistols, others elected to do their fatal work up close using a serrated knife to the throat or an ice pick in the ear. Whichever method they employed, they performed their bloody work with brutal efficiency.

Within two hours more than fifty unsuspecting congressmen, doctors, judges and other critical members of society were lying dead behind their mahogany desks or on their plush carpets.

As evening slowly overtook the workday, professional women began coming home, only to find their children dead. Other families sat around the dinner table to enjoy the delicious meals prepared for them by their attentive and loyal house-keepers.

By the time the word spread about what had taken place, before the police could even begin to formulate some sort of response, the women had all disappeared and assumed the alternate identities that had been arranged for them many years before.

*   *   *   *

The bullets never hit him because they had never been fired. Bam Bam opened his eyes and found the terrorist lying dead from gunshot wounds in the back of his head. He looked through the mangled front doors and saw Deputy Sheriff Bud Starling still holding his weapon in a two fisted grip, the barrel pointed directly at the dead guy on the floor; the smell of burned gun powder heavy in the air. Bam Bam holstered his weapon, his hands beginning to shake uncontrollably. Not from fear, but from the intense adrenaline that quickly began to leave his body.

Officers from every law enforcement agency in the county swarmed over the school and within ten minutes the grounds were secured and declared safe. News spread like wildfire throughout the community and terrified parents began arriving to take their precious children home to where it was 'safe'. As word got around that Bam Bam had virtually saved the entire school single-handedly, grateful mothers and fathers, with joyful tears streaming down their cheeks, sought him out and hugged his neck, thanking him profusely.

Bam Bam was leaning against Starling's patrol car running the events of the past half-hour through his mind. A paramedic had already attended to his cuts and he'd given a report to his captain. Starling nudged him and he looked up to see his son walk out of the front door of the building holding the hand of Mrs. Templeton. Upon seeing his father, the boy jerked his hand free and began running toward him. He swept the small boy up into his big burly arms, nearly crushing him. Bam Bam began to weep, thanking God above that his son did not always brush his teeth like he'd been told to time and again, and needed to go to the dentist today. "I love you son," he whispered in the boy's ear.

"I love you too, Dad."

He set the boy back on the ground, wiped the tears from his eyes and unshaven face, and then took his son's hand in his own. "Let's go home and see Mommy."

CHAPTER 40

▼

In rural North Carolina, Seyed turned onto the tree-lined street and drove toward the small building sitting at the far end of the cul-de-sac. It was painted in a multitude of bright colors and appeared to be a very happy place. He found a space and parked near the front door, removed a pistol from the console between the seats and reached for the door handle. Just then the front door of the building opened and an older woman came walking out with a toddler in her arms.

Seyed paused, watching her come down the steps and walk toward a blue Chevy Cavalier. She strapped the tiny girl into the child safety seat and then got behind the wheel and drove away. He waited for several more minutes before again reaching for the handle.

He stood at the foot of the stairs taking in his surroundings for a moment, and then proceeded up the steps and walked through the doors of the Tiny Tots Daycare in Mount Airy, North Carolina. He thought how poetic it was that he had been assigned this particular target.

He stepped through the door and saw an attractive young woman stapling what were obviously children's art projects onto a bulletin board to the left of a desk. *Talented kids.*

After a few seconds she noticed his presence and stepped down from the short stool she'd been working from. "Can I help you, sir?" she asked, smiling politely.

Seyed ignored her and continued to look around the room.

Still smiling, she asked again, "Can I do something for you, sir?"

This time Seyed responded by pointing the silenced weapon in his right hand at her face. With his left he opened his jacket revealing the eight sticks of dynamite strapped to his chest. She opened her mouth to scream, but Seyed massaged the trigger one time, and her world went black.

He could hear the playful laughter and frivolous shrieking of children coming from the room directly behind the dead body at his feet. Walking around the corpse, he slowly opened the door, stepped inside and quietly closed it behind him.

✳   ✳   ✳   ✳

The billionaire was confident the United States would never concede to *his* demands, and that was exactly the way he wanted it. The US was much too proud to lose face in such a manner in front of the rest of the world. To give in to a bunch of third world savages would be unthinkable and beneath them. For decades the Great Satan had pretty much done as it pleased, to whomever it pleased, and no one had really dared to take a stand against it. If the Germans, the Japanese and the Russians couldn't back them down, a bunch of terrorists surely weren't going to.

The only country that had stood a chance of defeating America in open combat was the former Soviet Union. The world had eventually learned the great *Bear* army was no more than a teddy *bear* when they allowed that Hollywood cowboy, Ronald Reagan, to defeat them without even firing a shot.

Even he, as much as it galled him to admit it, admired Reagan for the wily fox that he was. Reagan had done nothing more than spend the Soviets into bankruptcy by forcing them into an arms race they could not have possibly won. If Reagan, or someone like him, were in office today, things would no doubt prove to be a lot more difficult. The former president was never one to mince words. When he said he would do something, he meant it. While the rest of the world may have hated him for it, they took him seriously just the same.

Nothing had proved this more than the release of the American hostages held by Iran for nearly fourteen months back in '79-'80. Many credited President Jimmy Carter with the hostages' freedom due to the peanut farmer's patience and diplomacy while handling the crisis. Of course, the release of nearly eight billion dollars in Iranian money held by the United States and US assurances that Iran would be immune from any lawsuits resulting from the entire incident, helped greatly.

The billionaire knew it wasn't Jimmy Carter's negotiating skills and frankly was amazed the world had been so duped by it all. Some may call it a strange coincidence, but wasn't it convenient that after 444 days the hostages were released on the very same day Ronald Reagan was inaugurated as president? Before he had served even one day in office, his mere presence was already yielding results. America's enemies knew this man was different and that they were now facing a much more determined and cagey adversary.

The events going on now represented an entirely different situation. In his opinion, the current US president was not nearly as strong as Reagan had been. He was no more than a 'yes man' to the peaceniks that made up his party. How disillusioned President Nicholson was to actually believe peace could be achieved through diplomacy. Why did America believe so naively that just because they desired peace, so did the rest of the world? The Islamic world did not want peace. They wanted to see Israel destroyed and the Jews driven out of the Middle East and they would not rest until the victory was theirs.

The whole Palestinian issue was never about peace or getting back their land. Even Muslims knew the Jews were the rightful owners. The Palestinian issue was nothing more than a catalyst for the Islamic world to keep things stirred up and provide the justification, in the eyes of the world, to keep up the attacks. If it had been about land, then there was plenty of undeveloped land in other Islamic countries to accommodate the Palestinian people quite comfortably.

For roughly twenty years he had been meticulously planning the war against America. When he sat down in 1988 and presented his plan to the others, they were, to say the least, hesitant it could ever be accomplished. Even Saddam, the most diabolical one in the bunch, was doubtful more than twenty thousand true believers could be infiltrated into the US and their presence be kept a secret from the enemy for such a long time. He had questioned, "How do you hide thousands of warriors under the nose of the enemy without them ever finding out?"

The billionaire's answer had been to simply utilize America's loose immigration policy and wide open borders against her. Thousands of believers would simply walk across from Mexico and Canada and seek employment in America's vast service industry. Also, by utilizing America's fair hiring practices, several followers would get themselves hired with the former INS (Immigration and Naturalization Service). As INS employees, they would assist thousands of other Muslims gain lawful entry into the United States. After a year had passed, thousands more, who had no knowledge of the overall operation, would follow. Using these assets to occupy and drain the intelligence resources of the US government, other holy warriors would be able to slip in right under their noses.

The next question the billionaire had to answer was, how do you keep the Americans from stumbling onto the entire operation and taking it down before it could be implemented? The answer to that was simpler still. Each and every cell would operate independently from one another. That way, if the authorities did succeed in finding one cell, there would be nothing that could possibly lead them to any of the others. It had worked so well over the years that throughout the country several members of different cells even became fast friends. Some worked together at the same companies and shared weekend getaways together with their families. None had any idea the other was a part of the same holy war that they were themselves.

The billionaire was amazed, with a few minor exceptions; the entire plan was being carried out with the proficiency of a well-oiled machine. The grandest part of the scheme would be going into effect shortly and the results would be cataclysmic.

He turned on the television and switched the channel to CNN America.

"...the terrorist apparently walked in through the front doors of the daycare here in Mount Airy and wasted no time blowing up himself, the children and employees inside. Now...from what we are being told by neighbors and business owners in the area, there are normally about twenty to twenty-five children and at least five or six employees working here at Tiny Tots. We have not yet received any reports that there are any survivors. Firefighters are still battling the blaze and say it will be sometime yet before they will be able to get inside. The firefighter I spoke with said he did not see anything that would give him cause to be optimistic.

"Again, for those that are just tuning in, an unidentified person has only a short time ago walked into the Tiny Tots Daycare here in Mount Airy, North Carolina and detonated a bomb killing possibly as many as thirty innocent people. This is Monica Trotter, reporting for CNN."

*   *   *   *

President Nicholson switched off the television and looked dumbfounded over at Secretary of State Barbara Duncan. "Why in the world would they hit a daycare in the middle of Nowhere, North Carolina?"

"Sir, are you not familiar with Mount Airy?"

"No...should I be?" he asked a bit bewildered.

"Mr. President, Mount Airy is where they filmed the Andy Griffith Show," she said, somberly.

"What! Are you telling me not even Opie Taylor is safe?"

"It would appear so, sir."

*   *   *   *

Liquid propane trucks left the warehouses outside of Charlotte and several other large cities across America at exactly 12:15 PM Eastern Time.

*   *   *   *

On the outskirts of Los Angeles and Richmond, California, Corpus Christi and Houston, Texas, Lafayette, Louisiana and Pine Bend Minnesota several single engine planes were being readied for flight at small private runways. The planes had all been stolen over the past ten years and none had been flown since their theft. However, they had been well maintained and their would-be pilots had no doubts they would perform perfectly when the time came.

*   *   *   *

The caravan of SUV's and trailers arrived in Yreka, California and quickly located the last storage facility on the list. There they retrieved the sixth and final vehicle. The small group drove to a Round Table Pizza parlor and had lunch and then checked into a nearby Motel Six. There they would stay until receiving the final signal to complete their mission.

CHAPTER 41

▼

The small planes had begun taking off at 1230 EST and twenty minutes later, all twenty-five single engine aircraft were in the air and racing toward their targets. While all commercial aircraft had been grounded due to the recent missile attacks, the flight ban hadn't yet been widened to include private aircraft. This country was too wide open and today the Americans were going to find that out, one pilot thought.

*   *   *   *

Three liquid propane trucks drove straight down Highway 74, Independence Boulevard, and entered downtown Charlotte using the third street exit. The trucks passed slowly by the Mecklenburg County Jail and proceeded into the heart of the Queen City and North Tryon Street.

Two other trucks drove north on I-77 entering the John Belk Freeway, passed the Carolina Panther's NFL stadium on the left and moments later took the College Street exit and drove slowly into the business district.

*   *   *   *

President Nicholson was back in the Rose Garden wracking his brain for solutions, when he received word regarding the failed attack in Morgantown, West Virginia. *Finally,* he thought, *maybe things are gonna' start to go our way. It's about time we caught a break.* He tilted his head to the sky and said a silent prayer, then walked off toward the Situation Room.

*   *   *   *

The first truck slammed into the main entrance of One Wachovia Center, the bank's forty-two-story headquarters building, at over forty miles per hour, penetrating the structure by seventy feet before its driver pressed the detonator. The explosion was tremendous and tore through the first three floors of the building causing millions of dollars in damages and killing over three hundred people. A glistening sheet of shattered glass blew outward from the concussion, shredding the flesh from people walking along the street outside. Trees, light-poles and parking meters were twisted, bent and ripped from the ground and sent flying through the air like unguided missiles, tearing into passing cars, pedestrians and other nearby buildings.

*   *   *   *

The second truck repeated the same maneuver at 201 North Tryon Street, but this time the thirty-story IJL Financial Center was the target. The IJL Building was mostly used by the Bank of America and had more than three thousand employees, clients and visitors inside. The explosion was equally as powerful as the one at the Wachovia Building, and instantly another three hundred and seventy-five people were killed.

A huge fireball was forced upward through the stairwells and into offices as high as five stories above the blast point, setting ablaze office furnishings and the huge volumes of paper it takes to run a major corporation. Seventy more people died when the oxygen they so desperately needed was literally sucked from their lungs by the ravenous fire.

*   *   *   *

Abdullah Rahim was driving the third truck and heard the first explosion several blocks away and then only moments later heard the second just a block or so to the west of his current position. Looking in that direction he saw smoke and concrete dust shooting high into the air and people running as fast as they could from the area. The infidels would know Allah's wrath this day, of that there was no doubt.

Abdullah aimed his truck at the entrance of another building. This time it was the corporate headquarters of Bank of America itself. The truck pierced the exterior of the building and drove deep into the huge and exquisitely decorated lobby. When the thirty thousand-pound bomb exploded, huge chunks of marble were sheared from the walls and came crashing to the floor, crushing several people in their path. Another two hundred and sixty American citizens became the latest victims in a holy war that didn't seem to have any hope of being stopped.

*   *   *   *

Three thousand feet above the ground in southeast Texas, the pilot banked the aircraft hard to starboard, placing the small craft into a steep dive. He could hear the air traffic controller screaming at him through the radio to immediately alter his flight path because he had entered restricted airspace. The pilot knew exactly what he was doing and ignored the frantic voice now ordering him to comply or the F-15 fighters on an intercept course with him would have no choice but to shoot him down. *Let them try!*

Ibrahim reached over and clicked off the radio, silencing the infidel. He could see the target less than a mile away and at his current speed should be there in less than thirty seconds.

His timing had to be perfect. He glanced toward the airspeed indicator and then checked the altimeter. He did some quick calculations in his head and then reached over and pressed the red button on the aluminum control panel between the seats. *Just like in the movies, the button is always red,* he wryly thought to himself.

The timer on the fifteen hundred pounds of Semtex in the back of the plane began its thirty-second count down.

As Ibrahim pushed the throttle all the way forward, he glanced up to see one of his Muslim brothers in another plane approaching quickly from the opposite direction. He too was already in his terminal dive.

Time was passing so slowly. He'd thought his death would be over very quickly. But it seemed his last seconds were ticking away in slow motion.

*   *   *   *

The pilot in the F-15 Strike Eagle was racing through the sky at close to mach two, nearly fifteen hundred miles per hour. He had already received instructions that he was 'weapons free' and as soon as he acquired the target he was to blow it out of the sky.

Air National Guard Captain Eli Christmas, call sign Rudolph, had no problem with his orders as he reached up and flipped on the master arm switch. With all that had been taking place it would be nice to get a little payback. He checked the radar screen, which showed there were two slow moving aircraft flying steadily toward the facility that he and his wingman had been tasked with protecting.

Without warning, the computer notified him, with a steady tone in his helmet, that he had good target acquisition and was cleared to fire on the nearest plane.

Christmas didn't even stop to think before squeezing his right index finger one time. From under his portside wing the AIM-9X Sidewinder missile's engine ignited and erupted from the rail. The one hundred ninety pound, forty thousand dollar weapon quickly sped past mach one and raced through the sky toward the enemy aircraft.

Christmas could see the plane had already started its dive and that it would clearly be touch and go whether the missile could get to it before it got to the target.

*   *   *   *

Just before Ibrahim's plane struck the building he looked up to see the other plane explode into an expanding cloud of millions of tiny pieces of metal, glass and plastic.

Seconds later his own life came to an end.

*   *   *   *

Christmas saw the missile close with the target and blast the tiny plane from the sky. He felt absolutely no guilt that he had just ended another person's life. His only emotion was elation.

That quickly turned to shock and despair when he heard his wingman say his missile had missed and Christmas saw the other enemy aircraft crash into the command and control buildings of the Houston Fuel Oil terminal.

In only a matter of seconds it seemed the entire facility was transformed into one of the hugest conflagrations ever known to man.

Christmas radioed in what had just taken place. The air traffic controller responded by telling him two planes had just struck the refineries in Corpus Christi and that other attacks were being reported at several facilities in California, Minnesota and Louisiana.

Christmas hung his head and then, with nothing else to do, returned to his patrol sector.

✳   ✳   ✳   ✳

The fourth and fifth trucks waited five minutes before beginning their attack runs. The fourth one followed the path of the first and drove through the gaping hole already present in front of One Wachovia Center. The truck bounced over the curb and slammed even deeper into the damaged building than the first, and then in like manner blew up, shaking the entire building once again at its foundation.

People were steadily streaming down the stairwells in a mad dash for safety when the second truck forced its way into the building and exploded. More than seven hundred and fifty people were killed from that blast alone. Then ceilings and walls started to crumble and the death toll continued to climb.

Like the Wachovia building, people in the Bank of America building were rushing out of the mortally wounded structure. Unlike at the World Trade Center on 9/11, people were not taking any chances. Panicked employees were getting out just as fast as humanly possible. No one was asking questions about what had happened, they just wanted out. The terrorists knew this was likely to occur; in fact, they were even counting on it. They didn't have any illusions any of the buildings would be toppled, they simply hoped the lobbies would be so tightly packed with people trying to get out that it would become so congested no one could actually escape their doom. The freedom fighters were getting their wish.

When the fifth truck struck the building, the huge lobby was virtually crammed full of people attempting to push thru to freedom. Bankers, stockbrokers and office staff were in such a panic they were inadvertently trampling those who had tripped and fallen in their path. The huge bomb detonated, killing another fifteen hundred in a manner of seconds.

Huge fires raged for hours and fire captains, remembering the events of 9/11, refused to order their men into the buildings. Giant water cannons were set up and thousands of gallons of water were being pumped onto the buildings, but very little was reaching the destructive fires inside.

Unlike in New York, surprised people outside did not stand around and wait to see what happened. As fast as they could they were leaving the downtown area. Their wisdom would be rewarded. Five hours after the bombs struck, the Wachovia building, having been severely structurally weakened by two mammoth blasts, began to bend forward. After several more tense minutes the building buckled and went crashing to the ground and into a building across the street. Seventeen hundred people were still trapped inside when it fell. The building it landed on was mortally damaged as well, over a hundred more died, and hundreds were injured.

People trapped in the Bank of America building could see the top of the Wachovia building shudder and then disappear. All rationale rapidly vanished and terrified people actually ran through raging flames to escape. Very few made it through alive and none made it without living the rest of their lives horribly scarred.

Ninety minutes after the Wachovia Building collapsed so did the Bank of America building. Sixty floors of concrete, steel and glass came crashing down onto the streets, buildings and firefighters below.

The Queen City looked like a battlefield. What was once believed to be one of the prettiest cities in the country now lay in ruins. The first and fifth largest banks in the United States lost their headquarters that day as well as the lives of over seven thousand two hundred Americans. It would later be determined that if firefighters had gone in and fought the blaze, the fires could have likely been brought under control within a relatively short period of time, but who knew?

CHAPTER 42

▼

Friday

Day Twenty-Two

The entire National Security Council was already waiting in the White House Situation Room Friday morning when the president walked in at 6:05. He sat down, immediately reaching for his cup of coffee, taking a couple of quick slurpy sips. The lack of proper rest was taking an obvious toll on the leader of the free world. There were dark rings under his eyes and his hair had grown noticeably grayer in the past three weeks. But the most notable difference was the profound sadness in his eyes.

He pushed the cup aside with the back of his hand, sloshing hot liquid on the highly polished table. Jabbing the button on the intercom, he ordered, "Somebody bring me a Coke."

A few moments later an orderly came in and placed a can of the requested beverage on a coaster in front of the president. Picking up the cup, the orderly swiftly wiped up the spill and walked out as Nicholson took a long swallow from the bright red can. Setting it aside, he at last addressed the room, "All right people, give it to me."

The Chief of Staff, Cornelius Bennitt, had won the honor of updating the president on everything that had taken place in the past eighteen hours. He cleared his throat and began, "Sir...it's not pretty. The terrorists have hit us hard. They've attacked so many places it's difficult to know where to begin..."

"Why don't you start at the top of your list and just work your way to the bottom," Nicholson said, without the slightest bit of emotion in his voice.

"Yes sir," Bennitt said looking down at the folder in front of him. He puffed up his cheeks, blew out the air with a soft sputtering sound and then opened the folder and began. "Well, somehow they got their hands on more than two dozen, fully-loaded liquid propane trucks and rigged them with explosives. You have already been fully briefed about the buildings that were destroyed in Charlotte. In addition to those, the Philadelphia Inquirer building was bombed, as was the

John Hancock building in Chicago. They attempted to bomb the New York Stock Exchange but they failed to make it through the barricades and elected to blow the truck up in the middle of the street instead, killing more than fifty people. The damage to surrounding buildings was also enormous." Bennitt looked up from his notes expecting the president to have a comment at this point. Nicholson just stared at him stoically.

"Hospitals were bombed in Fort Wayne, Indiana, Boise, Idaho, Minot, North Dakota and Helena, Montana. While none of the buildings were destroyed, like the one in Redding, the damage is still severe and there are significant casualties." Again, he paused to allow Nicholson the chance to comment. Seeing none was forthcoming, from the president or anyone else around the table for that matter, he continued.

"Police Headquarters in Miami, Atlanta, San Francisco, Beverly Hills, Cheyenne, Wyoming and Colorado Springs were also bombed. Again, we still don't have any hard figures concerning casualties, but I have been assured they are quite substantial." By this time a dark mood had settled over the room, each man and woman trying their best to reconcile what they were hearing. No one wanted to accept this as reality. It had to be a bad dream. Nothing else made sense.

Bennitt wasn't even close to finishing his summary.

"One truck was driven through the front gates of Disneyland, and another through the gates of Disney World in Orlando. The parks were closed for business, and other than the drivers, there were no casualties."

"Then why hit them?" Gooden asked.

"More than likely they were selected for the emotional damage they would strike in people's hearts. Most every American has sentimental memories of Disneyland; I believe those memories to be the real target," Bennitt answered. "Two more trucks were detonated in two of the three tubes of the Lincoln Tunnel and two more in the Holland tunnel in New York City," Once again he paused to see if the president had anything to say.

A somber, "Go on," was the only reply from the president who was staring intently at an indistinct spot on the far wall and rocking softly back and forth, his arms folded across his chest.

"The damage to the Lincoln Tunnel was bad enough to keep both tunnels closed for at least ninety days…perhaps longer. Unfortunately, the North and South tubes of the Holland tunnel completely collapsed."

"What do you mean by collapsed? Please elaborate." Nicholson requested.

"They're completely flooded, sir."

"Please…continue."

"The New York Port Authority estimates there were more than eight hundred vehicles in the tubes when they were struck. They added that very few managed to get out." Bennitt wiped his forehead with a handkerchief. Even though the room was kept at a comfortable seventy degrees, he was perspiring profusely. He turned the page of his notes while everyone in the room sat quietly listening.

"Several oil tankers were also sabotaged. Two were sunk in the port of Long Beach and one in Pittsburgh, but those pale in comparison to the other three." Bennitt took a drink of water from the glass in front of him. Taking a deep breath, he sighed and continued. "The liquid propane carrier *Dante's Revenge* was blown up smack dab in the middle of Charleston Harbor; the explosion was so tremendous the ship was cracked completely in half. As you all know, at least you should by now, propane carries a much more powerful punch than gasoline does. The entire new propane-handling terminal was also destroyed, along with a significant portion of other harbor facilities including the majority of the cargo docks and several other huge cargo container ships."

"How did they get to the ships?" Barbara Duncan asked. "I thought we had tight security on them."

"We think the terrorists were equipped with scuba gear and…"

"What do you mean, you think…don't you know?" Gooden demanded.

"Let me put it this way; with half the harbor blown to hell and the other half still burning, it's the only thing that makes sense," an exasperated Bennitt retorted.

"Let's all keep our heads, shall we?" Nicholson said soothingly. "Cornelius, please continue."

"Yes, sir. While these are all terrible incidents, even worse is the tanker that was sunk in Houston. How they timed it so perfectly is still a huge mystery, but they managed to sink Exxon's *Distant Horizon* right in the middle of the Houston Ship Channel."

"How is that worse than half of Charleston harbor being blown away?" Minetti inquired.

"I can answer that one," Alexander offered. "With that ship sitting on the bottom of the channel, the Houston oil terminal is virtually shut down indefinitely. I'm not sure if Houston is the biggest terminal we have, but it's pretty close. That one is going to hurt us bad and the economy is gonna' take another huge hit."

"How bad is it?" Nicholson asked.

"The damage is under the water-line and as of right now over three hundred thousand barrels have been spilled. It's going to be an ecological disaster."

"What about the other tankers they hit?"

"As of an hour ago the two in Long Beach were listing badly, but I've been assured they should be okay. They're pumping oil out of the ships' holds as fast as they can and crews are working feverishly to contain what has already been spilled." Bennitt checked his notes. "The tanker in Pittsburgh is badly damaged and dumping oil rapidly, containment crews don't sound too optimistic there. As for the one in San Francisco, they sank it directly under the Golden Gate Bridge. The ship is about eighty percent submerged and emergency personnel have not been able to reach the damaged area to stop the spill."

"How much oil does that ship carry?" Nicholson asked.

"Sir, the ship is the Exxon *Monsoon*, it's categorized as an ultra large crude carrier and is designated as carrying in excess of four million barrels of oil."

"Four million barrels…" Nicholson uttered softly to himself.

"And sir?"

"Yes?"

"They hit it when the tide was coming in, the bulk of the oil is going to wash straight down into the heart of the bay. It will make the spill in Prince William Sound, Alaska back in '89 look like an overflowed toilet."

"How did they manage to blow six oil tankers?" Gen. Slade asked. "I thought those things had double hulls."

"Most of the newer ones do," Bennitt explained. "However, China's demand for more and more oil in recent years has resulted in a shortage of modern tankers; as a result, petroleum companies use what's available."

Nicholson interrupted, "Let's go on, Cornelius."

"Yes sir…at least twenty single engine planes packed full of explosives were used to sabotage several oil refineries as well. The terrorist's flew the planes kamikaze style."

"Which ones were hit?" Nicholson asked.

"They hit the Chevron refineries in El Segundo and Richmond, California as well as the British Petroleum refinery in Los Angeles. Then also struck huge refineries in Corpus Christi, Lake Charles, Louisiana, Pine Bend Minnesota and…"

"And what?" Nicholson prodded.

"Well, I guess it no longer matters that a tanker was sunk in the Houston ship channel."

"How badly were they hit?" asked Nicholson.

"They all might as well be total losses as far as we're concerned. While none were completely destroyed the damage is so significant they might as well be."

"How long until they can be repaired?" asked Gooden.

"Best estimates are at least a year…perhaps longer. Company officials say it's too early to tell until they can put the fires out and get in to survey the damage."

"What was the refining capacity of those refineries?" Iverson James asked.

Bennitt consulted his notes and did some quick math. "Looks like approximately five million barrels per day."

"How do our strategic reserves look?" asked Gooden.

"Down to less than twenty-five percent," Mims said.

"So basically you're saying we're screwed."

"Pretty much. I mean even if we could somehow increase petroleum imports, where are we going to refine it at?"

"Somehow we will make do, this country always finds a way," Barbara Duncan said matter-of-factly.

Nicholson turned toward Slade. "General."

"Yes sir."

"I want each and every one of our remaining refineries under tight military protection immediately. Direct that Patriot missile batteries be sent in and ensure there is a ring of troops around each one of them. General…I want security so tight around those places people will have to ask permission to fart!"

"Aye, sir!"

"Instruct our troops to shoot anyone attempting to gain illegal access and shoot down any unidentified aircraft that refuses to follow orders to alter course."

"Aye sir. Where do you want me to pull the troops from? We're still spread a little thin until reserve call-ups are completed."

"We've got fifteen thousand troops on the way home from Germany, use them. And draw up plans to bring home another ten thousand. We've defended other countries' borders for long enough, I believe it's time we started protecting our own."

"Aye sir. I'll get right on it. Do you want me to stay or go now?"

"Go ahead, go. Mark can bring you up to speed later." Nicholson rethought that and said, "No wait…not just yet, hold on for just a minute longer."

"Yes sir." Slade sat back down.

"How many lives did we lose yesterday?" he asked Bennitt.

"Early estimates are placing the number at around thirty thousand, however, those figures are just preliminary."

"Of course they are." Nicholson turned his chair away from the table so he could think for a minute. After several minutes of awkward silence, he turned back around. "Gentlemen, this has got to stop. We've been looking at this problem from a law enforcement perspective and that is simply not working. We've tried everything we can think of to end this, but our old ways will no longer work, perhaps they never have…at any rate it's time for something new."

"What do you suggest sir?" FBI Director Alexander asked.

"We discussed some options a few day ago and with the exception of a couple of you, you all disagreed with the proposal. Most of you thought it was blatant discrimination and in some ways I guess I agree with you. But unless someone can lay out an immediate effective strategy for stopping these monsters, then I think the time has arrived to begin rounding up all the Arab Muslims in this country illegally or on work or student visas and begin shipping them back to wherever it is they came from."

"How are we supposed to know where they came from if they're here illegally?" Minetti asked.

"You know…I don't think that's our problem and quite frankly, I no longer care. I ordered fifteen thousand troops be reassigned from South Korea to Iraq. That order was expedited and the troops have already been moved. Before they arrived, troops and engineers already in the country had begun constructing detainment camps to house the huge number of people we're going to be sending to them. We're going to take every one of the illegal Arabs that are in this country to Iraq. Once they get there, if they want to advise us of their true identity then we'll possibly make arrangements to get them home. Either way, it doesn't matter, but they're leaving this country."

Several of them, who had not been privy to the earlier discussion, sat there stunned, not sure whether to believe him or not. "Mr. President are you sure you want to do this?" Duncan asked cautiously.

"Want to…no. But I don't see as if we have any other choice."

Gooden cleared his throat before speaking, "Sir we also talked about other illegal immigrants, as well as Arab Muslims who have taken the oath of citizenship, but won't assist us in locating the terrorists. What is your decision concerning that?"

"I do not see any reason to just kick out all non-Arab illegal immigrants just because they're here. Besides, I'm not ready to open that can of worms just yet. They serve a vital function to our economy whether some people care to admit it or not. As for Muslims citizens who were not born here, if they wish to harbor and protect those that would do us harm, then I believe that they have violated the oath they took to gain their rights as citizens and they'll be deported as well."

"Sir, as you said, some of us were not present at this meeting you were talking about," Director James said, "Would you care to elaborate on just how we are suppose to determine which Muslim citizens are in league with the terrorists?'

Nicholson politely smiled. "Iverson, it is not necessarily a matter of finding those in league with them, that would probably be next to impossible. However, if we employ the GPS bracelet that Stuart proposed a few days back, then at least it would be possible to keep track of those wearing them."

"But those that refused would still have the freedom of movement to continue carrying out further attacks. What do you propose we do about them?"

"Those that refuse will either submit to wearing one in the interest of national security and the defense of their fellow citizens, or they will be deported."

"We can't do that sir. Those people have taken an oath and are now legally US citizens with all the rights that go with it," Barbara Duncan said alarmingly.

"Not only can we, we're going to. If they are choosing to hold the safety of a bunch of terrorists above the safety and security of this country, then they forfeit those rights. I further submit they took the oath in vain because they swore to renounce all loyalty to other countries and to defend the Constitution of this one. If they are refusing to fulfill their voluntary oath, then it makes perfect sense to me that they are also willingly abandoning the rights that oath provides."

"Sir," Duncan continued, "Muslims are killing because they believe they are following the wishes of their god. For centuries Christians have also killed thousands of non-Christians because they believed they were following the commands of their god as well. If you start casting out Muslims for doing it, will you treat professed Christians the same way? How can you persecute one religious group for following their beliefs and not others as well? What's the difference between the two?"

Nicholson sat staring at Duncan for what seemed like minutes, but in reality was only seconds. "I'll tell you the difference. When Christians carried out their brutal killings they might have believed they were carrying out the desires of the God of the Old Testament. But, if you have read the Bible you won't find any scriptural support for doing so…"

"That's my point!"

"Hold on a minute," Nicholson said, raising his hand in the air. "When these Muslim fanatics go about killing innocent people they also believe the same thing. However, when you read the Koran, you will find that they are doing exactly what Muhammad told them to do. His commands are to convert the infidels or kill them. There is no room for compromise, discussion or finding neutral ground. There is no provision for people sitting down, like we are right now, and discussing their differences. When the mandates of a religion sanctions the killing of anyone that fails to follow that religion, and then professes to be a peace-loving religion, I have no choice but to draw the line and say no, not in this country.

Now…unless someone has a better solution, then I suggest we get to work protecting the remaining three hundred million people out there who are depending on us to do so. Besides, how can we continue to allow people to live among us whose only desire is to slay us? Are we expected to just sit around waiting for Allah's justice to befall us? I, for one, say no." Nicholson was quiet for a moment. "Furthermore, the Patriot Act provides for the expulsion of aliens who may threaten the national security of the United States. We are by no means proceeding without the power of the law behind us."

"Do you think for one minute you're going to get the political support you'll need to push this through?" Duncan asked.

"Yes I do. I've already met with the majority and minority leaders of both the House and the Senate and have been assured of their complete support. In writing, I might add. This nation is in a severe state of crisis. In fact, we are at war and the battlefield is our country. We have no other choice. As I've said repeatedly, if anyone has a better idea, let's hear it. When I say better idea, I don't mean one constructed with political purposes in mind. The time for that has passed too. If we don't get on the offensive, we will lose this war, of that I have no doubt."

"But Mr. President…"

"No Barbara, there are no 'buts'. If we don't get a handle on this and fast, there won't be any rights to protect for anyone because there will no longer be a United States. The enemy declared war on us, not the other way around. We thought the enemy was overseas, in other countries hiding in caves, while all along, they have been here, on our soil, plotting, organizing, and waiting for the right moment to strike. And boy, did they succeed."

Sounding resigned to the fact he was determined to carry it out, Duncan asked, "So when do you foresee putting this plan into effect, sir?"

"It will take a few days to get everything into place. We have a lot of troops to deploy and aircraft to get into position. I plan on addressing the nation in a few days. That should give us adequate time to take care of all the logistics." Nicholson seemed to ponder what he wanted to say next. He reached for his can of Coke and drained the rest of it in one gulp, then took a peppermint candy from a dish on the table. He sat there and fiddled with the cellophane wrapper for several seconds, opened it and popped the treat into his mouth. "I am declaring a nationwide state of martial law effective Monday night at 9:00PM Eastern Time."

Martial law exists when the military exercises control in various degrees over civilians or civilian authority. More significantly, it may exist in times of war, when civilian authority has ceased to function or has become ineffective. The President institutes martial law in his capacity as the Commander in Chief, and has broad powers that he may invoke in the event of drastic emergencies such as an attack against the nation involving weapons of mass destruction. In most cases, however, soldiers are often placed at the disposal and direction of civilian authority as a supplemental police force and are subordinate to civilian management and judicial review. In cities across the nation concerned citizens had repeatedly petitioned the president to invoke martial law and return stability to the land. That request would now been honored.

"Until then, direct all state governors to set a curfew for 6:00PM. Only people performing vital emergency services will be allowed out after that. Our ports and refineries will remain open around the clock. We still need oil and other goods if we're to continue functioning as a country."

"Sir, do you believe for one minute that Arab Muslims are just going to voluntarily get in their cars, drive down to city hall and submit to being deported?" FBI Director Alexander asked.

"No I don't believe it will be that easy. I am hopeful, however, that once the great majority of Muslims, who are by the way good, honest and decent people, see that we are serious, they will submit to wearing the bracelets, for a time anyway, until we can root out the evil ones in their midst."

"I hope you're right sir, because if you're not the results could be catastrophic."

*   *   *   *

By lunch time prices at American gas pumps had shot above $10 a gallon. Local governments, already cash-strapped, began shutting down commuter buses. Taxi drivers parked their cabs by the thousands. Greyhound bus lines suspended all routes. Suddenly millions of people, who were fortunate enough to still have jobs, no longer had the means in which to get to them, except to walk or ride a bicycle. That is, if they still felt safe enough to risk going to work.

CHAPTER 43

▼

Saturday

Day Twenty-Three

The recovery of bodies continued in the wake of the latest round of attacks. People's fear and hatred were multiplying as quickly as the death toll. The face of America had changed dramatically and it no longer mattered that it was Saturday. Malls, theaters and most businesses were closed. Public parks were deserted. Friday night high school football games had been postponed indefinitely. After a small bomb went off on the loading dock of Yankee Stadium, Major League Baseball had written off the remainder of the season. The National Hockey League and the NBA were considering following suit; before their seasons even got started. School attendance across the country was down more than eighty-five percent and 'closed until further notice' signs were plastered all up and down Broadway in New York City. A second 'Million Man March' in Washington DC was cancelled, as were all luxury cruises on the high seas. America was afraid; terrorism was having its intended effect.

Then America got angry!

Armed citizen patrols canvassed residential neighborhoods across the country; a terrified populace had lost all hope and confidence in the authorities and the military's ability to protect them. Concerned fathers, deciding staying home was the only reasonably safe option, chose to barricade their families inside their dwellings.

As a hostile populace elected to take the law into its own hands, retaliatory attacks steadily increased. Muslim-owned businesses were vandalized and torched nationwide and there were simply not enough police officers to deal with the countless cries for assistance. In certain instances, when officers were dispatched to Muslim-owned businesses, they would conveniently have a flat tire or some other vehicular trouble en route. By the time other officers or firefighters could respond, it was too late.

Muslims, who were normally peaceful and law-abiding citizens, became enraged and started fighting back. Numerous incidents resulted in gunfire and several people died. These events did nothing more than fuel the hatred already firmly rooted and growing in people's hearts. Those who would normally never consider hurting anyone became violent. Across America war was brewing, with Muslims on the one side and Christians, Jews, Atheists and everybody else on the other.

As more and more call-ups were completed, soldiers and Marines were slowly being deployed throughout the country in support of the overwhelmed National Guard troops already in place. Most of the fresh troops were being assigned to big cities and other high value targets across the land. Very few were finding their way into Middle America. This angered the citizenry of smaller towns and they vented their anger in the only direction left to them, toward their Muslim neighbors.

Irate people banded together to drive Muslims out of neighborhoods and towns at gunpoint. Muslim homes were then looted and burned to the ground. When the more anti-social members of these bands saw that no one was being held accountable for their actions, murder replaced vandalism and Muslims began to die in large numbers.

*   *   *   *

The billionaire watched all of this unfold on satellite television and was quite pleased with what he was viewing. Although mildly saddened so many of his Islamic brothers and sisters were falling victim to the mob violence sweeping America, he knew it was a necessary sacrifice if Allah's objectives were to be realized. Soon Americans would demand their government pull its troops out of the Middle East. When this happened, Israel would stand alone, isolated. From there it would take little time for the Islamic world to unleash a holocaust on the Jews that would make the events perpetrated on them by Nazi Germany pale in comparison.

*   *   *   *

Mariska received the signal she was waiting for yesterday around mid-morning. When the television news stations announced truck bombs had detonated in several cities, she knew their mission was a go. The caravan was still in Yreka; however, the final objective was less than a two-hour drive to the south along

Interstate Five. They had pulled into the parking lot of an abandoned warehouse the day before to check over their equipment one last time. As best she could determine, everything was in order and she was reasonably, confident it would all work as planned.

She also decided it was time to inform the others of the remaining details surrounding their mission. When they returned to Motel Six, she gathered them into her room and filled them in on all the finer points of the operation. The men were awed and honored by what they had been chosen to do. Out of all the true believers in the world, they had been the ones selected. Now, each of them was even more determined to succeed than ever before and took vows before Allah they would not fail.

*   *   *   *

The men had been sitting in a warehouse in northeast DC for the better part of two days and their patience was wearing thin. They assumed once they stopped for breakfast Thursday morning it was to be their final meal. All had checked out the van, inspected the contents of the three large crates inside and were preparing to drive out the giant roll-up door when Yousef's cell phone rang. The caller ordered them to stand down and await further instructions and then quickly hung up.

They had not stepped outside the building since. Yousef was afraid if they all went out for meals they might be questioned and somehow their intentions would be discovered. He wouldn't risk that this close to the end, so he elected himself to go out and get their meals as the need arose.

Comfortable amenities were in anemically short supply. They slept on old tarps and used semi-clean grease rags from a barrel for pillows. There was nothing with which to pass the time, so they just sat and discussed over and over each and every detail of their plan. After a time even that grew old and each man gradually found their own space in the abandoned building to be alone with their thoughts. However, they did make sure to kneel toward Mecca five times a day and make prayer to Allah.

CHAPTER 44

▼

Monday

Day Twenty-Five

It was a bright and sunny morning with a cool breeze blowing in from the north off the still snowcapped Mount Shasta. *It is so peaceful up here,* thought Clinton Bowdry, *looking at this, who would believe a war was being fought all over the land?* A war fought against a faceless enemy who, without mercy and without warning, had struck at the very heart of the country.

He looked around, taking in the beauty of the towering trees and the joyful chirping sounds of birds singing loudly from their perches high up on the branches. In the middle of this serene beauty he grieved for his wounded nation. He wept for the thousands of families that had been ripped apart by the senseless violence. He worried about the safety of his own wife and children who were home waiting for his return. He wondered if life would ever be as it once was just a little over three weeks ago. Somehow, in his heavy heart, he knew that it wouldn't, couldn't.

Bowdry had been guarding the structure intermittently since the events of 9/11. Directly after the attacks, security had been substantially increased and no unauthorized personnel were allowed to even approach it. In the decades before the attacks people were allowed to pretty much come and go as they pleased. They were even allowed to take guided tours inside the facility. But, after 9/11 all of that changed. However, as time passed the events of 9/11 grew farther and farther from people's minds. When further *imminent* attacks never took place, security around the behemoth had been scaled back and its guardianship relaxed a bit. Years passed by and tours were again being allowed, as long as the party wishing to take one agreed first to pass a background check.

In light of recent events, Bowdry believed security should have again been tightened immediately. That had not happened until three days ago. Another guardsman was assigned to the security detail and the three of them were now standing ready behind the makeshift barricade that restricted vehicular access to the structure.

Each man was armed with M-16A2 combat rifles and 9mm pistols. Although they had all qualified with their weapons and could even hit a man-sized target with their rifles at three hundred yards, without a scope, Bowdry was convinced security was still too lax. In fact, their modest show of force was there more to ease the fears of a wary public than of any possible effect it might have in deterring a tenacious and well-equipped attacker. Were a concerted attack to occur, Bowdry believed he and his fellow guardsmen would fail miserably and the structure would be lost. Furthermore, he knew the structure to be so vital it should rate, at the least two armored Bradley fighting vehicles and a Patriot missile battery as protection. Even their presence wouldn't guarantee nothing bad would happen but at least they would have a more realistic chance of success.

Nevertheless, he and his two partners stood their post, alert to any signs of danger while a curious sightseer occasionally strolled by, taking in the imposing sight from a distance.

*   *   *   *

Mr. President, we may have just caught a break!" Gooden exclaimed.

"What sort of break?"

"Do you remember the damaged hard drive the FBI recovered from the terrorists in Redding?"

"I remember, what about it?"

"Analysts at Quantico just recovered this email fragment from it," Gooden said, handing it to Nicholson, who began quickly reading through it with a concerned eye. When he got to the end his head came up sharply.

"Is this for real?"

"We believe it is. With the info from the hard drive, in conjunction with other recent intelligence, we're fairly certain those are the most likely targets."

"If they succeed in this, it could wipe out thousands…hundreds of thousands more people."

"Yes sir, it could."

Nicholson collapsed into his chair, his head spinning. *As if we haven't already lost enough! Will these vermin ever be satisfied?* Nicholson noticed that his breathing was rapid and his hands were shaking. His heart had again taken up residence in his throat and had been making frequent visits there over the past few weeks. *When will enough be enough?* He reached for the pack of cigarettes in the desk drawer and shook one out. He slipped it between his lips and raised the lighter. Suddenly with angry disgust he threw the heavy lighter against the far wall shattering it and ripped the cigarette from his mouth. "Damn it all to hell! And damn them!"

A startled Gooden just stared at the president as he sat there seething with fury, his entire body quivering with bottled up rage; his eyes welled up with tears. A secret service agent swung open the door, an alarmed expression on her face, but Gooden waved her away.

"Mr. President, are you…?"

Nicholson shook his head and raised his hand silencing Gooden. Several minutes passed before the president regained his composure and spoke again.

"What are we doing to stop it? Are we even sure these are the actual targets, that this is not some sort of elaborate decoy?"

"As sure as we can be, sir. We have notified law enforcement agencies closest to the targets just in case our Marine Force Recon and SEAL Teams aren't able to reach them in time, because it will take a little while to get them there."

"Marines, Seals? Is that the only option available to us?"

"Yes sir, it is. This cannot be left up to the local police. They're just not capable, in our opinion, to handle it. The consequences are much too dire. We simply can't risk it."

"Very well, the second you learn anything, I want to know about it."

                    ✳   ✳   ✳   ✳

Mariska had assigned each warrior a different insertion point and approach vector, thereby greatly increasing his or her chances for success. There were several access points all over the northern part of the county from which to stage their attacks. As they entered the outer perimeter of the objective the first terrorist vehicle left the interstate, taking Antlers Road and turning left at the bottom of the off-ramp. Several miles further on two more exited and turned right on Lakeshore Drive. A few minutes later two more vehicles departed the caravan at O'Brien Avenue and finally Mariska saw Packers Bay Road and veered to the right.

Mariska followed the winding road until she reached her destination. Stopping, she scanned the area for anything that didn't look right. After several minutes she saw nothing that alarmed her. She waited for several more minutes until satisfied there were no nasty surprises lying in wait for her by the American authorities. She checked the time and decided further delay was not feasible. She placed her foot on the gas easing forward.

Like Mariska, each terrorist arrived at their destinations and timed the off-loading of their vehicles to coincide with the others. Starting at exactly 10:30 AM, the zealots backed up to their assigned loading ramps and began to quickly and smoothly off load their cargo from the trailers.

*   *   *   *

The ten *freedom-fighters* walked out of the small secluded house and piled into four vans and a Ford Taurus parked towards the back of the property in a large barn. The Taurus was the first to leave, a male and female riding inside. The car turned left and drove off toward the target. Ten minutes later the first van pulled away skidding its tires on the gravel driveway, five men inside all looking very grim. The remaining vehicles waited another five minutes before they followed the path of the first two. Their destination was less than five minutes away.

*   *   *   *

Clinton Bowdry sat under an awning drinking a Pepsi with one hand while using the other to fan his sweating face with a magazine. The cool breeze had stopped more than an hour ago and the temperature had rapidly shot passed ninety-five. Jonesy and Mick were standing guard at the barricade. They had all been taking turns rotating under the shade every fifteen minutes; it was the only relief they had.

"Hey Jonesy, what are you doing tonight?" Bowdry hollered from the shade.

"Not much. I'm getting something to eat and then going to the motel and sit on top of the air conditioner until my backside's got ice sickles on it and I ain't coming out till morning."

"I'll second that," Mick chimed in. "I don't know how these people living around here stand this god awful heat, it's like an oven. I can't wait until I get to rotate back to Vermont where wearing clothes is not such a drudgery. If it's this hot tomorrow you fellas might find me standing guard in a tank-top and Speedo."

"If you do, I'm going AWOL. I'd rather face a court-martial than spend a day staring at your hairy butt!" Bowdry laughed.

"Aw…you know you love me."

"Don't kid yourself. I don't like any man that much," Bowdry said as he watched another car pull into the parking lot a hundred yards away. "Besides, any self respecting man wouldn't be caught dead in one of those things. It just ain't proper."

"You know, they say it's not the heat but the humidity that gets you," Jonesy offered.

"Oh yeah?" Bowdry said.

"They say."

"Well, I'll tell you what, why don't you stick your head in a hot oven and I'll squirt ya in the butt with a water pistol. Then you tell me what's worse, the heat or the humidity?" Boisterous laughter ensued.

A couple of minutes passed before anyone spoke again. "Hey Mick?" Jonesy said.

"What now?"

"Don't you 'now what' me, you big lummox. What do you think of these towel heads runnin' around blowing themselves up?"

Mick scoffed. "I think they're clinically insane."

"I don't know, brainwashed maybe...but insane?" Bowdry said.

"Sure...I mean really, what man in his right mind would want to blow himself to pieces just for the privilege of havin' seventy-two women. I mean come on...can you guys imagine having seventy-two of them constantly ragging on you to talk to 'em, pick up your socks, listen to their problems without givin' them answers to their problems, mind you, and then take them shopping too? They gots to be nuttier than a Christmas salad to want that."

"I hear you man. I got one for you. What do the women get, seventy-two men? I can just see that working out real well." Mick said snidely. "Poor girl would probably volunteer to go back and blow herself up all over again just to get a break from it all!"

"And what about the ten and twelve year olds that are blowing themselves to hell...er...Paradise?" Jonesy asked.

"I guess Allah's promise of future considerations." Mick snickered.

"Or perhaps their very own build-it yourself rocket launcher," Bowdry laughed.

Yet another car came down the hill and entered the parking lot. "It's near a hundred degrees out here and they just keep on coming," Mick complained.

Despite all of the terrorist attacks of late, there were still a surprisingly large number of visitors today. *I guess people can only stay hunkered down in their homes for so long.* Bowdry looked at his watch and with a sigh reluctantly stood up. It would be another half-hour before he could again sit in the shade and the relative coolness it provided.

He walked toward the barricade. "Jonesy, it's yer turn in the cooler."

"I guess I better get my sweater first," he joked.

As Jonesy walked away, Bowdry looked around taking a quick appraisal of the area. He saw a man and what appeared to be his two sons in a large grassy area, about fifty yards away, attempting to fly a kite in the sporadic breeze. An elderly couple was sitting at a picnic table enjoying a quiet lunch together. Walking toward him was a young newlywed couple still clothed in their wedding attire. They strolled along hand in hand looking very much in love. He turned his head to the left at the sound of a county maintenance vehicle driving toward him. He thought it a little odd; one didn't normally see county vehicles at a federal installation.

"Hey Mick, what do you suppose they want?" he asked, pointing toward the van.

"Maybe they're here to build us an Igloo," he said with a big cheesy grin.

Bowdry glanced back toward the newlyweds as the van came to a halt in front of him. It took him half a second to process what he was seeing. That half-second almost cost him his life. The groom was drawing a pistol from beneath his tuxedo and leveling it toward him.

Bowdry's training in Army Special Forces was the only thing that saved him. On instinct, he drew his own pistol and snap fired two rounds from his hip toward the 'groom'. As he fired, the side door of the county maintenance van slammed open and four more armed men leapt out, raising rifles in preparation to fire. Without thinking, Bowdry dove behind a nearby concrete barricade as the men opened up in his and Mick's direction.

Bowdry came up with his pistol in his left hand, squeezing off three quick rounds toward the gunmen and ducked back behind the barricade. He looked to his left and saw Mick lying on the concrete with several holes stitched in a jagged line across his head and chest. He took a quick glance behind him and saw Jonesy clutching his M-16 rifle in his right hand while attempting to call for help on the radio with his left. Even if he got the call off, help was miles away. Bowdry knew they were on their own.

The gunmen were not letting up. Their constant fire was sending chunks of broken concrete whistling in all directions. Bowdry once again popped up and fired. A hail of bullets met him from three different directions. He saw as he collapsed to the ground that the groom was down. *At least I got one!*

Bowdry lay there gasping for every breath. His chest feeling like it had been run over by a truck. He could still hear shooting and recognized the sound of Jonesy's M-16 rattling away behind him, but it sounded as if it was getting farther away, though Jonesy hadn't moved. *Get them Jonesy,* he thought, *get the bastards.*

With great difficulty, Bowdry reached into his pocket and withdrew his keys. He looked at the tiny key chain and the picture he carried on it of his wife and two handsome boys. They were smiling at him; through tears he weakly smiled back and closed his eyes.

*   *   *   *

Shasta Lake is the largest manmade lake in the state of California. Located on Interstate Five, north of Redding, it has a surface area covering more than thirty-five thousand acres. Featuring a backdrop of rugged towering mountains, majestic pine and evergreen trees, it is a great location for swimming, boating and fishing. The lake encompasses over three hundred sixty-five miles of shoreline and is thirty-five miles long, making it longer than San Francisco Bay.

Six identically painted boats raced across the sparkling blue water at over thirty-five miles an hour.

*   *   *   *

The five men had finished placing the explosives the previous Wednesday. They were now in position and all they had to do was sit back and wait. From their individual positions they watched people going about their lives as if it was just another blistering hot day of work and fun. Unaware that their world was about to be shattered once again, they scurried about as if the war had moved on to riper pickings and would now leave them in peace. In short order they would learn how mistaken they truly were.

Each man held a remote detonator in his sweaty hands. The wait would soon be over.

*   *   *   *

Jonesy had taken cover behind the front fender of their security vehicle and was enraged to see both Mick and Bowdry were down. The shooters had taken up position on the other side of the barricades and were shooting back at him. He again called for help using the radio on his hip. *Why won't they answer me?* he thought. He chanced a look down at the radio and saw a random bullet had shattered it. Realizing no help would be coming, he rose up from behind the fender and fired again at the terrorists. The bolt on his rifle locked to the rear indicating he was out of ammunition. Jonesy reached for another magazine but his hand came back empty, he was out.

He looked back toward the center of the structure and decided he had to make a run for it. If he could make it to the tower, he might have a chance. Jonesy drew his sidearm and scattered seven quick rounds at the shooters, hitting one in the stomach and driving the others behind cover. He then turned and broke into a full sprint toward the tower.

Jonesy was a wide receiver in college and still had a bit of the old speed left. He pumped his legs for all they were worth and he had covered half the distance before the terrorists realized what he was doing. They stood and opened fire in his direction.

A sharp pain quickly developed in his right side and he felt like he was going to die. The painful memory of his two partners lying dead on the sun-baked pavement drove him onward. Ignoring the cramp and running in a jagged line, he pushed himself harder and harder. He could hear the sound of numerous bullets whistling by his head and ricocheting off the pavement. Still he ran. He was beginning to fade. He was losing speed. He couldn't make it. "No!" he yelled, he had to dig deeper and push even harder, if that was possible.

Suddenly the shooting stopped and Jonesy eased his pace just a little. Salvation was just forty yards away. He'd made it. As he ran the last few yards to the steel door he wondered, *why had they stopped shooting?* He glanced back over his shoulder as he reached for the door handle and safety. Jonesy's body was crushed between the tower and the bumper of one of the terrorist vehicles.

*   *   *   *

The six boats each arrived at the rendezvous point within five minutes of one another. Their pilots maneuvered the watercraft close together and then prayed Allah would continue to bless them with good fortune.

Mariska looked at her five companions, who until a few days ago she hadn't even known. Now they were gathered together, ready to become Shaheed, Arabic for martyr, for this great cause. The next victory would no doubt crack the spine of the Great Satan and send them all running for cover, cowering from Allah's wrath. She looked toward the objective and for the green flare that would signal it was time to go.

She looked back at the men. "I am proud to have served with you. For your sacrifice you will be greatly rewarded when you get to Paradise. You have all done well and I gladly go to my death with you as comrades for the honor of Jihad."

$$* \qquad * \qquad * \qquad *$$

The terrorist backed the vehicle away from the wall and Jonesy's twisted and mangled body crumpled to the concrete. Three other vans pulled up and the remaining seven terrorists got out. Their leader told the drivers exactly where he wanted them to park their vans and they drove away to comply.

When the drivers had returned to the group, they all retrieved huge backpacks from the remaining van and pulled them onto their shoulders. One of the men placed shaped charges on the door of the tower. Taking cover behind the van they blew the charges. The heavy metal door was left twisted and hanging at an angle from its upper hinge, giving the terrorists free access to the interior of the target.

They met no resistance as they got on the elevator and made their way down into the inner depths of the structure. Two of the terrorists had taken a tour just four weeks prior. Using watches equipped with GPS locators they knew exactly how far down to go before stopping the elevator. Each man struggled with the burden of one hundred-fifty pounds of plastic explosives on his back and the woman carried fifty. Two of the men had even managed to drag the heavy packs of their two fallen comrades along with them. Fourteen hundred pounds of C-4 carries quite a punch.

When the elevator doors opened they all got right to work. It took nearly ten minutes to finish their task, but finally all of the charges were in place. The timers were set and they all got back in the elevator to begin their ascent.

Five minutes later they were back topside and wasted no time climbing into their getaway van. The leader reached into the console and grabbed a flare gun and flare. He checked his stopwatch, and waited ninety seconds before continuing. Then he loaded the gun, pointed it out the window toward the clear blue sky and fired. The green flare shot high into the air. Upon reaching its zenith the little parachute within it deployed and it began to slowly drift toward the cool tranquil water.

*   *   *   *

Mariska saw the flare arc into the air and looked at her watch. She told the others to get ready as she began the two-minute countdown. She'd already agreed to go first. They all started their engines and Mariska's boat moved away from the others. She aimed her craft toward the target two miles away and then pushed the throttle all the way forward.

*   *   *   *

The driver whipped the van around and sped off back in the direction they'd come. Within a minute they were clear of the area and parked a safe distance away on a bluff affording them a good view of what was to come. In the distance they could hear the faint sound of sirens echoing through the canyon walls, but they were still far away and it would certainly be several more minutes before they arrived. The woman commented that one of the tourists must have called for help. Though help would no doubt arrive, it would get here far too late to matter.

*   *   *   *

"Sir, we were right...the terrorists were planning to take down four dams; Grand Coulee in Washington State, Shasta and Oroville dams in Northern California and Hoover in Arizona and Nevada," Gooden told Nicholson.

"Did we stop them?" Nicholson asked alarmingly.

"Seals, Marines and Army Rangers stopped them cold at Hoover, Grand Coulee and Oroville. The terrorists put up quite a fight but our guys mowed them down. Field commanders are reporting more than fifty dead bad guys and no friendly casualties."

"Did we take any of them alive?"

"No sir. Most of them were killed in the gun battle, and several of them jumped from the dams to avoid being captured."

Nicholson shook his head slowly, "What about Shasta?"

"It doesn't look good. Teams are on the way, but the place is rather isolated and it's taking some time to get there. Unfortunately we have reports that shots have already been fired."

"Will our people get there in time?"

"Unsure. I was told that two Apache attack helicopters were dispatched and they should be almost there, but ground troops are at least ten minutes out."

"If our people don't stop them, is it feasible the terrorists could somehow bring down the dam?"

"Engineers say it's highly unlikely but you never know. The terrorists that were trying to attack the other dams had a lot of explosives on them when our guys stopped them. Not only that, but they had several boats packed with enough explosives to blow the nose off the man in the moon."

"So…?"

"So sir, I'd say it's anybody's guess."

*   *   *   *

The heinous killers sat anxiously watching the events unfolding from the safety of a nearby hill that was normally used by tourists to take in the overall view. From their position they could easily see Shasta Dam, Shasta Lake and, far away on the northern horizon, Mount Shasta. Slicing through the water at high speed a mile and a half away were the six speedboats Mariska Jabril and her companions had so carefully snuck into the Lake Shasta area. Spaced a quarter mile apart the boats were making a beeline for the center of the dam. The water line was about sixty-three feet from the crest and that had all been carefully considered when her fellow warriors had planted the charges inside.

*   *   *   *

Flying close to one hundred fifty miles per hour, Warrant Officer Michael Jergenson and his co-pilot swooped down over the mountains in their AH-64D Longbow Attack helicopter. Skimming fifty feet off the surface of Lake Shasta down the Pitt River arm, Jergenson saw Interstate Five at the Bridge Bay Resort directly ahead. As they drew near, the war bird popped up and over the bridge and then quickly dropped back to just above the water passing more than two hundred houseboats moored at the marina to his left.

Jergenson found it difficult to believe he was back at Lake Shasta so soon. He and his wife had vacationed here with the kids the summer before and had thoroughly enjoyed themselves. He knew this trip would not be such a happy occasion. His wingman had developed engine trouble soon after takeoff and was forced to turn back or risk crashing. Now it was up to Jergenson and his co-pilot to handle the mission.

"Lobo...you ready?" Jergenson asked his gunner.

"Roger, Gator."

"10-4. The objective should be around this next bend to the left. Master Arm on," he ordered.

The gunner flipped up the toggle switch activating the weapons system. Hanging from pylons on either side of the Apache were eight 'fire-and-forget' Hellfire missiles and thirty-eight rockets. Normally the Apache could carry sixteen of the deadly missiles, however, external tanks had been installed to provide adequate fuel to complete the long flight from Idaho and eight missiles had to be eliminated from the weapons loadout. Rounding out the Apache's deadly punch were twelve hundred rounds for its automatic gun, located in the nose of the aircraft. The gun was linked to the gunner's helmet. Wherever he looked, the gun followed.

As soon as they cleared the cliffs to their left Jergenson saw six boats lined up, speeding toward the center of the dam. *That's got to be them!* He increased altitude to five hundred feet and pointed the nose of the Apache toward the line of boats.

"Lobo...target lead boat with missile, prepare to engage!"

"Are you sure that's them?"

"I'm sure, target the boat!"

"Roger! Hellfire selected. Target acquired. Prepared to fire."

*   *   *   *

Inside the van the alert leader saw the Apache clear the peninsula through his binoculars and zero in on his Muslim brothers on the water.

"Awad, get a missile...hurry!"

Awad sprang from his seat and sprinted around to the back of the van. Jerking open the doors he quickly opened a long green case and reached in. With a practiced hand he speedily assembled the Stinger missile inside and threw it up on his shoulder. Activating the seeker head he was quickly rewarded with a steady tone indicating he had good missile lock on the enemy aircraft. Awad squeezed the trigger ever so gently...

*   *   *   *

Inside the Apache an alarm began screaming in Jergenson's ear informing him that a missile had locked on to his aircraft.

Jergenson thought quickly. "Lobo, fire!"

The hundred-pound Hellfire shot from the launch rail of the portside weapons pylon and raced toward the lead boat at over mach one. Jergenson immediately jettisoned the external fuel tanks while banking the Apache to starboard and dove toward the surface of the lake. Increasing speed to full power he fired off six missile decoy flares and raced back the way they had come, hoping to put the cliffs between them and the missile.

Jergenson never knew whether the decoy flares or the heat-seeking missile jammer located just behind the rotor head had decoyed the missile, but the immediate threat was over and he was pissed.

*   *   *   *

Awad fired the missile and almost immediately saw the helicopter turn away, dive for the water and race away back around the peninsula. About the time the helicopter disappeared from view the lead boat exploded, sending metal and fiberglass shooting across the water and into the sky. The other boats continued toward the dam undeterred while Mariska Jabril's soul began its journey into the netherworld and an appointment with Allah.

*   *   *   *

"Lobo, did you see where that missile came from?"

"Roger, looks like it came from a van parked in a clearing above the dam roughly a quarter mile to the southeast."

"Good, let's go get him and we've got to hurry. Those boats are getting closer by the second."

This time Jergenson avoided the lake and flew dangerously fast through several narrow canyons until he found a road he was sure would bring them in behind the van from the down-stream side of the dam. Sure enough, as the Apache came tearing around the side of a high mountain and cleared a rise in the road, the van was directly ahead no more than a half mile away. Jergenson could see a figure standing to the rear of the vehicle, a missile launcher on his shoulder. The terrorist was staring back toward the lake just waiting for Jergenson to show himself. He was looking in the wrong direction. Jergenson smiled. *Just enough time to snuff these guys and then deal with the boats!*

"Lobo, select rockets. Let's light 'em up.

Lobo selected the requested weapon and targeted the terrorists' vehicle.

*   *   *   *

The terrorists watched the lead boat explode and knew their meticulous timing was now pointless. While the explosives in the vans on the roadway of the dam could be timed to detonate with the impact of the first boat, the ones inside were on a timer because a radio signal could not penetrate the millions of tons of concrete.

The terrorist looked down at the timer in his lap and watched the remaining seconds tick away. He could hear a dull rumble come from deep within the giant structure and felt the ground tremble as the fourteen hundred pounds of explosives wreaked their havoc.

*   *   *   *

Jergenson could not hear the bombs go off over the Apache's engine, nor could he feel them from a hundred feet in the air. However, he could see trees swaying from the shockwave and he knew something terrible had just happened.

"Lobo…fire!"

The gunner squeezed the trigger, rippling off ten of the Hydra rockets at the enemy below.

*   *   *   *

As the first boat hit the center of the dam, the terrorist leader sitting in the van pressed the remote detonator in his left hand. The missile holding terrorist standing at the back of the vehicle abruptly turned around and saw the hovering Warbird and snap-fired his second Stinger a half second before the airship's rockets struck the van.

The Stinger shot toward the Apache and once again Jergenson rippled off a half-dozen flares and darted back behind the rocky cliffs, barely escaping the missile that slammed into the rocks behind him.

Having wasted vital time and now free from danger, Jergenson pulled hard on the joystick and accelerated back toward the dam and the homicidal watercraft. The first thing he saw was that the rockets had torn into the terrorist vehicle and blown them all to bits. Jergenson quickly dismissed them and turned his attention toward the lake; all hell was breaking loose on the center of the dam.

The nearly three quarters of a ton of C-4 inside the dam created a shockwave so powerful that most other structures would have crumbled from the trauma, but not this one. This one would need a little help and the two Army warriors hovering a short distance away were getting a firsthand view as it was provided.

The construction of Shasta Dam was completed in 1945. Next to Grand Coulee Dam, on the Columbia River in Washington State, it is the largest dam mass in the continental United States. The dam was built using more than fifteen million tons of concrete. It is six hundred and two feet high, eight hundred eighty-three feet thick at the base and thirty feet thick at the top. The face of the dam covers thirty-one acres and is three thousand four hundred and sixty feet long. Shasta Dam holds back in excess of four and a half million acre-feet of water. So much concrete was used in the construction that its engineers claim it could take as long as a hundred years for it to fully cure.

Mansur's boat, packed with fifteen hundred pounds of explosives, struck the outside of the dam dead center, exactly opposite of where the explosive had went off inside. Already weakened within, cracks spider-webbed across the inside face of the monstrous structure. The sound of the dam cracking carried loudly over the surface of the water to the already alerted swimmers, picnickers and boaters.

Directly above where the two boats had struck sat the vans the terrorists had left behind. Each was stuffed with three thousand pounds of ammonium nitrate, the same explosive mixture used to take down the Alfred P. Murrah Federal Building in Oklahoma City in 1995. The van's huge load detonated with double the force of the explosion in Oklahoma. The combination of more than six tons of explosives hitting the dam from three different directions, in the same area, at the same time was devastating. Huge sections of the dam were ripped away, thrown into the water and into the air. The dam was grievously fractured in several places.

Millions of gallons of water surged into the interior of the dam applying even more force to the over-stressed behemoth. Qasim's boat struck in the same place as the last followed by Najjar's at quarter mile intervals.

The exploding dam was between Jergenson and the waterborne terrorists requiring him to fly a wide path to avoid the concrete missiles flying through the air. Precious seconds passed before he was able to place his sights on the sixth and final boat. Without being told, Lobo sighted in on the speeding zealot and let loose with the nose-mounted machine gun. Hundreds of tiny splashes skittered across the water as he walked his fire into the target. Less than a hundred feet from the dam, Hassan's boat blew apart.

Although the army warriors had managed to stop two of the boats, the remaining ones carrying three tons of explosives had struck the dam at forty miles an hour; any hopes that the dam would be able to hold vanished.

Shasta Dam was never designed to withstand this kind of onslaught. Engineers believed that even a 747 crashing directly into the face of it would not have toppled the giant. However, it was an entirely different story when nearly fourteen tons of high explosives were strategically placed with the sole purpose of destroying it.

Most curved concrete gravity dams were designed to last fifty years. After that they require extensive overhauls to ensure they are still strong enough to withstand the constant pressure of billions of gallons of water. Shasta Dam was now more than sixty years old and the old girl could simply not withstand this devastating trauma.

It started at the weakest point, the point of impact. Reinforced concrete began to slowly give way under the tremendous pressure. Huge sections began breaking away and falling over the three giant drum gates in the face of the dam. Under normal conditions emergency procedures would go into effect and the huge gates would be opened to release excess water pressure. These were not normal conditions. Uncountable millions of gallons of water flooded the inside of the dam shorting out computers tasked with this duty. The gates were not opened and raging water simply took the path of least resistance. Fifteen minutes after the attack began, a twenty-foot section in the center of the dam gave way; other, larger pieces soon followed and the dam, block by block, crumbled.

Enormous sheets of shattered concrete were dislodged and went shooting down the face of the mortally wounded giant into the water below. The power plant at the base of the dam was sheared from its foundation and sent hurling down the rapidly rising Sacramento River. Automatic alarms went out to the unsuspecting residents down stream. This included Redding, ten miles to the south, which lay directly in the raging tidal wave's path.

Still hovering a short distance away, Jergenson and Lobo helplessly watched the carnage unfold. They had failed their mission; who knew how many would perish? Jergenson activated his radio to report what was taking place. As he tried to convince the disbelieving operator hundreds of miles away he was serious, he watched, as huge houseboats and swimmers were sucked through the gaping maw that used to be Shasta Dam.

CHAPTER 45

▼

The population within the city limits of Redding is around a hundred thousand, however, on a normal workday that figure swells to around a hundred and twenty thousand, fed by the great number who drive in from the suburbs. Over half of these people are employed or live in the immediate downtown area.

Redding sits in a depression right by the Sacramento River. In fact, the heart of the city is all but surrounded by water. The river meanders along the northern and eastern sides of the city while Clear Creek runs along the entire southern edge, eventually converging with one of the river's estuaries. The only way out of town, without crossing a bridge, is to travel west toward the Trinity Alps and Whiskeytown Lake.

Ideally, when the alarms sounded, warning the citizenry to begin evacuation, they would have taken the western route and been assured of their safety. The problem was that people were by nature creatures of habit and few had ever taken the time to truly consider what they would do if ever faced with the current calamity. As a result, just as the terrorists desired, disorganized panic ensued.

Terrified people swarmed toward their cars and sped toward the six bridges that could take them safely out of the path of the crushing wall of water currently barreling toward them. Very few people had the presence of mind to take the western route. Residents in the Redding area had always been told they would have about two hours in which to get to higher ground in the event the dam failed. Of course that time estimate was based on an earthquake damaging the dam and its failure being imminent, but not immediate. However, it didn't include deliberate acts of sabotage that caused instant destruction. People had discussed the idea of someone sabotaging the dam for years, but no one could conceive that it could actually be toppled. While alarms had been sounded, the severity of the situation had not yet been made clear. Most people didn't even know what the alarms were for. For those that did know, many mistakenly believed they had a little time to rush home for irreplaceable valuables.

In short order, traffic snarled, backed up and city streets became a bottleneck. Fender benders and stalled vehicles quickly added to the bedlam. Watching the chaos from a distance, were five men whose orders were to wait for this very thing to happen before completing the final step in their diabolical plan. Knowing that cellular providers would be overwhelmed, the men kept in contact by way of walkie-talkies. They waited until traffic was backed up to the point no one was moving and within seconds of one another they each pressed their detonators.

*   *   *   *

The ABC News van cleared the security checkpoint a half-mile from the White House and was allowed to join dozens of other news vehicles tightly grouped together outside the fence beyond the South Lawn. The four men within, having used legitimate identifications obtained from an actual employee at ABC, quickly began setting up their equipment.

*   *   *   *

A motionless President Nicholson sat watching a live feed from Warrant Officer Jergenson's Apache helicopter video system as it hovered along above the mammoth wall of water surging toward Redding. Jergenson had chose to record the event because he didn't know what else to do.

With a bird's eye view, Nicholson could see what appeared to be another small dam downstream, later determined to be the Keswick Dam reservoir. In a matter of seconds it was enveloped by the wave. The concrete barrier was ripped apart, snapping like dry timber in a tornado and flung along in the ravenous path of the now-ferocious deluge that was the Sacramento River.

Nicholson watched as towering pine trees were plucked from the ground like so many weeds from a flowerbed. Massive boulders spun over and over on the very crest of the powerful wave. Seconds later the camera angle turned a bend in the river and in the distance he could make out a train trestle spanning the river high above the water.

Moments later it too collapsed under the brutal force of angry water lashing at its giant timbers. The massive wooded beams were splintered like toothpicks.

The five-engine freight train that was just starting its trek across the trestle suddenly found it no longer had tracks to glide along and plunged into the churning waters a hundred and fifty feet below, pulling seventy-six fully loaded freight cars along with it.

The President wiped a tear from his eye as he watched the giant boxcars being washed downriver violently twisting and turning towards the thousands of American citizens in their path.

"Mark, have they managed to evacuate the city?" he asked, knowing full well there had not been nearly enough time to get everybody out.

"Sir, the evacuation is in progress, but they've only had about fifteen minutes to do it," Gooden explained.

Nicholson glanced back over to the video screen and the mass carnage still unfolding.

*　　　*　　　*　　　*

Three panels slid slowly back on the roof of the ABC news van. Inside, men readied the M-47 Dragon missiles they had carefully smuggled through security, with the help of a Muslim brother on the security detail who had been planted a decade earlier. The Dragon was a medium range, wire guided, anti-tank weapon. Requiring only one operator, it could be used to penetrate fortified bunkers and other hard targets, in this case, the Oval Office.

*　　　*　　　*　　　*

Support columns on the vital bridges were sheared away by the explosive charges. Each of the bridges broke apart; fragmenting and plunging into the waterways they had only moments before spanned. All avenues of escape were suddenly gone, some of the fleeing motorists at last remembered the western route, but due to the clogged roadways couldn't get turned around to attempt the alternate routes. There was no time anyway. Hundreds were killed when the bridges were blown. Mass hysteria ensued. People abandoned their vehicles and began running, before realizing there was no place safe to run to.

Having no other options, thousands of people jumped into the water attempting to swim across the brutally cold, swift river. Hundreds of weaker swimmers drowned quickly. Thousands more would be caught by the giant wave before safely reaching the far bank.

*   *   *   *

From the safety of the cliffs north of town one of the terrorists sat watching the utter pandemonium he had so willingly created. Giving praise to Allah, he got into his vehicle and drove away to safety. He, like the others, had other missions to accomplish.

*   *   *   *

The monstrous wave of water crashed into the heart of the city at 1:37PM. The massive wall smashed into downtown with a force equal to that of the tsunami that struck the Indian Ocean in late 2004. Homes, business, cars and people were rapidly added to the trees, houseboats, train-cars and wildlife; all swept swiftly away to the south.

Within two hours the entire downtown area was submerged under one hundred feet of water. Very few of the more than seventy-five thousand people working and living there at the time made it out.

The destruction was not, however, limited to Redding. Ten miles to the south lay Anderson with a population of nearly ten thousand souls. Here people, like their neighbors to the north, mistakenly believed they had more time than they actually did. Many took the time to grab valuables, pictures and other items of great sentiment worth before fleeing. The tidal wave did not pause to give them the time they so desperately required, scores more were caught in its path. Close to two thousand more perished that would have survived had they left as soon as they received the warning.

The water continued south and wiped out the small community of Cottonwood and devastated Red Bluff fifteen miles further on. By the time the dam had spent its fury there would be two inches of water standing in downtown Sacramento, one hundred and eighty miles away.

In addition to the massive loss of human life, the devastation to California's agricultural industry was untenable. The economic impact to California was conservatively estimated at more than fifty billion dollars, but that was nothing more than a random figure plucked out of thin air. No single act of terrorism in the world's history came close to equaling the destruction caused by the demolition of Shasta Dam. It was truly the worst day in American history.

*   *   *   *

With the Dragon missiles on their shoulders, three would-be assassins stepped up on small benches and stuck their heads out through the openings. Quickly locating the huge windows of the Oval Office, they took careful aim.

*   *   *   *

On the rooftop of the Old Executive Office Building an agent scanning the area with binoculars happened to see the panels on the van slide back. Focusing his attention on the holes, he saw three figures rise up through them with what were obviously missile launchers on their shoulders.

Swiftly activating his radio he screamed, "Navaho! Navaho! Navaho!" The sniper to his right leveled his rifle toward the distant van, took quick aim and fired. The center figure was flung backwards and fell through the hole.

Before he could fire again the first missile exploded from the launcher. Three seconds later the second one followed.

*   *   *   *

Several secret service agents slammed open the doors of the Oval Office and rushed toward a startled Nicholson, still watching the indiscriminate slaughter striking America on the monitor. Without speaking, two of the huge agents grasped the president under his arms and lifted him forcefully from his chair. Rushing toward the door, Nicholson's toes brushed the highly polished marble floor about every third step.

*   *   *   *

Eleven seconds after the first missile blasted from the launcher it struck the thick bulletproof glass directly behind the president's desk. The thick barricade was shattered, but the warhead didn't explode. The terrorists had omitted one important detail from their elaborate scheme. The M-47 missile they had was the earlier version and requires 11.2 seconds to arm.

*   *   *   *

Just as the agents carried the president through the newly installed solid mahogany doors the second missile shot through the shattered window and hit the far wall opposite the president's desk. With the additional flight time the second missile exploded just as advertised.

Shrapnel blew in all directions, pulverizing the marble floor into a fine powder. The round walls were obliterated and the president's desk was blown through the window and onto the grass below.

A fireball shot through the open doors the president's protectors had just carried him through. No more than six feet from the doors the agents carrying him, as well as two others, had thrown Nicholson to the floor and covered him with their bodies.

The two agents on top died instantly. The two underneath received second and third degree burns. President Nicholson was knocked unconscious and bleeding profusely from a severe head-wound.

Three feet away from the president lay the body of National Security Advisor Mark Gooden, his head partially decapitated from a jagged piece of the heavy mahogany door.

*   *   *   *

Outside heavily armed agents cautiously approached the news van. In other vehicles all around the terrorists, legitimate news-people hunkered down hoping, praying that they were safe.

The leader of the assault team used a blow horn to order the occupants out of the vehicle with their hands above their heads. Several tense minutes passed before the side door of the van slid open. At first no one was visible except the body of the terrorist shot by the sniper. Then slowly, three other men stepped into view with their hands above their heads.

The detail leader had been instructed to take them alive if possible. America was desperate for information as to how they could stop this war and these three were the only potential leads.

The terrorists stepped down out of the van and stood still, apparently awaiting further instructions. The detail leader saw that one of them was clutching a cell phone in his hand.

"Drop the phone!" he ordered.

The killer didn't move.

"I said, drop the phone or I will order my men to open fire!"

This time the zealot smiled ever so slightly and moved his thumb a quarter inch to the right, detonating the thousand pounds of dynamite carefully hidden within the walls of the van.

CHAPTER 46

▼

Day Twenty-Eight

Thursday

President Nicholson stood gazing through the gaping hole in the outer wall of the Oval Office. Out beyond the South Lawn he could see countless twisted and burned out hulls of former news vehicles. He had been informed that many well-recognized journalists had perished in the ambush. Armored personnel carriers and M-1 Abrams main battle tanks now patrolled the perimeter of the White House, and no one was being allowed within a half-mile of it who didn't have at least five White House staffers personally vouching for their character.

He had no doubt that the entire world wanted to hear what he had to say tonight. They were eager to know just how the only remaining superpower was planning to deal with these attacks upon its homeland. The answer would no doubt please many and enrage countless others, but there was no help for that now.

It had been three days since his attempted assassination and the heinous slaughter of Redding, California. There were still random attacks occurring all over the country, although none of them compared to the ones of the week prior to Monday. He had also learned that more and more citizens were fighting back and taking the war to the streets. Bloody and violent skirmishes were taking place in just about every city and community in America. The term 'give me liberty or give me death' suddenly had a whole new meaning.

With the exception of a single pool-camera in front of him and its operator, he was alone. For as long as he could remember he believed true peace could be achieved through cool heads and diplomacy. He had also long believed the United States' insistence on having the strongest military in the world was a mistake; it would only draw hatred. While he still wasn't convinced that wasn't the case, he was now convinced it was time to look at things from a completely new perspective.

From day one of his presidency he had striven to change the way America conducted her foreign policy. If the US would just pull back its military and let others rule themselves the way they chose then all would be fine. Surely America's enemies would recognize our good will and call a truce. The events of the past several weeks had very cruelly forced him to see that was not a possibility. America's enemies were not just angry at the military and US foreign policy; they hated America's very way of life. *Their goal is not to change us, but to destroy us*, he thought. *No matter how much we try to placate them it will not stop. Each time we reach out in an attempt to arrive at a peaceful solution, it is only taken as another sign of weakness.*

Knowing his own family's history as being filled with racial hatred and bigotry, he found himself quite surprised at the position he now found himself adopting. He once believed it unthinkable he would condone the singling out of an entire race of people or a particular religion. However, that was a mindset from a different time and when he lived in a far different America. Today it was all changed. He knew it was time to take a stand, to draw a line in the sand and say 'here but no further'. He had indeed taken an oath to preserve, protect and defend the Constitution of the United States and that was just what he was going to do, let the chips fall where they may.

Sitting behind Mark Gooden's desk, which was brought in from his office, Nicholson bowed his head and said a prayer to the Almighty. *Please, give me grace and bless my words, oh Lord. Impart your wisdom upon me this night. If I ever needed it, now is the time. In your name, Amen.*

"Mr. President, it's just about time," White House Chief of Staff Cornelius Bennett said as he walked through the splintered doors. Following him were the hair and makeup people who quickly began touching up the president's face for public presentation. They also checked the bandage on his forehead making sure it was clean and secure before leaving the room.

"Two minutes until air-time. Are you ready?" Bennitt asked.

"I guess I'd better be. I'm told that a large number of cable television stations are pre-empting their programming for this one. Has that ever happened before?"

"I'm not sure, but I don't believe it has, at least not to this extent."

"Oh well, first time for everything I guess," he thought for a moment then asked. "Cornelius, are we sure we have the entire support of both parties? I sure don't want to be left hanging in the wind after this is over tonight."

"Mr. President, don't worry about it. Taking recent events into account, any congressman who splits off and goes against you at this point will be cutting their own political throat." The cameraman indicated thirty seconds until airtime.

President Nicholson took a drink of Coke and set the can down out of sight of the camera. He then adjusted his chair, made sure to sit up straight and reminded himself to keep his hands on the desk because he had a nasty habit of gesticulating when he talked. The cameraman raised his right hand above his head and began counting down, five...four...three...two...and pointed at him. The green light on top of the camera came on.

He had elected to deliver this speech from the Oval Office. Even though it had been destroyed, he felt that America and the world needed to see exactly what had happened. With scorched walls, two new glistening American flags and a large sheet of bulletproof glass standing behind him, he leaned slightly forward. "My fellow Americans, good evening," the president began, still a bit nervous, "It is with a heavy heart that I address you this evening. Over the past several weeks our nation has been the victim of numerous vicious and savage attacks. The despicable human beings that carried out these attacks have shown they knew exactly where, how and when to strike us, to ensure they caused the greatest damage to our infrastructure, our economy, our people and our national state of mind. At present we have lost over one hundred and forty thousand innocent American lives. More will surely follow as the battle continues, more of the wounded lose their fight for life and additional bodies are recovered from the carnage that used to be Redding, California and other destroyed buildings across the country."

Nicholson paused, swallowed hard and then plowed ahead, "The America I once knew is now gone, changed forever. In its place is one of fear, doubt and mistrust of practically everything and everyone. It is now a nation where people are afraid to go to work or to the store. It's a nation where frightened parents refuse to send their children to school or even out to play. We were once a nation possessing the strongest economy and fastest growing industry in the world, now were crumbling into that of a second-class country. That cannot be allowed to continue. That is not the America I will concede to live in."

"As a nation, we have attempted to be a friend to the entire world. In fact, even nations that have steadfastly opposed us and others that have proven to be our enemies, we still responded in their time of need. We have supported them with our finances and the very lives of the brave men and women of our armed forces when their safety or borders were threatened. At no time has this country displayed any intentions toward global conquest. We simply wanted others to share in the quality of life that we have been so blessed with. Even though we gave our help freely, expecting only friendship in return, they have eagerly accepted our help and all the while plotted our destruction. Therefore, all foreign aid, to any country that has publicly denounced this nation or has sided with our enemies against us, is hereby revoked immediately and indefinitely. The United States will no longer dump the hard-earned money of our people into corrupt countries, only to see them aid our enemies.

"In 1941, the Empire of Japan suddenly and without provocation attacked the United States at its naval base in Pearl Harbor. Their intent was to cause such extreme damage to our naval forces that we would be impotent to respond to them in like manner. Shortly after the attacks were carried out, Admiral Isoroku Yamamoto made the following historic statement, "I fear that we have awakened a sleeping giant and filled him with a terrible resolve." Yamamoto could not possibly have known how accurate that prophetic statement would prove to be. In four short years the Japanese Navy was virtually destroyed and their ability to wage effective war against the United States was decimated. However, the Japanese would still not relent and resorted to using Kamikaze attacks, much like the terrorists have been recently employing against us, in a last ditch effort to win victory.

"Long ago my forerunner, President Harry S. Truman was eventually forced to make a very difficult decision that he truly did not want to make. However, he made it because that was his responsibility as the leader of this great nation. He authorized the first release of atomic weapons on the cities of Nagasaki and Hiroshima, which instantly killed more than one hundred and ten thousand people, fewer than we have lost these past weeks. While many innocent Japanese lives were tragically lost, the decision he made no doubt saved countless millions of American and Japanese lives, because shortly after the bombs were dropped, the Japanese Empire surrendered.

"I do not claim to be the equal to the great Harry Truman; however, I find myself facing an equally difficult decision, like the one he did more than sixty years ago. Our enemy has chosen to attack us where we are the most vulnerable. They are attempting to drive us out of the Middle East through any barbaric and terroristic means they can dream up. While I have my own opinions of what the United States' involvement in the Middle East should be, I do not for one moment condone the violent acts they have employed against us. While we enjoy the freedom to disagree with one another as one of our greatest liberties, when faced with a determined enemy we must come together and set aside our differences. Only then can we face the threat as one country, one people, one United States.

"For years the leaders of many Islamic countries have shaken the hand of the United States with one hand, all the while stabbing us in the back with the other. These uncivilized and unfriendly acts must now be put to a stop. We have recently gathered solid intelligence that some Arab leaders have financed, armed, harbored and encouraged these terrorist organizations for years. That too must now stop.

"In this nation, if a young child breaks a neighbor's window we do not hold the child legally accountable, we hold the child's parent or guardian responsible for any and all damages. It is the parent's place to instill proper discipline in their children. If the parent refuses to correct the child then the authorities are duty bound to intervene. If the authorities find the parent is blatantly refusing to control the child's behavior, then the parent can be charged with neglect. In every instance the parent is ultimately held accountable.

"Just a few days ago I held an emergency meeting with the entire Congress and the National Security Council. In that meeting a unanimous vote was cast declaring unrestricted warfare against all enemies of the United States whenever and wherever they are found. The countries and heads of state that declaration involves are at this very moment being delivered, by US Ambassadors, a formal declaration of war. As additional intelligence reveals other enemies, they too will be added to the list.

"While I understand not all Muslims within our borders are guilty, the fact remains that the great majority of terrorists all have one thing in common. They are Arab Muslims. Not Christian, not Jewish, not Buddhists, not Hindus and not even atheists. The terrorists' religion is their common denominator. As I said, not all Muslims are guilty, in fact, a very small percentage are creating the problems. However, Muslims also believe it is wrong to inform on one another, no matter how much evil is done and that is simply unacceptable. The very protection this wall of silence is providing is why these savages have been able to continually carry out attacks with greater and greater success.

"To become a citizen of this country, for those who were not born here, you must fulfill several requirements. Upon meeting those requirements you must take an oath of citizenship. I, for one, never truly took the time to read it, because like most of us, I didn't think it applied to me. However, I discovered it affects us all more than we might realize. So that we all understand just what the oath says, I will now read it.

"I hereby declare, an oath, that I absolutely and entirely renounce and abjure all allegiance and fidelity to any foreign prince, potentate, state, or sovereignty of whom or which I have heretofore been a subject or citizen. That I will support and defend the Constitution and laws of the United States of America against all enemies, foreign and domestic. That I will bear true faith and allegiance to the same. That I will bear arms on behalf of the United States when required to by law. That I will perform noncombatant service in the Armed Forces of the United States when required by the law. That I will perform work of national importance under civilian direction when required by the law. And that I take this obligation freely without any mental reservation or purpose of evasion; so help me God. In acknowledgment whereof I have hereunto affixed my signature."

Nicholson paused and took a sip of water from a glass on the desk in front of him. "The oath they took swore them to protect this country from all enemies foreign and domestic and it goes on to say that they did so freely and without any reservations. There is no clause that allows them to neglect their oath as long as it pertains to other Muslims. We have not asked them to take up arms as their oath obligates them to. All they have been asked to do is report to the authorities any and all persons they know to be committing terrorist acts against their country and to wear a GPS locator bracelet so the authorities will know where each and every American Arab Muslim is. The Muslim community and their leadership have blatantly refused to assist the government in any way to apprehend the enemy among us. And that is completely unacceptable.

Some may claim that requiring GPS tracking is discriminatory. In some ways I will have to agree with them. Some may say that we are unfairly profiling Arabs. There I disagree. I say we are applying real statistics to real problems. Statistics reveal that ninety-eight percent of all the terrorists are Arab Muslim males between the ages of eighteen and thirty-five. With that in mind, I do not see the need to waste resources searching the handbags of silver haired retirees in a vain effort to be sensitive to terrorists' feelings. From this day forth, if you fit the terrorist profile, law enforcement will be taking an extremely close look at you and your activities. If you feel that is unfair, unacceptable, or insensitive to your feelings, then move to one of the countries that will no longer be receiving US aid. I'm sure you will be welcome there.

"The intelligence agencies of the United States have worked hard to uncover the origins of the terrorists that have either martyred themselves or were killed in the perpetration of terrorist's acts. The animals that attacked this country were not here for only a matter of days, weeks or months. Many of them were, in fact, here for years and even decades. Many of them had attained citizenship status. They had false birth certificates and social security numbers. They owned their own businesses, some facilitated by the financial aid of federal agencies, I might add. They worked among us while they plotted our destruction. The great majority even filed their yearly tax returns. Our enemy is here among us and has been for a very long time and we didn't even know it.

"Therefore, with great trepidation and sorrow, I announce today that each and every Arab Muslim who has entered this country illegally, or any Arab Muslim who cannot prove their right to be here legally, will be immediately taken into custody by federal troops wherever they are found and returned to their country of origin. In addition, any Arab Muslim that has attained legal status will be under the greatest scrutiny to verify they are who they say they are and that their purpose for being here is an honorable one. That order goes into effect immediately and has been approved by the entire Congress. Furthermore, any Arab Muslim who has taken the oath of citizenship yet refuses to do what is right and proper to protect this great land will be deported along with every member of his or her family. If they refuse to uphold the oath that gives them rights as citizens of this nation, then they forfeit those same rights and will no longer reap the benefits of its protection.

"As I said, some will argue that it is not fair to single out one group of people for such drastic treatment. I for one made that same argument not one week ago when the option was first presented to me. However, I have since changed my opinion. In war, sometimes innocent people are hurt and sometimes even killed and it has been that way since the beginning of time. You have all, unfortunately, seen many of our fellow citizens killed in the past weeks and they too were innocent. Did they have any less right to protection? As I said before, the one common denominator all the terrorists have is that they are Arab-Muslim. Because it has been a politically incorrect topic for so long does not make it any less true. This is no longer a matter for law enforcement to resolve alone. We are at war and we can either fight it like we want to win, or we can roll over and allow evil to triumph.

"Ladies and gentlemen, there comes a point in time when every civilized nation must come to the realization that the course of action they are following has proven to be ineffective. A time that says we must adopt the rules of war employed by our enemies against us. You know, I watched a movie years ago and to loosely quote one of the characters, he said that if your enemy draws a knife, you draw a gun; if he sends one of your men to the hospital you send one of his to the morgue. He was basically saying that if you're going to defeat an enemy's force then you must meet him with superior force and with greater determination and conviction. And that is exactly what we are going to do.

"My fellow Americans, when a surgeon performs an operation on a cancer patient he knows going in that in all likelihood some healthy flesh may be damaged or even destroyed if the operation is to be a success. However, he also knows to completely excise the cancer he must err on the side of caution and make sure it is all extracted. For if even a few malignant *cells* are missed, the cancer will continue to grow and in a very short time he will have to repeat the operation, if at that time it is not already too late."

"We as a nation are faced with the same dilemma. We have a cancer that is eating away at our land from the inside out. Some of the cancer is obvious and will be easy to remove. But some of it is hidden and this is the part that is doing the most damage. The time has come, and is long overdue, to perform an operation on this great land and remove the cancer that is hell-bent on destroying us. I know some healthy flesh will more than likely be harmed or even destroyed and I find no pleasure in that. It deeply troubles my soul when I think about it in any great detail. However, to save the body sometimes we are forced to do what was once thought of as unthinkable. The needs of the many must outweigh the needs of the few. We will rise to the challenge. We will meet the challenge. And we will be victorious."

He took another drink of water before continuing. "I now speak directly to those national leaders with which we have declared war. Through your deceitful actions you have brought great harm, fear and destruction to the great people of this country. I will not bother to name you directly in this national address but you know who you are. What should deeply frighten you is that *we* know who you are as well; and we'll be seeing you soon.

"Through your repetitive and numerous unfriendly acts you have now managed to re-awaken this long sleeping giant and again filled it with a terrible resolve. We have been asleep far too long, but our eyes are now wide open and focused. We will no longer just hold accountable your wayward children for events you have set into motion. We will no longer hold political correctness or international opinion above the safety and security of the American people. We will no longer explore avenues of peace with you when you only desire war. Therefore, from this moment forward, as long as I draw breath, the full financial, industrial and military might of the United States of America will be unleashed upon you. There will be no discussion and there will be no more compromise. You will be our friend or you will be our enemy, there will be no middle ground.

"With the stroke of a pen, just hours ago, I rescinded Executive Order 11905 signed by President Gerald Ford in 1976 banning the assassination of foreign heads of state. If you are our sworn enemy, either publicly or privately, you will no longer be allowed to hide behind your political positions."

"To all of you holy warriors who profess to be Allah's followers; you have either been filled with hate or brain-washed into believing that you're actually doing God's will. You believe that if you martyr yourselves by killing innocent people you will go to Paradise and be rewarded with seventy-two virgins. Rest assured that is not the case, as I'm convinced that many of your brothers and sisters who went before you were more than a little surprised to find out."

Nicholson paused and then seemed to deviate from his scripted speech. "You know, I find it amazing that throughout the ages many of the most despicable acts perpetrated against mankind have all been carried out by men with the name of God upon their lips." Nicholson took another drink and then continued.

"I know you fanatics will not believe that I am being sincere, so that leaves us very few options to dissuade you from further acts of barbarism. Therefore, since it is well known that Arab Muslims believe they must be clean before burial and you have absolutely no fear of death or imprisonment, you leave us with only one option. We have no other choice than to see to it that the remains of any terrorist who martyrs themselves or is killed in an act of terrorism against Americans or our allies will be buried with swine. If nothing else will scare you or deter you, perhaps knowing with a guaranteed certainty you'll go to hell, will. This policy is to be retroactive to the date of the first terrorist that blew himself up at the hospital in Redding, California.

President Nicholson paused to allow his words to have their full-intended effect. "However, there is an off switch to the retribution that is at this very moment coming your way. Starting right now you have exactly one week to completely dismantle every terrorist training facility operating within your borders. You are not to imprison those that you find in those camps, you are to turn them over to the United States and our justice or to those of our trusted allies. Furthermore, you are to publicly denounce all forms of terrorism in the name of Allah. I personally believe he is sickened by the very nature of what some Arab Muslims are doing and then claiming to do it in his name.

"You will arrange to pay reparations to each and every American who lost members of their immediate family during your barbaric *Jihad* against our people. Lastly, you will in one week provide the names and locations of each and every terrorist currently operating within US borders as well as those of our allies. You will also provide proof that they are who you claim they are. One week from today is the deadline. There will be no extensions. There will be no arguments and there will be no escape from American justice.

"Do not deceive yourselves into believing that the United States Government is again just posturing and blustering. Through the actions of the past two administrations you have seen that things have slowly been changing here in Washington. The American people are hungry to restore the liberty this land once promised and I, representing their government, intend to see they get it. If violence is all you want and violence is all that you understand, then so be it, violence is what you will receive. The great American General, George S. Patton once said, "No bastard ever won a war by dying for his country. You win the war, by making the other poor dumb bastard die for his." You have brought this upon yourselves. May God have mercy on your souls, because the United States of America no longer will.

"To the American people, let not your hearts be troubled and neither let them be afraid. The greatness of the United States will be restored. It will take a lot of blood, sweat and tears, of that I'm certain. But isn't that what it took for this nation to be born in the first place? Stand strong, stand together and we will prevail. Good night and God bless the United States of America."

A note from the author.

When I first sat down to write this book I had no idea what it would become. I had been thinking ever since 9/11 why had the United States not been struck again. Sure we are waging war against terrorists worldwide. We're throwing money, resources and lives at the problem hand over fist. But, have our efforts been so great that we are actually preventing further attacks? The more I thought about it, the more I began to believe there must be something more terrible in store for us and for some unknown reason it has not yet been unleashed.

Then I thought, suppose all of this time we have been looking in the wrong direction. What if we have been so absorbed with preventing the enemy from getting to our soil, we have virtually blinded ourselves to the fact they were already here: planning, plotting, preparing, waiting...

History tells us that throughout the ages some of the most successful military victories came from ingenious planning that involved elaborate sleight of hand and misdirection. Is that what America's enemies are attempting to achieve themselves? How vulnerable are we? Are our enemies prepared and in the position to take advantage of those vulnerabilities? I believe they are.

While this book is a work of fiction that spawned from the thrift shop of my own imagination, the possibility it could actually take place remains very real. If only a quarter of what occurs in the story were to happen, what would the damage to our society, our dreams and our futures be?

There are some that will say that I have gone overboard in my descriptions of the treachery our enemies are willing to go to in order to ensure our destruction. That surely no one could hate us so badly as to go to such lengths. If you are one of those naïve individuals, then please take the time to visit the website Michael-Savage.Com. Take a look at the beheading videos the host has made available there. Listen closely to the repetitive chants of "Allahu Akbar" as these peace-loving holy warriors savagely saw off the heads of innocent and defenseless men. These videos will provide you with a brutal glimpse into the rancid heart of our enemy. <u>Please note that these videos are extremely graphic and are not for the faint of heart! I cannot emphasize this enough!!!</u>

Perhaps if the mainstream media were to play these videos on the evening news, or maybe just the sound clips with a narrator providing a description of events, then no doubt the *brutal* treatment of *terrorists* at Abu Ghraib might not have seemed so egregious to the American public.

The evil intents of bad men and women can only be checked by the willingness of good men and women to intervene. Ignoring evil will not make it go away; it will only perpetuate and feed it!

I hope you enjoyed the story, because that is why I wrote it. I don't know what the eventual solution for our terrorism conflict is to be; however, I have taken great liberties in presenting what I believe to be both a fictional yet plausible option. I understand while some readers will take exception to some of the things I've written and others will bang a drum of triumph; offense to no one is my intent. Until the war on terror is eventually resolved, I urge each of you in:

Albuquerque	Atlanta
Bangor	Beverly Hills
Boise	Boston
Charlotte	Charleston
Cheyenne	Chicago
Colorado Springs	Corpus Christi
Dallas-Forthworth	Des Moines
Detroit	Duluth
El Sugunda	Fort Wayne
Fresno	Green Bay
Helena	Houston
Johnson City	Kalamazoo
Kansas City	Lake Charles
Las Vegas	Lexington

Little Rock	Long Beach
Los Angeles	Lubbock
Memphis	Miami
Minot	Morgantown
Mount Airy	Myrtle Beach
New Orleans	New York City
Norfolk	Oklahoma City
Omaha	Peoria
Philadelphia	Pine Bend
Pineville	Pittsburgh
Portland	Raleigh
Redding	Richmond
Riverside	Sacramento
Salem	San Antonio
San Francisco	Savannah
Shreveport	Springfield
Syracuse	Tallahassee
Tucson	Tupelo
Washington, DC	Wilmington

And those of you in every other city and community, big and small, that didn't make it into the book, to remain vigilant. They are here among us. They will strike. Perhaps they are right now!

978-0-595-37661-2
0-595-37661-4

7044232R0

Made in the USA
Lexington, KY
14 October 2010